DEAD CITY

Books by Shane Stevens

Go Down Dead
Way Uptown in Another World
Dead City

SHANE STEVENS

DEAD CITY

Holt, Rinehart and Winston
New York Chicago San Francisco

Published simultaneously in Canada by
Holt, Rinehart and Winston of Canada, Limited.

Library of Congress Cataloging in Publication Data

Stevens, Shane.
  Dead city.

  I. Title.
PZ4.S84554De   [PS3569.T453]   813'.5'4   73–1567
ISBN 0-03-010336-3

First Edition

Printed in the United States of America

1761701

FOR JOHN FOGARTY . . .
and the over the hill mob

*Woe to the dead city! It is all
full of lies and robbery.*

—THE BIBLE

DEAD CITY

1

HE LIVED ALONE in the Exchange Place Hotel, a squat six-story relic of a time when the city built itself out of dirty red brick, and the Hudson River nearby ran clean and full of angry fish. Whatever charm the hotel may once have had was buried in its musty drapes and darkened carpets, but Charley Flowers didn't notice such things. He kept his suit in a garment bag hanging in the closet, his shirts and socks in a shopping bag by the bed. His line of work sometimes meant a quick change of residence, and for him one Jersey City hotel was like another. Each one gave him the same feel about the dingy river town, with its factories and warehouses, railroad yards, rotting piers and truck terminals, wire-mesh fences and the endless rows of frame houses squatting on barren streets slowly leaking sounds. His windows looked out on alleyways strewn with garbage. In the dark halls people cursed or dropped wine bottles or cried over solitary loves or slashed the air. Soot the size of cinders hovered over everything, stormed the less accessible places, cut around corners and between buildings, and deposited itself on Flowers' windowpanes. He never opened the window. In his room the sweet, dank odor of too many years of too many people permeated every piece of furniture and every inch of space. His mattress was ripped, his sink busted, and his twice-weekly towels all had holes in them.

Charley Flowers was hired muscle working for the Jersey syndicate. Medium-tall, angular, not too muscular but tight-boned and thin-waisted, he gave the appearance of stamina more than sheer strength, of purpose and determination. His face, oddly handsome, was roughhewn and heavily creased. A dimple in the right cheek flattened out to a pencil line that ran down almost to the jawbone. There was a fullness to the lips and mouth, the nose was sculptured and imperious. His chestnut hair, worn long, covered his ears and curled up at the nape of the neck. It was mostly his eyes—cold steel-gray—that said what he was. Practiced before mirrors in imitation of Bogart, he could hold them open, staring intensely, for a full minute and more. He had developed the ability by taping his eyelids open and holding a lighted candle in front of them. It never failed to impress people.

Flowers had not been given a straight hit contract by the syndicate in two years, and now he was being used for loan-sharking and the like. Why he had been demoted to this kind of work at thirty-two was not entirely clear to him, and it made him uneasy. What troubled him was his inability to do anything about it.

Past rows of dilapidated stores along Montgomery Street, he made his way to the corner and caught the bus for Journal Square. He was going on another job, just punk stuff. Feeling a sense of depression at the thought, he absently looked out the window at the dark afternoon streets.

In a massage parlor on Sip Avenue, a few blocks from the Square, Flowers stripped down. He had a small bullet wound at the base of the spine, received while on a hit that went wrong, now turned an ugly brown, and a long jagged knife scar running down his left thigh to the knee. In a towel and a pair of paper slippers he walked around the narrow dimly lit room, did the bends a few times, farted loudly, and worked his way over to the metal massage table where he lay down. When the door opened, he turned his head and watched the girl as she came into the room. She wore a white sleeveless gown and a green comb in her hair, which was silver blue. She smelled of pine disinfectant. With a quick glance at the body, she went over to a painted cabinet and took from the top shelf a small jar and several hand towels. These she placed on top of the cabinet.

The girl turned then, occupied and morose. "You want a hand job or the vibrator?"

Flowers could see she wasn't looking at him. "I like human touch, you know what I mean? People don't touch no more like they use to."

She moved her shoulders in a slight shrug, indicating it made no difference to her. With the jar of cream she began rubbing down Flowers' private parts, working swiftly. She was chewing gum.

"You want my clothes off, or is it OK like this?"

Stretched out, already beginning to feel warm, his hands and face flushed, Flowers told her that he enjoyed looking at a good body.

The girl removed her white gown. She wore no bra. "You want the panties off, it'll cost you extra."

He decided he could see enough and told her so. She made a loud pop with her gum and went over to the cabinet to put up the cream, coming back with the hand towels.

Flowers was not circumcised and consequently had a harder time reaching orgasm, but he believed he felt it more and women enjoyed it better. He watched her face for any sign of this enjoyment, but all he could see was the movement of her jaws.

Eventually the girl asked him if he wanted her to take it and Flowers, unable to speak, merely nodded. He knew that would cost extra too.

When she was finished with him, she went over to the sink to rinse out her mouth, then returned to clean him with the towels. Afterward, he lay there a while in solitary ease before he slowly dressed and left.

At six o'clock Flowers stood on Hudson Boulevard,

3

around the corner from the massage parlor, waiting for his driver. He had on his one suit, a brown weave, and a green sport shirt open at the throat. He liked wearing the suit on a job, felt it made him look less conspicuous. Right on time a black Ford pulled over to the curb. When Flowers opened the back door, a lanky youth sitting in the front gave him a quick look, rolled up the window, and lowered himself farther into the seat. There was nobody in the back. Flowers got in, rubbed his hands a few times over his hair, grunted in satisfaction, and waited for the boy to say something. After that first glance he now sat very still, staring hard out the window. It was the pose of someone with a case of nerves, and Flowers, smiling tolerantly as he remembered his own younger days, invited him to talk, though he himself knew it wouldn't do anything to help the nerves.

The boy spoke up then, startled. "You a shooter?"

Flowers caught the edge in his voice. "I was. No more, least not right now. Nothing to it though, if you got what it takes. Know what I mean?"

His body half-turned, the boy nodded glumly, as if unsure of anything. Flowers, exasperated, turned his attention to the driver, Hymie Cole, whom he had known on several previous jobs, and they shared some small talk. After that, they rode in silence the rest of the way there.

Hymie Cole was a worrier. He worried when he had money, he worried when he didn't have money, he worried about his health, his wife, his kids. Now he was worrying about the job they had to do. Joe Zucco didn't want anything to go wrong, and he was big enough to get what he wanted. Hymie wasn't the smartest man in the world but he wasn't dumb and he was very careful. Zucco appreciated that. He also knew that Hymie would be able to get to Dominick Spina, and that was what he most definitely wanted. "Step on the little bastard," Zucco had said, "and make it good. Tell him you're with him, tell him you'll help him, tell him *anything*, but *get him*." Zucco's hand shook with anger as he gave Hymie the small bottle of blood. "If I hear about him walking around without crutches before next year, it's back on the street for you."

Hymie drove carefully. He had no intention of going back to street hustles, to penny-ante crime and cops and robbers. That was for the young hoods. He was forty-six years old, with a bad liver and maybe heart trouble, a disturbed wife, and two teen-age punk kids who wouldn't listen to anything he told them. The snotty brats, they'd have to learn the hard way. Why, he'd already forgot more than they'd ever know, these punk kids today. No, the street held no meaning for him anymore. Nothing. Life was hard enough without that.

They were almost there. Hymie had planned every detail, and still he was worried. Flowers, half asleep in the back seat, was OK, but what about this boy staring out the window next to him? He had never even been on a job. When Zucco gave out the job, Hymie had shopped around and come up with Flowers. Then somebody had talked Hymie into using the boy, who was owed a favor by someone else. Maybe some new blood here, he was told. Now he was sorry he gave in. If anything went wrong it was his ass. But it was too late to turn back now, Spina was set up. Dominick Spina, small-time jewelry fence—nickname Grandma Dom, given to him years ago for raping a young girl when he was dressed in matronly woman's clothing—this same Dominick Spina, this rapist, had had the temerity to do a little loansharking on his own. Not only that, but because of him one of Zucco's boys, who had the territory, was arrested. He must be mad, Hymie had thought evenly when he was told about it. But crazy or not, Spina had made a big mistake, and now he had to pay for it.

The parking lot was behind a row of stores, all of them closed this time of evening. Hymie pulled up next to Spina's car. For the past week he had clocked Spina's movements, his habits, everything about the man. He knew Spina worked late on Wednesdays, and wouldn't come down to the car until about seven-thirty. When he did, he'd be with his bodyguard, a young knife artist named Ginger. Hymie checked his watch. An hour to go. He slumped back in the seat and closed his eyes, worrying about his wife and wondering where he was going to get the four grand for the car he had promised that little tramp he was keeping on the side.

At seven-forty Dominick Spina and Ginger walked into the parking lot. Hymie, now alone in the car, took out his gun and checked the cylinders. The first one was empty. He put the gun under his jacket and waited until they were almost to the car before he called out. "Dom? It's Hymie." He slowly got out of the car, his hands showing empty. "We had a deal, remember? The four thousand I told you I needed?" Ginger, suspicious, stood still.

"Oh yeah, sure. You alone?" Spina barked. Hymie, around the car now and in front of them, said he was.

"Why didn't you come up to the office?"

Hymie, all smiles, spread his hands in a shrug. "I can't afford to be seen with you, Joe'd have my ass in a sling. You know how it is. Better this way, right?"

"I don't have that kind of cash on me," Spina hissed. "You must think I'm nuts."

Hymie drew his hands back, and in one swift movement the gun was out. Ginger went for his knife and Hymie pulled the trigger. It clicked loudly on the dead cylinder. "That's the only free ride you get, punk. The next one's in the stomach." Ginger shrugged, and dropped his knife on the gravel. "Now kick it away." Ginger was a businessman who had just come in second best in a business deal, but he knew there would be other business deals. He kicked the knife away. "Now take a walk for yourself and don't come back. You just lost a job."

Hymie turned his attention to Spina, whose arms were pinned by two men who had come around the other side of the car from the back. "See what I mean, Dom? You can't trust these young punks today. Ain't like it use to be with us, eh?"

"What you want with me?"

Hymie went over and picked up the knife and slipped it into his pocket. "Just some talk is all."

"What about?"

"This and that. Maybe how there's no way you can hide out from what you do. No way."

"I don't know what you mean."

Hymie took out a small bottle from his jacket. "You and me, Dom, we're getting old, you see what it is? We piss our lives away just trying to get by, while somebody else walks off with the cake. We sweat for a buck and some joker comes along and rips off a million. Sometimes that does funny things to a man, know what I mean? He gets careless and he gets a little greedy. And before you know it, he's stepping on somebody else's toes. But somebody else don't like it."

"I didn't do nothing. S'help me, I don't know what you're talking about."

Hymie shook his head. "No use, Dom. It's like I told you, there's no way a man can hide, no way at all." He opened the bottle and walked over to Spina and stood directly in front of him. "You got somebody real mad, Dom. And that's no good. Me, I'm not mad. Nothing personal, you understand. It's just a business thing and we got to do it. Now open your mouth."

Spina kept looking at the bottle. He knew what was coming and he began to tremble. Sweat poured out of him. His eyes, maddened, watched as Hymie put the bottle to his lips. "The mouth. Get your mouth open, Dom. We don't want to shoot you." Dazed, Spina obeyed and Hymie poured a little of the blood down his throat. When he started to choke, Hymie raised the bottle and poured the rest of the blood over the man's head, slowly, deliberately. Then, flinging the empty bottle into the darkness, he turned to the two men holding Spina's arms. "He's all yours."

Charley Flowers let go of Spina's arm, took a step sideways, and smashed him in the kidney. The boy turned him toward Flowers who uppercutted perfectly into his groin. Spina sagged, and was held up from behind as Flowers broke his nose. Spina screamed. Pounding his fist into the man's back at the base of the spine, the boy sent him pitching forward, and Flow-

7

ers drove him back with powerful blows to the face that splattered flesh and bone. Now the two of them took turns chopping Spina to pieces. They timed their punches, delivering them with full weight to do the most damage. Spina's face was pulp, his body torn rubber. The boy grabbed his arm and cracked it behind him, while Flowers caved in his ribs with sledgehammer hits. They were breathing heavily now. The screaming had long stopped, and now there was just the sound of escaping air as the body sank into the gravel. In the darkness it was indistinguishable from a heap of soiled clothing. The beating had taken four minutes.

Hymie, who had gone to the car and started the motor, brought back a bottle of brandy. He gave Ginger's knife to Flowers. "Here. Cut all around the pants leg up near the top, the right one." When this had been done, Hymie pulled the pants leg down over the shoe and off. Then he poured half the bottle of brandy on Spina's wooden leg and set it on fire.

Back in the car, headed toward Journal Square, Flowers took out a blue railroad handkerchief and wiped the blood and bits of loose skin off his knuckles. Traces of drying blood still remained, and these he licked and rubbed away carefully. "What's your name, pal?"

The boy again sat in the front seat. "Harry. Harry Strega."

"How long you been doing the muscle?"

"This my first job."

"No shit. How old are you?"

"Twenty."

Flowers nodded appreciatively. "For first time you done real good. I mean, a lot of guys freeze up the first few times, they worry about killing the hit. They don't know it takes a lot to kill somebody like that."

"I wasn't thinking nothing, just trying to do what I was getting paid for."

"That's what a pro is all about, kid. It's just a job like any other job, only some do it better than others, is all it is. You do it good enough to be in the business."

"I don't know. I guess it's OK if the money's there."

"Who got you for this job, anyway?"

"Just a favor."

Flowers grunted in understanding. "You should go see Joe Zucco, right, Hymie? He's always looking for good boys. No use wasting your talent."

From the back seat Flowers measured Harry in his mind. The kid had done good, no question about that. His hands were big, he had the power and he had the instinct. Now if he had the brains he might even make a good shooter. Looking at the back of his head, Flowers wondered if he had the brains. The face, when Harry turned around, told him nothing. Now that the initial nervousness was gone, it was impassive with its thin lips, high cheekbones, and guarded eyes. From his inside jacket pocket, Flowers took out a small silver harmonica and, aware of its incongruity here in the car, he played it softly with his hands held in front, shielding the notes from the others. Even so, the sound filled the car, masking all of them in a solemnity no one felt.

After dropping Harry on Hoboken Avenue, Hymie drove Flowers back to his hotel, letting him off around the corner. Flowers walked the block slowly, sucking in great gulps of air. Car rides always brought cramps to his legs. What he needed was to exercise them, so he walked on past the hotel to the store on the next street and bought a salami sandwich and a six-pack of beer. Then he picked up a paper and started back. The sun was playing dead in the west, wiping out the spent shadows of a dark and windy day. Debris lined the streets. In the harbor the hulks of a dozen deserted piers groaned in unison as brackish water slapped the underpinnings. Farther out, the Statue of Liberty, its halo of light shimmering in an eerie mist, patiently stood watch over a New York skyline held together by a choppy sea.

There was no one on the street. In the hotel lobby the clerk carefully slept behind a newspaper. Flowers walked up the three flights of stone stairs to his room. Once inside, he hungrily wolfed down the sandwich and two cans of beer. He was on a third when his neighbor asked him to see if the woman he lived with was really sick.

"Don't you know?" Flowers asked him.

"I can't tell for sure."

The man was small, shrunken, with a close-cropped head and elephant ears, and one side of his face was lower than the other. The woman was heavyset, older than Flowers, and she wore long black false eyelashes that made him look away.

"Do I look sick to you?" she asked him from her bed.

"I guess you do."

"There, you see?" she crowed to her companion. "He says I'm sick. What do you need, a death certificate?"

"He ain't a doctor. How does he know?"

"Why, you dumb sonofabitch, you the one brung him over here." She threw her head back onto the pillow. "I'm dying is just what I'm doing." She smiled at Flowers. "Joey loves me, he really does. I just don't know what I'd do without him. But sometimes he acts too stupid for words. He's got it in his head that I ain't sick, that I'm just faking so's I don't have to go to work tonight in that crummy dive. You ever hear anything like that, I ask you?"

"Been done before," said Joey.

"Not by me it ain't."

"You say."

"I know."

"Yeah, sure."

Flowers took a pull on his beer, wishing he were back in his own room. He swallowed too much and coughed. The woman looked at him. "Guess I'm just tired," he said. When he got no answer he put the beer can on the littered dresser.

She made a noise in her throat. "Joey?"

"Yeah?"

"Maybe you should call a doctor."

"What for, for chrissake?"

"For me, that's what for. Maybe I'm sick enough to need a doctor look at me. What's so strange about that?"

"Nothing strange about it."

"Anyone'd think you didn't give a good goddamn for me, the way you carry on. Is it my fault I'm sick, should I be sorry about it? OK, I'm sorry. Is that what you want? I'm sorry, so there."

Joey looked at her, then at the floor. "It's all right, Alice," he said quietly.

"It's all right, Alice. Is that all you can say? It's all right?" She punched the pillow behind her head. "I don't know why I ever tied up with you. You're always away on that stinking barge, then when you do come home all you do is mope around and nag me to death. You the one brung this on, I know you done it. Be just like you." She punched the pillow again, this time even harder.

"Maybe you ought to call a doctor," Flowers said. "She could be real sick."

Joey went over to the table and sat down, motioning Flowers to join him. "There's something funny here." He opened a big book.

"Funny? What's funny?" Flowers was seeing no humor at the moment.

"She thinks it's the flu. This medical book says people with the flu get pains in the back and legs. But she don't complain about any pains in the back and legs."

"Maybe she's too sick."

"I don't think so." He read some more in the book. "It says here they get red around the eyes. I don't see any red around her eyes."

"So her eyes are funny. What does that mean?"

"Maybe she's faking."

"How can she fake a thing like that? Don't she look like she can't get out of bed?"

"Maybe," said Joey mysteriously. "All the same, why don't she get pains in her back and legs like she supposed to?"

"You're nuts."

Flowers sat there for a minute deep in thought, then he got

up and went over to the bed. "Joey says you should have pains in your back. You got any pains like that?"

"No."

"He says you should have pains in your legs, too. What about that?"

"No."

"Maybe you're not too sick after all."

Alice turned her head away. Joey slammed the book he was holding. "I knew she was faking."

"My stomach hurts like I'm dying inside," she said.

"What about them other pains?" Joey asked. "The book don't say that your stomach should hurt."

"How the hell should I know what the book says. I just know how I feel, goddamn it."

Joey laughed derisively. "Come on, Alice, you ain't kidding me. You feel fine."

Just then she started coughing. She sat up quickly and hacked away for a moment, then she began to retch. Flowers watched as the woman threw up all over the sheet. When it was over and she slumped back on the pillow, Flowers got his can of beer from the dresser and walked over to the door. "You're nuts," he said to Joey on his way out.

Back in his room, lying on the bed in the darkness, he could hear the woman coughing again. It was always the same in these hotels, always the same crazy people, the same noises and fights, the same losers. He wanted to believe he was not a loser, he needed to believe in himself. But somewhere along the line he had lost the power to believe. At one time he could have been up there, he could have been somebody, he was sure of that. Now his life was going, and there was nothing he could do about it. Now he was just what he was and nothing more, and what he was was nothing. Hired muscle, an enforcer, a topcoat. He turned on the light. The paper was full of children stories, dog stories, marriage and divorce, home life and the price of meat, all the things he cared nothing about because his life was not like that. He turned to the obituaries; at least death was something he understood. Unsure of the meaning of his own life, he believed that from the obituary columns he could tell about the respect and honor, love and hate in which a person was held, not so much from what was said but what was left unsaid.

Flowers had killed his first man at seventeen in a crowded street behind Pershing Field, where high school football teams played on Saturday afternoons and bands marched on patriotic holidays. He and Johnny Lupo did the job for two hundred dollars, golden money to a green kid who never had anything. It was a bike kill. Lupo pumped the bike, with Flowers on the handlebars holding the sawed-off shotgun in a towel. Just two kids maybe on their way to a swimming pool. When the hit, who had been talking too much to the wrong people, came out of the house all he saw was a bike. He was a smart man and he wasn't going to let any shooters get close to him. As he walked down the stairs, Flowers jumped off the bike, cleared the gun, and cut his man down. Both barrels. Boom. The next second he was back on the handlebars, with the shotgun back in the towel. Around the corner he threw the gun in a waiting car, and walked away while Lupo pedaled on.

By the time he was twenty-five, Charley Flowers had spent two years in a reformatory and one in prison, had mob connections for whom he did odd jobs, and drove a truck for a living. In the next five years he prospered to the point where he was given several important hit contracts and a little bookmaking of his own. Word got around that he was dependable. Those years had been the peak of his career, though of course he hadn't known it then. Always expecting more, he couldn't believe that was all he was going to get. The realization came only after he badly bungled a contract, getting himself shot in the process.

It had all started out as a simple contract. A former state trooper named Jack Kenney had gotten a foothold into gambling in Hudson County and was leaning on some important people. They didn't like it. A contract went out on him and was given, through Philadelphia and Atlantic City, to Flowers. After two days of watching his prey, Flowers caught him in Union City late one night. He was waiting for a red light at the top of the viaduct. Pulling up alongside, Flowers quickly aimed his shotgun right at Kenney's head and pulled the trigger. Nothing happened. In his haste Flowers had not released the safety on the shotgun. He just froze there with his hand squeezing the trigger, and his victim looking down the long barrel resting on the open window. In the next second Kenney pulled out his own gun and sent a bullet crashing into Flowers' shoulder. A syndicate doctor quickly patched up the wound, but it lost the contract for him. Two weeks later Kenney was gunned down on Washington Street in Hoboken, waiting for another red light.

For Flowers it had been a mistake he couldn't believe himself capable of making. It shattered his confidence. By the time another contract was offered him several months later, his self-doubts had only increased. Yet he couldn't refuse the job. The hit was important, the most important he had ever been given. His target was the owner of a big showplace up by the Washington Bridge, who refused to cooperate with the syndicate, moving into Bergen County in a big way. Flowers stalked him carefully for a week, then waited patiently one morning with his driver in front of the man's sumptuous home. When the garage doors swung open at ten in the morning, Flowers hurriedly walked across the street with his gun in the folds of a newspaper, as though he were simply going to work. Intent on surprising the man in the garage, Flowers saw nothing and heard nothing, not even his driver's frantic horn-blowing. At the last second the blaring sound woke him, and as he turned a bullet struck him in the back and he crumpled to the gravel. The man's bodyguard came around from the other side of the house, gun in hand. Flowers had walked into a simple trap that anybody should have seen.

His intended victim soon came to an agreement with the syndicate that lasted for more than a year before he was shot twice through the head with a .30-caliber carbine by a syndicate shooter.

Flowers, meanwhile, spent months in the hospital and had two operations before he was pronounced healthy again. Word got around that he had lost his nerve, that he was no longer dependable. His numbers operation was taken away; his contracts dried up. Little by little he found himself being used simply for strong-arm work, paid by the job like any common hustler. Soon he was no longer a shooter but merely another muscle man.

He resented the loss. Whenever he thought about the past, which was as seldom as possible, his memories left him dissatisfied with the present. Worse still, he saw little of value in his immediate future. Without the opportunity of making a really big hit, there seemed small chance of achieving his former status.

In these two years since his fall, Charley Flowers had become a changed man in some ways. He'd given up the heavy drinking and woman-chasing. At least once a month he visited his mother, alone in a housing project, giving her a few dollars whenever he had it. He even returned to the Church, going to mass on Sundays when he got up in time, which was seldom. Since the shooting, Flowers paid more attention to religious feelings. On those days when he felt his life was over, he believed that maybe God would help him if only He could be persuaded.

Somebody slammed a door nearby and walked past the room, cursing loudly. Flowers threw the paper on the floor. Above his head on the wall was a yellow and white sign that read: YIELD. IT'S MORE FUN. Over the dresser mirror was another, smaller sign, this one red and white, that simply said: BAN DDT. Someone had crossed out the first D and added a small S at the end. Next door they were still shouting at each other.

HARRY STREGA WAS eighteen years and ten months old when he killed his first man, on a dirt road in the Central Highlands of South Vietnam near the Cambodian border. He had been in Vietnam four months without seeing action. When it came it was an ambush, as three M-48 tanks raced down a road near the Ho Chi Minh Trail toward Dakto. Vietcong rockets knocked out the lead tank, and Harry, a gunner on the middle can, climbed out of the turret hatch and worked the mounted .50-caliber machine gun. When his tank got hit, he scrambled over to the brush, picking up a submachine gun from a dead soldier. For twenty minutes he fired at the enemy, killing at least three of them before help arrived. In the next eight months he killed at least four more men in close combat. In between he learned about booby traps and mines, and saw a dozen of his friends die. One of them who didn't die had both his legs blown off by a mine. There was hardly any bleeding from the stump, the concussion cauterized the wound and the flesh just sucked up. Seeing this, the man next to him went berserk. It took four men and several shots of morphine to hold him down. Raving, he was taken away to a hospital in a straitjacket. Harry, made tougher, noted all this and came to a decision. By the time he left Vietnam for home he had been both the hunter and the hunted, and he knew which side he was going to be on in the future. It was an easy decision to make.

The funeral parlor was on the ground floor of a two-story stucco building with a low iron gate in front and iron bars on all the windows. On one side a parking area extended for the length of the building and continued around the back, ending at a retaining wall that cut off access from the apartment house next door. A separate entrance, through a small foyer from the parking area, led up a flight of stairs directly to the second floor. At the top of the stairs a heavy door opened into a large, windowless room. Setting his face in a mask of confidence, Harry climbed the thickly carpeted steps and opened the door. In the room a row of metal folding chairs was neatly stacked against one blue-and-white papered wall. Two men in dark business suits, one heavyset, the other short and muscular, turned as Harry walked in. The short, muscular man came over to him.

"Looking for somebody, pal?"

"You Joe Zucco?"

"What you want to see him about?"

"Charley Flowers told me to come over and see Zucco."

"Mr. Zucco," the man said simply. He glanced at his partner, whose face remained impassive, then looked back at Harry. "Charley Flowers send you?"

"That's right."

"OK, wait here. I'll see if he's in."

Harry relaxed, focusing his attention on the room. The heavyset man continued to watch him closely, his right hand now in his pocket. Harry looked over at him. "Nice day today."

"Yeah."

"My name's Harry Strega."

"Yeah?"

Harry pointed to the metal chairs. "Expecting company?"

"Yeah."

"You don't say much, do you?"

"No."

Harry, uncomfortable, thought about leaving but decided against it. He shifted his weight from one foot to the other. He hummed softly to himself. In a few minutes the short, muscular man called to him from a doorway. "In here, pal." He followed, and they walked through a second, smaller room into a third, outfitted as an office, where a man sat behind a huge mahogany desk. There was nothing on the desk but a gun. The man got up, keeping his eyes on Harry. Dressed in a dark business suit like the others, he was older, about fifty, taller and broader. He gave the appearance of solidity and iron strength. His features were sharp, his complexion dark, his voice cold. "I'm Zucco. You wanted to see me?"

Harry gulped. "I was told you might have a spot for me."

"Who said?"

"Charley Flowers mentioned it."

"You know Flowers?"

"I did a job with him the other night. Guy in a parking lot. Maybe you heard about it."

"Oh yeah, I remember now." Zucco, smiling, came out from behind the desk. "I hear you boys done pretty good."

Harry, saying nothing, stood his ground while Zucco walked around him.

"Tough boy, eh? Think you can handle it?"

"I think so."

"Do any muscle before this?"

"Only personal."

Zucco stopped in front of him. "Ever kill anybody? I mean for real, no accidents."

"I was in Vietnam a year. I got my share."

"Yeah? A war hero, eh?" Zucco went back behind the desk and sat down. He reached in a drawer and took out a fat cigar. "What else you do there?"

"Mine-laying, booby traps."

Zucco's head snapped up. "You mean like dynamite?"

Harry smiled. "That's one kind."

"What's another kind?"

"Anything sharp, a knife or even a pointed stick. Anything flammable, like a hundred different chemicals. All kinds of ways."

Zucco lighted the fat cigar, puffing on it repeatedly until clouds of bluish smoke swirled around his head. When he had it to his satisfaction, he grunted and threw the match on the floor. "Anything else?"

"I know karate pretty good."

The short, muscular man leaning against the wall with his arms folded made a derisive noise in his throat. Zucco seemed amused. "Gino here don't think much of that karate stuff. He thinks it's a pile of shit. What do you think?"

Harry stiffened. "It's helped me a few times," he said carefully.

"Maybe so, but not in this racket," said Zucco forcefully. "Here it's straight muscle. You break a guy's arms or legs or you cave him in, that's one thing. They understand that. You start fooling around with the fancy stuff and people right away get the idea you ain't serious. See what I mean? Then the whole idea of the muscle is lost. Then people got no respect and they don't do what you tell 'em. See what I mean?" Now it was Zucco's turn to smile. "Besides, it ain't healthy. You come up against street muscle and you lose every time."

"You sure about that?" Harry said evenly.

Zucco laughed. "You ain't faster than a speeding bullet, are you? I mean, you ain't no Superman, right? And you can't stop a knife or a baseball bat with your bare hands, right?"

"What about hand-to-hand?"

"This ain't the goddamn boy scouts," Zucco exploded. "Maybe that's where you belong."

"I only meant if it ever came to that," Harry explained hastily.

"You just make sure it don't never come to that." Zucco looked at Harry for a few moments, saying nothing, then he waved his hand with the fat cigar at the man leaning against the wall. "Gino, show the kid what I mean. But don't hurt him. I like him." He motioned to Harry. "Maybe I can use you on a few jobs here and there. But if you work for me you forget the fancy stuff. Just do what I tell you. I been in the business a long time."

Gino came off the wall. "In the other room," Zucco said curtly, getting up. "I don't want no blood on these Oriental rugs. Cost me a goddamn fortune." The three men, Harry in the middle, walked through a small storage room lined with filing cabinets. A handsome wood casket with gold handles lay on the floor. In a large sunny back room with holy pictures on the walls and a crucifix over the door, three more caskets were stacked against a wall between two windows.

"Take your coat off and make it easy on yourself," said Zucco. "And next time come around in something." He fished in his pocket. "Here's a couple bills. Here. Build yourself a real suit and get rid of those rags you got on. Go ahead, take it. I'll get it back."

Harry put Zucco's money in the pocket of his work shirt, snapped it closed, and took off his faded denim jacket. At six feet one, he was wide through the shoulders but thin in the chest and back. His forearms were muscular, tapering down to slim wrists at the end of a long reach. With an air of intensity, Harry stretched his legs a few times and decided not to use his feet because of the heavy work boots. Even so, he hoped he wouldn't hurt Gino too badly.

"You ready for your first lesson?" Zucco asked him gravely. "You can't learn everything now. Let's just see what you can do."

"Like what?"

"Tough boy like you? Just do your fancy stuff. Gino can take it."

Gino, his jacket removed, stood in front of a wide bay window with heavy green drapes open to catch the sunlight.

Looking at this man at least five inches shorter, but with

a body obviously rock hard, Harry had a moment of doubt but dismissed it contemptuously. He got into the karate position. Hands flat open, his body slightly bent forward from the waist, a tenseness in his shoulders and back, he waited in perfect pose while Gino shuffled over flatfooted from the window. Smiling broadly, Gino held out his right hand in a gesture of sportsmanship at the start, and Harry, uncoiling from his protected position, instinctively went to shake it with his own hand. For one moment he was unguarded, and Gino, bringing his short leg up swiftly, kicked him in the groin. As he doubled over, Gino's hand, now somehow with a gun in it, came down on the side of his head with the gun butt. It was a glancing blow, meant only to stun. Harry's legs buckled and as he lurched forward, Gino's knee came up in a perfect arc, catching him on the side of the jaw. He stumbled backward, crashing onto the floor. Gino, working rapidly, bent down and hit him several times in the kidneys.

"That's enough."

Gino, straightening himself, looked at Zucco, shrugged, stepped away, and smoothed down his shirt with the flat of his hands. Then he walked gracefully back to the window. The beating had taken no more than fifteen seconds.

Stretched out on the floor, bleeding from the mouth, one hand held shakily over his groin, Harry fought to catch his breath while Zucco, bending over him carefully so no blood touched his shoes, moved his fat cigar up and down in meaningful gestures. "It's like I was telling you, kid. This ain't a game. Right? You don't get a second chance. Right? There's no rules. You get the jump on the other guy or you get wiped out. Straight muscle, that's all counts in this business. So you can take a beating. So what? I got a dozen slobs can take a beating. Right? What I need are boys can dish it out, no questions asked. Now you learned something here, right? A street fighter's gonna win over a fancy dan every time. You work for me you forget the fancy stuff. Just do the job like you done with Flowers. That way everybody's happy, see what I mean? Nail your man so he knows what's going on. Then people respect you. Right?"

In the washroom Harry was helped by Gino, who held him up while he puked in the toilet bowl. "No hard feelings, pal."

Harry looked up at him. "No hard feelings," he said through broken lips.

"You got a hard head. Where you from?"

"Down the line."

"Where's that?"

"Hoboken."

"Tough town."

Harry spit out a clot of blood. "Use to be. What about you?"

"South side Jersey City."

"Any action there?"

"Same thing, mostly old people and niggers now. Last time I was there, me and this other guy, we grabbed this nigger in a hallway trying to get the pants off an old lady, she must've been a hundred. Yeah. He had a knife on him so we took him up to the roof and threw him off."

Harry was over at the sink now, washing the blood off his face. Gino, finished, zipped his pants and flushed the urinal. The sound of gurgling water seemed to soothe Harry's head.

"Zucco run things here?"

"Yeah, he's got the loansharking and some nightspots. Other things too, like cigarettes."

"He use a lot of muscle?"

"Everybody in the city uses muscle. Any city. How else you keep the sheep in line?"

"Or the other wolves," Harry said softly.

Gino smiled, a warm, flashing smile that showed his straight white teeth. "Now you learning, pal. Zucco's got his territory and his rackets in the city. Others got theirs. And everybody's wired into the rest of the state, and the state's wired into the whole East Coast. Nobody steps on nobody's toes without trouble. It's all organized now. Simple."

"Think he can use me?"

"Sure, you'll get used. He likes you, don't he? He looks at all the new meat. If he wasn't gonna use you for muscle, you wouldn't be here now, would you?"

Finishing up, the two men stood in front of the wide mirror, combing their hair.

"How's he know I'm OK?"

"You done the job on Spina, there's witnesses. If you wasn't OK, he'd get you nailed on a ten-year rap for that." Gino put his comb away and smoothed out his bushy eyebrows. "Besides, some people passed the word on you. That's all you need in this business." He walked over to the door. "Relax, pal. Just do the hits they give you and keep your nose clean. Work yourself up. It's like any business, see? You start with the small stuff and work up till you get a piece of a racket for yourself. Then you milk it for all it's worth. Just like any business, see?"

Alone, Harry carefully worked his bruised jaw over the sink, taking in and spitting out great quantities of water. The left side of his face was beginning to swell, his head already had a lump on it, his stomach and groin were made of lead, he was nauseous, pained, and exhausted, and he had never felt so alive in twenty years of living. It was something to do with being among real men, he told himself. A wave of exhilaration swept over him. He wanted to be like these men, hunters. No, he *was* like them. All he needed was to do it. Work himself up. It was just like Gino had said. Work your way up in the business world, and be a man among men.

Harry caught the Journal Square bus to Hoboken. He sat in the back of the half-empty bus, smiling inwardly, pleased with himself. Out of the army four months and he hadn't worked in all that time, didn't even look for a job. Now he was into something good.

He got off at Observer Highway and walked up Jefferson Street toward his rooming house. He walked swiftly, his work boots beating a staccato rhythm on the pavement. Face and head bruised and still hurting, he felt the need for a little quiet and maybe a few drinks. The Cozy Corner was just up the next street, on the same block where he lived. He hurried along. Overhead the day was turning nasty, as fingers of dark clouds spread across the sky. Birds nested in the rafters of low-slung tenements. In the streets whole armies of kids screamed and fought among cars resting bumper to bumper at the curb, some of them steel hulks already cannibalized. On every block, abandoned houses, their glassless eyes closed over with sheets of tin, stood mute testimony to the neighborhood.

There were only a few people in the bar. At the back end of the room, behind a collection of clean glasses, the elderly bartender sat on a stool watching TV, the sound turned low. Harry called him over and ordered a Scotch. He downed it quickly and ordered a second before the man had time to go back to his stool. On the third the bartender asked him what he was celebrating.

"I just feel good," Harry told him.

"That's for sure."

"Don't worry, I'll nurse this one."

The bartender shrugged. "All the same to me, mister."

At the shuffleboard table set against the opposite wall, a short, chunky man was casually sliding the puck down the board. He wore a plaid sport shirt, open at the neck, and flare corduroy trousers. His rounded face and blond wavy hair gave him a youthful appearance. He was alone at the board.

"I'm the best goddamn player in the house," he said loudly to no one in particular.

"Guess you are," answered the bartender.

The man came over to the bar. "You see?" He motioned to Harry. "He knows I'm the best. What about you, you think I'm the best?"

"How would I know?"

"One way to find out, friend." He pointed to the shuffleboard. "That is, if you're man enough to find out." Lowering his voice, he moved in closer to Harry. "I'll even make it easy for you to beat me. I'll spot you eight points in a game of fifteen.

All I ask is the last shot. Eight points! Why, that's half the game, more than that. What about it?"

"You're too good for him," said the bartender.

"You keep out of it, Frank."

Harry picked up his Scotch, took a swallow. He didn't like this loudmouth, and that crack about being man enough. He brought the glass down and banged it on the bar. The two men looked at him. "Why not?" he said. When no one answered, he downed the rest of the Scotch.

The man went back to the board. "Frank, where's the slick?"

"Ain't it slippery enough for you?"

"Not for me it ain't. When I work I want everything just right. That's OK with you, ain't it?"

"Sure, sure." Frank bent down and got the can. "Here you go."

"Bring it over, will you, friend? I have to warm up my shooting arm." He sent a puck skittering down the board. "We'll play for five dollars a game, just to make it interesting. How's that sound to you?"

The bartender put the can in front of Harry, his voice low. "Watch him," he warned, "he's a hustler."

Harry nodded and picked up the can. "Five's fine with me." He walked over to the shuffleboard. "How come you go last? Shouldn't we match for it?"

The hustler's face looked pained. "You already got half a game before you start, friend. I need a little something, don't I? With the hammer, least I got a chance."

"Hammer?"

"The last shot. If I go last every time, maybe I can shave a few points off your lead."

"Maybe you ought to give me more points," Harry said. "You sound like you know the game real good."

The hustler dusted the board with the slick. "Only played it a few times. You can ask anybody, honest." He finished the dusting. "There, smooth as a baby's ass."

"Smoother," said Harry cryptically.

"You shoot first, friend."

The two men took turns. In five throws Harry got the other seven points to win the game. The hustler shot three cliff-hangers for twelve points and sent two over the edge.

"See, what I tell you? You're probably too good for me."

The second game was a repeat, with Harry again winning in five throws. This time his opponent got ten points. In the third game Harry just beat him out fifteen to fourteen.

"Bad day," growled the hustler. "Look, what do you say we up the stakes just a little? Say, ten a game. I'm out fifteen clams already."

"OK by me."

In four games Harry won two and lost two, and was still ahead fifteen dollars.

"This is getting me nowhere," the hustler whined. "Suppose we shoot twenty a game? This way, maybe I can make some of it back if I get real lucky."

Harry nodded in agreement, thinking this was where the hustler would make his move.

He was right. On every shot his puck was nudged off the board by his opponent, who got a cliff-hanger almost every time. He lost the first three games without getting a point.

"My luck is changing," crowed the hustler.

"Sure looks that way." Harry was still smiling.

The hustler let him win the fourth game, fifteen to twelve. Then he swept the next four in a row. Again, Harry didn't get a point.

The hustler was all teeth. "My lucky day after all. That's a hundred and five clams you owe me, friend."

"You're real good at figures," Harry said, no longer smiling. "But you know something, you're even better at shuffleboard."

"Just a friendly neighborhood game. You want to pay me now?"

"Wait'll I go to the john."

Harry walked to the back of the room, made a left behind a partition and pushed the door open. After waiting a minute, he went over to the one window and raised it, making as much noise as he could. Then he quickly skipped back behind the door. There was a shout from the front and the sound of running feet, then the door was flung open and the hustler raced by him to the window. "Goddamn sonofabitch," he cried savagely, "he got away."

"I'm right here."

When he turned around, Harry was waiting for him. "You made a mistake hustling me. I don't like it. You made another mistake coming in here after me. You won't like that."

"It was a fair game."

"Maybe it was, but I ain't."

Harry, in front of his man now, suddenly brought his heavy-booted foot up and sent a crashing kick to the hustler's ribs. The next second he smashed the shoulder near the neck with an overhand chop. As the hustler screamed in pain, Harry calmly got his right arm in a lock and snapped it broken. The man's body went limp.

"Your hustle's over, *friend.* Get yourself something else."

Harry went over to the sink and blew his nose in a paper towel and checked himself in the mirror. He felt better already. He glanced back at the man's body on the floor before leaving. "Karate's still good for some things," he declared petulantly to no one in particular, "I don't care what they say." He closed the door softly behind him.

Frank and the other two customers were studiously minding their own business when he returned. "Guy had an accident in there," he said, pointing to the men's room.

"Happens all the time," Frank told him.

"He may need some help."

"There's a hospital up the street a few blocks he can go to. St. Mary's, it's called."

Harry picked up his change from the bar. "Real nice place you got here."

The elderly bartender shrugged. "Nothing's perfect, mister."

"Sure as hell ain't," Harry said pleasantly as he walked out the front door.

That night Harry Strega dreamed he was waking up; it was the banging on the door waking him up. Joe Zucco and Gino, come to get him.

"You're king," Gino said.

"King of kings," said Joe Zucco.

The man who had his hand in the paper bag said nothing.

Obsequiously, Joe Zucco and Gino bowed before Harry, fawned over him, drank toasts to his health, lavishly praised his every move. They laid out his clothes, helped him dress. When he was ready they accompanied him out the door, always a half step behind to show the proper respect. Downstairs, the car was waiting, a long black limousine. Gino opened the back door for Harry, who sat in the middle as befits a king. Settled comfortably in the now moving limousine, Harry was offered a fat cigar by Joe Zucco who promptly lighted it for him. At the touch of a button a bar came down out of the backrest, and the three of them drank heartily, amid high-spirited laughter and much good humor.

Soon the car stopped and they all got out, Harry last, with the door again held open for him. He was in a garden of marble statues and magnificent shrubbery. Fountains ran everywhere, and flowers of every color dazzled his eyes. In sheer wonder, Harry walked toward the far end of the garden, the others following. There, standing on an enormous open terrace, Harry looked out beyond its edge. Spread before him, the city was life growing out of a flatland bed, a vertical giant of neon assembly bays. There was a metallic ring to it, like a single penny in a beggar's cup. It was bright and hard and all the things he felt he understood. "I never been here before but I know all about it," he murmured.

"It's yours," Gino said.

"All of it," said Joe Zucco.

The man with his hand in the paper bag said nothing.

Harry turned toward the house, which was on a hill. The path leading to it took him through a grove of olive trees. He stopped several times to look at the trees, all of which seemed to be dying. At the house he was met by Joe Zucco and Gino, who escorted him inside. There was only one room. In the room, several hundred men dressed in dark business suits stood silently waiting. A way was opened for him through the crowd, each man nodding in a gesture of respect as he passed. At the opposite end of the room was a long table at which sat Joe Zucco and Gino. Between them was an ornate wood chair, empty. The two men rose as Harry sat down. In front of him on the table lay a gun and a knife, and a silver goblet filled with red wine. Joe Zucco picked up the long-bladed knife and pricked Harry's palm with it. As the blood flowed out, Gino put the gun in his hand.

"Kill him," Gino said.

"Kill him," said Joe Zucco.

Harry held the gun flat against his palm, the bloodied forefinger on the trigger. He shot Joe Zucco twice in the face, then turned the gun on Gino and blew away the top of his head. When he placed the gun back on the table, no one was in the room. He was alone. He slowly drank the red wine from the silver goblet. As he got up from the table, the man standing in front of him took his hand out of the paper bag. In it he held a machine gun. The bullets spun Harry around and he fell backward against the table, staining the white cloth crimson. Out of one blood-soaked eye he watched Gino pick up the knife and chop off both his hands above the wrists.

"You didn't make it," Gino said.

"You blew it," said Joe Zucco.

The chatter of the machine gun continued as Joe Zucco took the knife and cut off his head.

Harry woke up in a cold sweat. All he could remember about the dream was that some olive trees were dying. He thought he had been shouting something, but he wasn't sure. Turning over on his side, tired and uncomfortable but elated still at the thought of his being among the hunters, he tried to go back to sleep, believing that from now on he was king of the hill.

JOE ZUCCO WAS A VERY CAREFUL MAN. He had come up the
hard way in a hard town, and he always covered his tracks.
Now at age fifty-one, after more than thirty years of hustling,
he was a respectable businessman, owner of a funeral parlor and
a few other things, with hidden interests in a half-dozen companies and pieces of several local nightclubs and one in South
Jersey. That was the tip of the iceberg. Underneath was the real
money, coming from his loansharking, extortion, and, most
recently, cigarette bootlegging. It was a comfortable existence
and Zucco enjoyed it fully. He lived with his invalid wife in a
big house in Metuchen with white Grecian columns in the front
and a circular driveway entered through an iron gate. In back
of the main house were two guest cottages, with a swimming
pool in between, and several acres of woods for his dogs. In the
city he kept a floor-through apartment in the luxurious Plaza
Arms Hotel. He also owned a three-story townhouse near Journal Square, a turn-of-the-century building with a high stoop
where his mistress lived. In keeping with modern business practice, his visible outlay approximately equaled the visible intake
from his legitimate enterprises. Everything else, including the

townhouse and a house in Florida, was registered in the names of other people. The apartment was, of course, a business expense.

While Zucco enjoyed his gains, he was ever vigilant to reduce his losses. He promoted the right politicians, paid off the proper police, and constantly mended his fences. It was a full-time job.

He had also to defend his preserve from incursions by rival factions and to organize counterattacks. Though no full-scale mob war had occurred in Jersey for many years—indeed, was absolutely prohibited—proximity bred a certain amount of tension, which in turn caused problems and subsequent loss of revenue. This Zucco bitterly resented, but he saw no solution. He was only one of a half-dozen racket heads in the city, each controlling different interests, and his standing beyond the county was marginal. In the state syndicate he was at best a middleman, with very little real power. But he kept his mob connections clean, gave whatever was needed, and did whatever was asked of him from time to time.

For purposes of defense, as well as the more obvious reason of public manipulation in loansharking and extortion, Zucco employed a number of men whose specialty was the fist or the gun, or both. And, in truth, he himself was not above a little neighborly poaching if the odds were tightly in his favor. All this required manpower. Some of it, mostly professional, he kept around full-time. Others worked by the job. Still others helped out, when asked, in payment for past favors. Through political dealings, and with a fine eye for the future, Zucco over the years had built up a list of favors owed him by elevator operators in buildings that had no elevators, swimming instructors in schools that had no swimming pools, park attendants where there were no parks, and bridge operators where no bridges existed, as well as by those to whom he gave small positions or a bit of territory in pursuits outside the law. In all cases, payment was due on demand.

"An investment must always pay off," he said to those

seeking his help, and they, nodding attentively, always knew exactly what he meant. Waving the fat cigar in the air, he postured and preened, turning away from impossible demands, then with no advance warning, as though he had suddenly decided on a course of action, he explained why he was willing to invest. Each year, with the addition of this favor or that, some requiring more effort than others, and therefore a greater expected return, his list of investments grew.

Zucco waited patiently, knowing that the final payoff was always his. Meanwhile, he attended to his various interests with great care. Holding out the threat of physical injury or worse, he badgered and prodded his more recalcitrant loanshark victims into line. His extortion activities followed the same pattern. Concentrating mostly on restaurants and small nightclubs and lounges, Zucco presented himself as a peacemaker, after his men had assaulted employees and customers. For a price, he offered protection against threats and further assaults. His price was usually met by knowledgeable owners.

As with any entrepreneur, Zucco was always on the lookout for new business. He kept his ears open. He moved around the city as much as he could, picking up information. He read the papers. Each night, in his head, he would go over any prospects, as well as the day's troubles, resolving what was to be done. In the morning he did it.

On this bleak, overcast morning Zucco had much to do. The cigarette truck was coming in at ten-thirty, and Augie had set up a meeting with Harris for eleven-thirty. Before that he had to see the syndicate representative, who was in town just for the morning. And the afternoon promised to be equally busy. When his night man knocked on the bedroom door a second time Zucco got up, cursing, stretched like a cat, yawned a few times, and went in to shower. Ten minutes later he was picking out a conservative brown suit, one of a dozen he kept in the apartment. He had stayed up late the night before, drinking and visiting a few places with friends, and now he had a queasy stomach. He dressed hurriedly, white shirt, striped green tie, black shoes. He checked his wallet for money. The only other items in the thin calfskin billfold were a driver's license and pictures of his two daughters, taken when they were small, long before they married and moved away to California and Mexico City. He glanced at himself lovingly in the gold-framed mirror, decided he was still as handsome as ever.

"Hey, you, get up."

Someone moaned sleepily from the bed. He walked over and pulled back the covers. A blob of long blond hair, tousled from a night of lovemaking and deep sleep, lay over the upper part of a slim white body, its smooth, long legs jackknifed into the stomach. She was lying on her side, naked. Zucco put his hand between her knees and rolled her onto her back, then pressed her knees down straight. He looked over her body. "Jesus," he said softly, wondering if he had time for a quick one. He decided against it, there was no time. With his thumb and forefinger he squeezed a nipple and twisted it sharply. The blond head shook violently and a voice squeaked as soft blue eyes opened in startled fright.

"C'mon, get your ass up. The party's over."

The voice moaned dreamily, pulling the mouth together in a seductive pout. She wet her lips carefully, the tongue rolling sensually over the upper lip. Zucco, watching her, felt himself harden, and this made him angry. He didn't like women challenging him, especially little tramps like this. Christ, she couldn't be more than twenty-one, his own daughters were older than that.

"Do I have to get up?" she asked languidly.

Zucco didn't answer her. Standing at the edge of the bed, over her warm, inviting flesh, he unzipped his fly and with a deft motion took out his penis and began pissing on her belly. She screamed and jumped up to the other side of the bed and onto the floor. Zucco, laughing, tightened his kidney muscles to stop the flow, and walked into the bathroom. When he came out, she was almost dressed.

Still laughing, he opened his wallet. "Here's a bill for you, kid." He threw it on the bed. "Next time I say get up, you get."

With a hungry look she couldn't quite conceal, the girl picked up the hundred dollars and put it in her shoulder bag.

"I'm doing this I don't know why," he told her, "since I get all I want free. Maybe I just like to piss on you. Where'd I pick you up, anyway?"

"The Hot Spot. I was there with some friends."

"Yeah, yeah, I remember now." He went to the door. "Leave your name with Santos. He'll call you when I want you."

"Mr. Zucco?"

"Yeah?" He turned at the door.

"Last night you promised if I——"

"What about it?"

She swallowed hard and wet her lips again, not at all seductively. "You said you could get me a job on a TV show in New York."

"What's your racket?"

"I'm a dancer."

"Dancer, eh? Yeah, you got the legs for it. Nice jugs too. How old are you?"

"Twenty."

He made her take out pen and paper, and he wrote down a name. "Go see this guy, Santos will tell you where. If he can't get you on one of them shows right away, he'll fix you up with something." The name on the paper was that of Moe Davis, who had show business connections and ran the shuttle of girls from New York to Las Vegas. If a girl couldn't make it as a top-line hooker in New York, she was sent on to Vegas. From there it was all straight down. Zucco smiled to himself, thinking that Moe Davis would now owe him a favor. "Tell him I sent you. He'll take real good care of you," he said to the girl.

On his way out, he called home and asked the nurse how his wife had spent the night.

At ten o'clock Zucco sat alone in the last booth of a small luncheonette on Pavonia Avenue, near the courthouse. Two youngsters, the boy in a striped shirt and wearing a blue pork-pie hat, the girl in a print dress and red sweater, were in the first booth by the door, sipping Cokes and brushing hands on the table. At the counter Gino Agucci sat with his back to the booths, drinking a cup of coffee and watching the door. Outside, a man sat behind the wheel of a dark sedan with the motor off. He watched intently as a black car pulled up and two men got out. The first wore a lightweight topcoat and a brown velour hat with a snap brim. He was tall and lean and he had chiseled features. Glancing up and down the street, he spotted the man sitting in the sedan, noted him in his memory, and walked with cat steps to the luncheonette. The second man was shorter, heavier; he wore an expensively tailored gabardine suit and soft, black buckle shoes. He, too, glanced quickly in both directions before following the hat into the luncheonette.

Inside, the first man checked out the couple in the window booth, walked down the aisle, and nodded to Zucco before sitting next to Gino at the counter. The other man went directly to the last booth. He greeted Zucco warmly, and ordered pastry and tea from the waiter. "Coffee's bad for the nerves," he said apologetically, yet frowning at Zucco's cup. "Makes you all jumpy inside, know what I mean, Joe?"

At the counter Gino and the tall man sat in silence while the two men behind them spoke in low tones. They had already acknowledged each other's presence in gestures, neither man looking directly at the other, and now they were simply waiting out the meeting. It was a duty in which they had obviously had much experience. To an observer, they could easily have been two strangers sitting quietly side by side, yet each time someone came into the luncheonette their heads would turn in perfect unison toward the door.

At ten-twenty the public phone on the back wall cracked the room's quiet. Gino slid off the seat and answered it, then motioned to Zucco who came quickly.

"Yeah?"

"The package just arrived."

1761701

"What's it look like?"

"No problem."

"Okay. I'll be there in twenty minutes."

Zucco went back to the booth. "Business," he said energetically.

The other man nodded in understanding. "Joe, we're asking you to take this contract because it's got to be done around here. We don't want anything to go wrong."

"Nothing'll go wrong. I'll see to it."

"Fine, Joe, that's just fine." The man got up. "We'll be waiting to hear from you."

"You'll hear."

"Anything you need, let me know."

Zucco held out his hand. "Say hello to the boys for me. Tell 'em I said they got it soft."

"You come out sometime, Joe. Marian'll fix you a good meal. We don't want that you get skinny."

"Fat chance," Zucco said, laughing. "Yeah, I'll be out soon's I get things set around here."

"You do that, Joe. Be nice to see you. The boys been asking about you."

The tall man next to Gino walked to the door and opened it for the syndicate representative, who followed him out. The black car, doubleparked, was waiting for them. A minute later, Joe Zucco and Gino got into the dark sedan.

The meat-packing plant was on the city's edge, near the Holland Tunnel, a long, low brick building with a truck ramp in front and a motorized hook rail to bring the beef in. Along one side was a fenced-in parking area for the big refrigeration trailers that ran their cooling units even when idle. Around back was a second loading platform, used in earlier times when railroad cars had serviced the plant. Barrels of suet, enormous wood crates with ribbons of metal girdling them, and assorted garbage of every description now occupied the platform, spilling out onto the tracks, rusted and weed-blown. The building was old inside and out, but its location gave it the needed space for trucks and easy access to market.

Joe Zucco owned the plant, gaining control from the previous owners in a loanshark operation. Intending to modernize in order to get a big contract, but not having ready cash, they had originally borrowed thirty-five thousand dollars for which they were to pay back two thousand a week for twenty-five weeks. After eight weeks, needing more money, they borrowed another thirty-five thousand. The terms now were ten thousand dollars a month for ten months. But after two months they couldn't meet the full payment and were told that they would have to pay six thousand every month until they could make one payment of the remaining eighty thousand dollars. In addition to which, any part of the six thousand not paid in a given month was to be doubled and paid the following month, along with the regular six-thousand-dollar payment. In four months they ran dry and Zucco walked in. He had the promissory notes and he had the muscle. And for a total outlay of ten thousand dollars he had the business. He didn't bleed and bankrupt the company because it was moderately profitable, and while his name appeared nowhere on paper, most of the money eventually reached him. Under his ownership, the plant acquired an added value. It became the drop for his cigarette smuggling.

The dark sedan pulled off the macadam and swung in through the gate, passing two refrigeration vans before coming to a stop next to a diesel rig parked in back by the railroad tracks. Behind the diesel, uncoupled, was a corrugated aluminum trailer loaded with cartons of cigarettes worth a hundred thousand dollars.

Zucco went up the platform and into a small office, where he was greeted by two men. He eased himself gently into the ancient swivel chair by the rolltop desk. "Who's working this one?" he asked brusquely.

"Petey Buttons," said one of the men. "He'll be back at seven."

"What about the unloading?"

"This afternoon."

"Then get the truck the hell back."

"It'll be in Newark tonight."

Zucco pulled out one of his fat cigars. "What brands come up this time?"

"You name it, it's there."

He picked up a carton from the desk, took out a pack and opened it, and shredded a few cigarettes. "How can anybody smoke this shit?" He made a face. "No wonder they get cancer."

One of the men held out a match for his cigar. "You want us to bring in extra trucks for this one?"

Zucco shook his head. "Don't need 'em. This load's no more than any other time."

"Maybe less," said the other man.

"Maybe." Zucco thought for a moment. "I want you to get a close count from now on. I don't trust them bastards down there. Anybody'd push this shit has got to be a crook." Everybody laughed.

Outside, the trailer with the tax-free cigarettes looked inconspicuous in the truck loading zone. It had North Carolina and Virginia plates, and was driven to New Jersey by someone who didn't know where he would be unloading. If he were picked up on the way, he would have no information. At a specified truck stop in South Jersey, off the turnpike, the driver called a number to get his instructions. He was then routed to one of several closed garages around Newark or Elizabeth—these were legitimate businesses, and all knowledge of the truck and its contents would be denied if he were followed. There the driver's tour ended, and he waited until the empty truck was returned for him to drive back to North Carolina. The trailer remained in the garage overnight as a double check. The next day, a second driver, one of Zucco's men, would bring it into the city to be unloaded, then return it to the garage that same day. At the plant the cigarettes were transferred to meat trucks to be delivered to distributors around the city. The smuggling had been worked out by the combines of several states. Zucco, having seen the possibilities, got in on it early, and now controlled the operation in his area. There was hardly any risk, sales were good, and profits kept going up as taxes increased. Zucco was pleased.

Back in the car he checked his watch. He was running late. Almost eleven-thirty, the time for his meeting with Harris. "Step on it," he barked at the driver. "We still got to pick up Augie."

Leon Harris owned a men's clothing store, one of the biggest in the city. He was a flashy dresser and steady horse player. He was also a well-known ladies' man, the younger the better. Between following the horses and chasing the women, Harris had managed, over the years, to squander much of the store's profits. Now he was in trouble. His latest escapade, involving a sixteen-year-old girl, was going to cost him twenty thousand dollars to keep quiet and out of jail. He had nothing left. He owed too much to his creditors, and was unable to order any further stock or borrow from the banks. When someone suggested a private loan, Harris readily agreed to listen to terms.

The store was on a good shopping block, almost in the middle. Two large display windows, sheathed in soft brown lighting, advertised the latest fashions for men. Inside the store, heavy gray rugs and wood-paneled walls gave the feel of a successful men's club. Recessed lighting and angled mirrors were designed to flatter the body, and there were comfortable chairs and oak smoking stands at every turn. Walking toward the back of the store, almost a half-block deep, Zucco, impressed, wondered if he would be able to get a piece of the business for himself.

The offices were up a flight of carpeted stairs, all thin gauge metal and pitted glass doors. Credit, Orders, Shipping. The last office had a wood door and a girl with blue eyeshadow sitting at a desk guarding it. After a five-minute wait, which Zucco had expected, they were ushered in. Harris, coming around his desk to greet them, was short and somewhat paunchy, though his tailored suit hid it well. His face was flaccid, with thick lips and weighted eyelids. He wore two big rings on his left hand and his voice was almost falsetto. Zucco didn't like him.

"Leon," Augie began, "this is Joe Zucco I was telling you about. I spoke to him about your problem, and he thinks maybe he could do something for you."

Harris frowned, his eyelids snapping shut. "Just what do you think it is that I need done."

Zucco tightened inside. He knew it would be like this when he first saw Harris, bitch was written all over the man. Instead of playing it straight, he had to do a dance. Zucco knew the type, he had been through it all many times. Now once again, he had to play his part in the act.

He got up. "Augie told me you might be in need of a little extra cash, Mr. Harris, and I said I'd talk to you. Just doing him a favor, you understand. I guess he got it all mixed up as usual." He turned away. "Sorry to bother you."

Harris opened his eyelids wide. Zucco's voice told him he might have overdone it. "A man *could* always use a little more money in these times," he said quickly. "Perhaps I shouldn't be too hasty." He spread his hands in a helpless gesture. "It's just that I wouldn't want anyone thinking I'm *desperate,* you see."

"Of course," Zucco agreed. "Anyone could tell you ain't desperate, with the setup you got here." His eyes took in the room. "But like you say, a little extra never hurt anybody."

"You think you could be of some help with a small loan, then, Mr. Zucco, isn't it?"

"How small?"

Harris' eyelids slowly worked themselves up and down a few times before he spoke. "Twenty-five thousand should do it very nicely," he said finally in a whisper.

"How much?" Zucco shouted in mock surprise, turning another screw.

Harris wet his thick lips. Sweat glistened on his forehead. "Twenty-five thousand," he repeated softly. "That amount would be a big help right now."

Zucco said nothing for a few moments. He wanted the man to suffer; this kind of people had to suffer before they could feel anything was real. He hated them all, there was nothing in them to respect, nothing but weakness. Just a bunch of sheep.

"That's a lot of money," he said when Harris started squeezing his palms together. "It'd cost you two thousand a week for eighteen weeks."

Harris' eyelids popped open in pain. "Isn't that," his voice squeaked, "a little high?"

Zucco shrugged. "Money's tight, you ought to know that. Besides, I'm not even sure I can do anything for you. I don't have any money myself, you understand. But these people I know, they would have it."

"Would they lend it?"

"They might, if I ask them as a special favor. But they'd need some security for their money."

Harris looked annoyed. "The store is worth a good deal more than that."

"Not the store," Zucco said simply. "They wouldn't be interested in your store. The security is you yourself. Your body."

"Me?" asked Harris dumbly. "Whatever would they want with me?"

"If you didn't pay up, it wouldn't look right," Zucco explained. "Be bad for business. So they'd have to take it out on you." From experience Zucco knew that any threat to the store would scare Harris away, no matter how much he needed money. But personal danger was too unreal to the average person to take seriously. Later, if Harris couldn't keep up the payments, as Zucco hoped, and the interest kept mounting, the threats would become more real until the cumulative effect would be a personal fear greater than any concern for the store. Then Harris would be desperate. That's when Zucco would suggest giving the people a piece of the store. For Harris, it would appear to be the only logical answer to his trouble. And Zucco would be in business. If Harris paid off on time, it was still a hundred percent profit a year. There was just no way to lose.

On the way to lunch, after Harris had agreed to terms, Zucco calculated that if he had a million dollars on the street, he could take in maybe twenty thousand a week. A *week.* Zucco wished he had a million on the street.

Julie K was waiting for him in the Pagoda Gardens, seated at a table in the back drinking ginger ale. When Zucco came in, Julie K waved him to an empty chair. "You're late," he said matter-of-factly, then went back to checking the stocks in the *Wall Street Journal.* Every few seconds he would say, "I knew it." In between would come groans of dismay. In his short-sleeved pullover shirt and baggy trousers, with a balding head and a long cigar stuck in his mouth, Julie K didn't look like a stockbroker, which he wasn't. He looked more like what he was, a man who owned a trucking company and several big furniture stores, two small hotels in the Catskills, and a thriving business in fake antiques. Julie K played the stock market the way some men played the horses, lovingly, and often with more passion than skill. He was one of Zucco's oldest friends, they had grown up together when the city was tightly controlled by the toughest, most ruthless political machine in the country, run by a man who proclaimed himself the law. Coming out of the infamous North Ward, they saw the city elect corruption time and again. In return, officials didn't interfere with gambling or prostitution or a dozen other things, as long as they were done quietly and the city got its share. It was a sweetheart contract all around, and the Jersey syndicate grew immensely strong and prosperous during all those fat years. Julie K and Zucco, learning much from the city, grew prosperous too over the years. Now they were middle-aged men with investments and obligations, two friends who met every few weeks for lunch.

"I had business with some clown."

"Huh?" Julie K looked up from his paper.

"You said I'm late, and I'm saying I had business with this

dumb asshole who don't know what end is up. That's what I was saying."

Julie K tilted his head meaningfully. "Business is business. That comes first."

"What about you, you bandit?"

"Business." Julie K laughed. "If it gets any better I'll retire. Can't take the strain no more."

"You retire? C'mon, don't shit me, you wouldn't know what to do with yourself."

"No, no, I mean it, Joe. Everybody wants antiques, they think it's a safe place for their money. You know. So now I got a whole factory making antiques night and day, still ain't enough. I'm so busy I can't even play the market, that's how busy I am."

"Who says you ever could?"

Julie K put on a hurt expression. "Why you say that, Joe? I always got a few big winners in my pocket, you know that."

"So what you got now?"

"You looking to play? Is that why you ask?"

"You know me, Julie. If it's a sure thing, I'm always ready to take a chance. What's the fix for today? C'mon, you can tell me."

Julie K threw his hands up in disgust. "Bah, to me you'll never listen. For twenty years I tell you there's no fix. It's just what you pick up here and there. You read the papers, you study the charts, you follow the form."

"The form," Zucco snorted. "That's all you guys know. Without the form you'd be nothing."

The waiter came over and Julie K ordered for them. Pork lo mein, shrimp, lobster ding, chow sam sein. It was their usual fare at these lunches, hardly changing over the years. Each time, after the banter about the stock market, which Zucco would never play because it was not a sure thing, and Julie K couldn't help playing for the same reason, they settled down to talk shop. Though Julie K was not himself in the heavy rackets, his fake antiques operated interstate under syndicate protection, and his hotels in the Catskills were favorite playgrounds for the mob management in the area. He employed no muscle, having no need of any, and was never involved in the enforcement end of syndicate business but, like Zucco, he maintained correct mob connections, and never overlooked an opportunity to pay his respects. It was Julie K who, over the years, had steered Zucco to a dozen good extortion possibilities. Julie K had also been the first to point out to Zucco the enormous potential of cigarette smuggling, back when it was first starting up on an organized basis. Now he had another one of his money ideas.

"Printing," he whispered to Zucco. "Printing books."

Zucco always listened patiently to his friend's ideas. He never knew when one would be worth big money, like the extortion angle on homosexuals in executive jobs or the cigarette thing. Julie K was full of crazy schemes, but once in a while he made sense.

"What kind of books?" Zucco asked him carefully.

"Any kind. Don't matter what they are, just so there's a lot of them."

"I don't get it."

Julie K smiled. "These big publishers, Joe, they sometimes print millions of copies of these paperback books that sell a lot. Right?"

"So?"

"So whatever books don't sell, they're sent back to the publisher. And the publisher gives back what the distributor or store paid for the book." He stopped for effect. "Now suppose, just suppose you had a hundred thousand copies of a book to send back, and they cost you a buck each."

"A hundred grand," Zucco said quickly.

"See how easy it is?"

"Yeah," said Zucco thoughtfully, "but where'll we get a hundred thousand copies of a book? I mean, look, you got to set type and make plates and binding and who knows what else. It'd eat up all the cash. I know a guy prints up them dummy licenses and credit cards, and he says it's a goddamn bitch."

"For him, maybe. Not this."

Zucco was doubtful. "Where you gonna get a hundred thousand books?"

"You don't need them, Joe."

"Huh?"

Julie K beamed. "That's the edge you got. You don't need the books at all, not even one copy."

Zucco just looked at him, wondering if his friend had gone over the edge a little himself.

"Sending books back and forth would cost too much," Julie K explained, "so what they do is they get the distributor to send back only the covers. A hundred thousand covers means that many books."

"You mean all we got to do is print the covers?"

"Simple, eh? And you don't even use real engraved plates, just a cheap plate made by a photo mechanical process. It loses some detail but not enough to matter."

Zucco was impressed. "Maybe you got something, Julie. Maybe you really got something here," he repeated slowly.

"I know I got something here. You look into it. We can make a real kill on this one, Joe, and there's no risk."

"If it works out, you want half?"

Julie K sat silent for a moment, watching his fork scraping around the remains of the shrimp. "This one's a lot like my fake antiques, you know? It's a clean operation with no muscle, no threats." He looked up. "Yes, Joe. I think maybe we go partners on this one. There's a lot of money can be made here."

"If it works out," said Zucco.

"If it works out."

They were finished with their meal and were on the coffee when Fred Riley came over to sit down with them. Riley owned the Pagoda Gardens, winning it, so the story went, from a crazy Chinese in a crap game one night by making fourteen straight passes. Whatever happened, one day the Chinese was there and the next day, there was Riley. He wasn't in the rackets himself, but he knew everybody worth knowing in the city. That included Joe Zucco and Julie K.

"I just bought into another place down by City Hall," Riley said. "Got half of it from the same Chinaman owned this."

"That so?" Julie K's face, round, flabby, with thick bushy eyebrows and a big nose, was perpetually set in a look of total credulity. Short and shapeless, his heavy glasses constantly slipping down the bridge of his nose, where his hand repeatedly pushed them back, he now moved his fat thighs together and squatted deeper into his chair, preparing himself to listen to more crazy Irish talk.

"What happens if he loses it in a crap game?" asked Zucco. "There goes your money too."

"He don't play craps no more. I got him out of that."

"Can't trust them goddamn Chinamen." Zucco's eyes squinted in hard concentration. "One time I had this Chink into me for eight grand. Eight grand. He owns an import business and he lives in this big house with a million other Chinks, see? But he likes the horses, so every day he's at the track playing with my money. This goes on two, three weeks, then one day I don't see him and I send the boys after him. You know what he done? Know what he done? He died in his sleep. Never been sick in his life and he dies in bed owing me eight grand."

"That's when you should've done something," Julie K announced majestically.

"Like what? The sonofabitch was dead."

"You should've held the body for ransom."

"Could've worked," said Riley. "Like I knew this one Chinaman when he died they wanted to auction off his prick. He was a big ladies' man, you know, and they figured some-body'd want it to remember him by."

Zucco puffed hard on his fat cigar. "Tell you one thing, that's the last goddamn Chinaman dies with my money. Cut off his prick, eh?"

"No, that's the whole point. Even after he was dead, it was so hard they couldn't chop it off."

"So they just didn't try hard enough."

"No, they even used a meat cleaver."

"On what?" asked Julie K. "His prick?"

"Yeah, this Chinaman was dead and they tried to whack it off and they couldn't do it."

"What was the matter with the cleaver?"

"Nothing. The guy's prick was like a rock."

"That's the strangest thing I ever heard of, Fred. I never heard of anything like that. Once had a woman tell me about a Jap she was with kept it hard for three days straight. But he was alive at the time."

"Yeah, but wait'll you hear the rest of it. They can't do anything with it, see, so they decide to bury him, but when they get him in the coffin it's standing up so high they can't close the damn thing."

"This Jap was with the woman, he had a dong on him so big he could piss only when it wasn't hard. Or else he'd have to stand about four feet away. She said he couldn't ever piss in the bowl 'cause it'd reach right down into the water. Had to shit standing up, too."

"What about that nigger was barred from all the whorehouses years ago?" asked Zucco. "They say he use to come out the other side."

"Wasn't he the one had to pay double all the time?"

"Yeah, but listen, you ain't heard the end of this. They finally drill a hole in the top of the coffin and stick it through, see, so now he's laying in there with it sticking up out of the coffin and people are coming around saying what the hell is this? Everybody thinks it's the embalming fluid, so now you got a thousand Chinamen lined up to get a shot of the stuff. Meanwhile, the undertaker's saying nothing, he's pulling in the cash at fifty bucks a shot."

"Them goddamn Chinamen'd drink anything."

"Yeah but then when they get him to the cemetery, he can't be buried like that. All the remains have to be inside the coffin is the rule there. And they can't even take the top off to do something 'cause it's stuck tight around his prick. They were in some mess."

"So what they do, Fred?"

"What *could* they do? Took two workmen with sledge-hammers a half hour to level it off. The damn thing must've been made of solid stone."

Julie K silently wiped his glasses with his napkin. Riley drummed the table with his fingertips, grumped in his throat a few times, and started to whistle softly. Zucco blew a smoke ring. "This one broad I knew," he began, "had the whitest snatch I ever seen. It was so white it was transparent. You'd be pumping away, and you look down and you could see yourself coming inside her, clear as anything."

THE LUNCH lasted until almost three-thirty. At four o'clock, while Fred Riley was sitting in his tiny office in back of the Pagoda Gardens looking over the bills, and Julie K was on the phone in his factory ordering a new shipment of old wood dowels and homemade nails, a dark sedan pulled up to the side entrance of the Court Tavern and Grill in the downtown section of the city. Joe Zucco, with his bodyguard Gino Agucci in the lead, hurried up the three steps and through the street door, then up a flight of stairs to a second-floor meeting hall, bypassing the bar and dining room downstairs. They walked the length of the hall swiftly, soon coming to a much smaller room without a door. A long table in the middle of the room took up almost half the space. In one corner a closet, again with no door, held a few empty clothes hangers. An old Rosebud stove stood against one wall, unconnected to any gas line, its blackened and chipped surface giving an air of domesticity to the otherwise barren room. Peelings of dried paint mottled the ceiling, and on the walls successive coats of a yellowish white enamel served only to brighten the grime of years. The dark hardwood floor was bare, its thin planks pockmarked by use and disrepair. An overturned plastic ashtray lay on the floor near the stove. Several others were in use by the three men sitting in straightback chairs around the table. When Joe Zucco walked into the room, they stood up to pay respect.

"Where's Scottini?"

"He's waiting downstairs in the bar."

"Get him."

Johnny Apples, nearest to the doorway, dropped a cigarette on the floor and stepped on it as he got up.

"No, you stay. Hymie'll get him."

Hymie Cole turned toward Zucco, lines of surprise creasing his worried face. "Why me, Joe?" he asked in a quiet voice.

Zucco snorted. "You the one brung him in, right? You're responsible for him." He pointed his finger, his eyes narrowed. "Now you go get him up here."

Hymie rose from his chair without a word, passed behind Al Parry and Gino, who had taken the seat opposite Johnny Apples at the other end of the table from Zucco, and walked out of the room. His footsteps could be heard going down the hall.

Nobody said anything. Johnny Apples lit another cigarette, tossed the match at the nearest ashtray, and missed. Broad-shouldered and heavily muscled, with rows of black wavy hair worn long, Johnny Apples was one of Zucco's four top men. Not yet forty years old, he handled most of the details involving the use of muscle in extortion. Apples was known to have killed at least five men, one with his bare hands, and he boasted of never having spent a day in jail. Al Parry, a second Zucco associate, took care of most of the loanshark work. He was a thin, intense man in his early forties, with a low, syrupy voice that carried a lot of threat. In earlier years he had served time for murder. Hymie Cole looked after Zucco's hidden business interests, including the meat packing plant, a uniform company, a big gas station and truck stop near the Pulaski Skyway, and several local bars. But not the nightclubs. These were handled separately by Pete Montana, the fourth Zucco associate. The cigarette smuggling and big money loansharking were managed by Zucco himself, who also watched closely over the whole operation. Each man had tactical power in his own area but exercised it only by Zucco's wishes, and kept it only by achieving results. As with any well-run business, only results counted.

"Where's Montana?" asked Johnny Apples suddenly.

"He ain't here," Zucco croaked.

Nobody spoke again until Hymie Cole came back with Ray Scottini, who stood in the doorway quietly waiting to be told what to do. Scottini was a ferret-faced man of indeterminate age who had been on Zucco's payroll for about a year as ready muscle. To pay his way, Zucco, at Hymie Cole's urging, had given him a few loanshark accounts, but Scottini, not satisfied with this, had lately started hustling the numbers. This put him in direct confrontation with Alexis Machine, boss of the numbers trade in the city and no friend to Zucco. To make matters worse, Scottini had knocked over one of Machine's policy banks for six thousand dollars. Zucco, aware of all this, had allowed it to continue because he saw a good chance to test Machine's determination. Not specifically interested in the numbers for himself, knowing that only a full-scale local war could upset the balance of power in the city, he yet neglected no opportunity to probe for weakness among his various rivals. Now, however, things had changed. Ray Scottini, in a fit of rage, had shot one of his loanshark victims. The man was permanently paralyzed and his ten-thousand-dollar debt was automatically canceled. To Zucco, this was the same as theft or a double cross in a business deal. It showed him that Ray Scottini had no judgment and couldn't be trusted with the job.

Hymie Cole sat down, looked at Zucco, and ran his hand nervously across his cheek. Al Parry and Gino sat silently in rigid postures. Johnny Apples grinned at Scottini, his thick fingers stroking his Adam's apple. Scottini, shifting from one foot to the other, waited with hat in hand over by the doorway.

"Tell him to come up here," Zucco said in a low voice, looking down at his polished black boots.

Hymie nodded to Scottini, who walked slowly past Johnny

Apples to an empty chair next to Zucco. He stood behind the chair.

Zucco motioned to Gino. "Go get us a bottle of wine, say it's for me. And don't forget the glasses." He turned to Scottini. "You sit down."

Hymie wiped his forehead with his jacket sleeve. "Joe, that thing that happened. It was an accident; you know how these things go. Ray here just had a——"

"Shut up."

Nobody moved. Hymie, his hand gripping the table edge, aged five years. Al Parry stared straight ahead at the blank wall. Johnny Apples kept the cigarette in his mouth, almost burning his lips, because he didn't want to be noticeable. Scottini paled. When Gino returned with the wine, the room was as quiet as a morgue. He put a glass in front of each man and filled it from the green, dusty bottle.

"Ahh. Private stock," Zucco said suddenly. "Vino from the gods, eh?"

"Why not, Joe?" asked Johnny Apples, immediately catching Zucco's new mood. "You own the joint, don't you?"

"You shitting me? This dump ain't turned a penny since I got it. The way things are going, it owns me."

Everybody laughed in their wine. Zucco watched them, the glass raised to his lips. Then he downed the dark red liquid in one swallow. "Fill 'em again," he told Gino, "and get me another bottle. Only don't open this one." Pressing his lips together in sudden realization, Gino refilled the glasses and left the room.

Zucco turned to Scottini. "Now what's the trouble we got here?" Scottini's eyes sought Hymie Cole, but Zucco put his hand up. "You, I'm talking to you."

Scottini gulped. "No trouble," he whispered. "No trouble, Joe, just a little accident."

"No trouble," Zucco exploded. "Just a little accident. Everybody hear that? He says there's no trouble." His head snapped back to Scottini. "Your little accident cost me ten grand. You don't think that's trouble?"

"I can explain that, Joe."

"Can you explain ten grand?" Zucco shouted. "Where is it?"

"You know I ain't got it."

"I know you lost it."

Hymie Cole bit his lip but said nothing. Scottini's hand shook.

"The guy owned a paint company," Zucco said softly. "Who knows how high we could've got him?" He banged the table. "Who knows?" he shouted.

Somebody opened the back door to the bar and the sound of jukebox music drifted upstairs.

"And you, Hymie. You been in the life a long time now. How old are you? Forty-five, forty-six? How could you bring a *gavone* like this around, eh? Maybe you getting soft in the head."

"Joe, I can't be responsible for what a guy does just 'cause I brung him in. I mean, Al here should've kept an eye on him."

Al Parry glowered. "He was working on the accounts you got for him. He didn't come to me for no help. How'd I know what he was doing?"

"You should've known," said Hymie.

"You're his sponsor so you're responsible for what he does. It's always been like that."

"Shut up, all of you." Zucco's eyes blazed. "What you got to say for yourself?" he asked Scottini.

Scottini spread his hands. "The guy was leaning on me for more time for a payment. I already give him a few days extra. When I tell him no more, he gets nasty and tells me he ain't gonna pay nothing, 'not a nickel' is just what he said. Then he comes at me with this big wood club and I got mad, that's all."

"He didn't have no wood club."

"Well, it looked that way to me."

"So you shot him."

"Nothing else I could do."

The downstairs door opened again, allowing a few more musical notes to travel upward.

"There's something else." Zucco almost whispered. "Machine's people tell me you been sticking your big nose in their business. What about it?"

"There's enough for everybody is the way I see it," Scottini said with an air of desperate bravado.

"They say you owe them six grand."

"I took my chances for that dough. I owe them nothing."

"You got any of it left?"

"No."

Zucco shook his head sadly. "I don't know how you lived this long, you understand? You're a danger to anybody around you." He watched as Gino came in with the unopened bottle of wine. "Bring it here." He waited for the wine before continuing. "You pull a deal that could start a war around here, and all you can say is there's enough for everybody. Now you cripple ten grand on me. You know what Machine wants you for? He wants to hang you on a railroad bridge. Cut off your balls and stuff them in your mouth and rip you up the back and leave you off one of them bridges. Only thing saved you is you work for me." He got up. "Now I feel like doing the same thing to you."

Everybody remained silent as Zucco opened the bottle. He filled his own glass, then walked around to each of them and poured. Hymie Cole, Al Parry, Gino, Johnny Apples. He left Scottini's glass empty. "I don't want no more trouble around here," he said, returning to the head of the table. "We have enough going for us without Machine's trade. This town is split up and it's gonna stay that way, or else everybody'd come around taking whatever they want. If we ain't got any law around here, we got nothing. What I'm ruling is we give Machine back his six grand. Hymie, I'm holding you responsible for that. And I mean out of your own pocket. The ten grand, I'll take the bath on that. Now let's drink up and that's the end of it." He picked up his glass.

"What about me, Joe?" Scottini pointed to his empty glass. "You forgot me."

Zucco turned his head toward the ferret-faced man. "You?" He put his glass down. "Yeah, we can't forget you, right?" He took the man's glass, held it in his hand for a moment as if to pour, then returned it to the table, upside down. Scottini's face went white. Hymie Cole sucked in his breath like he had been hit. Al Parry and Gino remained impassive. Johnny Apples grunted in surprise. "You're through, finished, *finito*. You got no brains and I can't use a man got no brains."

"I made a mistake is all," Scottini whined.

"You made too many. I can't afford you no more."

"Please, Joe. Gimme another chance."

Zucco sat down. "You're out and that's it." He drank the wine before him. "If you fight it, you'll be fighting the whole organization. You know what that means. Is that what you want?"

Scottini was motionless in his chair, the glass turned over in front of him. His face had already broken apart and now his mind was picking over the ruins. "They'll kill me," he repeated several times in a soft scream.

"If I was you," Zucco was saying, not hearing him, "I'd get out of town before Machine's boys find out. Know what I mean?" He grinned cruelly. "Cowboys like you, I can get a hundred of them and they ain't worth a pound of piss. If you can't follow orders and work as part of a team, you're no good to me. We're running a business here, see? This ain't Capone's Chicago. This is big business and everybody works together, just like in the army or them big-shot corporations. Only this is bigger than any corporation. But a dumb greaseball like you, you think you know it all."

"I made a mistake," Scottini pleaded.

"Don't make another." Zucco looked down the table at Al Parry. "You pick up his accounts. Johnny, you help Al if he needs it."

"Joe, I got no money."

"You got your life. Take what I give you, or take nothing."

Zucco got up. The meeting was over. Everybody at the

table understood that Ray Scottini had been condemned to civil death. He would not be executed, at least not by Zucco. But he was deprived of all rights in the organization, having been expelled, and his property was inherited by the next of kin. The next of kin was the organization.

Zucco was at the funeral parlor at six-thirty. The body had been dressed in a black suit, pale shirt, and blue silk tie, the hands folded across the chest. On the left hand was a large onyx ring with a diamond chip in one corner. The casket, burnished bronze, rested on a raised platform of moss-green carpet. Heavy rose drapes closed off the background. A lithograph of Jesus hung on the wall. The viewing room, dimly lit by a glass chandelier, was burdened with flowers, wreaths of red roses and white and yellow chrysanthemums. Around the casket lay lilies, carefully strewn. Inside, the face of Joseph V. Flynn held a repose it had seldom known in life.

By seven o'clock the large room was filled with mourners, come to pay their last respects to the county political boss. At age seventy-seven, Flynn had died peacefully in his bed at home, thereby escaping the more dramatic fate frequently wished upon him by many people over the years. In death, he had left the city a political legacy that some thought difficult to live up to, while others considered it impossible to live down. Now he was beyond both praise and condemnation, and even those enemies of his who attended the bier did so with a touch of nostalgic regret—after making certain, of course, that it was really he in the coffin.

Monsignor Brennan of St. Mary's, Flynn's home parish, led the prayers for the dead. A silver rosary was entwined through Flynn's stiff fingers, and a Knights of Columbus pin adorned his lapel. He had received holy communion a few days before his death and the last rites immediately after dying. He was, in the eyes of his church, fit to appear before his God for judgment. To assist him on that far journey, the liturgy for the dead was now being said.

"Praised be God, the Father of our Lord Jesus Christ, the Father of mercies, and God of all consolation, he who comforts us in all our afflictions and enables us to comfort those who are in need."

"Blessed be God."

"Come, let us sing joyfully to the Lord. Let us acclaim the rock of our salvation. Let us greet him with thanksgiving. Let us joyfully sing psalms to him."

"Come, let us adore the king of life."

"For the Lord is a great God, and a great king above all gods; in his hands are the depths of the earth, and the tops of the mountains are his."

"Come, let us adore the king of life."

"His is the sea, for he has made it, and the dry land, which his hands have formed. Let us worship before the Lord who made us, for he is our God, and we are the people he shepherds."

"Come, let us adore the king of life."

Zucco watched from the crowded vestibule. He didn't like these rituals, considered them a barbarous custom of his church. For him a dead body was simply a thing to be buried, the quicker the better. Private mourning he understood; after all these many years he still mourned the death of his sister Carmella, killed by an incompetent abortionist when she was eighteen. But public displays of grief left him cold. And these religious rites, where everyone pretended the deceased had been a paragon of virtue, filled him with contempt. As he listened to the priest's words he couldn't help thinking that Flynn would need more than prayer to atone for his sins, and he wondered how many others were thinking the same thing. "If there's a heaven," Zucco muttered savagely, "that bastard's in hell right now."

"Grant, O Lord, that as we lament the departure of our brother, your servant, out of this life, we may bear in mind that we are most certainly to follow him. Give us the grace to make ready for that last hour by a devout and holy life, and protect us against a sudden and unprovided death. Teach us how to pray that when your summons comes, we may go forth to meet the bridegroom and enter with him into life everlasting, through Christ our Lord."

"Amen."

"Eternal rest grant unto him, O Lord."

"And let perpetual light shine upon him."

"May his soul and the souls of all the faithful departed through the mercy of God rest in peace."

"Amen."

Zucco stood there listening. His meetings with Flynn had been few, consisting mostly of brief exchanges at political affairs and an occasional word of greeting at a local nightspot. But his dealings with Flynn's political machine were long and continuous. Virtually nothing in the city moved without the OK of the machine. From the waterfront to construction, garbage to newsprint, the payoff—chicken soup as it was known—was a way of life. Any illegal activities simply raised the amount of chicken soup. While he never publicly proclaimed himself to be the law, Flynn continued the web of corruption woven by his predecessors. "If the people of this city want it a little bit dirty," he was fond of saying, "who am I to go against their wishes? But they must understand that even dirt has to be paid for." In true democratic fashion he taxed the dirty as well as the clean. Zucco, one of the dirty, had paid his share. But that was all yesterday. Now Flynn lay in a casket holding a rosary and the machine lay in shock holding the bag. Zucco wondered who would get the bag. The only thing he was sure of was that it would continue to be filled.

The service was over. Monsignor Brennan put his prayer folder away and consoled the bereaved. The men went out to the vestibule to smoke, the women crowded around the casket and family. Zucco, uneasy, walked down the carpeted hallway to the front door. He didn't like to be seen in the funeral parlor. He was the legal owner, had been for six years, but to him the business was just a front. He had bought it for a legitimate source of income but chiefly because it gave him access to the second floor, with its separate entrance, which he used as his headquarters. Since large numbers of people were always visiting funeral parlors day and night, the men he had coming around never aroused suspicion in the neighborhood.

Its other function was more recent. With the syndicate's dumping ground for executions accidentally uncovered on a pig farm in South Jersey, Zucco's funeral parlor, along with others controlled by the mob, provided a convenient means of disposal: double-deck caskets, with a legitimate body on top and the murder victim underneath in a false bottom. At the cemetery both bodies went into the ground but only one was recorded. It was a perfect method. The previous evening Zucco had watched Gino Agucci stuff Tommy Ryan into the bottom of a casket holding an eighty-year-old woman who had died of pneumonia. Both bodies were now safely buried. Boswell Earle, Zucco's well-paid funeral director, a highly respected mortician who shut his eyes to his employer's other business interests, knew of the occasional double casket, but considered himself not involved. He was never there when such things were done, nor was he ever asked to participate. His sole job was to run the funeral parlor at a profit, which he did with considerable success.

Outside, Zucco breathed in the dank evening air. He wished he could put a body in with Joseph V. Flynn, it would be sweet revenge for all the payoffs he had had to give the machine. But that was too dangerous, only ordinary people who died for an accepted medical reason and were buried in the ground could be used. Nobody of any renown, nobody who died under suspicious circumstances, no cremations, no mausoleums. He puffed on his fat cigar. Tommy Ryan was a fool, a stupid punk who shot off his mouth in public and tried to act like a movie gangster. He had insulted another, older member of Frank Taylor's organization in a bar. When he got slapped for it, he pulled a gun and made the older man lick his boots. Now Tommy Ryan was dead and buried. Taylor, who ran the city's drug traffic, had asked Zucco to bury the body. Zucco happily obliged, and picked up another favor due on demand.

When John Powers, Flynn's nephew and apparent political heir, came down the steps of the funeral parlor he was wildly angry. "What the hell are those New York detectives doing here?" he bellowed at a local police captain standing on the sidewalk. "And who sent for the goddamn state police?" The captain, who had known that out-of-town cops would be on hand to look over the mourners, denied any knowledge beyond the fact of their presence.

"Well, get them the hell out of here," Powers shouted. "They have no right to intimidate peaceful citizens."

The captain, only a few years away from retirement, was flustered. "What reason can I use on them?"

"Reason? You don't need any reason, you're the law here. Just order them out. And if you don't, I'll get somebody who will."

That was enough for the captain. He walked over to the knot of men. "You guys beat it out of the county fast or I'm gonna have to arrest you."

"You're kidding," one of the New York detectives said.

Now the captain was mad. "You think so, you're nuts, buddy. It's my ass in a sling, not yours. Now move and don't come back."

"I never heard of anything like this," someone said.

"You're hearing it," the captain snapped back. "And just to make sure you get the message, a police car'll follow you to the tunnel." He turned to the state police. "Do me a favor and just fade out of here. I don't want no trouble."

The knot of men loosened and all walked away toward parked cars, their faces tight and their eyes furious. The captain went back to Powers, who just grunted and returned inside. Standing there alone on the steps, the police captain mopped his forehead with a handkerchief and cursed Powers under his breath. Someone must have told him about the New York cops for sure. The captain was glad that Powers hadn't known about the FBI taking pictures from the drab telephone van parked across the street.

Zucco watched the episode from the shadows. He didn't interfere because he had nothing to fear from local or even state police. What he didn't find at all amusing was the idea that New York was interested in the city. He would have to check that. He had spotted the telephone van earlier but didn't regard it as significant. Groups like the FBI were always taking pictures of politicians, it was the new craze.

A car pulled into the driveway.

"Pete. Over here."

Pete Montana stopped the car, saw Zucco coming over, and waited till he got in before wheeling around to the back of the building, where he parked up against the retaining wall. He switched off the lights.

"You just get back?"

"About an hour ago, figured I'd try to catch you. What's the cops for?"

"You should've been here before, you want to see cops. How'd it go down there?"

"Club's doing fine. If the town goes for gambling we'll be in a good spot. But Meyer's still sore about the deal, thinks he should've been in on it."

Zucco grunted. "I'll take care of him. What's with City Hall, they coming around?"

"They're getting greased enough," said Montana. "The town needs the dough, so it looks good. But no timetable." He squirmed in his seat. "Jesus, I'm glad to get out of there, a week's too much in them small towns. No kidding, why all the cops?"

Zucco looked over at the funeral parlor. "Flynn's in there," he said quietly.

Montana whistled. "I seen in the papers he finally caved in, but why your place?"

"Powers figured it'd cause less noise this way. It's Catholic and it's the old man's parish, that makes it just a local boy kind of thing. Up on the hill there'd be too much commotion. Powers don't want no commotion, he just wants the old man buried."

"After all Flynn done for him?"

"What do you expect? All them politicians just a bunch of whores. Show money and they lay down till you turn your back, then they shove in the knife."

Both men sat in silence for some moments. The glow from Zucco's cigar ash was the only sign of life in the darkened car. With the windows rolled up tight, nothing could be heard from the outside. Or from inside.

"Jimmy Rye was in town this morning," Zucco said hoarsely, after a long puff on the cigar.

"Trouble?"

"Yacavelli. The syndicate's dumping him." He brushed an ash from his pants leg. "We got the contract."

"A favor?"

"A favor."

Montana rubbed his nose. "What's the beef?"

"He's using syndicate money on that turkey he's building in Newark. The city's changed hands and the project's dead, but he won't listen. They asked him to stop pouring money down a hole, but he says the city's gonna open up on gambling. He still thinks it'll be another Vegas."

"He's nuts."

"He don't know that."

"If he goes, won't that leave Newark to the niggers?"

Zucco shook his head. "Andy Boyle and Miriglia are all set to split his take. The niggers'll pick up nothing but the crumbs."

Pete Montana inched the front of his pants down, allowing his belly to nudge over it more comfortably. Two years younger than Zucco and a long-time associate, Montana was fast for his weight, which was ample. He was also the most trustworthy of Zucco's key men, a fact appreciated by Zucco. With an unprepossessing face and bland personality, Montana took his time about everything, often giving the impression of being a little slow-witted. But he was far from dumb, and he was a good listener. Now, as he cleared his throat, he believed he knew why Zucco had told him all this. "Who's gonna make the hit?" he asked.

"I can't take no chances on this one, Pete," Zucco replied in a surprisingly soft voice. "I'm giving it to you. Get whoever you need; set it up any way you want. I know from nothing. Just tell me when it's done." Zucco snapped the door handle. "Go get some sleep, you look awful. Must be all them broads down there, eh?"

He got out and went over to the front steps, where he watched Montana's car slowly pull out of the driveway and turn left into the darkness of the deserted street.

At ten o'clock he went home to his townhouse. It had been a long day. On the way he told Gino to get hold of the kid who had been in to see him last week. "What's his name? The war hero, you remember."

"Strega. Harry Strega."

"That's the one. Have him in the office in the afternoon, late. Now who we got to take Scottini's place?"

"What about Benny Roach? He's been looking to get in."

"I don't like the punk. He's too snotty."

"He's done a few good jobs."

"No."

Gino thought for a minute. "There's Charley Flowers."

"Flowers is OK."

"Use to be a good boy, but he can't take it when something goes wrong. No good in the clutch."

"He's OK on the muscle, ain't he?"

"Yeah, he's got some good years left."

"So give him a few of Scottini's accounts, see how he does. And tell him he don't get paid by the job no more now he's on the books."

His mistress was waiting for him.

"I might be going into the clothing business in a big way," he told her.

"I hope it's furs." Her long legs stretched in front of her, the slender hips taut, the graceful back straight, she was sitting on the living room floor doing her exercises.

"It's men's clothes, no furs. I got this guy that needs cash, see? He owns a big store but he blows it all on the horses. And he likes the play that little girls give him, that puts him behind. If I can only get him in deep enough I got a chance. But I need luck on this one."

While his mistress changed out of her black exercise tights, Zucco, Scotch and soda in hand, began to relax on the couch.

"If I can hook this one I got it made," he said toward the upstairs. "I'll get a deal with Baraca to supply me with the goods. He's got all them spics in his factories can make that stuff like nothing. All they got to do is put in the right labels and I can sell 'em for ten times what they cost. Who'd know? All the suckers want is a label so they feel they got something for the cash. It's like the meat racket. You stamp it grade A and they'd buy the worst shit off the rails. Or the booze, same thing. All they want is to think they're getting the real thing. Yeah, if I can swing this clothes thing I got one sweet deal here. You know what I mean?" Zucco waited. "Cindy?" He looked up, saw the bedroom door closed. Feeling foolish, he muttered to himself and went back to the couch. Goddamn broads, they never listen when you want them to. "What the hell you doing up there?" he shouted. "You dead or something?"

"What?"

"I said what're you doing up there?"

"I'm dressing."

"For what?" He took a swallow of the Scotch, wiped his mouth with the back of his hand. "We ain't going nowhere."

"All right, all right," she shouted.

Waiting, he finished the Scotch.

"You like me like this?" she asked softly from above. "Or have you seen it before?"

"Jesus Christ."

"You said we weren't going anywhere."

He watched her come down the stairs. Long slim legs, smooth and unmarked, coming to a perfect V of blond hair above the muscular thighs. A firm belly, still bronzed from the Florida sun. Above the belly button, more taut skin slowly rounded to breasts like Byzantine domes. She stood in front of him, naked, her long white neck softly arched, the red lips caught in a courtesan's smile. He felt himself harden for her for the hundredth time, or the thousandth.

"Jesus Christ," he repeated.

"You said that," she teased, the smile unchanging.

He could think of nothing else. Removing his pants right there in the middle of the living room, he pushed her down onto the rug, not thinking or caring about a woman's sensibilities. She was his, she had told him, and what was his was to be used by him. When he was with her like this, in these moments, he thought of no other woman, and each time he marveled anew at the experience. She was reserved, yet she did his bidding, feeling each spasm. He moved his hand over her, and in this moment her presence was startling. He was suddenly aware of the wetness of his own body, his forehead, his underarms, his thighs, his legs.

"Come to me," she whispered, and the sound of her voice was heard from a great distance.

IT WAS a narrow, ugly red brick building with a high stone stoop set between rusted iron railings that over the years had resisted every attempt, however noble, at destruction. The bent and twisted metal had given shape to local legends about two long-ago lovers turned to stone for their evil ways, forever guarded by a pair of iron devils. Neighborhood children were admonished to keep away lest they fall prey to the devil or hurt themselves on the gnarled mass, and so quite naturally every day saw them at play on the stoop, jumping, tumbling, sliding the rails, bruising, scraping, and cutting themselves with reckless ingenuity. At dusk and suppertime, they abandoned the sagging house for home, leaving it only the warmth of its electric fixtures. Inside, in the papered halls and painted rooms, lamps were lit and shades drawn as people of different persuasions came and went according to their needs, using the stoop only as a ferry to or from the world outside.

On the second floor of the rooming house, Harry Strega lay in bed in the darkness, masturbating. Flashes of girls he had known, disembodied faces, faceless bodies, ran across the mirror of his mind, some exaggerated in proportion, others distorted in action, all supine and bowing to his will. Stimulated, his hand moving in a practiced, rhythmic stroke, he thought of the girl in Ding Ho, a Vietnamese hamlet his company had stayed in one night, a miserable mud-mired village of several dozen huts surrounded by fields of wasted crops. It had been overrun and rerun by both sides: spent ammunition and fragments of equipment lay everywhere along the trail outside the village. The Americans had remained for most of the night before moving out, and long before their withdrawal across the blasted countryside in the face of enemy fire, the homes had been searched, Harry finding a young and quite beautiful Vietnamese girl. He had raped her, a slight child of about fourteen in a torn dress. He didn't know why he had done it, he wasn't even sure it had been rape. Finding her there, alone, being with her in the middle of a jungle war, a million miles from the containment of home, hating these people who hated him, he wanted only a little warmth and comfort and so he made love to her. She did not resist, she did not move but simply lay there as he held her closely. He meant her no harm. In another time and place he might have seen in her a schoolgirl and, noting her sexuality, been roundly ashamed of himself. When he entered her she said nothing, her eyes, unblinking, staring at him. Touching her, he felt an incredible flow of physical energy, lasting perhaps a minute from breath to breath as the rush left him. Excited wildly by her long dark hair, her small breasts, and soft, clear skin, he kissed her repeatedly, wanting her to feel the passion of his body as it sought the stillness of hers. The girl spoke only once, a single word as he, relieved, stood above her tidying himself. "Death," she had said in her native tongue, but he didn't know why she had said it or what she had meant by it.

He stopped the rhythmic motion of his hand. Other thoughts, defeating him, clouded his memory. A sergeant had taken the girl, used her brutally, not out of love as he had done, but in hate. He understood the emotion but could not understand why it had to be so. Afterward, the sergeant had shot her through the head. The company had lost nine men at the village, destroyed by an unseen enemy, perhaps the very people they had come to protect. It was a sordid war.

Harry got up from his bed, cursing himself, his memory, all that made him uncomfortable.

He ate supper in a diner down the block, pork chops and mashed potatoes and string beans for a dollar seventy-five. The food looked better than it tasted and he washed it down with two glasses of milk. By the time he had finished, the diner, run by two Poles, was closing. At this hour people were home from work, watching television, preparing for the next day's ordeal. Harry pitied them. Before going into the army, he had worked briefly at several jobs, liking none of them. It was the routine, the sameness, that paralyzed his will, making him unable to continue at any of them.

For this same reason he had hated his schooling, finding it dull and unrewarding, and continued only because the aunt with whom he lived insisted he remain in school. There was little for a sixteen-year-old to do anyway and so he went to Hoboken High, sitting in the park across the street on warm days, in neighborhood candy stores at other times, shying away from the jacketed gangs, going with this girl and that, doing his schoolwork which was really no work, and finally getting his diploma in a night of ceremony that saw him proposition a blond kindergarten teacher at one of the inevitable parties following the program. At a rugged six feet one, though somewhat bent from drink, he was accepted and woke up the next morning in the teacher's apartment, surprised but pleased. Thus began the first serious involvement of his young life, and while it did not last beyond the sexual flash, the kindergarten teacher soon moving on to other, fresher prey and he, fiercely proud, unable to protest, the brief affair filled him with a sense of power. In one stunning defeat he had learned all he needed to know about women. He became the predator, working on a biological urge rather than an emotional need, and in this way he was seldom touched and never pierced.

His aunt, disappointed in life and given to a melancholia that frightened the boy growing up, died in the summer of his graduation. She had once been married, he knew that, but not much more. Perhaps her husband had died or left her suddenly, she never would say, would never talk of him. She had had no children of her own, and when his parents, his mother her sister, were killed in an automobile accident—he was five then —the woman, alone, stoical, and resigned, took the boy to her home. It was an orderly, well-scrubbed rooming house that she owned. He slept in rooms of secondhand furniture, spotted dressers with loose mirrors and fluted legs, beds with stained mattresses and painted silver springs. When he rose for school each day his aunt was already well into her routine of cleaning the rooms and tending to the house, her surrogate child. At his bedtime hour she had not yet finished her work. It was a large house of three stories and a basement, eleven rooms in addition to their first-floor apartment. He seldom saw his aunt during the day, eating only supper with her in the small kitchen between his bedroom and hers. Gradually he came to accept her silence in the quiet of the house and the fact of his own singularity. His aunt neither encouraged nor discouraged him; knowing little about raising a boy she wisely, to her, let him grow by himself. She kept house. Sparse and angular, she carried herself with the unmistakable air of one who could be surprised by nothing but good fortune.

In the beginning Harry had fought her studied indifference with a child's fantasies of being the center of attention. With adolescence he took to secrecy. In high school his every move was so shrouded that his aunt finally assumed an active interest and began to demand explanations. By his last year he had run through every available stratagem for keeping her as uninformed as she had always been. "You never were interested before," he told her more than once when she hounded him for the particulars of his existence, and she, smugly satisfied and nodding to herself with pursed lips at the latest proof of her view of life, retired to await the next vindication.

He walked across town to the piers, passing the block on which he lived all those years with his aunt. He didn't look back. On Hudson Street he passed the Catholic church and the small park with its two rusted cannons forever facing west and the approaching redcoats. Wearing the new hundred-and-fifty dollar suit custom-built with Joe Zucco's money, each stitch and fold shaped to his body, he went down the cobbled road behind the ball field, carefully avoiding broken glass, crumpled paper bags, bricks, flattened cans, metal shards, and weathered pieces of lumber tossed along the roadbed. At the pier's edge gummy water foamed up coffee containers and bits of wood, colored rags, leaves, and an occasional prophylactic. On the water seagulls hopped and skipped, rising only to dive again. Harry stood on the rotting bulkhead between two covered piers, one used sporadically, the other a nightmarish twist of steel girders roofless to the blazing sky, unused and unfinished. This was his favorite spot in the city at night; from here he could see New York's magic lightshow in all its dazzle. The Empire State Building stretched before him, its upper torso bathed in white light that gave him a religious feeling. East across the Hudson the West Side Highway, with its thousands of moving eyes, loomed both north and south beyond vision. The water itself, dark and mercurial even where a spot of light announced a passing vessel, reflected the calm of the city from a safe distance. His eyes, adjusted now to the pinpoints of light within the dark circle, began to pick out shadowed objects across the river, ominous in outline. As curls of whitish water rode inward on slight waves, banged against the piles underneath him, eddied about, gave up their bits of debris, turned tail, and rolled out again, he continued to scan the far shore, at peace now with himself and the world.

At the other end of the ball field, the road down to the docks turned sharply left before veering back to the water's edge. Jagged, cemented rocks lined both sides of the road, forming guide walls. Moving slowly, his feet picking carefully over the old railroad tracks at the foot of the hill, Harry walked between the rock walls whose grotesque outlines, looking like stone Medusas in the dim moonlight, played havoc with his imagination. Coming to the park's edge, he sat down on one of the benches facing the water and, closing his eyes, inhaled deeply of the sea air. With his lungs filled and his back ramrod against the bench, he exhaled slowly through his nose. He kept breathing in this manner for a long while. After a time he got up and walked through the deserted park toward home, again passing the ancient cannons, the Catholic church, and the block on which he used to live, until finally he arrived back at the stone stoop guarded by the pair of iron devils, which he also had to pass before gaining the privilege of sleep.

At ten in the morning Harry brushed his teeth and fixed organic eggs for himself on the double-burner, looked over the newspaper furtively taken from outside his neighbor's door, and spent twenty minutes in the bathroom before putting on his street clothes and walking out of his building down the swept steps past the painted fence. He turned south on Jefferson Street. At the highway he waited by the bus stop until a green Ford pulled up. The driver, Frank Farrano, was a massive ex-longshoreman whom Harry had met the week before in Zucco's office. On the seat next to Farrano was a blue Pan Am flight bag, its shoulder strap wrapped tightly around the bag.

"That it?" Harry asked.

"That's it," answered Farrano.

"I never even seen that much," Harry said ruefully.

Farrano said nothing.

They rode in silence out the Holland Tunnel exit toward the turnpike. At Tonnele Avenue they turned right and continued on until they came to the Starlight Motel. Farrano steered into the parking area and stopped behind a powder-blue Cadillac. "Probably his." He shut off the motor. "The bastard's really raking it in."

"Will he be around now?" Harry asked cautiously.

Farrano chuckled. "Don't get nervous, kid. Just stay with me and keep your mouth shut and your eyes open."

"I ain't nervous." Harry scowled. "Just like to know, that's all."

"He'll be here," muttered Farrano, getting out of the car. "Today's their payday so he's around somewhere."

"You forget something?" asked Harry.

"What?"

He pointed to the bag.

"Christ," Farrano said, reaching into the car. "Maybe I'm the nervous one." He chuckled again, a fat man's laugh that got caught in the folds of flesh at the throat. Surprisingly fast for his three hundred pounds, Farrano put the flight bag under his arm and waddled toward the motel, Harry a step behind.

In the lobby, once past the potted palms and vending machines and dry goods counter, they went through an archway under a small neon sign that spelled out Cloud Nine, the nightclub-lounge attached to the motel. Inside, all the lights were on, even those behind the bar and over the bandstand. Chairs were still piled upside down on the tables and large green sacks of refuse were lined along one wall by the kitchen door leading to the service entrance. The walls of the huge room were arched and covered with blue imitation velvet and silver stripes. Overhead, the balloon ceiling lamps, in various colors and sequined for light diffusion, rotated airily from slender black poles, their movement casting constantly changing patterns on the parquet floor. The room was empty.

"So this is what it looks like in daylight," Harry mused, feeling almost as if he were in some kind of silent church. "Sure is quiet."

Farrano was not impressed. "Don't do nothing for me, but the suckers must go for it all right." His booming voice echoed in the cavernous room.

"Where is he, you think?"

"How should I know? Maybe in the office, wherever that is."

Both men stood there, helpless, in the middle of the floor, their feet fixed firmly while their heads swiveled in all directions. Farrano held the bag in one huge hand while Harry, out of place, kept his hands in his jacket pockets.

"We're still closed. Can't you fellas see that?"

Two heads turned toward the voice. An old, white-haired man, holding a silver pail, was standing by the entrance.

"Can you tell us where's the office, pop?" Farrano asked loudly. "We want to see Mr. Green."

The old man bristled. "No need to shout, I can hear you. My ears is good as when I got 'em." He put down the pail. "What you want him for?"

"Got some business with him," Farrano said in a lowered voice. "He's expecting us."

"Don't know's he's in yet." The old man pointed. "You go through there and up a little stairs. Last door you come to."

Farrano was already moving. "Thanks, pop," he said over his shoulder. Harry, right behind him, turned back at the door. The old man was nowhere to be seen.

"He's gone," he whispered urgently to Farrano.

"Who?"

"The old guy."

"So what? Maybe he's working 'stead of being so goddamn nosy." He was halfway up the stairs.

"Maybe," Harry reluctantly agreed.

The hallway was lit by a single red bulb, naked in a ceiling fixture. The door at the top of the stairs, a solid slab of wood with a gold-plated handle-lock combination, was open several inches. Farrano carefully peered in, keeping the bulk of his considerable body behind the door. It was a liquor closet, small but well stocked, with rows of shelves neatly arranged by brands. "Private stuff," Farrano said softly. "He must stay around here a lot."

Harry looked in. "Enough here for a liquor store. You think he sells it on the side?"

Farrano was already at the second door, which was locked. He noiselessly turned the handle several times. Nothing. Fishing in his pocket he brought out a small piece of clear plastic which he pressed up against the door jamb at the lock. The door didn't open. "Double-locked," he muttered disgustedly, a surprised look on his face.

"Probably a linen closet or something," Harry whispered.

"Yeah," said Farrano suspiciously.

They stood in front of the last door. Farrano squared his enormous shoulders, almost covering the whole doorway, knocked loudly once, and turned the knob.

"Come in."

The man was tall and thin, his gaunt face and large bony hands tight-skinned. A Zapata moustache framed large white teeth. He was dressed only in pants and slippers.

"We're looking for Phil Green," Farrano announced pleasantly. "He around?" His eyes searched the otherwise empty office.

"I'm Green. What's on your mind?"

"You?" Farrano's mouth dropped in surprise.

"Me," Green said, frowning. "What's the matter, something you didn't expect about me," his voice got tight, "white man?"

Farrano's eyes narrowed to pinpoints. He licked his lips, wanting to take this nigger apart. How the hell could a nigger own a joint like this anyway? Something wrong somewhere. He saw Green standing there smirking, and he shrugged off his thoughts. Business is business.

"My name's Jones," he said politely, "and this is Mr. Smith. We're here representing your new partners."

"My what?"

"We're here representing your new partners," Farrano repeated slowly.

Green's face suddenly looked scared. Nobody said anything. From a second room behind the office a toilet flushed and a moment later a mellifluous voice, babbling incessantly, approached. She was blonde and sensuous, blue-eyed, long-legged, wearing only a half slip and panties. Three heads turned at her entrance. Harry almost wet his pants. Her breasts, snowy white and perfectly arched, were the biggest he had ever seen on a slim-bodied girl. He had heard about such things but believed them possible only in fairy tales and movie stars. Now he was seeing them in the flesh and he still could hardly believe it. Even Farrano, whose weight compelled him to find sexual interest mostly in a woman's mouth, was impressed.

"Oh." Her voice had a hesitant quality to it, as though doubting its own strength. "I didn't know you had company, Phil." She crossed her hands over her breasts, succeeding in covering only the nipples.

"Go get dressed," Green snapped at her. "I'll be there in a minute."

Harry stared as she backed out of the doorway, giving him a smile as she turned and disappeared. "Goddamn," he said loudly to himself.

Farrano grinned lasciviously. "Some piece, eh? You must be doing all right here."

Phil Green, recovered, played it hard. "What's this about partners?" he sneered. "I don't have any partners."

"It's like this, Mr. Green," Farrano began. "The people we represent think this place is too much for one man to handle. Too much business and too many worries. You see what I mean?"

"So you're going to help me handle it," Green replied sardonically.

"That's the idea. Only it's not us that'll be here, like I say we just represent the people who asked us to talk to you."

"And who might they be?"

Farrano spread his hands in a gesture that indicated the question was of no importance. "Just a group of businessmen who don't want to get involved in all the red tape and technicalities. You'll meet them sometime."

"And they expect to just walk in and take over, is that it? I mean, just like that?"

"Oh no, Mr. Green, no sir. You misunderstand. The people we represent don't want to take over anything they don't own. That wouldn't be right. They just want to protect their interest is all."

"They don't have any interest in this place. I own all of it."

"Up to now that's true, yes sir." Farrano opened the blue flight bag and dumped its contents on the desk. "There's twenty thousand here. It's all yours, every dollar. This is a legitimate business deal."

"What's it for?"

"A partnership. You see, Mr. Green, nobody wants to take over your whole business."

"No, they just want to share it with me."

"Now you got the idea."

Phil Green snorted. "I gross this much every week around here. Every week." He picked up a stack of bills. "This is chicken feed, even if I wanted partners. Which I don't."

"Do yourself a favor and take it, Mr. Green," said Farrano in almost a whisper. "It's the only offer you're gonna get."

"Is that a threat?"

Farrano spread his hands again. "You been around, you know how these things go. Either soft money or hard ground."

"I'll take my chances."

Farrano's sigh boomed around the room. "Mr. Green," he said sorrowfully, "don't you think maybe you're taking on more than you can handle? I mean, this place is OK now but you never know."

"I'm doing fine on my own."

"You're not interested in the twenty grand. Is that final?"

"That's final. Now get out of here, I have work to do. And take that money with you."

Harry helped Farrano scoop the piles of money back into the bag. "You're a marked man," Farrano said to Phil Green on his way out the door, the bag under his arm again. "Don't say you wasn't warned."

All the way down the stairs and back through the night-club and motel lobby, Harry kept searching for the girl they had seen in Green's office, thinking maybe she had slipped out another door and was waiting for him. She had, after all, smiled at him. But she was nowhere to be seen. Even as Farrano pulled the car out of the driveway onto Tonnele Avenue, Harry craned his neck back for one last fruitless glance. When he tried to talk about her, Farrano wouldn't listen. "She goes with niggers, don't she?" Harry admitted she did. "So she ain't worth shit." That made Harry laugh.

"You mean you wouldn't grab her juice if you could? You wouldn't stick your head between those balloons she got, just 'cause she gives it to niggers?" Farrano told him to shut up. "Anybody'd let that go is nuts," Harry said. Farrano said nothing.

While Harry sat in silent thought about the girl, Frank Farrano thought furiously about business. The nigger would have to be softened up; some rough stuff on his employees and customers should do it. If business got bad enough he'd come around; they all did. He hoped Zucco'd give him the job; he didn't like the nigger making all that money and having the white bitch. But if Pete Montana handled it, he wouldn't get the nod because Montana didn't like him, the crummy bastard. If Johnny Apples handled it, everything'd be OK. He decided that Zucco would let Johnny Apples take it, and then he'd be in on it. He stole a quick glance at Harry. Nothing there, he told himself. The kid's big but his head is into the tramps too much. No good for business. He pressed his foot down on the gas and wiped Harry out of his mind, thinking only of the linguini and clam sauce that his mother, God bless her, was making for him right now at home.

ON A WARM AFTERNOON, still in the grip of the girl from
Cloud Nine, Harry rode with Lucy Berg on the train to Coney
Island, fifty minutes across the foot of Manhattan and down the
arm of Brooklyn. At Church Avenue the train roared out of the
tunnel into gray skies stretching over rows of disabled houses
with uneven roofs, all solemn in the pensive air. Television
antennae looped downward over cornices and drainpipes.
Along the elevated subway tracks, blackened switches changed
automatically, sending unseen instructions to other parts of the
network. In the first car, his palm flat up against the motor-
man's door for support, Harry watched the houses fly by while
Lucy, at his side, stared straight ahead out the front window,
her neck occasionally rubbing against his outstretched arm.

Lucy was a doctor's daughter, a plain girl with thick hair,
a bobbed nose, and heavy, sensuous legs that Harry wanted to
stroke. He had started dating her in high school because he was
told she had a crush on him, and he needed something easy at
the time. The first half-dozen dates with Lucy, he had struck
out. This confused and angered him, especially since he knew
of several others who boasted of having made it with her. He

kissed and fondled her when they were alone on the leather couch in her father's waiting room but he could get no farther. Sensing in his infinite adolescent wisdom that it was a lost cause, at least for him, he broke several dates with her and remained aloof in class. After two weeks of such treatment she cornered him in the hall and asked him to come over to her home that night because she had a surprise for him. Curious, he agreed. When he appeared at the house she led him downstairs to the waiting room, sat him on the couch, and disappeared into the doctor's empty office. In a few minutes she returned with his surprise. She was naked. To Harry at that moment she looked beautiful. He quickly removed his clothes and they lay together on the couch until, uncomfortable, they shifted to the shag rug on the floor. There, with his feet propped against the baseboard heater and her backside pressed against the shag, Harry and Lucy celebrated their bodies. Afterward, flushed with success and filled with gratitude or love, Harry asked Lucy why she had waited so long to express her feeling for him, and she calmly told him that she had had warts on her vagina. When he sleepily asked if they were contagious, she calmly told him yes. When he asked, somewhat more alert now, how she could be sure they were gone, she told him she wasn't at all sure but she didn't want to lose him and so she took a chance. For the next few weeks Harry checked himself daily for warts. He didn't understand how Lucy could have been so unfeeling.

The train pulled wearily into the Coney Island station and shuddered to a stop, the doors clanged open simultaneously, releasing hordes of wild children and childlike adults in a festive spirit. The smell of the sea was everywhere, rolling invisibly across the cemented dunes. Giant apartment houses built on sand brooded over the shore while lesser houses hovered nearby. On the boardwalk that snaked its way along the beach's edge, small shops cajoled and sold their wares to people with few cares, at least for the day. Gulls performed their feats of levitation at the waterline, careful to preserve their distance. A warm breeze, wafting gently across the land, tickled bare torsos lying lazily on the drying sand.

The sky was clearing to the west. For Harry, slowly unwinding in the warmth of Lucy's familiarity, the day gradually became a respite from his new life of excitement. He still had almost a thousand dollars from his army savings, and he just knew that he'd be making lots more doing jobs for Zucco. Best of all, he'd be around the big money and the beautiful women that came with it—like the girl at the Cloud Nine club, Miss Balloon. Now that was what money got, and he was going to get his share. He nuzzled Lucy's breast with his mouth, his head resting on the flat of her stomach. They lay close together on the littered sand, halfway between the boardwalk and the water, he in Levi's and a work shirt, she in a two-piece bathing suit. Her breasts looked mountainous from his angle of vision, rounded peaks rising from a fleshy plain, ripe to burst free from the constricting top with the very next breath, yet he knew, or thought he remembered, that they were merely of average size and shape. He hadn't seen Lucy since high school, accidentally meeting her again on a local bus after three years. She was going to college. He told her he would call but he didn't for a month, finally calling late one evening out of loneliness and sexual frustration. She would not see him that night, of course, and could not for at least a week. Too busy with schoolwork. Angered, Harry hung up on her. Several weeks later he again called her late one evening. This time she agreed to meet him on the weekend. Now as his finger absently traced circles on her belly, Harry wondered if it was worth all the trouble.

For hours the sun came and went at the whim of moody clouds. In between huddling together and brief bouts of fitful sleep, voices nearby each time awakening them, they changed positions, stood and yawned, exercised their bodies, and collected seashells, all of them cracked. Lucy eventually put on her sweater and took off her top in a single, swift female movement that has long mystified the less dexterous male. His arm around her, Harry slipped his other hand under the sweater, all the while murmuring sounds and blowing kisses in her soft, grainy ear.

The sky gradually darkened; the inscrutable bleatings of the seagulls softened and ceased; people picked themselves off the beach, trudged up the boardwalk steps, and disappeared into civilization. The starry points of the big dipper flashed on in the galactic distance where infinite clouds of dust roamed the curve of time. A stillness hung over the world and in its midst the stretch of beach was lulled to sleep by the soft slurp of silvered water.

Harry and Lucy lurked together long into darkness. His mouth against hers, their bodies pressed together in a lover's embrace, they lay motionless in the cooling sand, oblivious to the passing of time or rolling of waves. Her tongue between his teeth was serpentine, darting about with small, deceptive thrusts. His hand upon her breast slowly kneaded the pliant flesh, the fingers stretching and relaxing in tandem. They were alone on the beach. When the night air cooled, Harry put his jacket around Lucy and pulled her even closer. He was aroused by this plain girl, wanting her submission to him, the submission of her body to his. He kissed her savagely, biting into her lip, holding her head tightly between his hands. His sudden urge made him realize where they were but he found he did not care. He wanted to possess Lucy because of all the good things he remembered about her, but also because she was the only girl next to him at the moment. He tried to think of her as the girl at Cloud Nine. Her pallor became rose-tinted, her frayed hair silken, her face animated, the breasts became balloons, the body smoothed and curved to perfection. In the moonlight she looked beautiful to him, just as she had looked when he had first seen her at the club. Excited now, he thrust his hand under the sweater, pulling it up as he drew his face near to kiss the voluptuous swells. His hand squeezed her breast as his mouth flopped down to gorge itself on the nipple. With uneven ardor he squeezed and gorged on a fantasy of his own making, interrupted only whenever he opened his eyes. In his deepening passion Harry kept them closed. His mind soaring, he felt constrained by the limitations of flesh. He alone in all the world possessed the woman of all dreams, and this he accepted as right and proper. Stiffly, with one leg crossed over hers and his pants already unzipped, he began prying Lucy's brief suit downward, his trembling fingers brushing the perfect body of the perfect woman, when Lucy's hand touched his, holding it in mid-motion.

"No."

Defeated, his mind punctured and his ego shot, he opened his eyes and saw Lucy staring at him. She let his hand go and he watched it crumble into the sand. She pulled on her suit, fixing it into place.

"Is that all I am to you?"

"How can you ask that?"

"We don't even know each other."

"We knew each other years ago."

"That was years ago."

"I just wanted to get close to you again."

"You were never close to me."

"What do you mean? Didn't we make it together all those months?"

"And when someone else came along you were gone."

"What about you? You didn't waste any time getting somebody."

She looked hurt. "I did it just to show you it didn't matter to me. But it did, it really did."

"And now it don't."

"I didn't say that."

He pouted. "Anyway, I want to be with you again."

"I'll bet."

"Well, I do."

Lucy lay there a long time, not smiling, unmoved. Harry waited, wondering what more he could say, or if he should say anything. He slowly removed his leg from hers, hoping she wouldn't notice, twisted his body until there was sand between them. He fidgeted with his hands, zipped up his pants, and stared, unseeing, up at the sky. The waves slapped the beach with a monotonous hum. Off in the distance shadowy figures on the long pier cast crab nets and fishing lines into the murky water. A silhouette moved imperceptibly out at sea.

"Harry?"

"Umm."

"Did you mean it?"

He rolled over on his side, facing her. "Mean what?"

"What you said about wanting to be with me again."

"Sure I meant it. You think I'd say something like that if I didn't mean it?"

She didn't answer. After a long moment her fingers moved up his pants leg, coming to a stop at the crotch. Noiselessly the zipper was opened. She put her hand inside, touching him, cool flesh against hot. Squirming, he tried to straighten himself. He grew big at her touch. With desperate movement he worked the swimsuit down to her knees, then brought his foot up to slide it down her legs. "Is it safe here?" she asked as Harry, unhearing, frantically removed her hand from inside his pants, freed himself, and rolled on top of her. He shut his eyes, trying to conjure up the fantasy again. The girl from Cloud Nine came into his vision, smiling, willing, inviting. She wrapped her arms around him, her fingers pressing into his back, and he thrust himself forward, kicking, clawing the sand at her shoulders, thankful that he had played his cards right. He moved with her body, locked with her in mortal combat. He quickened, growling from somewhere deep within. There was a tightening of muscle. As his breath came in staccato bursts of blinding light, he groaned and a ship at sea sighed mournfully.

Darkness returned. Breathing huskily, their heads thrown back onto the disheveled sand, Harry and Lucy lay still, each lost in a separate reality. He was surprised at how good he felt. Was it like this years ago? He couldn't remember but he didn't think so. Or maybe it was just the moonlight and the beach. He raised his arm to the sky, touching stars with his finger.

"Did you really miss me?" Lucy asked him.

"Sure I did."

She beamed at that. She had liked Harry in high school and had thought of him often. Was that love? She didn't think so, but she felt good being with him. At least until real love came along. Slipping back into her swimsuit, she pulled her sweater down and turned over onto her stomach, her head next to his.

"God, I was so horny."

"Me too."

"Let's do it again," she said lewdly.

He laughed. "On a public beach?"

"That didn't stop you before."

"It was hard before."

She squeezed his arm. "So I noticed."

On the boardwalk somebody passed with a radio blaring country music. They said nothing for a while, listening to the disappearing sound. A dog ran furiously in the soft sand, its owner lost in the shadows underneath the boardwalk. When the air turned chilly, Lucy brushed the sand off her thighs and put on her skirt. Harry eyed her approvingly.

"I could stay here all night, you know?"

She shook her head. "I got class tomorrow."

"I didn't mean we would," he said irritably, "just that it'd be nice."

"When it's warmer. Anyway, I'm hungry."

"All right, all right." He picked up his jacket and shook it violently. "Goddamn sand is everywhere," he growled.

"It's a beach, remember?"

"How could I forget?" Putting on his jacket he slipped his hand under her dress.

She slapped at him playfully. "What was that about a public beach?" she teased.

"Who said that?"

"You did."

"Not me."

"You."

He shrugged. "When it's soft a man'll say anything."

"And when it's hard," said Lucy with a laugh, "you'll do it anywhere, is that it?"

"You got any complaints?"

She thought for a moment. "Oh, I guess it was all right for a beach."

"Ever do it like this?"

She made a face. "Too sandy for me."

"You got no romance in your soul," he said gravely.

"Maybe not," she agreed. "But right now there's a lot of sand up it."

Laughing, arms entwined, shoes and socks in hand, they trudged to the boardwalk, where they put on their shoes, and continued on to Nathan's, sitting in the small indoor compartment at a corner table. After reading the menu on the wall Lucy wanted to order one of everything. "Sex always makes me hungry," she said disarmingly. "The more I get the more I eat." Harry, watching her, wondered how she would look in ten years. He silently vowed not to be around to find out.

On the train home she dozed against his shoulder. At her home she invited him in. "We can go in the waiting room. Nobody's there now."

"And do what? You already been laid," said Harry.

Tired of her, wanting only to get away, he had decided on the direct approach. All her old ways had now come back to him and he knew nothing less would work; she was very forceful once she saw something she wanted. Some girls were like that; they couldn't just be grateful for the sex and leave things alone.

"You think that's all I'm interested in?" she screamed at him, and he saw her eyes blaze out of control. He suddenly wished girls could be more like men. "I never should have gone out with you again," she said on the verge of tears. "You haven't changed one bit."

Harry stood there, his hand on the gate. While Lucy sputtered on, he grimaced and bared his teeth and stared down at the ground. He had been through it all before, standing there at the gate, listening to her bellow in rage.

He remembered the feeling, like he was drowning. He was back in high school, going around with her and getting steady sex. At first it was enjoyable. But after a few months he began to get restless, to feel that he was somehow being used. It was the sameness of the relationship that bothered him. Sex with her became mechanical; everything they did together they had done before, said before, thought before. It was maddening. Yet she seemed to thrive on this very sameness, as though her life had been set to this course and there was nothing new to which she aspired. He began to resent her. He noticed how she led him about, expecting him to do her bidding. He discovered she couldn't stand to have her plans upset. Worst of all, she took him and their relationship for granted. He felt no such assurance. As the days dragged on, he became increasingly convinced that he did not want to be so committed, to her or to anyone. After all, it was only the sex that interested him. But he knew she would not understand that. Finally, in desperation, Harry told her it was over. Standing there at the gate after spending half the night with her on the waiting-room floor, he told her there was someone else. Within a week there was. And after that one, another and another.

Reluctantly, his mind returned to the present.

"How could you just stand there and pretend you don't hear a word I'm saying?"

"Huh?"

"I asked you if it's true?"

"If what's true? What are you talking about?"

"That you just use a girl's body and then throw her away like she was a rag doll."

"Oh, for chrissake." He suddenly saw that he had changed a great deal. It was she who was still in high school, playing her little-girl games. He sighed heavily. She would never change. He had been through death and had killed, and here she was talking to him as though she were still sitting in class with her legs crossed. In the middle of a sentence he put his hands gently on her shoulders, leaned over, and kissed her tenderly on the forehead and walked away.

"Harry?"

He was already past the next house when he turned.

"Will you call me?" Lucy asked softly.

"For what?"

"You know, just to be together." She fluttered her eyelids suggestively. "It was really good."

Looking out for the future, he said he would.

THE HIRING HALL was jammed. Men eased their way back and forth, lounged with friends in corners and against walls, swore loudly, smoked endlessly, and retold lewd stories hoary with age. At the front of the hall, gangs formed to work the ships tied up in port. As names were called, men came forward quickly and filed silently past the desk and out the door. Others took their places until the overflow spilled into the streets. In the early morning gloom, shadowy men, capped and buttoned, their baling hooks slung around their necks in defiance, milled about in good-natured confusion. Among them walked Charley Flowers, making his appointed morning rounds.

In the month since he had been given part of Ray Scottini's loanshark operation by Al Parry, Flowers had opened a dozen new accounts on his own. All of them were small, mostly along the waterfront and in slum neighborhoods, but they showed his determination to succeed in his new responsibility, and he was proud of that. He had worked night and day for weeks now, and his diligence, it seemed to him, couldn't fail to pay off handsomely. But it had been sheer frustration at the start. Scottini had terrified his accounts. He had neglected business and antagonized friends and contacts. After several weeks of steady talk and some heavy leaning, Flowers had nudged the accounts back in line and smoothed over much of the bad feeling left by Scottini's actions. In his brown suit jacket and low-waisted chino pants, Flowers made the rounds of his territory, lending here, collecting there. He liked the work, especially the handling of money. He had no complaints.

The sky turned soft with whitish puffs of clouds as he passed a parcel of men, their faces frozen in smiles of camaraderie. They called out to him in good humor, all of them known to him.

"Ahh, must be nice to just walk around for a living, eh?"

"Yeah, that Charley got it made, all right."

"Just walking around with money."

"And ready to give it to anybody needs it. Don't forget that."

"Loan it, you mean."

"Same thing."

"He's all heart, that Charley. Don't care nothing about money."

"Don't mean a thing to him."

"Charley Money is just what he is, all right."

"Yeah, at six for five."

"Charley Money."

The work whistle blew. Men streamed through the gates onto the piers. Night lights were turned off as motors revved up, whirring sounds transforming a peaceful landscape into bedlam. In the crisp light of dawn all the moving bodies had a starkness to them. They kneeled and squatted and pulled and heaved, and, from where Charley Flowers stood outside the gates, they seemed to be working in slow motion, each movement having a monotonous finality of its own. After a while he turned away and crossed over to the hiring hall, quiet now save for the angry buzz of unhired workers and the steady hum of paperwork, and stood alone inside the doorway until approached by a young man in work clothes and wearing a watch cap.

"Charley Flowers?"

"Yeah."

"I'm Pete Marino. John Lewis said he'd talk to you about me."

"Sure. What's the problem?"

"I need two hundred fast."

"How fast?"

"Today if I can get it. It's an emergency."

"Always is. You work with Lewis?"

"I'm relief man in his gang."

"Work steady?"

"Steady enough."

Flowers retraced his steps past the metal front door, Marino following him out. On the steps they looked across at the docks and beyond, the ships silhouetted against a dingy sky. Nobody was within hearing distance. "Lewis spoke to me. It'll cost you forty for the first week interest," Flowers said, "and the interest is piled on top of the loan. You understand about that?"

"I got no choice."

"Maybe you should go to somebody else, a relative or something."

"No good. I need it now."

On the ships men were already loading and unloading cargo, the winches and booms moving in practiced rhythm. Orders were yelled, curses shouted. Flowers paid no attention to any of it as he peeled off two hundred in twenties. "Be seeing you next week," he said simply, giving the bills to Marino.

Stuffing the money in his jacket pocket without counting it, Marino squared his watch cap and turned away. "I ain't going nowhere," he said disconcertedly over his shoulder.

Back in the car, leased from a syndicate dealer, Flowers went over the next few stops in his mind. Two gas stations, only blocks apart, for collections. No problem. Then a few local stores. Business was bad and everybody needed money. A hundred here, three hundred there, it added up. He took out his notebook and wrote in it: *Marino 200W.* That was all he needed to know that Wednesday was Marino's day to pay. He slipped the car into gear and slowly drove over two sets of cemented railroad tracks, past the iron picket fence, brick guard posts, and tiers of wood sleds, past the booms of ships describing so many giant spiders at work, past the small hiring hall, its sandstone front pitted from the corrosive action of sea and air, across rows of massive planks shielding an underwater cable, out past truck graveyards and between two enormous wire-enclosed generators. On the asphalt roadbed again, he turned left and headed inland. At Erie Street he parked in front of a diner and leisurely ate double portions of bacon and eggs and home fries. Everything was burned and the grease at least a week old but, growl hungry, he hardly noticed. Finding the car ticketed at the curb, he tossed the parking ticket in the gutter after looking at the police officer's name. It was illegible. He made his several stops without a hitch as the sun weaved in and out of sight. After checking his papers and cash—notebook with latest figures in the shirt pocket, cash in two piles, folded double and rubberbanded, in separate jacket pockets—Charley Flowers headed for the Court Tavern and his weekly meeting with Al Parry, where he would have to turn in most of the fat rolls of money. It was a duty he found unpleasant.

He arrived early at the Court, found no one upstairs in the meeting hall or in the small, doorless room, and sat downstairs in one of the booths across from the bar. In the next booth was a tall, intense, thin-lipped man whose cold eyes watched Flowers over his raised glass of beer. Seated across from him, his back to Flowers, was a stocky Spaniard who hummed softly to himself as he drank tequila. Lost in his own thoughts, Flowers noticed neither man. With pressed lips and a deepening frown he squirmed through two beers and twenty minutes. He fed quarters to the jukebox, said a few words to the bartender, and played with his beer mug. When Parry finally came in, he was just about all played out.

In the next booth the tall, intense man said something to the Spaniard without seemingly moving his thin lips. The Spaniard nodded.

Al Parry signaled Flowers to follow him upstairs. Putting

his empty mug on the bar, Flowers failed to see the two pairs of eyes follow him as he walked to the rear, through the door, and up the stairs.

In the small, doorless room the two men sat at the table, Parry watching as Flowers took out the rolls of money. There was a stillness in the room as befits the presence of such sums. Shorn of their rubberbands, the two piles seemed to inch upward on the table, stretching after their confinement. Flowers stared at them for a long moment. In his mind was a suspicion that he would never get to where this kind of money would regularly be his to keep.

He shrugged off the despairing thought and opened the notebook, reading out the figures for the week's operation. Mouth dry, he stammered, paused, lost his way, made mistakes, corrected himself, and, breathing an audible sigh of relief, finished in about five minutes. By his figures he had done better than the week before. Smiling broadly, he closed the notebook and stuck it back in his shirt. With his right hand he shoved the two piles of money, twelve thousand dollars, toward Al Parry.

"You been doing a good job," said Parry in his syrupy voice, "better than Scottini ever done, the rat-faced little prick." Stung to anger, his memory pained, his pride hurt, Al Parry cursed silently, sitting there at the table with twelve thousand dollars in front of him, his eyes narrowed to slits as he remembered the abuse he got from Zucco. It had all been Scottini's fault.

"How come he's still breathing?" Flowers, nervous around Parry, brought out the silver harmonica he always carried. "Know what I think? I think Machine's got something special in mind for him." He toyed with the harmonica, grateful to have something to do with his hands.

Parry roused himself. "Just do your job. That's all you got to think about. We'll take care of the rest."

"I do my job."

"Don't get careless."

Downstairs the rear door opened and closed noiselessly as two men slipped through it unnoticed in a bar now almost filled.

With unhurried deliberation Parry counted out the money, making individual stacks out of each thousand. Four thousand was the new bank for the week, used to make loans and buy protection. The remainder was the previous week's collections. Sometimes, when bonuses were paid or inventories checked, or a heavy favorite ran in the money at the track, whole debts were wiped out at once, and the week's take would grow to prodigious amounts. Flowers had been on the go all week collecting money and canceling debts. He had also found time to make new loans, which was the lifeblood of the business. Anything up to a thousand needed only his OK, over a thousand required the approval of Al Parry. In his one month on the job Flowers had lent out more than seven thousand dollars. He expected to do even better. There were whole untapped markets in the city, such as his mother's housing project, if he could only get something like that organized. Lost in contemplation, excited by grandiose schemes, he did not hear the footsteps pad across the meeting hall or enter the room.

"Everybody just relax."

Still busily counting the money, Parry raised his head in surprise. "What the hell is this?" he demanded uncomprehendingly.

"What's it look like?" asked the tall, intense man. "This is a gun in my hand and that's money on the table. Maybe it's a holdup."

The Spaniard giggled.

Al Parry still couldn't believe it. "You know who I am?" he asked softly, his voice full of knives.

"We know who you are."

"You must be crazy."

"Shut up." The tall man walked over to the table and scooped up a stack of bills. "How much is here?"

"A thousand," answered Parry.

"I mean all of it. How much is on the table?"

"Twelve thousand," Parry whispered.

"Louder."

"Twelve thousand."

"That's better. Twelve grand, eh? Not bad." He turned his attention to Flowers. "You. What you got to say?"

His body rigid, hands flat on the table, Flowers couldn't take his eyes off the gun. For one awful moment he was again on the hit that had almost cost him his life two years before. He had lately come to believe that what had happened then was merely a bad break that could have happened to anybody. He had even felt his old confidence returning. Now he was not so sure.

"You. What you got to say?"

Flowers felt the anger rising within him. He had worked hard all week, Al Parry had just complimented him. Now it was all for nothing. His bad luck was following him, and there was nothing he could do with that gun pointing down his throat.

"I'm talking to you, pal. Where's your manners?"

"I hear you."

"So you ain't deaf. You carrying any heat?"

"That's a dumb question."

"Gimme a dumb answer."

Flowers raised his arms from the table. "I got nothing."

The tall man motioned to the Spaniard, who ran his free hand lightly over Flowers. There was a jagged scar across his palm and only the stump of his pinky. Finished, he checked Parry in the same desultory manner, obviously expecting to find nothing. While thus occupied, the tall man put the stacks of bills carefully in his pockets.

"Who sent you?" asked Parry suddenly. "Who you working for?"

Nobody spoke.

"How'd you know where we'd be?"

Still nothing.

"Who tipped you off?" Parry whispered in his deadliest voice. "Tell me and the money's yours."

"Looks like it's ours already," said the tall man.

"You'll never live to spend it."

Twelve thousand dollars in his possession, feeling easy and a little relieved, the tall man walked up to Parry. "Who's gonna stop us? You?"

"We work for Zucco," Parry stated simply.

"I'm shaking."

"You will be."

"Listen, Parry, we're just doing a job, see? If you want to figure out who set you up, that's your business. Just stay out of our business. Nobody's getting hurt here, it's just a friendly exchange. We keep the money and you keep your health. Don't make no more out of it than that, OK?"

"We'll be watching for you wherever you go," muttered the angry Parry, the veins in his neck popping out.

"You do that."

Both men laughed.

"Scottini," said Flowers.

"Huh?"

"Ray Scottini."

"What about him?"

"He tipped them off."

Al Parry stared at him.

"Who else knew we'd be here today? And that I'd have the week's money?"

"Go on."

Flowers pointed to the tall man. "How'd he know your name unless someone told him?"

"That's right," Parry exclaimed. He turned to the man. "What about that, was it Scottini?"

"Like I say, we're just doing a job. Whatever you want to think, that's up to you."

"But you don't deny it."

"We don't say nothing, and that's just what I want you to do. Sit here nice and friendly-like for five minutes while we go down them stairs and out. If you get us stopped there's gonna be some loose blood around here. Follow me?"

"Let's tie them up."

"Don't need it. Zucco don't want no trouble with the papers, so he'll keep it quiet."

The tall, intense man and the Spaniard with the missing pinky walked casually out of the room. "Remember, Parry," said the thin-lipped man from the doorway, "give us five minutes or we give you forever."

The two men sat quietly at the table, trained professionals. Parry unstrapped his watch and propped it against an ashtray in front of him. This done, he leaned back in the chair. "Ray Scottini." He repeated the name several times. "I never trusted the little prick. Something wrong about him."

"He done it."

"Yeah, I thought of him right off. Same as you. He's the one set it up all right."

"But what about them other two guys was just here, where do they fit in? They ain't no bums."

"That's for sure."

"They didn't bat an eye when you threw the organization at them."

"Why should they?"

Flowers hooded his eyes in suspicion. "You mean they're—"

"Sure, they're part of it."

"Who?"

"Who got knocked over for six grand? Who was out to get Scottini?"

"Machine."

"Machine."

"But why didn't he just do a job on the guy?"

Al Parry smiled tolerantly. "Better this way. Machine gets his cash back, and more. He shows nobody can knock over his boys and get away with it. And he fixes it so now we got to take care of Scottini."

"They didn't say nothing when we mentioned his name."

"Machine must've told them to make sure we know who done it."

"We know."

Parry strapped his watch back on. The five minutes were up.

"Let's go."

Downstairs, Parry called Zucco from the bar. When he hung up the phone his voice was shaky. "He wants to see us at five. At the office."

"Was he mad?"

Parry didn't bother to answer. "He says don't be late."

They walked to the front of the bar and stood close together, blocking the sun angling in through the small green squares in the stained-glass window. Hands sweaty, the back of his shirt soaked through, Charley Flowers cracked his knuckles. "What about Scottini? What's Zucco gonna do with him?"

"Where he's going, he won't bother nobody no more," said Parry slowly, a touch of awe in his cold voice.

Flowers stood there glued, feeling the sweat running down his legs, and Parry stared out at the green glass. "He won't bother nobody no more," he repeated, as though already speaking of the dead.

Flowers remained in the Court Tavern after Al Parry left. Standing in the shadowed corner at the foot of the L-shaped bar, he looked out at the long file of men lined up at the trough, elbows and arms caressing worn wood, feet resting on yellowed rail. A pair of battered men in truckdriver jackets and caps with the name of their outfit in red script, drank double boilermakers. Next to one of them Flowers saw some furniture slings. A lone seaman with tattoos up both arms stared moodily into his glass. Flowers ordered a beer. Men were leaving as others stepped up to take their places in constant rearrangement.

"You had enough," the bartender intoned to a man weaving back and forth. "Go home and sleep it off, mac. Come back tomorrow and you can start all over."

"Got no home," came the pained reply. "Woman threw me out again."

His empty glass was taken away by the unsympathetic bartender. "No more for you today."

"I'm an old man." He bared his rotting teeth to prove it.

The bartender took out his false upper plate in a deft motion and held it in his hand. "I'm older. Now go on home."

The lower lip, wet with saliva, drooled over. Slowly the old man's hands relaxed their grip of the bar's edge and he stood on his own. With a shuffle of feet his body turned toward the light and he swayed down the long march, past boozers and winos, workers and talkers, past people out to kill time and others looking to kill themselves. As the old man negotiated the door he turned and caught Charley Flowers watching him. He started to say something but changed his mind in mid-mouth and staggered out the door to the street.

"Who's that?" asked Flowers, pointing to the door.

"Nobody at all," said the hurried bartender, "just some old lush lives somewhere around here."

Flowers nursed his beer for another twenty minutes and then left without tipping the bartender. The old man had reminded him of his father.

Easing the car into traffic, he headed for Journal Square and the massage parlor, where he tipped the girl five dollars because she told him that men who were not circumcised were the best lovers. Afterward, he got a haircut and a face massage, lying under the hot towels for a while. He refused a shave, wary of anyone with a blade getting that close to his throat.

On the Square large display signs in store windows announced Memorial Day weekend sales. Flowers bought a blue and white striped Western shirt and went home to his room in the Exchange Place Hotel, where he showered and shaved and put on his new shirt and his one suit. Polished and pressed, he drove to St. Ignatius Loyola, parking at a bus stop across the street from the church. Inside the darkened vestibule he hesitated for a moment, unsure of exactly what it was he wanted to do. The door behind him opened and he hurriedly pushed through the heavy inner doors. With a swipe at the holy water he genuflected, his knee hardly bending, and walked solemnly up the side aisle, careful to hug the anonymity of the shaded wall. In the pews across both aisles lurked several dozen people, mostly old and weathered, some kneeling, others sitting tightly or sprawling, the women wearing dark shawls over bowed heads, their dry and cracked lips moving in dreadful supplication for some unfulfilled miracle known only to them and their God. Reaching the first pew, directly across from the confessional, Charley Flowers half-sat half-knelt, his eyes closed, his hands joined, his lips unmoving.

Afterward he ate garlic bread and drank cheap port in the back of a candy store down the block, his shirt collar already wilted, his jacket and pants losing shape swiftly. As he feasted, Pop Terminello, the store's ancient owner, told him for the hundredth time of the days when candy was two for a penny, in giant glass jars and mottled apothecary jugs always cool to the touch, pie à la mode had two thick gobs of vanilla dripping over the sides, and lemon ice was scooped out of a big steel drum packed with dry ice and came in one-cent, two-cent, and three-cent daisy cups.

Warming to talk of a time so long before his own, Flowers lingered in the back room, feet resting on an upturned orange crate, jacket off and shirt opened, baggy pants bunched up at the seat. As the old man rambled on, the stories became more episodic and fanciful until finally they turned to pure imagination. If he ain't nuts then I am, Flowers thought, and hoped he wouldn't live that long. Then he changed his mind. If the breaks only came his way for a change he'd be around for a long time, maybe move up in the organization and be another Zucco.

His mind wandered around the tiny room, its walls festooned with the covers of old comic books now faded to splotchy reds and greens. He recognized some of them, others were about heroes and villains he had never known. Batman, Plastic Man, Sub Mariner, The Spirit, Human Torch, Green Lantern, Blue Bolt, Action, Doll Man, The Ray, Green Arrow, Captain America. He couldn't imagine anyone reading them. They had no real sex or violence; it was all just make-believe. Even the words were fake half the time. He decided that people just had nothing better to do in those days. But what about now? Was his life going to end up as useless as these stupid comics hanging on an old man's walls? Was this all he'd ever get of his life, cheap hotels and cheap women, men who feared him and others whom he feared, nothing his and everything smelling goodbye? The thought depressed him again. He slumped in the chair, his head resting on his chest, hands looped over his belt. He felt himself doomed. Hopeless and afraid, he wished he were already dead. Slowly, with mighty heaves of breath, he fought the shakes to a standstill, eventually regaining an outward calm. He was even able to smile at Pop Terminello's incessant ruminations again. Hanging still on the walls, the comic books looked down upon him, their covers aglow with the titanic struggle between good and evil.

At four-thirty he uprooted himself and left the store. On the way out, the old man, lonely, asked him where he was going and all he could say was: "I don't really know."

SUCCESS IN HIS BUSINESS, according to Joe Zucco, came only through a combination of fear and respect: fear of a double cross and respect for the consequences. Take away these two bulwarks, he believed, and organized crime would be impossible. To be sure, other elements were needed in the mix and so a whole series of rules and regulations had evolved over the years. Police and reporters were never harmed willfully; territories were never violated; women were never told anything. An organizational structure was established, with a chain of command. Certain cities were declared open to all, certain areas off-limits to killings. Kidnapping within the organization was outlawed; a code of silence was instituted. All of these, and more, became indispensable in the daily conduct of business. But the bedrock, the foundation on which all else rested, was the certain and unshakable conviction that the double cross— the ultimate weapon—was unthinkable and therefore unusable. What kept its unthinkability uppermost in everyone's mind was the hideous consequences of such an act. Not just death, but a slow, agonizing death of the most painful sort. And not just a painful death with ritual mutilation but, if tactical considerations permitted, total disappearance of the body and permanent uncertainty and sorrow for family and friends.

In his earlier years Joe Zucco had made a number of mistakes which proved embarrassing and even occasionally dangerous. He also had made some other moves which could have proved fatal. He had misused organization funds; he had ruined some important business opportunities; he had once even killed the wrong man. With a cool abandon he allowed a witness to get to the district attorney with knowledge of some of his business associates, each of whom was ahead of him on the ladder of success. Later, he himself plotted against a rival faction, bringing death and destruction to both groups but furthering his own ambitious plans. But once having achieved his intended position, he instinctively saw the virtue of the old proscription against the double cross, and immediately became a zealous defender of the faith.

Now Zucco's belief in the code of proper conduct was awesome in its intensity. He demanded total loyalty and brooked no interference with his orders, perhaps remembering his own past. It was a practical necessity at best, and though he was not seriously threatened, he was never entirely at ease. Sharpened by this ambivalence, he brooded over his flock like a mother hen. He was their strength. And they were his weakness. Some had no concept of loyalty or were too unstable to take orders or too unreliable to carry them out; some were physical cowards or emotional misfits; some were mental defectives or were kill-crazy or just plain crazy; others were too dishonest even for the organization, or too idealistic or moralistic; still others died or were killed or went to jail or moved away or woke up in cold sweats, were crippled, lost eyes, became cancerous or otherwise diseased. Some couldn't handle the life and so were set free; others couldn't handle anything outside the life and needed innumerable small favors from Zucco to get by, all of which he infallibly granted, not as a bond of friendship but as a tie of loyalty.

With a cold eye and a warm temper, Zucco watched them

all. When something happened and one of his men made a serious blunder or, worse, committed some act of perfidy, he took it personally, felt betrayed, stormed and ranted in public and displayed all the emotional exaggerations and purposeful displeasures of any feudal despot faced with hostility or even a speck of disobedience. At such times Zucco's paranoia and showmanship were impressive to behold.

Seated now at his desk in the office atop the funeral parlor, with Al Parry and Charley Flowers standing nervously in front of him, Zucco felt the rage spread over him. He had given Ray Scottini his life when he could easily have wiped him out for placing the operation in jeopardy and losing thousands of dollars. For his magnanimity he was repaid with dishonor and deceit. Scottini, whom he had taken in as a member of the family, and for whom he had opened the doors of opportunity, had betrayed him and brought disgrace on his head. Scottini, this *schifozia,* had been disloyal. He had double-crossed the organization. He would pay for it, and pay dearly. Now, by God in heaven, he would suffer for his infamy.

"I want him dead," Zucco bellowed, banging the desk with his fist, shaking the room. "Dead, you got that? I want the little punk destroyed," he shouted wildly. "I let him get away with something once, and this is how he repays me."

Al Parry, unblinking, kept wetting his lips, standing there hollow-eyed in front of a mad Zucco.

"Okay, I was fooled. I'm a soft touch, I listen to a guy's got problems. So I let him go. I let him go," he raged, "so he can double-cross me." Bang. He slammed the desk again with his fist. "No more. I say no more." He picked up a knife and jabbed his thumb, letting the drops of blood drip onto the floor. "In the blood of my ancestors I condemn this pig Scottini to die. May he burn in hell forever." He stood up and with his foot he ground the fresh blood into the floor. "Scottini is dead," he declared simply. And sat down again.

Calmed after the symbolic rite, his anger dissipating in the face of action, Zucco attended to business. He regarded these bursts of outrage, real though they were, as pieces of showmanship to keep his men in line. It was, he thought, one of the many duties of a leader, and he accepted the burden silently, and with a grandiloquence worthy of his position. As he directed, managed, plotted, and pushed the business of the organization, he felt much as any captain of industry functioning at his peak. There was a job to be done and, after that, another and another, always under pressure and with insufficient time. A leader had to take care of business.

"I want Scottini to disappear. No body. That way his widow can't remarry or get no insurance for years. Serve her right for being around the little bastard."

"How you want it handled?"

"Like I told you on the phone, use the meat plant. Get yourself a good knife man for the job. He can work with Charley here."

"What about the other two, you want them?"

"What other two?"

"The ones got the cash from us."

"What I want them for? Just get me the little rat that set it up." Zucco's eyes turned furious. "And Al, listen to what I tell you. I want he should suffer so he knows what he done. You just make sure he dies slow, you know what I mean?" He got up. "Go chase yourself awhile. I want to talk to Charley here."

Flowers now understood what had happened. The two men were from Alex Machine's organization and Zucco couldn't get to them without starting a war. They had acted on Machine's orders, trying to get back the six grand taken by Scottini in the policy bank. If Al Parry was right about Hymie Cole not having the cash to give back, it was natural that Machine would try to get it the only way he could. He promised Scottini his life for the setup, knowing that Zucco would then be forced to take care of him. Scottini, probably crazed with fear, took the deal. Now he was holed up somewhere, waiting for the inevitable.

Zucco came around the desk. Smiling, he faked a short jab

to Flowers' chin in a playful manner and quickly put an arm around his shoulder. "Charley boy, I didn't get a chance to tell you I'm glad you with us. Been busy as hell, you know how it is. Everything comes up at once in this business. Now this Scottini thing. You didn't have no idea Machine was gonna pull this, eh, Charley?"

"No sir, first thing I know was the gun on me."

"Sure, sure. Just checking all the angles, you understand. What about Al, was he surprised when they walked in?"

"Sure he was. I mean, he looked plenty surprised to me. Hey, you don't think—"

"I don't think nothing. What's the matter with you? You got one of them suspicious natures gonna get you in trouble if you don't watch it."

"But you just said—"

"I said nothing. All I'm doing is seeing what happened. So you and Al was surprised when they come in. Did they mention Scottini?"

"No."

"Who thought of him?"

Flowers wanted to say that he did but he wasn't sure what Parry had told Zucco. "We both did, me and Al."

"And they said nothing."

"No."

"They didn't mention Machine?"

"No."

"Twelve grand's a lot to lose," Zucco said, his eyes thoughtful, "on top of the ten the little rat's cost me already." He looked at Flowers. "I want you to take care of this thing fast. Find the prick and nail him. Al'll tell you where to look for him, it won't be hard."

"Suppose he left town?"

"He ain't."

Flowers grunted. "I'll find him."

"See that you do." Zucco again put his arm around Flowers' shoulder. "I'm giving you the job 'cause they tell me you use to be a pretty good boy. I need somebody like that. You ain't scared, are you?"

"I ain't scared."

"Good, good. Once a shooter, always a shooter, eh?" He went back behind the desk. "See Al on your way out. He'll fill you in. And tell him to get somebody else on your accounts for a few days. Give him the book."

Flowers walked to the door.

"Charley."

He turned.

"Do a nice job, no slips on this one. Scottini's days are over."

"He knows it."

"Don't prove him wrong."

Zucco watched Flowers disappear behind the closed door. He had never had a son, not a legitimate one, and he constantly found himself measuring the young men in the organization against what he imagined a son of his would have been like. Not surprisingly, they always seemed to him inferior. Like this Charley Flowers. Not bright enough to lead, not fast enough to take, not tough enough to hold. Just an average monkey good for muscle and some easy pickings. Not at all what his son would have been, or what he had been in his youth. Zucco often thought of his own younger days, especially when he had troubles. At such times he had to fight the urge to go out and smash heads and settle problems as he once had done. No longer was this proper, for he had become too important a man. Now he left to others the actual physical contact, keeping buffers between himself and any possible trouble, and he was forced to spend his rage vicariously, allowing other, younger men to do what he had once done so well. Men like Gino Agucci and Johnny Apples and a dozen others. Over the years he had picked his favorites and charted their performances like so many racehorses, some better than others, none quite up to his expectations. Several, indeed almost like sons to him, he had lost and he bitterly resented that aspect of his life. Zucco, his huge hairy arms resting solidly on the empty desk top, closed his eyes in sad reflection. Chris was one of them, a thin, moody youth with quick reflexes and a smile of gold. Shot down in front of church.

They had stood together on the church steps, Zucco and Chris, waiting for the car. Younger then, and a little thinner in the waist, Zucco had just bought the funeral parlor and was paying his respects to the local pastor at St. Mary's. Chris was ostensibly his bodyguard but he was really much more, a right hand, his confidant and ally. They waited impatiently in a light drizzle as a blind man came tap-tapping up the block, his dark glasses and long, thin white cane visible proof of his affliction.

On the bottom step Zucco stood facing the approaching blind man, with Chris turned the other way. There, watching the man's rapid stride, his head erect and moving around, his one hand in his pocket, Zucco noticed an odd thing. The blind man had stepped around a puddle no cane could have forewarned. It was a small thing perhaps, that had a quick and simple explanation, but as wary calculations were being made in his suspicious mind, a gun snapped and Chris was hit in the side by a bullet meant for Zucco. Chris pitched forward into his opening arms, staggered sideways shielding Zucco just as the second shot tore into his back. Both men fell in a tangle of arms and legs. When Zucco loosened himself and peered up cautiously, the blind man was gone. He stretched Chris out as people ran over. He rubbed his hands, he patted his cheeks, he screamed for a doctor. Chris moaned once and his head slipped downward, the side of his face striking the street, saliva running along the edge of his mouth and mixing with the wetness of the pavement. His eyes, glassy, remained open as his body went limp.

Zucco was still squatting next to him when the police came. A doctor wasn't needed, only the undertaker. Zucco let go of the dead hand. He stood up and waited bareheaded in the rain until the ambulance arrived. The intern bent down and felt for a pulse. With a hurried motion he glanced at the wounds as the body was piled onto the stretcher. Shaking with rage and grief, Zucco stood there, unexploded, watching the ambulance speed away in futile haste.

No more than ten minutes had passed since the two men had been talking on the church steps, waiting for the car. Then one of them was gone. Two policemen in rainwear remained with the other. He clenched and unclenched his fists, he moved his lips silently. After a time he was taken to the local precinct for a statement. Of course he had seen nothing. Already known, he was released to mourn in private.

Zucco got up from his chair and paced restlessly between the desk and window. These memories always unnerved him, even after years of feeling sorrow or guilt or both. The shooting had not been his fault, he had himself survived only by luck. But he didn't know why. Why him and not the younger Chris? The thought vexed and haunted him. He told all who knew of the shooting that Chris had instinctively pivoted in front of him to shield him, but he could never really clear his own mind of the suspicion that he had ducked behind the wounded man after the first bullet. To ease such feelings he bought the widow a home in Florida and gave her a large sum of money. He also gave her the name of her husband's killer, a young ex-con who was paid to do the job on Zucco by a revengeful business rival. Both disappeared and were never seen again. At the funeral large wreaths of flowers bore the simple inscription: "From a Friend." Gradually over the years the memory of the man faded, became blurred with the faces of other men and other shootings, but in times of towering rage, when Zucco felt that he was being double-crossed, the image of his almost-execution and the face of his almost-son returned vividly.

Now was such a time and Zucco was once again experiencing all the impotence of rage and dread of uncertainty, and as he yelled for Gino to come in, his face contorted, he sensed the recklessness that was his life and wished for the millionth time that it could have been somehow different. It was, he had long ago convinced himself, simply a matter of controlling his remarkable temper. Yet this was no simple thing to do, and only with age was his fury more manageable. In his earlier years Zucco had used his ferocity as a weapon, bludgeoning people into doing his bidding. He was crude, violent, and immensely effective. Men feared him and women fawned over him.

When he was thirty he was grossly cheated by an associate in a business deal, and his reputation as a knowledgeable young racketeer was virtually destroyed. With a ferocity remarkable even for him, Zucco killed the man and cut off his head and limbs. The dismembered body he sent to the man's family and the limbs to enemies of his. Then he held a dinner for various people in the business, during which the head was baked and the skin removed. After everyone had eaten, the head was brought to Zucco at the table. In front of his astonished guests he cut a hole in the temple, shook out the brains through the hole and proceeded to eat them. Everyone at the table got the message. Joe Zucco was not a man to be tampered with.

In succeeding years, as age mellowed him, Zucco acquired the polish and tact required of business leaders. He learned much about corporate structure and how to separate himself from street activities, about banking and taxes and the law. He acquired some patience and a pose of sympathy for the troubles of others. He dressed fashionably and dined comfortably. He contributed to the proper charities, he courted the proper politicians. Yet all of this grace, most of it no longer a facade but a part of him, all of it cracked in the sum of his anger. Then he was once again the man who could eat the brains of his enemies. In those moments he fought to regain control, aware that the awesome anger had served him well in his youth but was a liability to a leader of the community. He afterward regretted each such incident and resolved that it never happen again. Now as he moved back to his desk, abandoning the useless pacing that only contributed to his anxiety, Zucco believed he had his rage under control. He no longer felt impotent or uncertain. Scottini would be taken care of swiftly, and he would take care of any other loose ends. Machine bracing his men involved no real loss of prestige since it was merely a reply and not a challenge. He would cease hostilities, though the blow would someday be returned at a time and place of his choosing. Like the tiger, he would stalk and wait. Meanwhile, the money was lost. The thought almost destroyed his resolve to control his anger.

Gino came into the room on cat's paws, silent and wary. He waited for Zucco, who had his chair turned to the window, gazing out with unseeing eyes. Zucco felt the presence and swung around.

"Get Hymie up here," he said abruptly. "We got things to talk about."

"You want him now?"

"Now."

"He ain't got the cash."

Zucco squinted up at Gino.

"He didn't have it for Machine," Gino explained.

"If he done like I told him, this wouldn't've happened."

Gino shrugged. "Scottini would've bought it some other way. He was looking for it."

"Now we're looking for him."

"No problem. You sending Flowers?"

Zucco nodded. "He can do the job."

"If he got his nerve back," said Gino quietly.

In the other room Al Parry told Flowers all the places Scottini could be hiding. "You'll find him. Machine's people already know a contract's out on him so the word's out. He won't have nowhere to hide. Besides, for what he done he'll be looking to get it. All them punks are like that. Guilty streaks straight up their backs."

"What happens when I get him? What you want done with him?"

Parry told him.

Leaning against a table, feet spread apart and arms folded, Flowers popped his ears, stunned. "Jesus," he kept repeating to himself. "Jesus."

THERE WERE FIVE OF THEM in the car. They rode north past Five Corners, past Journal Square and the business section, the frame houses and solitary high-rises, then onto the Tonnele Avenue cutoff for the highway. At the wheel, his immense gut folded under and around, was Frank Farrano. Next to him sat Johnny Apples, taciturn and deadly. In the back, wedged up against the corner behind the driver, Harry Strega rubbed elbows with Art Hammis, whom he had met on his first visit to Zucco's office. On the other side was Axel Gregor, a former wrestler and circus strongman, who could knock down a half-dozen men with one sweep of his iron arms. While Gregor and Hammis rested their huge bulks in semi-slumber, Harry, warm with excitement, stared straight ahead with Farrano and Johnny Apples.

"This'll be a cinch," said Farrano. "Nothing to it."

"Is that so?"

"Yeah, these niggers can't take it. You blow on 'em once they fall down, right?"

"Wrong."

"Ehh?"

Johnny Apples placed one large paw on the dashboard, turning sideways. "You keep thinking like that and somebody's gonna slice you up and down one of these days. A nigger's no different from nobody else. You got to watch them all the time. Everybody. You got to watch everybody all the time."

"Sure, Johnny, sure," Farrano said quickly. "I only meant the niggers fold up faster. But we'll watch everything all right." He screwed up his face in thought for a moment. "Hey, you know something? I'd like to have a piece of this joint. Kind of settle down and just work the one trick, you know? Maybe I'll ask Zucco if I can get in on it."

Johnny Apples said nothing.

A string of diesels groaned up a grade and the car swerved around them. "What about that, kid?" Farrano said, eyeing Harry in the rearview mirror. "You remember Big Tits. How'd you like to get that? Think you could handle that kind of work?"

"I can handle it," said Harry.

"Ahh, she'd smother you first time she got your face between them."

"By then she'd be choking from where her head'd be."

"Now you're talking. But you'd want to split that one too. Lots of red meat there."

"I'd split her. I told you I could handle it."

"Yeah, but you want to watch you don't smother. Now me, I just like 'em to get on their knees and be midgets so I don't go for the big tits and all the rest of it. But that broad's a lifesaver, you know what I mean? She's all hole."

The parking lot was almost full when they turned off the highway. Red and green neon blazoned the Starlight Motel in both directions. Farrano pulled the car into a spot against a chain fence in back of the motel, cut the motor, and doused the lights. In the silent darkness they waited. Harry flexed his right hand repeatedly, pulling the fingers tight into a fist. Next to him Art Hammis and Axel Gregor sat motionless. The minutes stretched as Harry, increasingly nervous, fidgeted in his seat, crossing and uncrossing his legs. His mind was suddenly caught by the incongruity of the moment—the utter silence and total darkness so near to light and sound in the nightclub a few steps away—and the potential for destruction that always lay just beyond the edge of light. He marveled at the ease with which the other men accepted the situation, wished he could be so unimaginative. Contemptuously he dismissed the wish. He was just as hard and tough and unimaginative. Yet a disquiet overtook him, a feeling that he was somehow not quite like the rest of them.

"You all know what to do."

Harry jumped, stunned by the sudden voice from the darkness. Nobody else moved.

"Art, you take care of the outside. And remember, nothing serious. You just want to scare them away. Nobody gets hurt."

"I got it."

"You better. Just bang them up a little and send them on their way. Frank, you and the kid are at the bar; Gregor's in the kitchen. I'll be upstairs."

"Right, Johnny."

"OK, let's go."

Johnny Apples, lumbering forward heavily, jacket open, tie pulled up tight to the throat, head low, and chest out, led the way across the lot and into the canopied entrance of Cloud Nine. The big room was at least three-quarters filled at the tables, with a full bar and three working bartenders. A small band was playing in front of a crowded dance floor. Laughter and loud voices threatened to drown out the music. Among the drinkers and diners were men planning to touch women and women planning to be touched by men, not necessarily those seated next to them. Others, intent on merely having a good time, table-hopped or just relaxed and observed. At the bar two drunks were engaged in a heated debate regarding the virtue of a lady not present. Several near-drunks were rapidly trying to catch up, while still others circled on blue plastic-covered stools or drummed absently on the bar with their fingers. His nervousness gone now, Harry eagerly took it all in. He liked bright lights and noise and the spontaneous gaiety of nightclubs, and he enjoyed looking at the women all dressed up and down. In the hundred-and-fifty-dollar brown weave, soft leather buckle boots, and striped shirt with green pearl snaps, he believed himself suited in worthy fashion as he followed Farrano toward the bar, walking confidently in measured strides. His height and bearing did not go unnoticed, nor did Farrano's three hundred pounds immediately in front of him. With each turn of head, a woman's eyes opened or a man's narrowed. In apparent nonchalance, Farrano waddled forward, his enormous arms describing an arc in wild swing. While Gregor ordered a table for one, Farrano and Harry went over to the bar as planned. They stood behind two stout young men with elbows planted firmly on the wood. One wore a dark pin stripe, the other a safari jacket with big patch pockets. A peasant scarf dangled loosely from his neck. The pin stripe had dark sunglasses that he kept putting on and taking off.

Harry ordered drinks, squeezing his arm past the scarf to get them from the bartender. "I'll bet Big Tits is upstairs right now," he said to Farrano in a low voice. Farrano, taking his glass, downed the Scotch in one gulp. "I'll bet she's up there walking around naked."

"She's not walking around. A broad like that, she's strictly a bed-and-blow job. You get yourself a place like the nigger got here and she comes with it. A dozen like her. They come out of the walls."

"You really think so?"

"It's a cinch."

"All I need is a place like this." He laughed.

"The nigger got it, ain't he?"

Harry nursed his drink while Farrano had another. At a table sat Gregor, ordering a steak dinner. His small table for one was close to the kitchen doors.

"Maybe we should go up and see. Just for a minute, I mean." He took a swallow of his vodka and soda. "We got time."

"You crazy? With Apples up there?"

"What does he care?"

"He cares plenty. There's real cash here and if he blows it, Zucco'll have his balls for breakfast. Apples don't like that." He downed the second Scotch. "One time somebody screwed a deal on him and he almost killed the poor bastard. Beat him so bad with a baseball bat he was crippled for life. Broke all his bones. He's one mean sonofabitch and if you cross him your ass won't be worth shit." Farrano was sweating all over from too many people and not enough air. He mopped his stringy hair with a handkerchief. He pulled the shirt away from the folds of flesh at his middle. His eyes watered, his neck dripped, his mouth was hot and dry, and his armpits were flowing in torrents. At age thirty-eight, he had been on Zucco's payroll for six years, working his way out of ships' holds and off the docks. Tonight he was involved in a deal that he hoped would set him up for a while. Like Johnny Apples, Frank Farrano didn't want anything to go wrong. "You stay here with me. This ain't no cunt hunt we're on."

"Didn't say it was."

"So don't act like it. When you work for the organization you do what you're told." Farrano mopped his head again. "You want to know what makes a really good hit man? I'll tell you."

Harry said nothing.

"He keeps his mind on business. Don't matter what comes up, all he thinks about is the job. That comes first all the time."

"I think about the job."

"You don't keep your mind on business, soon you don't have no business."

"I keep my mind on business. That's always first with me."

"The job is what counts."

"I do the job."

"You got to do the job. Or somebody else'll do it, and you're nowhere."

"I do the job same as you."

"Just keep your mind on business."

Harry downed the rest of his drink, frowning at the thought of Farrano telling him what to do. Who the hell was he anyway, the fat slob? He was lucky Zucco would give a job to a fat man like him. Only reason he's not upstairs is because he knows Big Tits wouldn't handle his fat. Furious now, Harry banged his empty glass on the bar, accidentally nudging the young man in the scarf.

"Easy, sport. You woke me up."

"Go to hell."

The scarf swiveled sideways on the stool, facing Harry. He was heavy enough, his girlfriend was away, his work was boring, and he had had too much to drink. Mostly he had had too much to drink. "You got a loose mouth, sport."

"Your mother too."

"Not yet, not yet. It ain't time yet," whispered Farrano. "We got to wait till we get the signal." He turned to the scarf. "Don't mind him. It's just the drink."

"He's got a loose mouth."

"Yeah, yeah, nobody's perfect." He looked at Harry. "What are you trying to do?"

"I don't like fags around me," Harry mumbled.

"For chrissake, take it easy. You'll queer the whole deal."

"Who's he calling a fag?" shouted the scarf. He got off the stool, buckled a bit, and held onto the bar as he straightened himself.

"Relax, will you? It don't mean nothing."

"I'm gonna take him apart."

"Listen, sonny boy, sit down while you still can. Do yourself a favor."

"When I want your advice I'll ask you."

"I ain't asking, I'm telling. Now just crawl back on your high chair and mind your own business."

"Out of my way, fatso."

Farrano had time for one quick glance at Harry. "You dumb sonofabitch," he said, with disgust etched in his face. Then he kneed the scarf in the groin and smashed his head against the bar. "Don't come back here," he said, "it's bad for you."

Harry was already on top of the scarf, beating him to the floor, as Farrano turned on the pin stripe. The dark sunglasses smashed on the bar with one blow of his huge fist. "Stay out of here, it ain't healthy for you," he repeated between blows.

One of the house bouncers, tall and thin with a broken nose, tried to grab Farrano around the neck but he was picked off and thrown over the bar, his well-shod feet crashing into a row of expensive bourbons. The sound of breaking glass was accompanied by the rush of movement at the bar. People ran or ducked to the floor. Women screamed. A second bouncer, paunchy, middle-aged, wearing a bow tie and ruffled shirt, lunged at Harry and was promptly kicked unconscious with one blow to the head. Two patrons, intent on stopping the carnage, grabbed Farrano from behind, pinning his arms. With one heave he shook them loose and banged their heads together. "If I ever see you in here again I'll rip your arms off," he told them as he dropped their limp bodies. Hesitating, his eyes seeking out his next victim, he mopped his brow with one hand just as a bottle came crashing over his head. Dazed, Farrano staggered a moment before turning to the bartender, who now cringed out of reach behind the bar. He shook himself violently, trying to clear his head. "Don't still be here next time I come around," he said to the terrified man. And he made the death sign across his throat.

Upstairs, Johnny Apples was sitting in Phil Green's office explaining the advantages of a partnership. "You get a bundle now for yourself, and you get protection so nothing goes wrong."

"Like what?"

"Like anything. Suppose your garbage ain't collected. We control that. Or you can't get food or liquor. Or you have union trouble."

"I don't have any union trouble."

"But you could."

"I can always find booze somewhere."

"But maybe it won't reach you."

"I can hire private trucks for the garbage."

"Not if you can't get drivers."

Phil Green leaned back in his swivel chair. "You got all the answers," he said with a tight smile.

"We been in business a long time."

"Not long enough." Green stood up. "I don't want any part of the rackets and I don't want any partners. I like it just like this."

"Everything'd be the same."

"Nothing'd be the same. I'd have your people looking over my shoulder. First time I closed my eyes I'd be out."

"No way. We operate legitimate. You do your job, we do ours. Nobody gets hurt."

"I told your muscle last week it was no deal, and I'm telling you the same thing. No deal."

"Is that your final word?"

"That's it."

Johnny Apples sighed loudly, picked off a piece of imaginary lint from his sharkskin trousers before uncrossing his legs. "I was hoping it wouldn't come to this," he said with genuine sorrow in his voice. "We don't want no trouble 'cause it's trouble for us too. But you leave us no choice."

"Meaning?"

Now Johnny Apples stood up. "Meaning don't be surprised if you lose your customers, and your help don't show up and the place gets a bad name. Don't say you wasn't warned."

Green was about to answer when someone rapped loudly on the door.

"Come in," he shouted impatiently.

The door opened and a head stuck in. "Phil, there's a riot downstairs."

"What?"

"Guys are all over the place busting heads. You better get down there."

"You don't waste no time, do you?" he growled at Johnny Apples on his way out.

Alone in the office Johnny Apples silently cursed everything and everybody. What's the matter with Farrano, how could he be so stupid? The goddamn clown. And the rest of them, why didn't they wait till he got to the bar and gave the signal? Suppose Green had taken the deal? This'd blow it for sure. Those stupid pricks, he'd break their heads for this.

In the small hallway, lit only by a red bulb, the middle door, slightly opened, caught his attention. He peered inside. The room held two daybeds, one on each side, a large work table, and several straightback chairs. In one corner was an oval sink. The walls, papered in a series of horizontal lines, had no pictures hanging on them, no mirrors, nothing. On the table were some small metal tins and a few spoons and pieces of rubber tubing. Three candles lay next to an ornate candleholder with gold filigree. One look was enough for Johnny Apples. The room was a shooting gallery, the only thing missing was the hypodermic needle, and he knew that would be wrapped in gauze somewhere in the table drawer. He took a step toward the girl on the daybed. She lay there naked except for panties, her head slumped into the crook of her arm. She was beyond normal sleep. Apples whistled softly to himself, he had seldom seen breasts so big on such a small-waisted girl. Even with her stretched out flat, they were impressive. What he could do right now with her, he thought lasciviously. Too bad she was on the junk.

He closed the door and walked quickly to the stairs. This changed everything. The nigger was probably on it too, so he needed his supply, he'd do anything to get it. Now the deal was a sure thing even without the heavy muscle. He could hardly wait to tell Zucco about their good luck.

Downstairs, he saw a bartender crash a bottle over Farrano's head. He felt sorry for the bartender. Next to Farrano he caught a glimpse of the new kid battling a mustachioed Negro. He couldn't see Gregor but from the noises in the kitchen he was doing his job. Picking his way carefully along one wall of the emptying room, Johnny Apples reached the exit where he skirted a milling throng of excited females and walked into the darkness toward the car.

Back in the club, three men jumped on Harry and Farrano. The first one, short and stocky, was thrown over a stool. An arm tight around his neck, Harry came down hard on the second man's foot. When the grip loosened he spun around and snapped the arm down. The man tried to butt him in the mouth but was stopped with a flat hand to the throat. Gasping, he stood there helpless as Harry sent a fist smashing into his jaw.

The band had stopped playing. Shouts and screams filled the air. On the stage a woman in a black satin gown was at the mike asking everybody to remain calm, but no one listened to her. Trying to shake himself free of the third man, Farrano stumbled and fell to one knee. The man twisted off him and Farrano scooped him up around the waist and battered his head into the bar. The man slithered to the floor.

"That's enough," said Farrano. "Let's get out of here."

In the kitchen Axel Gregor had held most of the staff at bay for the five or so minutes that the fighting had been in progress. During that time he had succeeded in throwing a half-dozen of them to the ground, wrecked at least part of the kitchen, and scared the rest out the side door never to return. Johnny Apples had said give it five minutes and Gregor was very good at his work. Several waiters were still grappling with him, their hands around his immense shoulders. Another leaped upon his back. Thrust forward by the impact, Gregor fell down, taking all with him. He got up swiftly, his superb condition, the result of three hours' daily exercise, giving him very quick reflexes. As he turned around, he was struck on the side of the head with a frying pan. Enraged, he lashed out at his tormentor, sending him sprawling into a cart of prepared salads. Gregor sensed it was time to go. Using the cart as a battering ram he mauled all who got in his way. With a monumental shove he sent the cart flying through the kitchen's double doors. He was right behind it.

"Don't work no more for this place or I be back," he shouted in retreat. Nobody followed him.

At the bar Farrano's fat hands were around somebody's neck, trying to clear the body out of the way. He neatly side-stepped a chair someone threw at him. He had been punched, kicked, bitten, and banged over the head. Liquor had been poured on him. He was sweating, he was tired, and he was looking to get out. As he moved away, he bowled over a short man with a chair, creeping up on Harry.

"C'mon, let's go, let's go," he yelled and Harry, hearing him, turned and was struck from behind. Thrown forward, he was shaking off the blow when something smashed into his mouth and broke it open. Doubling over from shock, he felt himself being held up by Farrano, who had bulled his way through two men. Farrano braced him against the bar. "You OK?"

Holding on desperately, warm blood filling his mouth, Harry tried to answer. With a swoosh of air he spit out a tooth. Strings of blood and spittle ran over his chin and down his striped shirt with the green pearl snaps. Farrano was still holding him, looking at his mouth. "Don't talk," he said in a growl, thinking perhaps it was a broken jaw. Taking Harry under his arm he pushed toward the exit, blood splashing over him. Near the doorway someone stood in his path. Another someone stepped up. Farrano stopped, intent on getting a firm grip on Harry before running over the two men, when Gregor slammed into them from the side. They didn't get up. "Follow me," he shouted to Farrano, his demonic face menacing anyone within striking distance. Harry staggered forward, trailing blood across the room and out the door. Then he was in the night air and Farrano was shaking him.

"Spit out your mouth. Leave it open if you can."

He did as he was told. Head bent over, he let fly a few more teeth and balls of blood. He hacked away, feeling as though his insides were coming out. Globs of blood-flecked spittle collected at his feet.

"Can you talk?"

He raised his head and slowly worked his jaw. "I think so," he said carefully. "Just a lot of blood and stuff." His tongue slipped into new places where teeth had been.

"What hit him?" asked Gregor after they started back to the car.

"Who knows? Maybe a chair or something."

"I think it was a bottle," Harry croaked through bloody lips.

"No, a bottle'd leave cuts," said Farrano, "a lot of small cuts. You don't have that."

"How can you tell what he got with all that blood?"

"Don't matter. Long's it ain't a broken jaw," said Farrano, and he took hold of Harry's arm.

With Farrano on one side and Gregor on the other, Harry trudged on to the car, where Johnny Apples sat in the bucket seat fuming with impatience and eagerness. In his exuberant mood he forgot all about breaking heads for starting the massacre without his signal.

Art Hammis was behind the wheel, his foot gunning the motor. "What's the matter with him?"

"Caught one in the mouth."

"For chrissake, I thought he was such a hot-shot."

"It ain't nothing. Just a bunch of blood."

Harry was pulled into the back seat and dumped in the middle. Johnny Apples turned around and stared at him.

"What happened?"

"He was cold-cocked, just one of those things."

"You want to be more careful." He scowled at Harry and turned back.

Harry put his head down between his legs and coughed up more blood that spilled over the edge of the seat. Art Hammis watched him. "He's getting blood all over the car, for chrissake."

"So what? It ain't yours."

"Shut up and drive."

As the car roared forward, Harry was pushed back into the

seat. Blood still filled his mouth. He figured he had lost about three teeth. Taking out a white handkerchief he emptied his mouth into it and, when it was soaked with blood, he ripped off his silk tie and used that.

10

ART HAMMIS had nailed six of the club's customers. He had stood directly in front of each victim in the parking lot. After explaining that the Cloud Nine was no longer a good place to be, he had warned the man not to come back. Then swinging loosely, he tapped him with a light blow to the jaw, not hard enough to hurt but easy enough to remember. One man had returned the blow, catching him on the side of the head. Surprised, Art had reacted instinctively and a few seconds later looked down to find a bleeding and battered body. Worried by what Johnny Apples would say, he had shoveled the unconscious man under the nearest car.

In the darkness Hammis had stalked each man carefully before pouncing. After the sixth such assault he had seen people streaming out of the club, and so he returned to the car. A few minutes later Johnny Apples had appeared. He ordered Art behind the wheel. "If them clowns ain't out soon, we go."

"Everything all right?" asked Hammis.

"Sure, sure."

"Is it a deal?"

"It will be," Apples replied, thinking about his discovery.

On the highway afterward, Hammis had concentrated on

getting away quickly from the Starlight Motel. He passed the circle going north and then cut off to one of the side streets leading up to the Boulevard. Turning left on the Boulevard, the car soon became lost in traffic. They were safe.

"Where now?"

Johnny Apples checked his watch. Too late to call Zucco, it would have to wait till tomorrow. Anyway, he wanted to tell the story face-to-face so he could build up his role and take all the credit. Not that he didn't deserve it. Joe had already told him he was in for a piece of the club, but maybe this would increase his slice.

"Johnny?"

"What?"

"Should I stop?"

"No."

They rode in silence for a while. Johnny Apples scratched his nose in thought. He was already doing pretty well from his share of the extortion end of the business and a few small things on his own. Now with what he'd make out of the club he'd be OK. Not bad for a kid from the railroad flats along the river who quit school in the eighth grade. He laughed softly, remembering himself as a boy.

"What's funny?"

"Nothing. Just keep driving."

In the back seat Harry Strega kept his mouth closed, bloody saliva filling it until the cheeks puffed out. Next to him sat Farrano in his bloodied toga, totally disheveled and reeking of sweat. Axel Gregor, who never allowed himself to sweat, fingered the rising lump on his head from the frying pan. He regarded it as a personal outrage. When Harry, in sudden realization, frantically indicated he had to empty his mouth, Gregor gave him the large Mexican bandanna from around his own neck. Earlier, on his way past the bar he had seen Harry making a few good moves until dropped from behind, and now Gregor looked him over with a brotherly interest that Harry in his agony missed. "How you feel?"

"I'm OK," said Harry. "Just sore, I guess."

"You let somebody get behind you. Forget it. That happens to all of us. Next time keep your back against something and if there's nothing you can back up to, just keep circling to your left. Ain't that right, Frank? Look at me. I been doing this twenty years and tonight I get banged over the head just like I know nothing. How about that?"

"It happens."

"That's what I mean. Happens all the time and there's nothing you can do about it."

"What about me?" croaked Farrano, silent until now. "That bartender rapped me over the skull with a bottle."

"Did it break?"

"Goddamn right. Can't you smell it?"

"Scotch, ain't it?"

"Shit," said Farrano through layers of smiles. "Ain't even my brand."

"Yeah, but we done good anyway. I know for a fact half the kitchen help won't be back. And you had them moving out at the bar too. You seen it, Johnny. The guy that stopped Harry, he should've been dumped outside. But nobody was hurt too bad, and now we got them on the run."

"Bet your ass," Farrano agreed. "A sure thing. Next time all we do is show up and they'll run."

"Won't be no next time." Scowling, his big beefy face florid, Johnny Apples turned around to look at each of them.

Here it comes, thought Farrano, he's gonna blast us for not waiting for his stupid signal, the crummy bastard.

"The nigger's a junkie. He's got a shooting gallery up there."

They all stared at Johnny Apples. Farrano didn't think he had heard right. "Who's a junkie?" he asked suspiciously.

"The nigger, you lunkhead. That middle room upstairs is where he coasts. How come you didn't spot it when you was up there?"

"It was locked, Johnny. All we seen was the liquor closet and his office. Ain't that right, kid?"

Harry gulped down some bloody saliva. "It was locked all right. You even tried to get it open."

"Yeah, and the nigger looked OK when we seen him. I didn't spot nothing."

"Me neither."

"Who else was with him?"

"Just a broad with big boobs, and if she's a junkie I'm Snow White."

Johnny Apples lashed out at Farrano with one hand. "You dumb wop," he shouted. "Who you think was in that room sleeping off a charge, eh? Take a guess. Go on."

"You mean that bitch—"

"Yeah. That's the one, Frank."

"Christ, Johnny, how'd I know?"

"How'd you know," Apples replied sarcastically.

"Well, we ain't exactly in the junk business. I mean, if I was working for Frank Taylor maybe I would've seen something."

"So maybe you should work for Taylor."

Farrano started sweating again. "What we do now?"

"Nothing, we do nothing. Joe'll work through Taylor to cut off the nigger's supply. When he starts screaming I'll talk to him again. Even if he ain't into it heavy, he's got that bitch and whoever else he's dealing. He'll come around. Only now it'll be a fifty-fifty split."

"So it came out all right, Johnny."

Johnny Apples squinted at Gregor. "Yeah" was all he said.

Art Hammis was cruising at normal speed, hitting a red light every nine or ten blocks along the Boulevard. After several lights in silence, Johnny Apples directed him to turn left. Several further turns placed them in front of a white Georgian house with colonnades and a trellised portico. Jalousies were at every window, yet the gabled roof, whim of a long deceased owner, pointed to an earlier age. Each of its three floors had twenty-foot ceilings, with crystal chandeliers in almost every room. The house was well kept. Scrubbed each week to perfection, it had the look of fresh paint and the feel of fresh linen. Nobody called it home, yet a family of sorts did reside in the house, well known to a select clientele of moneyed and important men. To all of these gentlemen callers the place was known simply as The Greek's.

They waited to be admitted outside the massive oak front door. Johnny Apples and Farrano, recognized, were allowed entrance, with the others their guests. In the front hall Harry noted a strange and overpowering odor. "What's that smell?" he whispered to Farrano.

"Spanish fly," Farrano shouted back. "Ain't you never had none?"

Everybody laughed and Harry, embarrassed, coughed into Gregor's orange bandanna.

In the small barroom they sat under a picture of a young nude girl with long blond tresses kneeling before a naked man with his enormous phallus buried in her brightly painted mouth. The figures were life-size. Other equally large paintings covered the room's walls, each depicting similar sexual intimacies in vivid detail.

Harry sat between Farrano and Gregor, their hulks dwarfing him at the table. Art Hammis and Johnny Apples were facing him. Hammis had been riding Harry about his mouth until told to shut up by Farrano, and now Art poked a finger at him, expressing a concern for the injury that Harry could see was not genuine. "You should be home with that mouth."

"I'm OK here," said Harry.

"The hell you are. You don't know these girls. While they doing you, you got to do them. That's the way it is today, goddamn broads want you to make them feel good too. Ain't that right?" He looked all around, winking broadly. "Ain't that right? And when they don't get it, they let you know goddamn quick." He poked his finger again at Harry. "Now how you gonna make them feel good with that mouth? You gonna bite them with your tongue?" he asked amid howls of laughter.

"No," Harry said evenly after a moment, "but if I have to, I'll gum them to death."

That broke up the table, even Johnny Apples had to laugh. Farrano slammed his ham hand down. "You got him beat," he said with tears in his eyes. "I didn't think it could be done but you got him beat."

Gregor agreed. "Art likes to give the needle, ain't that so, Art? It's time somebody stuck it into you."

"Who cares?" Tight-lipped, his heavy, soft face brooding, Art Hammis stared at the paintings on the wall.

Johnny Apples called the barmaid over, his voice exploding like a machine gun in the hush of the empty room. When she appeared, Harry looked up at the girl in the painting. They were alike. He wondered if she had been the model for the painting.

She stood next to Johnny Apples, dressed in nothing but a fluff of diaphanous material that showed even her birthmarks.

"Give us a couple bottles of Scotch, and some glasses."

"What do you like?"

"You got White Label?"

"Sure."

"No White Label for me," said Hammis, petulant. "Give me Black Label. I ain't gonna drink piss."

"No Black Label. Don't have it."

"Why not?" Raising his upper lip into a sneer, Hammis pushed his face toward hers in a menacing gesture.

"They don't stock it here," she said to Johnny Apples, avoiding the other's gaze. "I can only give you what they got."

"Forget it," said Apples. "He don't know the difference anyway. Art here, he just likes to shoot off his mouth."

"I can see that."

Angered, Hammis grabbed between her thighs and squeezed until she yelped. "Easy with the cracks, honey. I can always come back alone for you. You know what I mean?"

Unsure of herself now, she retreated to the bar where she conveniently ran out of trays. In the hall she asked one of the male help to identify the group at the table.

"What are they, bartenders?"

One look was enough. "Joe Zucco's gorillas. The one in the million-dollar suit is a top ape."

"Who's Zucco?"

"You never heard of Joe Zucco? Where you from?"

"Little Rock, Arkansas."

"Go back home while you still can. And stay clear of guys like that. They're all mobbed up."

When she returned to the table with the setups, Harry asked her if she had posed for the painting. Blushing, she told him no.

"It looks just like you. Really."

She was flattered of course, even if the pose was one she wouldn't want displayed in public. In private, well, she wouldn't mind meeting a man with one that big. Who would? For something like that she could do as good as the girl in the painting. Better.

"You work here regular?"

"Just two nights a week."

"If I come back sometime I'd like to sit down with you."

"Can't. Not in here."

"Outside then."

She somehow found this one different from the others, she didn't know why. Younger and slimmer, certainly. Better looking too, even though his mouth looked all puffed up. He seemed more gentle, yet he had the same smell of danger that stimulated her. "Maybe," she said in her best seductive manner, shaking everything she had as she left the table.

"She ain't one of the whores," said Farrano, filling up the glasses.

"How can you tell?"

"Easy. She ain't upstairs."

"So she does it outside and keeps the cash," Hammis said spitefully, still trying to needle Harry.

Harry smiled. "Hell, when I take 'em out they pay *me*," he boasted. "Always been like that 'cause I got what they need."

"What's that?"

Harry gazed up at the painting. Their eyes followed his.
"Who you think," he said quietly, "is paying who?"

"Huh?"

"That's what I mean."

The two bottles of Scotch, and another two after those, were finished by the time they shakily ascended the carpeted stairs to meet their ladies of the evening. They had come for that purpose and at least three of them were not to be dissuaded. Art Hammis quickly drank himself under the table and had to be carried out. He was deposited in a cab. Axel Gregor, who did not sweat and never got drunk, also never frequented prostitutes. He walked home, never riding on public transportation if he could help it.

While others took pleasure in the carnal, Gregor sought release in the physical perfecting of his body. Over the years he had seen men of astounding physical prowess become wasted hulks through the misuse of alcohol and women. All his adult life Gregor had watched carefully that he did not succumb to the two temptations. On those rare occasions when he allowed a woman to visit him, it was only to feel the differences of her body, to explore those secret passages with his organs of touch and taste, but never to divest himself of any of his balancing fluids. Even as a youth he had trained himself to overcome the debilitating effects of the purely sexual on his body. He had believed even then that one day he would be the world's strongest man, the first man to have a perfect body. He had known it was inevitable, if only he trained hard and with total devotion. Thirty years later he realized the futility of his ambition. The strongest man was always someone else, the perfect body was always just beyond reach. Yet the iron habits of a lifetime were not to be put aside so easily. The one time he consummated a union with a woman, in an abject despondency midway in his life, had been for him a time of agony. He had felt weak, defenseless, ravaged, used, terrifyingly lost, and he knew then that if he ever gave himself to another woman it would have to be done against his will. He would have to be chained and beaten and kicked and whipped and tortured with secret devices, and then he would still resist until his body was drained of all its strength.

Upstairs on the second floor, Frank Farrano passed out two minutes after hitting the bed in Carol's room. Carol had been with Farrano before and knew of his desires. Not to be deprived of her tip, which from Farrano was always generous, she struggled his baggy pants down to his knees and proceeded to masturbate him, thankful to the Virgin Mary that she did not have to do more. After ten minutes she gave up. He was deadweight and impossible to arouse. Mixing a solution of water and granulated sugar, she dripped the milky, sticky substance on his private parts and shorts so there would be evidence that she had done her job when he awoke. She then sat down in the comfortable chair to read a book.

On the third floor Johnny Apples and Harry Strega occupied adjoining rooms. Johnny Apples had chosen his favorite redhead, a young Irish girl with small breasts, and was now attempting to describe to her in drunken detail all his sexual fantasies. She listened politely, knowing that when he was finished he would mount her in simple fashion and would shortly thereafter be asleep.

Next door Harry, having had much to drink, sat on the edge of the bed listening to a slim, dark-haired Italian girl tell him of the time her parents insured her virginity. She was seventeen and leaving her village for a job in Rome. The two-thousand-dollar policy cost her parents two dollars a month, and each month an agent of the insurance company visited her in Rome, where he carefully checked her virginity. By the third month he had violated her policy.

The girl's voice was soft and soothing to Harry's alcoholic nerves, though he found it difficult to follow her words. "When I complained to the insurance company that my parents should now be paid the money, they sent another man to look into my virginity. He checked it for months, probing everywhere, each time promising that he would send in a report. He never did.

I wrote them letters they never answered. I even sent them a picture a girl friend took of me to show I wasn't a virgin any longer. They asked if I had any others like it." She put out the light and stood naked before Harry. "I told them I wanted no more agents because they didn't know what they were doing. I mean, if they couldn't tell I wasn't a virgin." She undressed Harry while she talked. "Then one day the owner of the company came to see me." She pushed Harry down onto the bed. "He apologized for the delay and said he would examine me himself." She got on top of Harry. "He examined me for a whole week before he had to go back to the office. He told me there was nothing wrong with me, that I was indeed a virgin. I asked him how that could be and he said nature was very mysterious." She moved up and down on Harry. "So I wrote my parents and told them not to send the company any more money." Harry suddenly sat upright, sending her sprawling backward. His confused mind couldn't quite grasp how she could be a virgin and do what she was doing to him, but if she was a virgin he wasn't going to dishonor her. He respected virginity in women.

"What's the matter?" asked the girl.

"You're a virgin." He tried to get up but instead sank back on the bed. He had a feeling he was drunk.

"Don't be funny."

"You're a virgin," he repeated. He looked at her crotch, trying to see if she really was a virgin but it was too dark.

"Do you want to examine me too?"

"I believe you."

"But I'm *not* a virgin."

"How do you know?"

"There's one sure way to find out."

"What way? What way to find out?" asked Harry. And she jumped on top of him and impaled herself on his penis, erect and massive. Harry's tight body leaped upward against hers and the noise of their involuntary movements drowned out the guilty voices within him, castigating him for violating the insurance of this young girl working on the third floor of The Greek's fashionable brothel.

Harry woke up at five in the morning, alone in bed. The house was quiet. Shaky from the drinking, his reflexes shot and his memory gone, he dressed slowly and walked unsteadily out of the room. There was no one in the hall, no one on the stairs. On the ground floor he stumbled toward the front door, opened for him by some shadowy being who bade him good night. Once on the street, Harry shook his eyes open and tried to pull himself together. He weaved up the corner, intent on asking someone where he was. He saw nobody. The night air was crisp, the sky clear as he breathed deeply, hanging onto a light pole. His mind functioning, his memory returning, Harry checked his pockets. Nothing was missing. He looked up and down the block but saw nothing familiar. Let's face it, he told himself, you're lost. With a weary shrug he sat on a stoop. "Goddamn," he shouted, "where the hell am I?" Nobody answered him. After a while he got up and plodded onward, determined to find his own way.

Twenty minutes later he hit Palisade Avenue, crossed over, and sat on a park bench. The alcohol was wearing off and his mouth was beginning to hurt again. He was tired and he was lonely. He squirmed into the bench and was soon asleep. In his dream he was in a helicopter with Frank Farrano and somebody with no face. The girl with the big breasts wouldn't tell them if she was a virgin. She gave only her rank and serial number. With her was a Vietnamese girl, they seemed to be friends. Farrano and No Face kept questioning the Vietnamese girl in English. They knew she didn't understand a word. When the craft was so high that only the treetops were visible, they threw her out of the helicopter. She screamed going down. Then they turned to the girl with the big breasts. Terrified, she told them she was a virgin. When she took off her clothes there was a grenade between her legs. She pulled the pin.

The rain woke him up, a light shower that left the next block dry. He shrugged himself off the bench and started walking. His mouth hurt fiercely. To the east dawn was cracking, pushing westward the weight of night. Two blocks farther on, Harry hailed an empty cab and gave the driver his address. As they sped down the viaduct he gazed with dead eyes out at the pulsing landscape that seemed to be sucking him into its maw. After a while he wasn't seeing anything.

"This is it, pal." The driver turned around to check if Harry was awake. "End of the line." He lowered the radio.

"What?"

"We're here."

"Oh, yeah. Right."

With bowed head and resigned manner, Harry paid the fare, stumbled out, and inched past the iron demons guarding the stone stoop. He crept silently up the stairs to his room, flung his clothes off in the dark, and crawled under the blanket. He couldn't sleep. His perfect world was slowly slipping away, he didn't know why or how. His mind circled itself, staring unseeing at whole patches of his vacant past. He changed his position a dozen times. Nothing helped. For the first time in his young life, Harry sensed that he might not be all the things he had always expected to be. For the first time he sensed that he might not make it. With his fingers he traced the soreness in his mouth. It was a bad omen, a very bad omen, and he didn't know what to do about it. Feeling sorry for himself, tears welling up in his eyes, Harry couldn't control the groans of defeat that escaped his throat and fell into the silent room.

11

SEEKING OUT HIS MAN, Charley Flowers went through a dozen flophouses and shadowy tenements, in each one hearing of yet another place where Ray Scottini might be hiding. In the daytime he prowled the bars around Garfield Avenue where Scottini lived. For three days he followed the trail across the city, up Communipaw and Newark avenues, down Garfield, along the Paterson Plank Road, in the railroad yards and parks, and around the industrial slag heaps and sand piles where homeless men congregated in droves over barrel fires and told tall tales, cursed their luck, picked their scabs, shared bottles with one another, and lost themselves in the anonymity of total freedom.

Everywhere the word was out on Scottini. No one could help him now. It was just a matter of time.

After a fruitless night and sleepless morning in bed with a shapeless blonde who insisted her name was Leo, Flowers showered and dressed, threw Leo out of his room, and took the car over to his brother Albert's house. In the heavy midday traffic along Grand Street he stalled several times, sending shouted curses out above the traffic's roar. The big tractor-trailers, twenty-six tons loaded on fourteen wheels, zoomed mightily by, shaking the earth in their dust. With recurrent bursts of profanity and a cautious gas foot, Flowers managed to ease the car forward. Eventually he pulled up in front of an ancient clapboard house with a green and white open porch and four rickety steps leading to it. The exterior had not been painted in forty years, the roof leaked, and all the downstairs windows had broken shades. Upstairs, several of the windows no longer opened. The frame sagged in the middle, the rain gutters were hanging off, and the basement flooded whenever it rained hard. Yet the house had undeniable charm in an old-worldly fashion. An elderly widow ran it as a boarding house, two meals a day and parlor privileges. She was not averse to allowing men of questionable character or certain reputation to live there, though the weekly rent was raised according to notoriety. Her six rooms were usually filled.

On the porch, a sandy-haired man in a leather jacket and steel-tipped boots, his pants flared at the bottom and the shirt half unzipped to reveal a hairy chest, waited patiently as Flowers parked the car and got out.

"What are you so happy about?" Charley Flowers demanded, irritable after the hard drive.

"Why not?" said Albert, smiling. "Today's our lucky day."

"Says who?"

"We'll get him today. I feel it." He took out a long thin knife and began to clean his nails.

"Ever been wrong?"

"A few times. Not much."

"I got a hundred says you're full of shit."

The smile stayed on. "It's sucker money."

"So take it."

"You been took."

The screen door opened. "You coming back later?" asked the widow from the doorway. "If you ain't, I'll clean your room."

"Go ahead. Just don't throw out them two babes I got tucked away in the bed," Albert said in a bantering voice.

The widow clucked in her throat. "You should be ashamed

of yourself, talking to an old lady like that," she crowed, obviously pleased.

"What old lady? I don't see no old lady."

"Ah, go on now. You'd talk the pants off the Blessed Virgin." She put her hand up to her mouth. "Oh, Mother of God, what have I gone and said now?" She shook her head sadly at the evilness of the world and went inside. Even Flowers, bad mood and all, had to laugh.

"She like that all the time?"

"All the time," said the other, "even when she sleeps."

"How would you know?"

"How you think?" He put his knife carefully back in his pocket. "She's hot for me."

Flowers trudged down the porch steps and continued on to the car, watchful to stay on the narrow cement strip between two small plots of grass. He wanted no animal dung on his shoes, and being from the city he naturally believed that all greenery was infested with dog, cat, bird, and sundry other droppings. His scrutiny of the grass was successful and his shoes emerged unscathed from the sidewalk. Unfortunately, he didn't notice the dog shit in the gutter until too late. Screams of anguish were of no help. His rage was so great that for a moment he considered taking out a contract on the dog. When his senses returned, he cleaned the shoes on the curb, slowly and methodically, then stepped gingerly to the car. One of the doors had a long gash in it, the work of destructive kids. The right fender was dented. There was a wheel cover missing and the aerial was bent.

"You coming, lover boy?" shouted Flowers.

"Why not? Today's my lucky day."

Albert was a knife artist, one of the best in the city. At thirty-six he was an acknowledged master craftsman. He could cut a man to any desired depth from a skin break to the bone, slice overhand or underhand, peel skin by the layer, and do all of it with either hand. His wrists were extremely flexible, his hands incredibly fast. In his pocket he carried a five-inch Harwood made of fine Swedish steel, able to slice paper or cut tin. Perfectly balanced, the knife never needed sharpening.

As a boy growing up in Bayonne, Albert had developed a rheumatic ailment that kept him in the house most of the time. With little else to do, he began playing with knives. The feel of the knife in the flat of his hand, or with his fingers tightly wrapped around the handle, excited him. He discovered his natural affinity for the weapon, and over the years he developed speed and great accuracy. By the time he reached manhood he had outgrown both his ailment and his native shyness. He had also killed a man in a bar fight, almost eviscerating him in the process. The victim was a neighborhood bully with a long assault and rape record, so nobody mourned or even appeared surprised. Albert claimed self-defense and witnesses corroborated. He was freed. In the next few years he killed several other men in the same manner, all of them for money. As his reputation grew, he prospered. The mob found him efficient and dependable, and began funneling jobs his way. Married and settled down, his future looked secure. Then his luck ran out. He knifed a man in a bar less than ten blocks from the first killing, but this time it was not self-defense. Nor did it have any mob connection. Police saw it as a simple grudge killing. He got seven years for manslaughter and was lucky to get that. Two years later his wife divorced him and moved away.

In his fourth year at Trenton State Prison, Albert got into a violent argument with another convict over a slim young boy whom they both fancied. A half-dozen cells separated the two men, preventing immediate physical contact. But nothing could prevent the screaming. "I'm gonna kill you. You hear me? I'm gonna jam my blade up your ass so far it'll come out of your hair."

"Just stay away from my boy, you hear?"

"Your boy? He's mine, I seen him first."

Albert gripped the bars. "You're messing with the wrong man, Steers. I'm warning you, that kid's punking for me."

"Like hell he is. I'm getting him first."

"I'll cut you into ribbon."

"What? What you gonna do?" Steers raged. "I'm gonna chop your goddamn head off is all's gonna happen. In the shower. I'm gonna chop you in two in the shower."

"You're dead," Albert screamed.

Everybody, including the guards, heard the argument. Nobody, including the guards, did anything about it. They encouraged it, in fact, by their silence; they wanted the two men to fight it out. It would be at least a temporary break in the monotony of prison routine.

The next morning they let Steers out first to go to the shower. When Albert arrived, folded towel under his arm, he undressed and went around the corner to the shower head, still carrying the towel. Steers was waiting for him. As Albert turned on the water Steers rushed across the wet, smelly room and lunged at him, a long blade in his hand. Albert spun quickly and caught the man's arm in its downward swing. Twisting it back, he came up behind Steers. With his other hand he pulled his own weapon, a short-handled kitchen knife, out of the folded towel. Bringing it up swiftly, Albert plunged it into the side of Steers' neck, snapped it around, and cut his throat from ear to ear.

Steers, unbelieving, died on his feet, his eyes wide, blood streaming down his front, his knife slipping from his grasp to clatter onto the shower floor. Albert stood alone in the room, naked, covered with blood, his blade still in his hand as the guards rushed in. Satisfied that at least one was dead, they beat Albert into submission and took him away. For the Steers' killing, self-defense though it was, Albert received an additional three years and lost any chance of parole.

At age thirty-five, ten years after he entered Trenton State Prison, Albert Flowers walked through the prison gates to freedom. He settled in Jersey City, visited his mother in the housing project to which she had moved from Bayonne years earlier, after her husband died and both her sons were in prison, and then asked his younger brother for a mob connection. In the year since his release Albert had been given a few strong-arm and bodyguard jobs, acquiring the reputation of a good worker who kept his mouth shut.

Seated now in the car with Flowers at the wheel, Albert knew they would find Ray Scottini. The feeling was so strong it was real, it had to be. They'd find him and do the job, and Albert's reputation would grow. He was pleased with himself. Everybody'd talk about this one for a long time, of that he was sure. His lucky day.

A siren screamed past them on Grand, police on a mission. Both men cursed automatically. Flowers guided the car through a string of trucks in both lanes, nosed out a bus lumbering into a bus stop, and raced past a red light, leaving pedestrians shaking fists.

"You always drive like this?" Albert asked sarcastically.

"Only around you."

"Yeah, I notice by all the dents."

"Amateurs."

He skirted around two cars abreast, crossed the dividing line, and made it back inches before a car sped by in the opposite direction, its horn blaring frantically. "Amateurs."

Albert paled. "And they put me away for just one kill."

On the side streets Flowers drove somewhat more carefully. "Where do we start today?" he demanded suddenly.

"How should I know?"

"You said we'll find him today."

"We'll find him."

"So tell me where."

"I don't know where." Albert thought hard. "You remember that cunt he use to live with? In that bar the other night?"

"What about her?"

"Maybe he's back with her and she was lying to us."

"Not a chance. She was scared shitless."

"You got a better idea?"

Flowers squeezed the car past a truck double-parked in the middle of the block. He turned left at the corner. "I think his wife knows where he's hiding."

"So what? Even if she does, she ain't telling us."

"Maybe we can change her mind." He pulled up in front of an old yellow brick tenement off Garfield. The street door was open.

Albert read the listing. "Apartment seventeen it says here."

"Christ, that must be the top floor."

They walked up the crumbling stairs full of noises, passing broken banisters and brown-flecked walls, a century's grime etched into every crack and crevice. At the fourth landing they rested, out of breath.

"Wouldn't do this every day."

"No way."

One more flight and they stood in front of number 17. On the door was a metal 7 but the 1 was missing, though its imprint could plainly be seen in the faded paint. Flowers knocked and waited a moment, then knocked again, harder.

"Who is it?"

"City inspectors," Flowers said gruffly.

The door opened a crack. "What you want?"

"Mrs. Scottini?"

"Yes."

"We're from the city sanitation checking on rats and we got to look around. Can we come in?"

"I was just resting."

"It won't take long."

The woman hesitated. "Where you say you from?"

"Sanitation."

"You don't look like sanitation."

"How do they look?" Albert asked politely.

"Maybe you better come back when my husband's home," said the woman.

"When'll that be?" Flowers demanded.

Suspicious now, she tried to close the door but Flowers put his foot against it and kicked it open wide, splintering the wood where the chain had been loosely attached. Frightened, she backed up to the wall. "What you want with me?" she asked in a squeaky voice, her dark hair disheveled, her eyes sunken and face hollow. "Go away, please."

"We're business associates of your husband," Flowers said, ignoring her. "We got to locate him. It's very important."

"He's away."

"Where away?"

"I don't know. Out of town somewhere."

"We happen to know he's still in town." Flowers motioned to Albert. "Check the other rooms." He put his face close to the woman's. "If you tell us, it'll save everybody a lot of trouble. We just want to help him, but we got to find him first."

"I don't know where he is."

"That's too bad. If we don't get to him, he may be killed." Flowers watched her face. He believed she already knew that her husband was in trouble. "How long's he been gone?"

"A few days."

Albert returned. "Nothing but a baby in a crib."

"Yours?"

The woman nodded, fear in her eyes.

"Boy?"

She nodded again. "He's only a year old."

"Let's all go into the front room," said Flowers, "where we can talk better."

They walked through the railroad flat to the front room, the woman first. On the way Flowers stopped at the crib and played with the sleeping baby for a moment. Mrs. Scottini watched him, dazed. He picked it up in a bundle of bedding and carried it into the living room and over to one of the two open windows.

"Nice kid you got here."

"Please let him go, please."

"I'll let him go right out that window," Flowers snarled, "if you don't tell us where's your husband."

"I don't know, I don't know," the woman pleaded, hysteria creeping into her voice.

With one hand Flowers raised the weatherbeaten window

higher, then sat on the windowsill. He placed the baby on its edge. "If you don't tell us, he goes."

"No," the woman screamed, "No, not my baby."

"Tell us," Flowers yelled.

"I don't know," she cried.

Flowers picked up the baby and held it in the air outside the window. "This is your last chance. Tell us or I drop him right now. We're not fooling."

"He didn't say where he'd be, just that he'll call and—"

Charley Flowers dropped the baby.

The mother howled like an animal, a strangled scream that burst out of her throat. She hurled herself toward the open window after the baby. Flowers grabbed her around the waist and pushed her backward, sending her sprawling onto the floor. She rose immediately, insane fury on her face, the edges of her mouth foaming, her hands clawing desperately in front of her as she rushed again toward the window. Flowers hit her in the face, crashing her again to the floor. She lay there, semi-conscious, legs askew, blood trickling down one corner of her mouth.

In the next room a baby cried.

Albert, startled, jumped violently. "What the hell was that?" he shouted in confusion.

"A baby. What's it sound like?"

Running into the room, Albert found the baby in the crib. He picked it up. "How'd it get here?"

"Been there all the time," Flowers said softly. "I just took the kid's pillow and wrapped it in his blanket."

"But why?"

"We had to see if she knew where Scottini was, right?"

"So she don't know."

"Wrong."

"What wrong?"

"She knows, and now she's gonna tell us." He waved his arm. "Bring the kid in here."

The woman, still on the floor, lay like a broken doll. She was glassy-eyed and oddly quiet.

Flowers took the baby and stood over her. "Mrs. Scottini, can you hear me? See what I got?"

She lifted her head and looked up at him, her eyes registering an object in his arms.

"That's right, I have your kid here. See, he's OK." He showed her the baby's face, peaceful now and no longer crying. "I threw out his pillow before, but he's OK. Can you understand me?" He spoke slowly. "I want you to tell me where your husband is or I'll throw the kid out the window for real this time." He walked to the window. "Tell me where he is and we'll go away."

The woman, drained of all emotion, spoke in a dull, flat voice, her tongue thick, her breathing irregular. "He's in the railroad yards on Caven Point Road. In a tool shed."

"You know where that is?" asked Albert.

"Sure. Not far from here."

"Then we got him."

"Maybe." Flowers pointed to the phone on the table next to the silver and blue tufted couch. "That the only one here?"

The woman stared at it, as though uncomprehending. "Yes," she whispered finally.

"Pull it," he said to Albert. He went over to the woman and handed her the baby. Sitting on the floor, she cradled it in her arms, unbelieving.

"Don't go out for a couple hours," he said close to her face. "Don't talk to nobody. And don't try to get in touch with him or we'll be back. You won't like that."

Flowers straightened himself, and he and Albert walked back through the apartment and out the door. Moments later they were in the car and headed for Caven Point Road.

"Would you've done it?" Albert asked suddenly.

"Done what?"

"You know, throw the kid out the window."

"We found out what we wanted, didn't we?"

"Yeah, but suppose she didn't tell us?"

"But she did."

"But suppose she didn't? Would you've done it?" Albert insisted.

Flowers was silent for a long time, steering the car carefully over the potholed road leading to the railroad yards. He wished Albert would shut up instead of asking dumb questions. He wished he were somewhere else. "I was scared," he said at last.

"Scared of what? That she'd call your bluff?"

Flowers shook his head. "Scared that it wasn't a bluff."

In her apartment Mrs. Scottini sat on the floor, cradling her baby. Moaning softly, a strange rhythmic dirge of oo-new oo-new, she rocked back and forth from the waist, her legs, unmoving, crossed beneath her. Horrified at the conflict of having to choose between her precious infant and the husband whom she loved, maddened by the sight of her baby being thrown out the window to its death, her whole world destroyed in one swift moment of terror, she now sat on her living room floor, her fragile mind snapped beyond recall, and toyed with the doll in her arms. A slight woman with only one kidney, orphaned as a child, sickly all her life, her son was the only child she could ever have, according to the doctors. Now he was dead and her husband was gone and all she had left was this toy doll. Her grief, utterly unbearable, turned to frenzy as her shattered mind rushed headlong into the vacuum of infinity. Lifting the doll over her head, now crying, she slammed it down against the floor with all the force of her absolute madness. Then, laughing hideously, she raised the doll again and again by its stubby little legs, each time crashing it to the floor. By the third blow the child was dead, its skull caved in, the neck snapped. After a dozen such blows the battered little body, most of its bones broken, was soft pulp encased in a blue and white sleep suit wet with fluid. The small face and head were no longer recognizable; blood and bits of flesh were pasted to the floor and flung everywhere about the room. The woman, exhausted and splattered with blood, dropped the sodden object and screamed. Her mind blown asunder to the farthest reaches of time, the demonic mother raced to the window and plunged outward, howling to the wind, following her infant son down, down to the silence at the end of the world.

On the silent roadway, a shed loomed ahead of the car. "We're almost there," said Flowers. "How you want to handle this?"

"Just go in and flush him out. What else can we do?"

"You want to take the back?"

"No good. You got the gun, I'm sticking with you."

"You never carry one?"

"I never even handled one," Albert admitted sheepishly. "They scare the shit out of me."

"You're nuts," Flowers said. "You can chop a man to pieces without a look, but a gun scares you."

"That's how it is."

"That's nuts." He parked the car on the dirt road about fifty yards from the shed. They had a clear view of three sides of the building. "He must've seen us by now."

"Suppose he scoots out the back?"

"Be a bitch to get him with all the track around here. He could go 'most anywhere and we'd never see him."

"So let's move in behind and then come back."

Flowers started up, inching ahead cautiously. The road veered to the right of the shed and he followed it past, braking to a stop several dozen yards on the other side. "Let's make out we're the cops," he said to Albert. "He might go for it."

"OK by me."

"He ain't gonna give us no trouble anyway."

"How you figure that?"

"He knows he done wrong, and he knows he got to pay for it. Else he'd be long gone out of here."

"I don't know about that. A man'll cling to life, don't matter what he done or what he's up against. I learned that," Albert said quietly, "all them years in prison."

The two men got out of the car noiselessly and crept to the

edge of the windowless building, Flowers' gun in his hand. The door was closed. Flowers unlatched it and kicked it open slowly with his foot as he stepped aside.

"We're the cops, Scottini. Come out with your hands up."

Nobody answered.

"You hear me? Come on out."

They waited a few moments.

"We're coming in after you."

Step by cautious step they walked into the one-room shed. Tools were everywhere on the workbenches, on the floor, on the walls. There was a battered mattress set against one wall and a half-loaf of bread and some cans of vegetables on one of the benches. There was nobody in the room.

"What now?" Albert wanted to know.

"I can't figure it. He must've been tipped, but how?" He looked around. "No phones here."

"Maybe she was lying to us."

Flowers shook his head. "Too scared."

"Maybe he left and didn't tell her."

Lost in contemplation of the mystery, neither man noticed the arm holding a gun in the doorway. The first shot brought them back to reality.

"Hold it, we're cops in here," Flowers shouted, dropping to the floor. Albert was already down. Neither one was hit.

As Flowers hurriedly whispered a plan to Albert, a second shot banged the wall over their heads.

"Goddamn it, we're cops. I'm coming out," Albert shouted. "I have no gun. I'm coming out with my hands up."

Flowers' plan was to drop Scottini when he showed himself to check out Albert. He'd wound his man rather than kill him, since Zucco wanted another kind of death for him.

It was a simple plan.

Albert held his hands high and began to move away from the corner toward the open door. As he walked hesitantly forward, the gun arm no longer visible in the doorway, he kept repeating his story. "Man, you're all wrong. We're cops. We're cops."

When he got outside, hands still in the air, Albert stood still. Scottini would have to come to him. Flowers, crouched in the corner, the gun steady in his hand, waited for his man to step into the light.

"Man, you're all wrong. We're cops."

Flowers heard the voice respond a second before the shot, a high-pitched voice that had a hysterical whine to it.

"That's too bad."

BANG.

Stunned, he watched as the bullet tore into his brother's guts, slamming him backward against the door frame. His eyes had a fearful look in them, his hands shook uncontrollably. He opened his mouth, trying to breathe.

BANG.

The second shot ripped through his throat, pulverizing tissue and muscle, and sending gushes of blood streaming down his chest. He was dead, a lifeless hulk slowly slipping to the ground, the look of fear still in its glazed eyes.

Charley Flowers had made a mistake. Scottini, totally desperate, trusted nobody and was ready to kill anybody. He was a frightened animal, maddened enough to destroy everything in his way. Flowers' mistake had cost the life of his only brother.

"Al."

It wasn't a question or even a name so much as a spontaneous scream hurled out of a stupefying shock, a scream shouted at the split second that Flowers tore himself out of his crouch and through the doorway, coming up in a ball at his brother's side, gun in hand. The shot came late and splintered wood harmlessly over his head.

He squeezed the trigger wildly, his direction off, scattering three shots. Something crashed around the building's side. Uncaring, unthinking, he rushed forward, turned the corner. A man was running away from the shed, toward the tracks. Flowers caught a glimpse of the face.

Scottini.

He raced after him. Twenty yards, fifteen, ten. Scottini, breathless, slowed up. Flowers came on like a demon out of hell. They were jumping over tracks now. Ten tracks, eight, six, four. Scottini suddenly turned, Flowers almost on him, and pulled the trigger right in his face. The gun clicked. A five-shot .38-caliber police special, it was empty.

Scottini broke apart. Out of breath, out of bullets, he fell to his knees on the hard earth, gasping, sniveling, out of control. Flowers steamrolled into him. Coming up feet first, he kicked Scottini in the guts and shoved the gun against his head, finger on the trigger.

Scottini screamed.

Flowers didn't move. His mind, his hand, his finger stopped. Something in the man's scream caught his awareness. He wanted to hear that cry again. An image of what Zucco intended for Scottini came into his mind, and he gloated at the thought. Turning the gun around in his hand, he clubbed Scottini over the head with the butt. As the man lay on the ground unconscious, Flowers kicked him in the face, breaking his nose.

In ten minutes he had Scottini safely in the trunk of the car, a gag in his mouth and baling wire wrapped tightly around his wrists. He then carried his brother's lifeless body, laying it gently on the floor of the back seat. Numb with grief, Flowers sat in the car a long time before he slipped it into gear and slowly eased away from the deserted yards. He drove slowly, mournfully. All the way back he kept thinking that this hadn't been his brother's lucky day at all, unless death itself—free from all needs, peaceful, beyond pain—was luck. He wasn't sure of anything anymore.

At the meat packing plant Flowers pulled around to the back. He left the bodies in the car and called Al Parry from the small office by the rear platform.

"The girl has arrived."

Twenty minutes later Parry was in the office. When he was told about Albert's body in the car, he blew.

"You dumb sonofabitch, how dumb can you get? Why'd you bring it here?"

"What else could I do with it?"

"Leave it there, that's what you should've done."

"What about when they found him?"

"So what? Nobody seen you with him."

"The old lady where he lived, she seen us."

Parry snorted. "Are you kidding? She don't see nothing."

"What about Scottini's wife?"

"What about her?"

"She seen us all right."

"How she gonna say anything? She's dead, ain't she?"

"Dead?"

"Sure. Didn't you do a job on her? It was on the radio coming over here."

"We didn't touch her."

Parry looked disbelieving. "Joe ain't gonna like that. You never hit the wife and kids. It just ain't done."

"We didn't do nothing to her," Flowers whined.

Parry was on the spot. Zucco would crucify him if they hit Scottini's wife and kid, it broke the code. But he hated Scottini so much, if he thought they had nothing to do with it, he'd rejoice that the whole family was wiped out. He'd consider it a piece of luck. Cursing Flowers bitterly to himself, Parry knew what he had to do.

"OK," he muttered savagely, "the radio said she must've went nuts and killed her kid and then jumped out the window. We leave it like that. Joe don't have to know you was even there. Understand? That's how you gonna play it."

"Sure, Al, sure." Flowers, relieved, knew that if he was in trouble with Zucco so was Parry. "What about my brother?"

"He goes the same as Scottini."

"Jesus, Al, that's kind of rough."

"Don't Jesus me," Parry exploded. "You screwed things up enough already."

"I done my best."

"Your best, shit. I told you to get Scottini on the quiet and do a job on him here in the plant. I give you a knife man, right? Did I tell you to knock off his family?"

"I didn't," Flowers protested.

"No? What you think, she done the job on the kid herself? Eh? Is that what you're telling me?"

"I don't know what she done."

"I know," Parry screamed. "I know what you done. Did I tell you to get your brother shot up? Did I tell you that?"

"It was an accident. Scottini was waiting for us."

"There are no accidents." The veins were popping in his neck. "When I give you a job I want it done right. Now you just gonna hand him over to the cops, is that it? Maybe take out an ad in the papers?"

"I didn't mean that."

Parry let his anger subside. There was nothing he could do now, and he had to be cool to face Zucco. "What did you mean?" he asked quietly.

"Can't we just leave him there like you said?"

"Leaving him was one thing. It's too dangerous to go back, maybe somebody heard the shots. Maybe the cops are all over the place right now. You want to walk into that?"

"How about the river?"

"Better this way. He's here now, no chance of anything going wrong. He goes like Scottini. That's final."

Waving his hands in a helpless gesture, Flowers gave up. Parry was right, there was no sense walking into trouble. If the cops found the body they'd question him since he was the brother, and he didn't want to go through that. Who cared what happened to a dead body anyway?

"I'll get you another knife man," Parry said. He glanced at his watch. "Six now. I'll have him here at eight."

"What should I do?"

"You stay here with the car. When he comes, do the job and get out. The guard'll lock up when he makes his rounds."

"He know about us?"

"No sweat. He's on the payroll."

Parry walked out of the office and down the platform steps, Flowers behind him.

"Where you got Scottini?"

"In the trunk."

"Make sure he can breathe. This is a revenge job, remember that. Joe wants him alive for a while."

"He can breathe."

"You just make sure."

Bending into his brown and tan Buick, the buzzer sounding until he strapped on the safety belt, Al Parry settled himself expansively in the contoured leather bucket seat, lifted his rear slightly to emit a noiseless fart, grunted in satisfaction, and burped mentally. He would soon be at dinner, eating his way through his favorite Chinese foods. He would let nothing spoil it, not even a lunatic of a would-be shooter who couldn't do anything right.

"See that nothing else goes wrong on this job. I'm holding you personally responsible for the rest of it."

Flowers stood between the two cars looking wistful, his brows knit in exaggerated attention. "Yeah, Al. Sure. I'll take care of it."

"You do that." He laughed cruelly. "You just do that, big shooter man."

"Up yours, you fish-eyed bastard," Flowers murmured at the departing car, wishing he could run it into the river with Parry in it. He went over to the other car and yanked open the trunk lid. Scottini was still unconscious. "Least I got you to pay for my brother."

He slammed the lid and trooped back up the stairs to the platform, where he stood motionless facing the car with two dead men. After a while the sun gave up over Newark and sank along its western rim. Flowers was barely conscious now, his gaze turned inward to a remote past when he and Albert were kids growing up in a fourth-floor walkup in Bayonne. Four people in two rooms, no bath, no heat, no hot water. An icebox in winter, a furnace in summer. The toilet was down the hall, a long, narrow corridor that stank of urine and stale sex. Everything was damp, everything dark. There were potholes in the floors, cracks in the walls, rusty water, leaking pipes, escaping gas, and roaches and rats. Cement bags were sewn together for sheets, anything was sewn together for clothes. Father, a day laborer, nightly drunkard, held out until both boys escaped to prison. Mother, spirit long broken, escaped to religion and a housing project on state aid.

It was seldom that Charley Flowers consciously thought about his early life. It was too painful. He simply hoped, in the best American style, to better himself.

When the black Ford pulled in through the gate, its turn signals flashing hypnotically, Flowers was still lost in the past, standing motionless on the platform, eyes staring vacantly. He did not notice the car's arrival until it braked to a stop next to his, in the same space where Parry had been two hours earlier. The motor was turned off, the lights switched out. He watched as the driver kicked open the door.

"You Charley Flowers, right?" Ginger asked from the driver's seat. "Al Parry told me to come over. Said you had some work for me."

"You're the big knife man," said Flowers simply.

Ginger walked over to the metal steps. He kept his eyes on Flowers. "Ain't I seen you somewhere? We ever work together?"

"Not together."

"Somewhere."

"Dominick Spina."

"Hey, that's right. Spina." He laughed. "You done the job on him all right."

"You were his bodyguard."

Ginger laughed again, a shrill, horsey laugh that spiraled into a nasal cough. "Yeah, well, can't win 'em all. Hey, no hard feelings, pal. It's just business."

"No hard feelings," said Flowers. "Like you say, it's just a business thing. Nothing personal."

He went to the car and by the light of the moon lifted out his dead brother's body, carrying it in his arms into the plant.

12

AMID a cacophony of imagined shrieks, squeals, grunts, groans, moans, howls, yelps, squeaks, in the midst of a sea of unimaginable smells—pungent, acrid, stinking, fetid, rank, putrid, musty—Charley Flowers gently placed the body of his brother on the cement floor of the slaughterhouse chute. His face, impassive, hid an odd mixture of confusion, anger, and guilt. As he went with Ginger to get Ray Scottini, he felt the first waves of an immense depression roll over him, a wash of unspeakable despair, and he became suddenly chilled to the bone.

The plant was closed, for its men worked only the morning shift. In the darkened pens the animals dozed fitfully, unaware of what was to come with the fugitive arrival of the throat slitters, skull stabbers, snout beaters, chute pushers, rump slicers, leg crushers, pipe wielders, vat handlers, electric prodders, and stunner gunners. Sneaking in during the morning's earliest hours, the men daily summoned up the courage needed to kill dumb beasts. Perched on a ledge above the pen, armed only with a thick, short-bladed knife, the skull stabber would wait for the hapless cattle to be forced into the pen, stabbing each one in the base of the skull as it passed within reach. Whenever he missed, which was often, the animal was beaten to death or hacked to pieces. In the pig pens the throat slitters worked more rapidly; the animals, still squealing, were dumped into vats of boiling water. At the other end of the process were the sausage machines, huge monsters of insatiable demand that were fed enormous quantities of meat, fat, gristle, and grind.

In the car Scottini, now conscious, was lifted out of the trunk and prodded, pushed, kicked, and dragged up the stairs and into the plant. Hands still bound behind his back with baling wire, he was unceremoniously shoved along the animal ramp and down the chute into the slaughtering pen. The gag was removed from his mouth.

"What's your name, pal?" Ginger asked in a friendly tone, and Flowers bent over the sprawled figure, trying to prop up the body against the side of the pen. He kicked at it viciously. "Hey, I'm talking to him," said Ginger, but Flowers ignored him as he lashed out again. Ginger winced. He didn't like personal emotion, it wasn't good business.

"What's your name, pal?"

Scottini, his nose broken, wheezing desperately, squinted up at his tormentors. Coagulated blood framed his nose and mouth.

"You got a name?"

"Where am I?" The whisper was barely audible.

"I'm asking the questions, pal. What's your name? You can tell me that, can't you?"

Scottini looked at him blankly.

"It don't really matter none." Ginger flashed a smile. "Just I like to know who I worked on. Like with the babes. I always got to know their names."

"You keep score?" Scottini whispered with false courage.

"No use getting nasty, pal. Ain't gonna help none." Ginger took out his knife, opened it carefully. "So what's the name?"

Scottini wet his lips. "Ray Scottini," he sniveled.

"Scottini. Yeah, I heard about you."

"Heard what?" he asked hopefully.

Ginger grinned, not at all friendly. "I heard you was a dead man."

Off to the side, Flowers, listening, bent down and grabbed Scottini by the throat, his face distorted by hate. "Your wife and kid are dead, Scottini, you hear me? They jumped out a window."

Scottini stared up at him dully. Flowers pulled him up on his feet. "Now it's your turn. You killed my brother and you gonna get yours right here." Shaken by uncontrollable anger, Flowers kneed the man in the groin and hit him full in the face, again and again, until stopped by Ginger. "Easy, man. Parry said he should feel the knife. The way you going he ain't gonna feel nothing."

His hands shaking, his facial muscles twitching, Flowers forced himself to let go of Scottini, who slumped to the floor. Kicking him viciously once more, Flowers spat on him and walked away. "Take him," he said to Ginger.

Fondling his knife, silver-handled with a long, very thin blade, Ginger purred softly to himself. He loved to inflict pain, as long as it was done for legitimate business reasons. The passion, he found, was too intense to be wasted on purely personal motives. But to get paid for it, to combine pleasure and profit, was for him the height of joy. At such times he was in his element, and he found the excitement of his work even more stimulating than when he allowed his sisters to perform fellatio on him. It was not everybody, he believed, who was lucky enough to be able to do the thing he loved best. Ginger considered himself a very lucky man.

At the far end of the chute, where the ramp turned left to the stock pens, Charley Flowers sat next to the body of his brother. In the distance, down past the chute and into the slaughtering pen itself, he could see Ginger stripping the clothes off the doomed man. He didn't like Ginger, there was something deadening about him. He was too sure of himself, he didn't seem to get emotional about anything. It was as though he were a machine doing the bidding of whoever paid him.

Flowers suspected the man had no feelings, no loyalty. While they both had killed, Flowers saw, or thought he saw, an important difference. For him it was just a job, and he took no personal pleasure in destroying anybody. In a moment of rage he might harm someone, willfully and with glee, but that was excusable, and he always felt rotten afterward. Even with Scottini, even that. He was already sorry that he had found pleasure in tormenting the man. If someone had to be taught a lesson or even killed, that was one thing. But to find pleasure in pain and death was abnormal. Psychopathic. He had known men like that. He believed Ginger to be one of them. No, he'd never trust a man like that, never turn his back on one.

Despair engulfed him and he lowered his head between his bent legs. Everything was going wrong. His whole existence was slipping away from him and he didn't know how to stop it. He needed someone and had no one. Now even his only brother was gone. They had never been very close, barely tolerating each other as youngsters. But during the past year they had gone out drinking a dozen times, and Flowers had begun to feel an affection for the man that he would never have believed possible. Now it was over. He thought of his mother, a small, heavy-jowled, sad-faced lonely woman with hesitant eyes and a disappearing voice. They were never close either, and his thoughts of her usually lacked any real fondness, but he now determined that he would see her more often. He had neglected her, he told himself, only because his work kept him so busy.

AARRRH.

The scream stunned Flowers. His head bolted upright, his toes curled in antediluvian preparedness, his hands assumed a defensive posture, all instinctively. For a split second he was once again a jungle creature, his animality responding. In the instant metamorphosis his blood ran cold, the hairs at the back of the neck bristled. He blinked. He had returned a million years. "Jesus H. Christ," he said aloud.

The screaming continued. Ginger was slicing flesh from Scottini's body. Wielding his knife like a surgeon's scalpel, he stripped away layers of flesh from the man's sides, his back and arms, his thighs, his abdomen. Each slice was placed carefully on top of the preceding one on the floor.

Flowers covered his ears with his hands. When that didn't work, he tried to bury his head between his legs. He stuck his fingers in his ears. Nothing worked. He counted out loud and couldn't get past ten. He tried to sing but forgot any words he ever knew. He cursed, swore, yelled, and shouted meaningless sounds, and pounded the sides of the chute. He decided that he was going mad and the screams were in his own head. He was about to run out of the plant, forgetting all responsibility, when the screaming stopped.

Ginger, oblivious to all outside noise, continued to slice flesh from the unconscious man, held up by a rope strung loosely around the neck and tied to one of the high beams atop the pen. He hummed softly as he worked at his trade.

Walking down the chute, Flowers decided that it was Ginger who was the mad one. When he got inside the slaughter pen he saw the neat pile of flesh on the floor. At least twenty pounds of flesh had been sliced from the body while still alive.

"He's dead," Flowers said unemotionally.

Disturbed, Ginger stopped humming. "Just unconscious," he said. "He'll come to."

"You done enough. Finish the job and let's get out of here."

"What's the hurry? I enjoy my work."

"The hurry is I say it's a hurry. Finish it up and I'll get you some chickens you can bite the heads off."

Ginger measured his antagonist, his eyes clicking data. They'd meet again sometime when things were different. Then he'd teach this wise guy a final lesson.

He smiled warmly. "Whatever you say, pal. It's your job."

"Don't forget it."

Flowers went back up the chute to sit by his brother's body. Looking at the corpse, its eyes glazed over, the mask of death already hardening on that once handsome face, he wondered if Albert had been anything like this Ginger. He couldn't have been, Flowers assured himself. They both were knife artists but that was all.

"I don't enjoy killing a man," Albert had said once as they sat in a bar late one night drinking to their bad luck.

"Me neither," Flowers had replied.

"But I don't think it's wrong either," continued Albert. "Lots of people need killing. That's just how I feel."

"Me too," agreed Flowers.

Now he was not so sure about Albert. Maybe all knife artists enjoyed their work. It was so different from using a gun on somebody, or breaking bones, or cracking a skull. The knife was such a personal thing. A knife could gouge out eyes or cut out tongues or chop off hands or cut off testicles. It could do what Ginger was doing to Scottini.

Flowers stared at his brother's face. "I really didn't know him at all," he mumbled. And despair gripped him all over again.

In the pen Scottini's throat was slit, the blood gushing out and spilling over the floor. When the body was bled dry, Ginger boned the carcass, just as though it were a pig's.

To Flowers, the screams he had heard were no different from the imagined shrieks and squeals of the animals being led to slaughter. He had a sudden vision of two-legged cattle prodding humans into pens and down the chute. The groans and cries were maddening. He opened his eyelids to release the vision, and in his mind's eye saw himself once again in the Knights of Columbus.

He was at the initiation rites. There were about forty prospective members, of whom he was one. He had been advised to join by several business associates who pointed out the advantages of membership. To be accepted in the Catholic fraternal organization, one had to be of good moral character. All applicants were supposedly screened. Hence, membership was an automatic religious and fraternal endorsement of one's character, and had distinct public relations value in a city that was itself a Catholic stronghold. Of Flowers' Catholic associates in the rackets, a goodly number, including some of the leadership, were members of the Knights of Columbus, never joining in any of the activities but wearing the lapel pin and letting their membership be generally known.

At the initiation rites Flowers was placed in a room with other prospective members and kept waiting in a line until tempers were short. Eventually a regular member appeared who began talking against certain minority groups. His speech became increasingly offensive.

"We don't want no wops around here. They're all gutless. The only good wop is a dead wop, right? The men are all lazy bastards, good for nothing but street cleaning. And the women?" He laughed lewdly. "We all know that every wop woman is a disgusting whore that'd fuck for the devil himself."

That was too much for one enrollee who broke ranks and rushed forward, a knife gleaming in his hand. "My mother's a wop," he screamed as he lunged for the speaker, who bolted out the door. Other members dragged him, still screaming, from the room.

Flowers did nothing. He had been told about the rites.

Eventually, after more argument and fighting and supposed bloodshed, the forty of them were herded into a tiny windowless room that could comfortably hold about a dozen people, perhaps a few more standing tightly together.

It was the slaughter pen at the meat plant. Suffocation by numbers, animals packed together. No air, fearsome noises, maddened cries. But these were people. Some fainted with no room to fall, some screamed because of their claustrophobia. Others cursed or prayed, thinking everybody, including God, must be mad.

Even Flowers, who had been warned, believed that something must have gone wrong.

Then the door opened and a giant of a man, heavyset, with the chest and arms of a wrestler, stepped into the room, accompanied by two other burly men. In his hand was a gun, which he held level in front of him.

"I want a three-foot-wide path right down the center of this room," he shouted. "Three feet. Now move it."

It was an absolute impossibility, of course. There were not even three inches of space.

After more shouting and pushing and screaming, the giant insisting that he wanted the path cleared, somebody went for him and the giant shot him. The sound was like a cannon's roar. Bang. Blood splattered all over.

Everybody panicked. Like a bunch of cattle spooked by a fearful noise, they stampeded. Pushing the giant and his assistants back, they bulled their way out of the room, kicking, scratching, clawing, spilling out into a huge meeting hall where several hundred faces were turned toward them, silently watching.

Flowers, out with the crowd, stayed along its edge. Others, excited, incensed, aroused, got up on chairs and began berating the seated members for allowing such death and destruction. Some wanted the police called; some decried a Jewish plot; some just flopped down, bewildered.

After a long while, after oaths and denunciations, acrimony and chagrin, order was finally restored and everyone seated. It was then revealed that no one had been killed, no one shot. The participants in such events were actor-members, the weapons props, the blood fake. All that had occurred was planned for the greater glory of God, and to show the new members whatever it was they needed to know. Flowers never did find out what that was.

A dinner was then held as the final event of the induction ceremony. And Charley Flowers was welcomed as a member of the Knights of Columbus, with all the rights and privileges appertaining thereto, including the lapel pin and a life insurance policy.

Seated now near the slaughter pen, Flowers shuddered at the similarity between man and beast. Down the chute Ginger finished boning Scottini's carcass, removing every last piece of flesh from the skeleton. In a large meat pan he carried all the flesh to the sausage machines. Piece by piece he stuffed all of the meat into one of the sausage machines, then pushed the button and ran it through. In a few moments Scottini's remains were ready to be packaged and sold over the supermarket counter.

"What about the skeleton?" Flowers asked him.

"Just a bag of bones," said Ginger lightly. "I'll bag it here and take it with me."

Flowers didn't ask him why.

Ginger stepped on the skeleton, breaking and crushing it.

"What about that?" Flowers pointed to the gruesome pile of flesh on the floor.

"I'm a skin collector," answered Ginger with a bright smile. "I'll take that too."

They walked back to where Albert's body lay.

"I want you to do this fast," declared Flowers, his voice shaking. "No skin collecting or bag of bones. And don't slit the throat, you got it?"

"Can't."

Flowers' eyes narrowed. "Can't what?"

Ginger looked amused. "You can't bone anything without first you got to slit the throat. You got to get rid of the blood."

"No other way?"

"No other way, pal. That's it."

Flowers hesitated. He wanted to take his brother's body and throw it in the river. Anything would be preferable to this; it was sacrilegious was what it was. But Ginger would tell Parry and he'd be in big trouble. He couldn't take the chance.

"OK," he said, defeated. "You do it fast. No frills, just do what you have to and get it over with."

"Sure thing, pal. I understand."

"You got any brothers?"

"Nope."

"Then you don't understand."

"But I got sisters." He laughed excitedly. "Boy, you should see them. Knockouts, both of 'em. Tits the size of watermelons. I been with them lots of times. Sort of keep it in the family, you know."

Flowers wanted to kill him, to stab him, strangle him, drown him, crush him. He pulled out his gun and shot Ginger six times. Only he had no gun now, it was just his finger and Ginger didn't even feel it.

"Just do it and hurry up."

He walked away because he didn't want to see any part of it.

When Ginger was finished boning the body he took the meat pan again to the sausage machines. On the way back, he asked Flowers what he wanted done with the skeleton.

"I'll take it and throw it in the river."

"You know, if you wanted to sell it, they pay good money for—"

Flowers' look froze him in mid-sentence.

"Just trying to help."

"Don't try."

Covered with blood and gristle and flecks of flesh, Ginger took his time washing up. Flowers, waiting for him, called Al Parry, who had just arrived home.

"The movie's over," he announced.

"How were the seats?"

"Good."

They bade each other good night, and Parry soon went to bed. He had had a busy day.

At about the same time two men walked out of a local meat-packing plant, each carrying a brown bag. They left in separate cars.

They had had a busy night.

13

EVERYTHING LOOKS GOOD, Harry Strega kept telling himself as the hurt slowly left his broken mouth. I'm doing all right, he would reassure himself, and everybody likes me. But he wasn't really sure of any of it. Each day he would stand in front of the dresser mirror, running his tongue over the jagged opening where three teeth had once been, fingering the wound and cursing bitterly at the bad luck that seemed to dog his steps.

"Can you make it the way it was?" he would ask the dentist each time. Aware of the vanity of youth, the dentist would cheerfully nod assent. Harry knew better. After a while he stopped his unreasonable demands and just sat glumly in the porcelained chair.

During the days he walked the streets, long mournful walks that took him up and down hills and across a half-dozen neighboring communities. Sometimes he just sat in bars or played endless games of pool with other young idlers. At night he watched television in his room, his dulled face matching the flatness of the screen. Against his better judgment he spent other nights with Lucy Berg, on the floor of her father's waiting room. It was, he reminded himself desperately, better than masturbating.

"I think I love you," Lucy told him one electric evening as they struggled in the darkness, her right hand feverishly fondling his tightened testicles in rhythmic squeezes. "I really think I do."

Harry felt himself go limp. Outside, a passing car, its muffler in dysfunction, screeched to a stop at the corner. A pair of hurled obscenities quickly followed, then the roar of the motor.

"I said I love you," she shouted above the din.

"I heard you."

"Well?"

"Well what?"

"Haven't you anything to say?"

"What can I say? You love me, that's your business."

"I *think* I do."

"So you *think* you do. What about it?"

"Don't you care for me at all? Not even a little bit?"

"Sure I care for you."

"No you don't."

"I do."

"If you really cared for me, it'd mean something when I say I love you."

"You only said you *think* you do."

"Same thing."

"Would I be here if I didn't care for you?"

"All you want is free sex."

"That ain't true."

"You men are all alike."

Harry felt suddenly betrayed. "What about you?"

"Meaning what?"

"Meaning don't say you don't like it."

"Women are different. We don't need it like you do."

"That ain't the way you act sometimes."

"Like when?"

"Like right now," Harry replied vehemently, "when you have your hand on my cock."

With an air of feminine superiority, Lucy deftly removed

her hand. "Some things," she said matter-of-factly, "are hardly worth holding."

For a long while they lay together, their bodies not touching. The stillness of the room muffled even the ticking of the grandfather clock set against a wall opposite the couch. In the hush, their breathing came slower and deeper until a rhythmic pattern began to appear, and it was this more than anything that lulled their eyes closed.

"Harry? Wake up."

"Hmm."

"Wake up, it's late."

"Oh, yeah. Right." He turned over, facing her, his belt open, his pants still unzipped. "Guess I fell asleep."

Her eyes, diamond cat-slits in the moonlight, showed concern. "Harry?"

"What?"

"Are you in any trouble? I mean, something real bad?"

Feeling a spasm of surprise and anger, his voice yet gave no hint of anything amiss. "Why do you ask that?" he said evenly.

"I don't know. You seem so restless."

"Got a lot of things on my mind."

"You were fidgeting in your sleep. And moaning, too."

"Did I say anything?"

"No. Mostly just noises."

"Guess I just had a bad dream."

"You sure that's all it was?"

"What else could it be, for chrissake?"

"You're not working, are you?"

"Not right now."

"Where do you get the money to live?"

"I still got some savings left."

"What about your teeth?"

"What about them?"

"How'd you lose them? I mean, they just don't fall out at your age, do they?"

"I already told you, I fell down and hit my mouth on a

goddamn stoop." He spoke quickly, irritably. "Why all the questions?"

"I just don't want anything to happen to you. That's why I'm worried. I care for you even if you don't care for me."

"I do care for you."

"If you really cared, you wouldn't let me worry like this."

"Worry like what?" shouted Harry, thinking that all women were absolutely crazy and a man didn't really stand a chance.

"You don't have to scream at me, I can take a hint. I mean, if you don't want anyone to care for you that's your business. I certainly wouldn't worry about anybody like that."

"I want you to worry," he assured her, defeated.

"Some men are like that. They think about nobody but themselves. If a girl tries to look after them, they run away. Just kick her down and run."

"I'm not like that," he pleaded, his belt still open and his pants still unzipped. "Not like that at all." He gently picked up her hand and placed it inside his pants. "Not at all." He held it there firmly.

"You do care for me, don't you?"

"Sure I do," he whispered.

"You want me to worry about you."

"You bet I do," he purred, and removed his hand from hers.

"And take care of you."

"Umm. There's something needs taking care of right now," he cooed in her ear. His swelled muscle flexed in her hand.

"I want to take care of you. Make you feel good." She tightened her fingers around it and inched her head down until her face was next to it. "Make you feel good all over."

His body went rigid as her mouth fastened onto his penis. With practiced strokes her hand moved in a rhythmic fashion that matched perfectly the circular movement of her tongue. Exquisitely excited, his body now unbearably tense, he waited for the colored lights.

Later, much later on his way home, Harry reflected on all that had been said and done earlier. He marveled at the incredible duplicity of women. They were an absolute paradox he would never be able to resolve, of that he was certain. Naïve and cunning, clever and stupid, all in one and all at once, they ran on something other than logic, something no man would ever be able to fathom. They were unknown and unknowable, an alien race from another planet. Consequently they could not be trusted. He would not trust them, any of them. He would use them as needed but no further. Yet they had this incredible power over men, the power of their bodies. It was a power they used consciously, willfully. Or unconsciously, without thought. No matter. He, like most men, had to seek them out. Either that or masturbate himself, which was at best a poor substitute. There was no escape for him, for any man. Sex made everything illogical. For a little sex he had to give up his time, his freedom, his life. He was forced to listen to gibberish, to look at nonsense, to play games, lie, cheat, maybe kill. It was just monstrous, this price he had to pay. He resented every extra minute he had to spend with them to get what he wanted, what he needed. The whole thing was unfair, inhuman. Walking down the deserted street, his shoulders hunched over in preparation for any attack by wild animals, he cursed women for being what they were.

The next day Harry resumed the hunt. He called up Frank Farrano for the address of The Greek's. Then he went there. The girl from Little Rock was not working days. When would she be on? Who wants to know? Joe Zucco. Oh, for Mr. Zucco. Sure thing, let's see now. Ahh, here we are. Colie Rogers, works Wednesdays and Fridays. At night? Yes sir, nights. OK, I'll be back. Make sure they know me at the door. Of course, and thank *you,* sir. At least, thought Harry as he walked away, you can still count on a man to act sensible.

Two nights later he sat through her shift, drinking stingers on the rocks at the small bar. Afterward they walked to Journal Square. In the early morning gloom they passed lovers on benches and stoops, and in parked cars. Everything seemed so natural to him. They ate an early breakfast at Bickfords on the Square, eggs and jam and tunafish salad. After a lot of coffee and small talk, they took a cab to her apartment in a brown brick building facing a little park. It was dawn before their lust was stilled, and they drifted off to separate sleep.

When Harry returned to his rooming house late in the afternoon, Farrano was waiting for him, his massive body stretched across the front seat of the car, bands of sweat running down his beefy face.

"We move soon," he said simply.

Harry, alert instantly, nodded in agreement. "Been almost two weeks. I was wondering when we'd go."

"Joe talked to Frank Taylor. He'll drop the nigger for one big buy from us."

"How big?"

"Don't matter. All that counts is the nigger'll have to come to us after this."

"What's Zucco want us to do?" Harry unconsciously lowered his voice at the mention of the name. "Go back to the club?"

"First thing is we deal for the junk."

"When?"

"Soon's I hear from Johnny Apples. Then Apples sees the nigger again and lets him know the new setup. He gets from us or he gets nothing. Nobody else'll touch him, he won't be able to get it anywhere. That makes us partners."

"Suppose he don't go for it? He don't seem to scare easy."

"He'll go for it. All them junkies need the shit or they cave in." Farrano wiped his face on the sleeve of his shirt. "Even if he ain't on it much, he's hanging around with them. Like that Big Tits we seen that time, right? He'll go for it 'cause there ain't nothing he can do. And once we suck him in, we take over."

"You mean Zucco and Apples take over."

"Same thing."

"How you make that?"

"This a business, ain't it? So every business got people at the top that get the heavy sugar. Joe worked himself up to boss, so he gets the most. Johnny, he gets his share too. And the rest of us do the work. But if they wasn't there at the top, there'd be no business. You can't have everybody working and nobody raking it off the top. What kind of life would that be? Long as they around, we get our share. So they really working for us. Besides, there's nothing says we can't be the boss, right? All it takes is everything you got and putting yourself on the spot all the time to get knocked over. Me, I make too big a target up there."

"Not me. I'd love to get with the real big money and all the women that follow it around. I'd know what to do all right."

"Sure, sure. You and Capone."

"Well, I would."

Frank Farrano grumped in his throat. "So how's your big mouth? Got any teeth left?"

Afterward, Harry lay on his bed thinking of big money and big women and big cars and big houses, all of them his. He drank a bottle of milk, made a salami sandwich, and watched television. He went to sleep with it on. The next day he kept his door open a little so he could hear the phone in the hall downstairs when Farrano called.

Two days later the deal was set. One hundred thousand dollars for eight kilos of pure heroin. The price was higher than it should have been between business associates, but Zucco had already made a connection in Newark to take most of the drug off his hands at a profit. The rest would be fed to Phil Green of the Cloud Nine until he was no longer in control of the club. All Zucco needed was one foot in the door, and it was only a matter of time before he took over. As with his other nightspot interests, Zucco tolerated no permanent partnerships.

"The only thing is you got to work fast," he had told Johnny Apples. "Frank says we can't string this thing out or word'll get around that we're in the junk business. Make him look bad."

"How long's he give us?"

"Six weeks, eight maybe. But he don't mind a few extra buys on the side, long as they're small. So keep forcing the shit on Green till he can't back out. Don't take no money. When he finds he can't get it nowhere else, he'll come to you. Then we got him in the squeeze."

"What about the Newark end?"

"Gino's got that covered. He'll make the delivery."

"Yacavelli ain't gonna like you moving in on his town."

Zucco, being a cautious businessman, and by nature secretive, didn't want too many people knowing what the mob had in mind for Sam Yacavelli. "Don't worry about Yacavelli," was all he said. "He won't give us no trouble."

Taking Zucco at his word, Johnny Apples set the wheels in motion. He met with Frank Taylor's lieutenant and they mapped out the strategy for the drop. A straight exchange was agreed upon, the drugs to be paid for on delivery. Each party had the right of inspection at the time of the delivery. A site was quickly chosen, agreeable to both. All that remained was the date.

"Thursday's good," Johnny Apples suggested. "Thursday morning."

The other man nodded in agreement. "Who's making the delivery?"

"You want to look him over?"

"I'll send one of the boys to check him, just so he knows who to expect on Thursday. What's his name?"

"Frank Farrano. Heavyset, built like a brick shithouse. You can't miss him."

"Have him in front of the hospital on Baldwin Avenue at four tomorrow. You know where that is?"

"I know where."

"He'll be carrying a rolled-up newspaper. There'll be somebody waiting for him." The man took out a dollar bill and tore it in half. "Give him this. My guy'll have the other half."

A thought suddenly occurred to Johnny Apples. "Why go

through all that? Why don't me and you just meet on Thursday and get it over with?"

The other man smiled, a slow, indulgent smile that wrinkled the lines of his pockmarked face. "You don't know the drug game, friend. This ain't gambling or running whores to Hoboken. You get a drug bust and you got one heavy rap on you. Look at Genovese in New York that time. Me, I been in the business twenty years and I don't have a single bust. Handling the stuff, that's for the little guys. Anything goes wrong they get the rap and nobody's hurt." He leaned close to Apples. "This Farrano you got. If he takes a fall, who cares? Right? Long's it ain't you." His smile disappeared. "I didn't get here from there by taking chances. That's strictly for the punks."

Going away, Johnny Apples found himself with a new respect for the drug combine. He cornered a thought in his mind that he would have to look into the business. That kind of money, he told himself all the way home, might be worth the risk. Turning into the gravel driveway of his eighty-thousand-dollar home on a wooded acre in Englewood Cliffs, Johnny Apples wondered how he could get to Frank Taylor. During dinner and afterward, having a half-dozen drinks with friends in the game room, he kept returning to the thought. He went to bed late and got up late, shaved, and put on a sweatshirt and sneakers. In the basement gym he did sit-ups for fifteen minutes, then worked on the oars. After a cold shower he leisurely dressed in expensively casual clothes. As he sat down to breakfast, his mind turning over the vast sums that could be made in drugs by the right people, a man stood on Baldwin Avenue with a newspaper rolled up under his arm.

"You Frank Farrano?"

The voice belonged to a swarthy man of average height and weight, bushy brows, sharp nose, a scar running from the right cheekbone to the mouth. His eyes, hard, giving no sign of friendship or trust, stared at the newspaper wilting under the massive arm.

"I'm Farrano."

"You got something for me?"

A second massive arm reached into a shirt pocket and pulled out half of a dollar bill. The swarthy man examined it carefully, matching it with his own half. Satisfied, he folded both halves neatly and slipped them into his jacket. "Let's take a walk," he announced.

When the call finally came for him, Harry was dozing, fully clothed, in a chair. It was the second day he had not left his room. Awakened by the landlady's shouts above the din of the TV, he raced down the stairs.

"Yeah?"

"That you, kid?"

"Yeah, Frank."

"It's set for tomorrow morning. I'll pick you up at ten. Be ready."

"Right. Ten o'clock."

When he hung up the receiver, his landlady, Mrs. Fugazy, was waiting for him at the foot of the stairs, her large print smock yellowed with age, the metal curlers in her frowzy brown hair strengthening the sharpness of her ancient face.

"You're leaving your door open," she said.

Harry, stooping with hands in pockets, feigned concern. "I was waiting for this call. It's important."

"Everything's important. It's important that my roomers aren't bothered when they're passing your door."

"I don't bother them."

"Your open door bothers them. This is a quiet, respectable house. People want to come and go in privacy."

"So the door's open for a day. Big deal." Harry shuffled the change in his pocket. "What they got to hide, anyway?"

"Two days it's open. And they got nothing to hide. They just don't want to be bothered with people spying on them."

"Spying? Who's spying? I just kept it open so's I could hear the phone."

"All right, now you heard the phone so you can keep it closed. Closed, I say." Mrs. Fugazy wheeled around and marched to her open door. "If you don't like it, Mr. Strega, I'll just have to ask you to leave. I can't have the neighbors talking about my roomers. It's bad for business."

"I'll make sure it's closed after this, Mrs. Fugazy."

"Thank you, Mr. Strega."

"And I won't spy on your roomers ever again."

"It's not a question of spying. Most of them are quiet men who just want to be left alone. Nobody likes to be bothered by anyone else. They all think they have secrets. If you'd been in rooming houses as long as me, you'd know what I mean. I got to think of them. It's good business, otherwise I wouldn't care, you understand. If no one bothers them, they stay on. An open door bothers them."

"So I won't bother them no more."

Mrs. Fugazy nodded in silent victory. "So why you stay here if you got no secrets?"

Back in his room, Harry banged the door shut, turned up the TV sound with an angry twist of the wrist, and spitefully left the warm water tap running in the sink. He fixed a sandwich for himself, opened a can of ginger ale and brought it over to the bed, the can cold against his skin. When "Gilligan's Island" came on, he went to change channels and the selector knob came off in his hand.

14

ON ERIE STREET the diesel tractors rumbled past day and night, pulling their twenty-ton trailers loaded with perishables for the New York–New England market east under the Hudson River on the red cobbled roadbed of the Holland Tunnel. Or turned west across the Jersey flatlands past the burly shoulders of Pennsylvania and down the arm of Middle America. Truckers swore, smoked, slammed their air brakes squealing against the slick streets and crowded corners, cars, red lights, unleashed dogs, and children, their dodging bodies anticipating some immediate goal. Along the Erie and Lackawanna Railroad tracks roared boxcars and flatbeds by the mile, screaming diesels shaking the earth. The buildings, the factories and houses in the area were blasted beyond belief. Garbage lined the oiled gutters, clogging sewers. Collection trucks appeared and disappeared without warning. Spanish immigrants came with huge, hungry families. Sometimes a house suddenly caught fire, sending blankets of smoke billowing across uneven roofs. Whenever the rains came, whole streets disappeared. Occasionally during a fierce rainstorm a city sprinkler mysteriously arrived to wet down the streets further. At election times there was always the promise of continued good service by city officials who raced through the area counting votes.

On Thursday morning Frank Farrano slowly cruised past the delivery point. Harry Strega sat next to him. The building was a four-story frame house on Erie Street near the elevated railroad tracks. Flanking the entrance were a pair of narrow stores with dirty glass and weathered wood doors, one of them framed by metal rails for a missing gate. One window was cracked, a long, jagged scar that ran almost top to bottom. Both doors were fastened with padlocks.

"Looks deserted enough," Harry said after they had passed the block for the third time and were parking around the corner.

"Enough for what?" asked Farrano, scowling.

Harry turned to him. "Think it's a setup?"

"How the hell do I know?" Farrano chewed a piece of loose skin off his thick lower lip. "Could be anything. That's a lot of dough we got right here."

"They wouldn't cross Zucco, would they?"

"Are you nuts? For a hundred grand they'd rip off their own mother." Farrano backed into a space behind a van. "Can't trust them bastards to do nothing right."

"What's wrong with them?"

"They dealing drugs, ain't they?"

"So what?"

"So I don't trust them. Too much easy money in drugs, too much temptation. You don't know who your friends are in that game, you don't got no friends. You can't trust nobody."

"I still say Taylor don't want trouble from Zucco."

Farrano pushed on his door. "You got a lot to learn." He kicked it out wide and turned around to face Harry. "Frank Taylor's got as much say as Joe. If he thinks he can sink him, he'd do it. All he needs is to know he can get away with it. If he can do it fast and clean, nobody'd bother him. But if he muffs it, everybody be down on him like a shot."

"So it's taking a big chance."

"Sure it's taking a chance. But they're all looking for that chance. Taylor, Machine, all of them."

"Zucco too?"

Caught by surprise, Farrano suddenly laughed. "Yeah, him too." He backed out of the car ponderously, still laughing. "Hey, you ain't so dumb at that."

The small car shuddered as Farrano's bulk eased itself out. Floorboards groaned, seats sagged, the A frame rolled and pitched. For a moment it resembled a lifeboat in choppy water.

"You know what to do," said Farrano from the street, and Harry nodded. "Give me room to get there, then come by in fifteen minutes. Look for my signal. If it's wrong, get out fast, and get hold of Apples."

Harry slid behind the wheel as Farrano slammed the door and walked off. On the seat was an attaché case with one hundred thousand dollars stuffed inside. The money had been given to Johnny Apples only an hour before by Joe Zucco himself. When Zucco handed over the money he had said only two words: "No mistakes."

Harry slipped his hand along the case, black with silver clips and a silver lock. He snapped the lock open and slowly lifted the lid. A hundred thousand dollars in twenties, fifties, and hundreds lay in front of him neatly stacked in twenty even piles.

"Jesus Christ," he said to the empty car. Picking up one of the stacks of bills, he let the cool green paper run over his thumb. Most of the bills were old, the hundreds newer. He had never seen that much money, never even imagined it. "Jesus Christ," he repeated, wetting his lips.

Around the corner the morning sun was strangling the west side of Erie Street, leaving the east shaded and cool. There were about a dozen people on the block: deliverymen making their rounds; neighborhood women sitting on crumbling stoops, rested after ridding themselves of husbands and children. Three men in grimy work clothes were chopping a hole in the street next to a load of sewer pipe.

"Plenty rock here," shouted the worker handling the pneumatic drill, his short peasant frame hunched over the trip hammer. Roaring to life with an ungodly whine, the drill dug into the street. Clouds of bluish dust were thrown in the air, concrete cracked, the earth opened, splintering into fragments, and settled in uneven shapes and formations as the drill moved on. The other two workers followed, spreading apart the loosened dirt with pickax and shovel. Frank Farrano watched them carefully, his body alert, hands tense at his side, as he passed. He was a professional, doing a tricky and dangerous job, and he was taking no chances.

"How's the street department?" he called out suddenly.

All three workers turned toward the shout, looked him over briefly before deciding that he, too, must be a worker.

"It stinks," said the man with the shovel.

"Too mucha boom-boom-boom," said the man on the drill. "No good."

Farrano laughed. "The city should give you more money, more *danaro*," he shouted, walking away satisfied.

"*Si. Danaro.*"

"*Prestatore di danaro*," said the third workman, holding the ax rigid. "*Strozzino.*" And he spit expertly into the crack of concrete.

Up ahead, Farrano was almost at the house. There was nobody by the entrance, one step up from the sidewalk. The outer door, painted a garish red, was closed. Above, a large black dog was sleeping on the rusted fire escape. Next to it were two green plants, their leaves flopping over the edge. A stringy mop hung upside down on the railing. Farrano stopped, glanced up at the facade of the building. Old weathered brick, the mortar lines long smoothed over, gave the house a look of solidity that belied its age. Cornices lapped over the roof line into scrollwork popular before the turn of the century. The window frames, some of them not painted for generations, were mostly rotted and many of them had putty missing. On the upper fire escapes cardboard boxes and sodden crates of indescribable contents filled all available space, contrary to city fire regulations. With a jerk at the shoulders to straighten his back, Farrano pushed open the street door and walked into the building.

The inside door, hanging from its upper hinge, was jammed against the wall by a single spike driven through it and into the wallboard. Both doorknobs had been hammered off, the rosettes still in place with bent screws. A naked lightbulb in the high ceiling illuminated the area to the stairway. Beyond this the hall lay in darkness. Walking loosely with surprisingly soft cat steps, his apelike arms at the ready, Farrano crept past the faded yellow walls, their upper sections plastered with obscene scrawlings, past the linoleum-covered stairway on the left where the hall widened, past the broken and gouged mailboxes. Behind the stairs he passed a half-dozen garbage cans overflowing with feasting insects.

Suddenly he stopped, his eyes now tuned to the darkness. Ahead of him lay the remainder of the hallway, perhaps thirty feet, again narrowed. At the far end was a door, closed and bolted. Midway along the hall were two more doors, one on each side. In front of the doorway on the left a figure stood motionless.

More startled than fearful, having expected somebody, Farrano approached cautiously. The door was closed. The figure, tall, appeared to shift its stance as he drew near. For a long moment neither man spoke. From the front of the hall could be heard the barking of the dog on the fire escape, announcing its wakefulness. Upstairs, someone slammed a door. A truck rumbled past.

"Anything I can do for you?"

The man was young, hard-faced, his eyes set deep behind menacing brows. On his jacket he wore a tricolored button.

"Farrano."

Without a word the young man stepped up and ran his hands expertly over Farrano's body, seeking a gun. Satisfied, he turned and knocked softly three times. Noiselessly the door was opened.

"Go on in."

Farrano stepped into the room. A gooseneck lamp was suddenly switched on, its light directed toward him. He was in a big kitchen. In front of him was a long table with the lamp. On the other side of the table was someone in shadow who watched him carefully. Behind him the door was bolted. Turning around, he recognized the swarthy man with the scarred face whom he had met on the previous day.

"Let's get down to business," said the scarface.

Farrano looked toward the third man. He couldn't make out the face but he sensed something was wrong. "Yeah, sure," he said nervously, the sweat already coursing down his back, his thighs, his fat calves. "You got the stuff here?"

"You got the dough?" asked Scarface.

"First I get to look at the stuff. That was the deal."

"OK, OK," said Scarface impatiently, "but where you got it is what I wanna know."

"Not on me," Farrano said softly.

Scarface stopped dead. Farrano stood very still. The seconds dragged on, seemingly endless as no one moved in the big room.

"Where's the money?" croaked the third man suddenly from behind the lamp.

Startled, both men looked into the light.

"Where's the money?"

Farrano cleared his throat. "The other man's got it. I didn't bring it in here with me."

"What other man?" insisted the voice. "Apples didn't tell me about nobody else. Just you was gonna bring it."

"Johnny didn't think you'd care," said Farrano. He spoke slowly, respectfully. "Johnny figured this way we'd both be safe. I can check over the stuff here, then you go with me for the money and I'll come back while you count it. This way nothing can go wrong." All the while Farrano was thinking furiously. The third man had to be Frank Taylor's lieutenant, he was the only one who would've talked to Apples. And the only thing that could bring him out was the double cross. Apples said he wouldn't be at the delivery, but here he was. That meant the double cross for sure. Farrano felt that he was standing in a pool of sweat. They'd take the money and he'd never be seen again. Taylor's man would be in a hundred grand and Zucco would never really know what happened. Except for one thing.

"What's a matter?" whined the voice. "Zucco don't trust us? He think Frank'd try to cross him? Why should we do that? We all got to live here together."

Except for one thing. He, Farrano, had crossed them up by leaving the money with the kid. He didn't trust them, most of them were Irish anyway. Even Johnny Apples was fooled by them. But he wasn't fooled, he was right all the time. He was smarter than Johnny Apples. He should be where Apples was.

"How can we keep doing business if we don't trust each other, eh? Answer me that."

"Sure we trust each other," Farrano lied. "But it's just good business to check everything out so we don't make no mistakes. That's all it is, just good business."

"So where's the guy with the dough?" said Scarface.

"He'll be passing here in about ten minutes. If I'm outside he'll stop and give me the money. After I give him the stuff." Farrano didn't mention the signal he had with Harry.

After a long silence the voice sighed, a heavy, regretful sigh that began deep in the diaphragm and was pushed upward and through the nostrils. "OK," it said, "let him have the package."

Scarface walked over to a cabinet hidden in darkness and came back with a small square package wrapped in white paper and tied with heavy brown string. Farrano opened it. Inside were sixteen transparent plastic bags, each containing a half-kilo of heroin. These he placed in succession on the table. From his pocket he took out a small glass ashtray and a Murine eyedropper bottle that had been sterilized and refilled with sulfuric acid. From each plastic bag he put a few grains of the fine snow-white powder into the ashtray. He then squeezed the eyedropper of acid over the heroin in a simple test of the drug's purity. In a few seconds the heroin turned a reddish hue.

"Looks pretty good," Farrano said, closing each plastic bag again.

"What's this pretty good?" the voice snarled. "Where you gonna get better?"

"I've seen lots better," Farrano lied. "If it was really pure stuff, it would've turned dark red right away. But this is good enough for what we need."

The voice chuckled unexpectedly. "You know what you doing, Farrano," it said smoothly, "but we know what we doing too. See what I mean?"

With the heroin repackaged, he was ready.

"Go with him, Al. Bring the money here."

Farrano, package in hand, turned toward the door just in time to see Scarface pull out the gun. A heavy .45-caliber automatic. He checked the magazine and released the safety.

"What's that for?" Farrano said evenly.

Scarface showed his teeth. "Just in case anything goes wrong. You don't mind, do you?"

"The deal was no cannons."

"So we're changing it. Just like you done."

"Nothing's gonna go wrong."

"You better hope it don't." Scarface slipped the gun under his belt. "You just better hope it don't, 'cause if there's no dough out there, you go."

"What he means, Farrano, is if Zucco tries to double-cross us, you get it first." The voice was now cold, distant.

"There's no double cross." Farrano was tempted to say more about a cross but he decided against it.

"That's good. Then we can do business again sometime."

"Yeah, sure. Apples'll be in touch with you."

"Johnny Apples," purred the voice. "My, my, what won't Zucco think of next?"

Scarface threw the bolt back and held the door open. Farrano stepped into the hall past the guard, past the infested garbage cans and broken mailboxes, the cheap linoleum steps and dirty words, past the nailed inner door and out the red front door, Scarface following, his hand on the gun.

At the corner Harry was turning into the block for the second time, moving slowly past the delivery site. Halfway up the block he spotted Farrano standing in the street, waiting. That was the signal. If things were wrong, he'd be waiting on the sidewalk instead. Harry pulled up slowly, stopping right in front of the two men. His right foot remained unpressed on the gas pedal. Through the open window Farrano handed him the package, and was then given the attaché case with the money. Without even a glance at the other man, Harry drove away.

In the street Farrano gave the money to Scarface, and both men returned to the building, Scarface again following. Inside, the case was opened by Taylor's lieutenant, still hidden in the shadow behind the lamp. Only his hands were in the light as he counted the money. He looked through every stack, counting some fully, others hardly at all.

"It's all there," Farrano said once.

Nobody answered him.

For what seemed an eternity Farrano stood motionless, rooted to the spot. He couldn't think of anything, and all he could feel was the gush of water all over his body. He was drowning in sweat. Several times he looked down to see if there were puddles at his feet. Whenever he bent his head, his eyes misted from the wetness around them. Determined, he clamped his teeth together. Finally the count was over.

"Let him go."

With a wave of the hand he was dismissed. Scarface opened the door and Farrano waddled down the long dark hall into the daylight. He got a cab to the rendezvous point on the other side of town, where Harry picked him up.

"Looks like I won," Harry said.

"You lost."

"You're here, ain't you?"

"You lost. The double cross was on all right."

"How do you know?"

"Taylor's man was there. Only way he'd be there is for the cross."

"But it didn't work."

"Only 'cause I didn't go in with the money."

Harry, taking no chances, was driving very carefully. "You sure about Taylor's man? Maybe you made a mistake."

"No mistake. He said he talked to Apples. It was him all right."

"So the only thing saved you was I had the money."

"That's the way I seen it. I can't prove it, but I say that's what happened. But what I can't figure," said Farrano, "is why Apples trusted them so much. He should've knew better."

"Maybe he's got other things on his mind."

"That's right," Farrano said mysteriously, "that's just what I'm beginning to think."

15

"YOU DON'T KNOW what it's like to lose your own brother that way."

"I know," said Hymie Cole.

"What do you know? How could you?"

"I had a kid brother die on me when I was your age. Younger even."

"Shot down like that?"

"Spinal meningitis. He went inside a week. And he never been sick a day in his life."

"It ain't the same."

"The hell it ain't. When you die, you are dead. So what ain't the same?"

"It ain't the same. My brother didn't die in no bed. He didn't have clean sheets and people around. He got it right on the street. On a stinking goddamn street that ain't even a street next to the railroad yards. And nobody around either. Just him and the bastard that done it. I seen it. I seen him get it right in the guts and then get his head blowed off. I was standing right there and I seen him get it. And I couldn't help him, you know what I mean? It all happened so fast. Too fast."

"Nothing you could do," said Hymie, looking at himself in the cracked mirror, his head half-bald, ears prominent, nose flattened by too many punches, his eyes buried deep in darkened sockets that gave him the appearance of a ferret in distress. For a moment there he had the sensation of watching some strange animal gazing back at him. Shuddering, he shrugged off the feeling and turned his attention to his companion, whose head was sunk midway to the bar so that the chin almost rested on the burnished wood. The head, thus suspended, blocked his view of the men playing liar's poker on the other side. With a sense of futility he turned back to the mirror and his own thoughts. He was going nowhere in the rackets. He didn't have the power or the resources of Pete Montana or Johnny Apples or even Al Parry. They each had things going of their own, they were making money for Zucco and making money for themselves. Pete Montana's nightclubs and the gambling operation in South Jersey would probably pay off big, Apples was doing good in the extortion end of the business, and Parry in the loansharking. Even Zucco had things going with the cigarette smuggling and big sharking, along with everything else. Everybody was big potatoes, everybody but him. All he had going was a five percent rakeoff from taking care of Zucco's hidden business interests. It wasn't enough, not nearly enough. He didn't have a big house or expensive clothes or beautiful women hanging around, he didn't even have any money in the bank. What he had was a crazy wife and two punk kids. If something big didn't happen, if he didn't get a break soon, he didn't know what he would do. Not only that but he was always being asked to take care of other people's shit. Now here he was sitting in a stupid bar with a drunk because Al Parry said maybe he could straighten Flowers out. Not that he minded in a way, he liked Charley Flowers. It was just that he could think of better ways to spend the day.

"Shot down like a mad dog. He didn't even have a chance. First in the gut, then in the head. I seen the whole thing."

Hymie looked around again. The men were still playing

liar's poker, cursing and baiting one another. Across the sawdust-strewn aisle a half-dozen drinkers were lined up at the food rail, munching on hot roast beef sandwiches or hunched over a dozen clams on the half-shell or a plate of steamers.

"I couldn't *do* nothing. One minute he's standing there big as life. He's talking easy to the bastard. Then bang, he gets one. Bang again. The next minute he's dead. I seen the look on his face when he caught the first one. I can't forget it. You ever seen that look?"

Hymie nodded, his mind on other matters. He had to get something else going for himself, he just had to. Even clipping a little on the side from Zucco didn't help that much.

"It's like they know they're dead but they can't believe it. I see that look every time I close my eyes now, that's why I'm drinking the booze like this. I can't stand to see his face all hurt and breaking apart. It ain't right."

Unable to resolve his own monumental difficulties, Hymie was listening again. "It ain't right you should get yourself messed up," he said. "That's what ain't right."

"I ain't messed up. Who says I am?"

"Everybody says so. Al Parry says so. He says you ain't been doing your job these last few weeks."

"He's nuts."

"Is he? He says the collections are falling behind. You know what that means?"

"What?"

"It means you'll be out on your ass in another week. He'll get someone else for the job, or he'll cut you down so small you won't be making spit. Is that what you want?"

"I tell you I can't think of nothing but my brother buying it like that. I should've done something."

"Like what?"

"I don't know. But I should've been able to save him. I mean, I had a gun."

"So you had a gun. Big deal."

"Sure it's a big deal. If it was you and you had the gun, you would've saved him, I bet."

"Maybe yes, maybe no. The point is he's dead and you're here slopping up the booze. That don't make sense."

"Easy for you to say."

"I'm saying. Al likes you and he wants you should take care of the business."

"He hates my guts. What he'd like is to bury me."

Hymie gave a disbelieving snort. "If he wanted that, you'd be long buried."

"No, I wouldn't."

"What do you mean?"

Flowers picked up his empty glass. "I know too much."

Hymie's ferret eyes narrowed. "No kidding. What about? C'mon, you can tell me. I won't say a word to no one."

"I'm empty."

"Huh?"

"Empty. I got no drink."

"Oh yeah, sure. Hey, bartender, down here. Just one."

"Ain't you drinking?"

"I got a bad liver, can't take too much. Now what's this about you knowing too much?"

"Who says?"

"You just said."

"That's right. I know too much."

"What about?"

Flowers leaned over. "Scottini's wife."

"She's dead."

"That's right. She's dead."

"She jumped out the window. Her and the kid."

"I know that. You know that. Everybody knows that."

"So?"

"So Parry don't know that."

"I don't get it."

"He thinks I done the job on her and the kid. Me and Al before he got hit."

"You? What's the point?"

"If Zucco finds out we done it, Parry's in big trouble 'cause you don't never touch the family."

"Did you do it?"

"No."

"Well, then what the hell—"

"But Parry *thinks* I done it."

"But if you tell Joe, you're in the same trouble as Al. Don't he know that?"

"Sure he knows that."

"So?"

"So what?"

"So why's he think you'd tell Joe?"

"Tell Joe what?"

"That you done the job on Scottini's wife and kid."

"I didn't do it."

"But Parry thinks you did."

"That's right."

"So he hates you 'cause you might tell Joe you done what you didn't do."

"Yeah. *No.* He hates me 'cause I might tell Joe I done what I did do."

Hymie toyed with his empty glass. "You're nuts, you know that. Nuts as a fruitcake."

Flowers wasn't listening. "And besides that, I put him on the spot by getting my brother killed. Like I wanted it, you know? He thinks I'm just a bum."

"Maybe he's right."

"Thanks a lot."

"What you expect? You're drinking like one, ain't you?"

"So I'm still a little shook up."

"Booze won't help."

"Won't hurt none either."

"It's hurting already. You got to get your book in shape and take care of business. If you don't—"

"Parry cuts me loose. I know."

"You can't blame him."

"I blame him."

"He'd do it."

"Are you kidding? He'd love it."

"Then why give him the chance? Cut the booze and get back on the job like you suppose to."

"Did he send you to tell me that?"

"He asked me. Anyway, Al ain't the one caused all this. Scottini did. Blame him you gonna blame anybody."

Flowers sucked in his breath. "Scottini," he whispered.

"Yeah, Scottini. He's the one got me all this trouble. I should've known that from the first minute."

"How?"

"He's a northern wop, ain't he?"

"How should I know?"

"Sure he is. From around Naples somewhere. All them northern wops are the same, nothing but trouble. That's 'cause they ain't even Italian. What they really are is Swiss. They just say Italian 'cause it sounds better."

"Better?"

"Sure. Who wants to be Swiss? That's like being some kind of cheese. So they make out like they Italian. Then everybody gives them respect. See what I mean?"

"What are you talking about? If they ain't Italian, who is, for chrissake?"

"Nobody." Flowers drained his glass and banged it on the bar. "There ain't no Italians."

Hymie gave up. Here he was, forty-six years old, with a bad liver and a bum heart, with a wife who was nuts and two punk kids who were nuts, with no money and everybody passing him by; here he was wasting his time in a bar with a drunk who was telling him there were no Italians. This was how low he had come. He felt like a geek in a circus. Picking up his glass he called loudly for another drink. Hell, if he had to listen to a drunk he might as well be drunk himself.

"You take the Sicilians. They ain't Italian, they don't want no part of Italy. For two thousand years they don't want to be Italian. They fought against Rome same as anybody else who come on their land. All they want is to be let alone and be

Sicilians. Call them cheese-eaters and they cut your heart out."

"But they're part of Italy now," Hymie tried to reason.

"Just a passing thing. Don't mean nothing. Like I tell you, Sicilians ain't Italian. They may be wops but they ain't Italian."

"And the rest of the wops in Italy?"

"Just a bunch of cheese-eaters."

Hymie took a long pull on his brandy. "If there's no Italians, why they call it Italy? Tell me that."

"I guess 'cause it sounds better than Wopland."

"Why don't they just call it Sicily and Swisserland?"

"That's coming. A few more funerals and a couple good elections, and they gonna get what they want."

Both men ordered another round and drank it in silence.

"Only trouble is they don't want it."

"Who?"

"The Swiss wops. They don't want to be Swiss wops."

"What they want?"

"They want to be Italians."

Both of them had another round.

"Hell with 'em."

"Who?"

"The Italians."

"Which Italians?"

"I don't know."

The two men sat in silence for a long time. Drinks came and went. Bartenders changed shifts. In the back of the long low-ceilinged room, men played the bowling machine as if their lives depended on it. The phone behind the bar rang incessantly and urgent messages were relayed. From the neon jukebox, its glass face full of numbered teeth, came the mournful wail of unrequited love. After a while, one song melted into another until only the moments of silence in between were heard.

"I miss him," Flowers announced suddenly.

"Who?"

"My brother."

"Oh."

"I keep seeing his face."

"Don't look."

"He was a good man, smiling all the time. Never done nobody bad. It was a woman messed him over."

"They do it every time."

"His own wife too. She cut out on him when he went to the can. Just took off one day without a word to anybody. Took him six months to find out she went to someplace called Omaha."

"Where the hell is Omaha?"

"I don't know but everybody told him to send a couple boys after her, but he said no. He still loved her. She messed him over so bad he still loved her even after that. Nobody could figure it, except that she must've cunted him right out of his mind."

"They're all cunts."

"You can say that again."

"They're all cunts."

"If they didn't have that thing between their legs there'd be a bounty on their heads."

The bartender bought them a round which they drank swiftly.

"They ain't worth a shit."

"Who? The wops?"

"Not the wops. Women."

"Same thing."

"They always looking to piece you out. Let them get close enough and they'll chop you into garbage. That's a fact. All they good for is to screw, and even then you got to watch they don't shove a blade in your back. Me, I just use them mostly for blow jobs. They real good at that and you don't have to turn your back on them."

"Not unless you're double-jointed."

"Where we went wrong with them, where we went wrong was teaching them what that cunt was for. We never should've done that."

"When we do that?"

"Adam and Eve. He should've just stuck it in her mouth and got a good blow job."

"Maybe he did."

"Not good enough."

"But how would the race survive?" asked Hymie, a fresh drink in his hand. "Go on, tell me that."

"Easy. We'd just screw them while they were sleeping."

"Suppose they woke up?"

"We'd knock them out first."

"So they'd be awake for a blow job and asleep for screwing."

"Sure. That way they'd be OK to live with and they wouldn't be bitches like now."

"But suppose they got mad and kept their mouths shut?"

"You ever see a woman keep her mouth shut?" said Flowers, picking up his drink.

Baffled, Hymie turned away to the mirror but all he could see was a face staring back at him. There was something wrong with what Flowers was saying, but he couldn't put his finger on it. Something about zapping his wife and jumping on her bones. It sounded good but what to do with the body? Maybe dump it in the river. No, not that. Why should he do that to his wife? She was a little nuts, sure, but he had a certain affection for her. He didn't want anything to happen to her. And here was Flowers telling him to do some kind of job on his own wife, to jump on her bones and throw her in the river. Flowers must be crazy to talk to him like that.

"You must be crazy to talk to me like that."

"Huh?"

"I don't go for that kind of talk about my wife."

"What?"

"I said you can just shut up with that talk."

"You're drunk."

"*I'm* drunk? What about you? You're sitting there drunk as a pig."

"What? What did you say? I heard you call me a pig. You better watch your ass, old man."

"*Old man?* Listen to me, boy, I can take you apart and not even feel it."

"Go on, you couldn't take a watch apart. Who you kidding?"

"If I get up off this stool you'll be sorry."

"Shit, if you get off that stool I'll be amazed."

"Ready for another?" asked the bartender smoothly, his voice oozing authority.

Both men shoved their glasses forward and waited in silence while they were refilled. Then they drank in unison, slow gulps out of unsteady hands. The bowling machine still worked, the phone still rang, the jukebox still sang. All seemed in order.

"What were we talking about?"

"I don't know. Some dumb wop or something."

"Who needs it?"

"That's what I say."

"Let's get out of here. I know a couple places we can have some real fun."

"Good idea. Ain't nobody here worth nothing."

"Nothing but slaves and grifters around here anyway."

"I wouldn't give them the sweat off my balls."

"Me neither."

"You know something? We the only ones in this whole place that got any class."

" 'S funny. I was just thinking the same thing." Hymie reached for his glass and knocked it over. Sadly, he watched the brandy spill on the bar. "Even got trick glasses," he mumbled to himself. He closed his eyes and waved the displeasing scene away. His head began to hurt.

"Ready?" Flowers slid off his stool and caromed against the bar. Straightening himself, he weaved uncertainly toward the door, with Hymie bobbing and juggling behind him. Nobody glanced their way or paid them any attention. Outside, the air was quiet. A heavy blanket of haze had settled over the city, bathing the evening lights in softness. Hymie Cole and Charley Flowers surged down the street, staggering, bumping into each other, reeling and twisting like two sailors on shore leave.

"How you feel?"

"I think I'm drunk."

" 'S okay. I'm drunk too."

Flowers giggled. "How'd that happen?"

"I don't know. We must've been drinking."

"Me too."

Both men erupted in drunken laughter that carried them up the block and around the corner. In zestful good spirits, neither one noticed the tall shadows behind them. As they crossed the street the first shot shattered Hymie's spine, spattering bone, sending him crashing face downward against a parked car. At the sound Flowers jumped, lost his balance, and tumbled onto the sidewalk in a heap. Two more quick shots ripped into Hymie's falling body, one puncturing the neck, the other gouging out his left eye. As Flowers, instantaneously sober, hugged the pavement, Hymie Cole's lifeless body slipped off the car to the curb, his bloodied head falling into the gutter inches from Flowers' terror-stricken face. In desperation, Charley Flowers closed his eyes.

16

JOE ZUCCO didn't like to be kept waiting. He had a noon appointment with Moe Davis and here it was almost twelve-thirty and no Davis. It was, he felt, one more sign that this was going to be a bad day. When he had awakened at ten, he was informed that his invalid wife had spent another restless night. A few more nights like that and she would have to be returned to the hospital for further treatment. Bone disease, he had learned these past ten years, was no laughing matter for the victims or their relatives. Loving his wife in his own strange way, he felt wholly protective toward her. He had bought their present house and the grounds, much too large for any couple, because she had seen the place on a drive some eight years earlier and had desired it. He secured the best medical treatment, constant nurses and companions. Because she loathed hospitals he paid a physician a handsome annual fee to look in on her. He cared for her needs as best he could. About the only thing he couldn't give her was any part of himself, or any of his time.

Zucco looked at his watch. Twelve-thirty and still no Davis. He scowled and swiveled his chair a half-turn to face the windows. A nice day, too nice for everything to be going wrong. At eleven-thirty in his townhouse apartment, after a drive into the city that featured a tire blowout on the New Jersey Turnpike and a twenty-minute delay, he was informed by his mistress that she was going to have a baby. His baby. He couldn't believe it. He sat there listening to her and he just couldn't believe what he was hearing. What was the matter with women? Was the world going mad? His first impulse was to choke her, then when she started to cry he wanted to laugh. He finally decided he was the one going mad, and so he left rather hurriedly. Now as he looked back upon it, he saw that he would need more time to think this one out.

He checked his watch again. He would give Davis another five minutes, no more. Woman trouble was one thing; it was constant, it was to be expected from the nature of the beast, and no man who was a real man was free of it. But business problems had to be dealt with promptly and firmly before they got out of hand. He was beginning to suspect that the problem of Alexis Machine was getting out of hand. Machine was evidently becoming ambitious in the wrong places. His anger over the Scottini thing was understandable, even justified, but it should have been defused by the stickup his men pulled on Al Parry. Now by killing Hymie Cole, Machine had worsened the problem. Granted that Hymie had been the weakest link in the top command, if nothing were to be done about his killing, as nothing had been done about the stickup, Machine would simply become increasingly bold. It was the old badger game of one more push.

Zucco sighed. Something would have to be done. But what? He didn't want to start a local war. It was forbidden, it was frowned upon, and, worst of all, it weakened both parties. Nobody won. The Gallo brothers had proved that years ago. Look at what it got them: a bunch of coffins and a lot of grieving widows. Blood on the streets. Big deal. No, a local war was not the answer. He would have to take care of the problem of Alexis Machine another way.

Gino Agucci opened the office door. "Moe's here."

Zucco swung his chair back. "Send him in."

"Apples called. He'll be here three-thirty."

"What about Pete?"

"Five-thirty, like you said."

"Parry?"

"No answer. I'll keep trying."

"Tell Al I want him here at four."

Zucco watched the departing bodyguard. A good man: solid, safe, dependable, along with Pete Montana, his most trusted lieutenant. He wished he had a dozen more like that. When the word came in on Hymie Cole the previous night, Gino had held the news of the shooting until the dinner party at the house was over. Nothing could have been done at the moment anyway. Afterward, he waited patiently for orders, ready to do whatever was needed. A very smart man. Zucco intended to let Gino take over some of Hymie's duties on the hidden companies, at least temporarily. The rest he'd handle himself for the moment. The whole legitimate end of the business was getting out of hand; what he needed was a legal expert. Something would have to be worked out, and soon. The only reason he had let Hymie run the companies over the years was because Zucco was the father of Hymie's two adolescent boys. Years before, he had been attracted to Hymie Cole's wife, a beautiful black-haired woman with giant tits and the wettest pussy he had ever seen. Their affair lasted for several years, during which time both sons were born. Hymie knew of the arrangement, of course, and since he couldn't have any children of his own he accepted them. When Zucco finally tired of the woman she first tried to kill herself, afterward she became increasingly strange. Her husband stood by her, and Zucco saw to it that Hymie Cole was given a soft spot in the organization. With some talent he eventually carved out his own place. Now he was gone. Zucco knew the wife would have to be put away and the boys sent off to school somewhere. He would make a call and it would be done. Complications, always complications, he mused as Moe Davis walked in on him.

"Sorry I'm running late, Joe. It's a bitch getting here from New York. Just a bad day all around."

"For all of us."

"Yeah, I heard about Hymie Cole. Big trouble?"

"Nothing I can't handle."

Davis sat on the couch by the window. At five feet two, balding, overweight, wearing thick glasses, he hardly looked like a ladies' man, yet he had access to thousands of young beauties. Running girls between New York and Las Vegas kept him busy, but he was good at his work and received few complaints. While Davis was semi-independent, his operation was under syndicate protection interstate. Consequently, he knew all the right people. Like Joe Zucco.

"What's on your mind, Joe?"

"I need something special."

"Like who?"

"She's got to be fourteen, no more."

"Getting to like them kind of young, ain't you, Joe?"

Zucco let Davis have his little joke.

"But she's got to look at least eighteen."

Davis whistled. "That ain't easy."

"That ain't all."

"What else?"

"She's got to be a virgin."

Davis removed his thick glasses, breathed on them, wiped them with a special tissue he secured from his breast pocket, and returned them to their proper position on the bridge of his nose. "What's the gag?" he asked softly, glancing up at Zucco.

"No gag."

"You want a virgin."

"Not only she's got to be a virgin, but she has to come from a good family that can stand some investigating."

"Ah, now I see. The old squeeze play, eh?"

Zucco didn't answer. Davis knew better than to expect any answers in his business. Nor did he particularly want any.

"Can you do it?"

Davis pulled out a fancy cigar in a silver metal container. He fussed with it a few moments before lighting it from a small gold lighter that was initialed C.D. After a few expansive puffs he settled back into the couch, his stubby legs dangling over the edge.

"It'll cost you, Joe."

"So it'll cost me. Can you do it?"

"I think I might be able to do something for an old friend."

"How old?"

Davis laughed, a short puny laugh. "You know me, Joe. I'll do the best I can for you."

"Just remember I've sent you some good ones."

"Maybe a few grand for the kid's parents should do it."

"When?"

"I'll let you know in a couple days."

"Sooner the better."

"You'll hear."

Twenty minutes later Joe Zucco was sitting down to lunch in the Pagoda Gardens. Across from him was Julie K, with his ginger ale and his *Wall Street Journal.* Like the old friends they were, they discussed the ups and downs of business. Julie K had heard of Hymie Cole's death. It saddened him. "He was a good man," he said simply.

Zucco agreed.

"What about the two boys?"

"They'll be sent away somewhere."

"And the mother?"

"She'll have to go to an institution."

Julie K nodded. He knew about Zucco's affair of years ago. He also knew enough not to ask who was responsible for the killing. It had nothing to do with him and was therefore none of his concern.

"I might be going into the clothing business soon," Zucco announced suddenly.

"A good stable business to be in," said Julie K with surprising gravity in his voice. "I sometimes wish I'd gone into it

201

when I was younger. People always need clothes." He fingered his threadbare jacket. "Men's, I hope."

"Yeah, don't worry. You'll get some fancy rags out of it."

"Rags I always got. From you I want better."

The two men ate their usual fare in silence for some minutes. Julie K wondered what kind of a deal Zucco was working to get into clothing. It was, as he knew, a very rough field, and one he had several times considered entering. But he hadn't the stomach for it. Unlike Zucco, he was not ruthless and iron-willed. All he owned had been secured through manipulation and guile, through deals of one kind or another. Julie K loved deals. While he might be a coward physically, he was a lion when it came to dealing in business matters. It was his strength, his drive. In his several business deals with Zucco over the years, Julie K noted that he had always come out better than even. This filled him with pride. In a straight business deal he considered Zucco no match for him.

"Have you thought about that little deal we discussed a few months back?" Julie K asked.

"What's that?"

"Printing phony book covers and getting refunds for them."

"Oh yeah, I remember. I tell you, I been so busy I ain't had a chance to think of anything. Let me look into it soon's I can."

"No hurry," said Julie K, wondering how his old friend could pass up a proposition like that.

Sitting there, Joe Zucco was thinking of anything but books. He wondered how his old friend could even suggest such a deal at a time like this. Here he was involved in everything from booze to protection. Maybe even clothing. He had a dozen things going and a hundred things to watch. He felt like a juggler. What he needed, really needed, he decided, was a little luck with Leon Harris. If the sex nut went for the fourteen-year-old virgin, the trap would be sprung. The sucker would be shown pictures; the girl, much under age, would be ready to testify. Harris'd have to pay off, with more money borrowed from Zucco. Then the squeeze would be on, the winner assured.

All in all, a sound business investment and a really good deal.

On the drive back to his office, Zucco got a sudden idea from something Julie K had said at lunch about the basis of all business contracts. What was it? If somebody wants something bad enough, they're prepared to give up something else to get it. That's it. If somebody wants something bad enough, they're prepared to give up something else to get it. The mob wanted Sam Yacavelli bad enough so they should be ready to make a deal, or at least to return a favor. To make it even better, it would cost them nothing. By the time he reached the office, Zucco, beaming, believed he had found the answer to his most pressing problem of the moment.

"Gino, get hold of Jimmy Rye. Tell him I got to see him right away. Tonight if it's OK. Tell him I'll drive down there and meet him anywhere he says. If he can't make it tonight, tomorrow."

"What if he wants to talk to you?"

"I'm out. This got to be done in person. If he ain't around, leave the message."

A fresh cigar in his mouth, Zucco sat quietly in his chair, carefully thinking his idea through until Johnny Apples was ushered into the office promptly at three-thirty.

"I want in on that club," Zucco declared simply. "It's bad for business if some punk slips by. Gives the others ideas. I don't like they should get ideas."

For the next half-hour the two men plotted and planned the overthrow and destruction of Phil Green of the Cloud Nine. He had been graciously offered money for an interest in the club. He had been politely informed of the consequences of an uncooperative attitude. He had been warned and threatened. His customers had been intimidated. Nothing worked. He had refused all deals. Now he would have to pay the price.

"You got the drugs. Tell the nigger the word's out on him. He won't get a taste nowhere but what we give him. What we give him is partners. Tell him it's a straight business deal. Nobody gets hurt."

"What if he don't go for it? I mean, how far should I push him?"

Glowering, Zucco looked toward the window. "We give him money, he don't take it. Now we give him the drugs. If he don't take that—" He spun around to Apples. "If he don't take that, we give him nothing. You push him till he don't push no more."

Most of the eight kilos of heroin bought from Frank Taylor had already been sold, at a good profit, to a Newark supplier, taken there furtively by Gino Agucci. Having thus had most of his hundred thousand dollars returned through the Newark sale, Zucco believed himself already ahead in the matter of the Cloud Nine. Phil Green would get his drug supply from Zucco, who would mark it against his share of the club. A special deal with Taylor for small future shipments was all worked out. Within six months Zucco's men would be running the club. Green would then be eased out. And Joe Zucco would have one more pin in his organizational chart, one more source of income.

He studied Johnny Apples, sitting by the side of the big desk in his three-hundred-dollar suit and fifty-dollar shoes. "You doing pretty good, Johnny. You come a long way. Big house, nice clothes, fresh money in the bank. Not like the old days, eh? Be a shame to lose all that, know what I mean? You don't want to get careless."

Johnny Apples, shaking inside, said nothing. He didn't know if Zucco had something specific in mind, or was just talking in general. How could Zucco know what he had been thinking?

"What's this about Taylor's boys planning a double cross? They expect to catch you sleeping or what?"

"There was no double cross, Joe. Just Farrano thought they might try something so he kept the money in the car till he got the stuff. You know how some guys get, all nerves." His laugh sounded hollow.

Farrano. The crummy bastard must've told Joe about switching the money so they couldn't pull a steal.

"You should've thought of that, Johnny. That's why you here and not on the docks pushing a hook. Suppose one of Taylor's people got ambitious and knocked over the drop? That's all it took. Then it would've been too late, see what I mean? You got to plan for these things. A guy don't plan, we begin thinking maybe he got other things on his mind. We don't like that." Zucco smiled, a thin crease that cut across his jagged cheeks. "You don't got other things on your mind, do you, Johnny?"

Apples swallowed hard, wetting his lips. "Nothing, Joe. Honest. I'm doing great. Everything's fine."

"That's what I been telling you. Ambition's a wonderful thing, just so it don't get away from you." He got up. "Take care of the nightclub thing. I want that in the operation."

Apples left, sweating profusely, cursing himself, Zucco, Farrano, everybody he knew. But mostly Zucco. He was a devil in disguise, always making people sweat around him. And he was able to read people's minds too. Steaming down the steps and out the separate entrance of the funeral parlor, one thing was clear to Johnny Apples. If he ever double-crossed Zucco, he'd have to do it without thinking. And he wasn't about to do that yet.

Upstairs at the window, Zucco watched Apples get into his expensive car and drive away. He was a good man but he would have to be watched so his ambition didn't get him in trouble. Farrano was right about one thing. Apples didn't plan for any double cross. He didn't have the guts for a cross of his own, at least not now, so it was carelessness. Zucco didn't like that. Carelessness could destroy anybody, including him.

Gino came in with Al Parry. "That guy said yes for to-night."

Zucco nodded. "Sit down, Al. I'll be right back."

In the outer room Gino gave him the details. Jimmy Rye would be in Philadelphia all evening and should be free after eight. They'd have dinner and stay over and then play some golf in the morning.

"He give you a time and place?"

"The Shoreham. He'll call you there."

"OK. After I see Al, we go to the apartment, then back here for Pete and straight out the turnpike. Use the Cadillac."

Back in the office Zucco listened while Al Parry gave him the week's loanshark figures. Everything was in order. "Except for a couple hard legs who act up now and then. Nothing serious. And that Charley Flowers that was in the hit on Hymie."

"What about him?"

"Since his brother got it, he been boozing too much. Ain't been doing the job right."

"Hymie getting it like that should shake him up OK."

"If it don't, I'm gonna dump him. Far as I'm concerned, he ain't nothing but bad luck."

"Gino says he got some good years left in him."

"Gino's nuts."

"Maybe. But go easy on the kid, I might have use for him soon."

"Be a mistake."

Zucco ignored that. "What about this knife artist you got? He any good?"

"Ginger? Yeah, he's real good. He does a job and he can keep his mouth shut. He's better than Flowers' brother ever was."

"So you don't like Flowers. You already told me that." Zucco got up. "Send Gino in on your way out."

By the time Pete Montana arrived at five-thirty, everything was set for the trip southward. The big Cadillac was gassed up and ready to roll, Gino at the wheel. "You're coming," Zucco told Montana as he rumbled out the door and down the office steps.

"Where?" asked his surprised associate, hurrying after.

"Philadelphia, where else?" came the reply.

Except for a brief discussion of the Yacavelli plans, neither man spoke much on the drive down the Jersey Turnpike. Years of furtive living in a closed society had conditioned them to silence. It was a state of being for which they had great respect. Alike in temperament and physique, almost the same in age, both men distrusted those who talked for lack of something else to do. They had much to do, most of it in silence. Gino, fully aware, did not interrupt their composure.

The ride was uneventful. Constantly exceeding the speed limit on the turnpike, the sleek machine got them to Philadelphia well before eight.At the Shoreham they registered in the suite reserved for them, and had a bottle and setups delivered to the rooms while they awaited the call from Jimmy Rye. It came at nine. By ten-thirty they were dining at the exclusive Rounders in Paoli, where a private room had been set aside for them.

At the big table against the polished bronze wall were Joe Zucco and Pete Montana and Jimmy Rye. With them, his face shrouded in flickering candlelight, sat Edward Alphonse Barone, the voice of authority for the Jersey syndicate. Zucco had met him only once, briefly. Pete Montana knew neither man and thus had to be introduced properly by Zucco as a "friend of ours." Jimmy Rye greeted him immediately. Barone, acknowledging Montana's credentials with a nod of his leonine head, said nothing. Nearer the door, at a smaller table, sat three men, all of them alert, one of them Gino Agucci.

The dinner and discussion lasted two hours. Barone was attending because he wanted to know what was delaying Zucco's move against Yacavelli. "It's costing us every day he lives. What we need is we don't lose too much more. There's no way out, we gonna have him killed for us."

"You mean I'm gonna have him killed for you."

"So what's the delay?"

"Nothing," said Zucco, lighting a fresh cigar. "Pete here has it all set to go."

"When?"

"Very soon."

"How soon?"

"Soon. Any time now."

Barone appeared satisfied. "How many men?"

"Two."

"Yacavelli's sharp. He knows we ain't happy."

"Don't matter, we'll get to him."

"No mistakes," said Barone. "It's too late for mistakes."

Zucco was momentarily annoyed. "I don't make mistakes," he announced somewhat grandly.

Pete Montana, watching the split-second flicker of Barone's eyes, thought that Zucco had just made a mistake. He wondered if it would ever prove fatal.

Slowly during the course of the dinner, without in any way suggesting a deal or even implying any connection to the Yacavelli job, Zucco broached the subject of his visit. He was having trouble, serious trouble that had to be corrected. His most valuable man was dead, his associates held up, his workers threatened and beaten and harassed. It was all the work of one man, a man whose ambition was driving him crazy, a man who would destroy all of them if he wasn't stopped. "It took us years to get our own kind organized in this country. Many of us died in the struggle. Whatever power we now have we have only 'cause those who come before us recognized that without law we couldn't exist. Do away with laws and rules, and we crumble. Turn this country into a jungle, and we all die. This man I speak of wants to turn my city into a jungle. He don't care that local wars are forbidden. He don't care that we could lose everything we own. All he cares about is getting power for himself. More and more power. Till nobody is left but him." Zucco paused, bent down to sip from his glass of water.

Pete Montana, fascinated by yet another side of his friend, urged him on with a tight smile.

"Why do I care? I ask myself. I could easily settle the matter. I could take things into my own hands and remove this threat. It would not be difficult. But I say no, I will instead go to my friends and ask for the law. The law must be upheld before all else. Without the law we're all animals again in the jungle. This I refuse to be." He was passionate now, his face dark and angry.

"I waited after the first attack. I said to myself, maybe he don't know about it, maybe some punk's getting ideas. But then other things happened. Now I see it's a plan. I'm being pushed. Still I wait, hoping he will return to the law. Then my associate is killed, gunned down. I can't wait no longer. Now I say to myself, I must go to my friends for the law and have this disagreeable matter taken care of, once and for all."

Barone cleared his throat. "What do you want from us?" His smile was cruel, brutal. "This ain't exactly something for the National Commission, you know."

"What I want," Zucco said gravely, ignoring the sarcasm, "is to take care of the problem in my own way."

"Your way could start a war."

"It's already started."

Barone inclined his head toward Zucco. "We don't like things like this. Even a local war can get out of hand."

"I can do it with no trouble." He snapped his fingers. "Just like that. No war, no nothing."

"How?" asked Jimmy Rye.

"Yes," said Barone. "How will you do this magic?"

"Only one way." Joe Zucco lowered his voice to a whisper. "He goes the same way as Yacavelli."

Barone didn't like the idea. Suppose something went wrong? Suppose other cities did the same? Suppose anything? Zucco answered his objections at length, in a calm voice and with an outward show of respect. Nothing would go wrong, he would give his word on that. The syndicate would not be asked to do anything. There would be no local war. Best of all, afterward the syndicate would be given a better rakeoff. By midnight Edward Alphonse Barone was listening with interest. By twelve-thirty he had agreed in principle. "But you wait till he makes one more move against you. If he don't, you don't. That's it. That's what I tell the boys."

That was good enough for Zucco. He knew there'd be another move, even if he had to make it himself.

He already had an idea.

On the long drive back to the city the next afternoon, after a night of drinks and a morning of golf, Joe Zucco lounged lazily against the luxurious softness of the car's leatherette backrest. He was content. Not even the acrid smoke or pungent aroma of the Jersey Meadows could distract him from his victory. Sam Yacavelli, mob boss of Newark gambling and a big drug merchant, was a dead man.

And so was Alexis Machine.

17

THE NATION OF NEWARK lies at the heart of the industrial East. Insurance companies, food-processing plants, electronic and petrochemical complexes are major industries. Truck terminals dot its highways, freight and passenger rails crisscross its arteries. A large airport services the constant flow of traffic. Along with its business properties, Newark provides recreational facilities for its four hundred thousand inhabitants: parks, playgrounds, swimming pools, and a dozen public and private golf courses. One of these, located in the Valhall section of the city near the South Orange border, is set amid a gently rolling landscape of cropped trees and trim bushes, away from the clogged streets and commercial distractions of the business district to the north. A private facility, operated strictly for its exclusive membership, the Mountain Valley Golf Club caters to its members in a fashionable two-story clubhouse of stucco and teakwood at the entrance to the course. An unguarded driveway off a main street leads to a parking lot, with the clubhouse a short walk away. Inside, members find a small restaurant and bar, a game room, television area, and library, and individual lockers. Upstairs are two gyms, a small swimming pool, a squash court, and a steam room. On weekends the facilities are enjoyed to their fullest, as busy executives relax away their cares. But during the week, especially in the mornings, a stillness settles over the clubhouse and the greens. Few members appear and fewer still lounge indoors.

It was precisely this reason that occasioned the appearance each Tuesday morning at ten o'clock of Sam Yacavelli, a valued member of the club and a man of obvious means. With his bodyguard always unobtrusively nearby, he changed his clothes at his locker, played a fair round of golf, returned for a quiet lunch, and departed in the early afternoon. He seldom brought guests. He was courteous to the small weekday staff, though somewhat loud and demanding, and he always left a sizable tip. They looked forward each Tuesday to his arrival.

On this particular Tuesday morning the front door of the clubhouse opened and two men walked in. They stopped at the reception desk.

"Can I help you?" the manager asked them.

"Maybe," one of the men said. He turned to his companion. "Can he help us?"

"Maybe," said the second man.

Sunlight streamed through the window behind the reception desk. A lighted chandelier hung in the center of the small hallway. The two men at the desk looked around casually. From his vantage point the manager coughed delicately, indicating impatience. He had been working on a crossword puzzle when they entered.

"Does Sam Yacavelli get here on time?" the first man asked.

"Mr. Yacavelli is a man of habit."

"That's nice. But does he get here on time?"

"I've never known him to be particularly late," the manager explained, a note of annoyance in his voice. "You can usually set your watch by his movements."

The first man looked at his watch. "I make it a quarter to ten."

"Thirteen to," said the second man.

"Same thing."

"Not if you hanging by it," the second man said. "Not hardly likely."

"Do you gentlemen have an appointment with Mr. Yaca-velli?" the manager asked. "He usually doesn't see many people here. And he hardly ever has any guests."

"He'll see us. There ain't a chance in the world he won't see us."

"You're friends then?"

"Let's just say we're the friendly type, eh? That way you can't go wrong."

"Will you be playing golf with Mr. Yacavelli?"

"There won't be no golf," said Ginger. He was dressed in a tailored suit, tight at the knees and shoulders, with a double vent in the jacket. His powder-blue shirt had a small snap collar and patch pleats. A striped tie matched the folded handkerchief in his breast pocket. He wore black buckle boots.

"We don't like golf," said the other man. He was shorter than Ginger. His suit, though of a darker shade, was similar in design and cut. Black boots completed the costume. Standing at the reception desk, they looked like two IBM salesmen.

"Who's around today?" Ginger asked.

"None of the regular members yet," the manager said. "We only open at nine-thirty."

"I mean who you got *working* here?"

"You mean the staff?"

"That's just what he means," said the other man. "How many staff you got?"

"Five."

"That include you?"

"Yes."

"Some luck, eh?" Ginger asked his companion.

"Sounds good so far," came the reply.

"When's the crowd get here?" Ginger asked.

"Looks like there ain't no crowd," the other man said. "Least not on weekdays, anyway."

"That's right," the manager said.

"You sure about that?" Ginger asked the manager.

"Quite sure. The weekdays are invariably less hectic."

"You sure know a lot of big words, don't you? I'll bet you went to college, some big fancy college."

"I went to Princeton," said the manager.

"No shit," said the other man, "You hear that?"

"He's a Princeton man," said Ginger. He turned to the manager. "Where's this Princeton?"

"Why, right here in New Jersey."

"How about that," Ginger said. "Been here all the time, eh? Now ain't that something."

"I know where Princeton is," said Charley Flowers.

"You too? Maybe you're a Princeton man same as him."

"Fat chance of that," Flowers said.

The manager, somewhat alerted now, attended to his professional duties at the desk. Behind his polished eyebrows he watched the two young men carefully.

"You said you were with—ahh, what company was that again?" he asked Ginger.

"Don't you remember?"

"I'm afraid not."

"You got a bad memory," Ginger said. He reached over the desk and took the plastic pen from the manager's fingers. It was a black plastic pen. He snapped it in two.

"You write too much." He dropped the pieces on the desk. "See what happens when you write too much?"

"I—I don't know what you mean."

"You forget who we are. Maybe we don't like that."

"Maybe he was only kidding," Flowers said.

"Sure, you were only kidding. Ain't that so?"

The manager, bewildered, nodded in agreement.

"You can talk to us," Ginger said to him. "We like smart people. You don't have to be afraid of us."

"I—I'm not afraid," said the manager.

"You hear that, he ain't afraid." Ginger looked over to Flowers. "When you go to Princeton, you ain't afraid of nothing. That's what it is, see?"

"Maybe," Flowers said. He walked around the desk.

"That's what it is all right," said Ginger mysteriously.

"Where's the rest of the help at?" Flowers asked.

"Yeah, that's a good idea," Ginger said. "We ought to check them out, too."

"What for?" the manager asked.

"For nothing."

"You better tell us where they are," Flowers said. He gave the manager a tight smile.

"What do you want with them?"

"Don't ask questions," Ginger said. "Just tell us where they are."

"Three of them are in the restaurant."

"And the other?"

"Upstairs."

"Upstairs where?"

"He could be anywhere."

"What's he do?"

"Take care of the various rooms."

"He stay up there all the time?"

"Mostly. He just comes down for lunch."

"What time?"

"Usually at twelve-thirty."

Flowers turned to Ginger. "We don't have to worry about him."

"OK by me. What about down here?"

"What are you going to do?" asked the manager.

"Never mind that," said Flowers. "Tell us about the downstairs help."

"What for?"

"Just tell us about them."

"Is this a robbery?"

"No, this ain't no robbery," Ginger said in disgust. "Do we look like a couple of punks?"

"Easy," Flowers said to him. "Why get yourself all worked up? You," he said to the manager, "tell us about them."

The manager knitted his perplexed brows. "Two of them serve food to the members. The third mixes drinks."

"What about the cook?"

"Cook? What cook?"

"The cook that cooks the food."

"There is no cooking allowed on these premises," said the manager with an authoritative air.

"If nobody cooks," Ginger asked suspiciously, "what in hell are you serving to all them members?"

"Our cuisine is delivered each day, of course. Fully prepared. It comes from several of the best continental restaurants in the area."

"Another fried chicken joint," Ginger said to Flowers. "I might've known."

"When they're not serving nobody," said Flowers, "where are they?"

"There's a small room in back of the preparation area. They usually remain there."

"Ever come out here?"

"Certainly not," said the manager indignantly. "The help is not allowed in the front of the house."

"How do they come and go?"

"There's a separate entrance for the help in the rear."

"What you think?" Flowers said, looking at Ginger. "Leave them or what?"

"Long's they stay in the back they OK. Less work for us." He walked across the narrow hallway to the coat room. "Looks like we was steered right about this dump."

"Looks it."

"Yeah. Empty and quiet. Couldn't be better." He came back to the reception desk. "I'll stay here on this side. You take the coat room."

"What about him?" asked Flowers, tilting his head toward the manager.

"He's gonna stay here with me like a good boy," Ginger said, smiling at the manager. "Ain't that right?"

"What are you going to do?"

"You hear that?" Ginger said. "He wants to know what we gonna do."

"What's he think we gonna do?"

Ginger looked over at the manager, standing nervously against the wall on one side of the desk. "Well, you got any ideas?"

The manager said nothing.

"He ain't talking," Ginger called out.

"It's got something to do with Mr. Yacavelli, hasn't it?"

"He says it got something to do with Yacavelli."

"Tell him he's right."

"You're right," Ginger said. "It got a whole lot to do with Yacavelli."

"You're going to—" The manager's face suddenly showed startled awareness.

"Kill him," said Ginger. "We're gonna kill Sam Yacavelli."

"Right here? In the *clubhouse?*" the manager screamed in horror.

"He comes here every Tuesday morning, don't he?"

"Yes, but—"

"So this is where he's gonna get it."

"But why?"

"Why's anyone get it? 'Cause somebody don't want them around no more."

"And that's all?"

"What else? He must've done something wrong, and somebody don't like what he done."

"Hey, knock it off," said Flowers from the coat room. "He'll be here any minute."

"Don't tell me what to do," Ginger said viciously.

"Somebody should."

"Just so it ain't you, pal. 'Cause I don't like you."

Flowers looked at his watch. "He should be here by now," he said angrily, telling himself that he'd settle with Ginger later.

"You just act natural," Ginger said to the manager. "When he comes in, just be yourself. You got that?"

"I'll try," said the shaken manager.

"Sure you will. You're a big Princeton man."

They waited in silence. Outside it was spring. The sun, slowly working itself across the manicured grass, dressed everything in warmth. A slight breeze rustled the fairway leaves. In the coat room Flowers took out his chrome-plated .38-caliber revolver. He checked the cylinders.

At eight minutes after ten a brown Cadillac turned into the driveway. Two men sat in the front seat. A minute later the car's approach was heard in the clubhouse.

"He's coming," said Flowers from the window next to the front door.

"You sure it's him?"

"Brown caddy? Two men? It's him."

Ginger opened his precision-honed knife of Swedish steel. He pressed the tip of the blade against the manager's back. "Greet him when he comes in just like nothing's wrong. I'll be right here behind you." He moved over a few steps to a side wall that concealed him from the entrance. "Remember," he whispered, looking into the manager's frightened eyes, "one bad move and I chop your head off."

"Get ready," Flowers said from the coat room.

"We both take Yacavelli," said Ginger. "Don't worry about the cannon, he'll fold soon as he hears the shots." He slipped the knife back into his pocket and pulled out a black .45-caliber automatic. The big gun felt heavy in his hand. He didn't like guns, didn't normally use them, but Pete Montana had insisted. It was that kind of a job, he had been told. He still believed a knife would do better.

"Here they come."

A cool gust of air blew through the narrow hallway as the front door opened. Two men entered, both tall and broad-shouldered, both wearing business suits and casual shirts. The younger man had on a brown fedora. He entered first, carrying a new set of golf clubs in a soft leather bag. The other man carried nothing.

"Good morning, Mr. Yacavelli."

The older man grunted in the direction of the reception desk and the manager. He took several steps down the hallway, followed by his bodyguard. As they passed by the coat room Charley Flowers stepped out behind them, gun in hand. He quickly shot twice. Yacavelli stumbled forward, crashing to the floor dead. At that same instant Ginger, from behind the reception desk, aimed the automatic at Yacavelli and pulled the trigger. Nothing happened. Yacavelli's bodyguard, startled into action by the shots from Flowers' gun, spun to his left as his own gun came out. What he saw was Ginger, confused, rushing out from behind the desk, desperately working the automatic. With a shouted curse he shot Ginger twice in the stomach. Unaware of Flowers behind him, he went to shoot Ginger in the head as Flowers cut him down with three shots. Two hit him in the upper back and neck, the third ripped through the back of his head, squirreling out the front over the left eye, spilling brains and oozing tissue.

Flowers put the empty revolver in his pocket and carefully crossed the hallway. Ginger, hunched over the desk, still clutched the automatic. As the gun was lifted out of his shaking hand, Ginger slipped slowly to the floor, landing on his knees. His eyes showed surprise; his mouth, foaming, tried to form silent words. Flowers looked at the automatic, then at Ginger dying on the floor. "You poor bastard," he said, shaking his head. He put the gun to Ginger's ear and pulled the trigger. Nothing happened. The safety was on. Flowers laughed, he couldn't help it. He pulled the magazine out. Fully loaded. He laughed again, slipped the gun into another pocket. Ginger was dead because he didn't know an automatic had a safety. That was very funny. For a mistake like that he deserved to die. Except he wasn't dead. Yet.

"C'mon. I'll help you out to the car." Flowers pulled Ginger up a bit and flung a slack arm across his shoulders. In this manner he dragged the stumbling man to the door. He would have liked to leave Ginger to die, but it was too dangerous. There were other ways.

"You didn't see a thing," he shouted to the petrified manager huddled on the floor behind the desk. "Remember that. Say anything else and we'll be back for you."

The sunshine was golden on the grass as he drove out of the almost deserted club. His watch said ten-thirteen. Seven shots had been fired in a few minutes, and in the clubhouse lay two dead men. Propped up next to him was a third.

Coughing his guts up, spitting blood bubbles, Ginger tried to whisper.

"Don't talk," said Flowers. "We'll be there soon."

"Where?" the voice croaked.

Flowers didn't answer. Driving up U.S. 1 he decided he had done a good job. Yacavelli was dead. That was all Pete Montana and Zucco cared about, that the job get done. What happened to the shooters didn't really interest them. Nevertheless he felt good. He was on his way again. Maybe now they'd give him more jobs and a smell at some real money.

He looked over at Ginger. That made him feel good, too. The man was dying fast. At first Flowers had thought of taking him to the meat plant and getting rid of the body in the sausage machines. It would be only right, he told himself. But it was too risky in the daytime and he knew nothing about knives anyway. He decided instead to dump the body in the river. Weight it down and sink it. He wished he could sink it a dozen times.

"Where?" croaked the voice again.

He still didn't answer. At the next intersection he took the cutoff for Bayonne.

"Need a doctor," Ginger gasped after a while. "Get me doctor."

"You need a miracle is what you need," Flowers muttered under his breath. He drove as fast as he could.

Fifteen minutes later he was near the Bayonne docks. He headed the car for a deserted stretch of waterfront, full of rotting piers and abandoned sheds. For many years, going back to his own childhood in Bayonne, it had been a favorite dumping ground for local mob kills. It was easy to get to, and the tide swiftly took the bodies out to sea, or at least far enough from prying eyes on shore.

He inched the car right up to the end of a bulkhead. Turning off the motor, he got out and walked around to the other side. Waves lapped at the rotting piles underneath his feet.

"This is it," he said, opening the door. He shook Ginger back to consciousness. "End of the line for you."

"Huh? What's this?" the bloody mouth asked.

"This is where you go for a little dive. You like the water, don't you?" Flowers laughed, a thin cruel laugh that got lost in the open air. "You gonna play sink or swim." He pulled the almost-lifeless body out of the car. "And you know what? I don't think you gonna swim."

Ginger, dazed, in shock from pain, a step away from death, had one last moment of awareness. As Flowers dragged him, stumbling, toward the water's edge, his hand slipped into his pocket and came up with the knife, opened. With a final desperate lunge, lacking any strength or even direction, he whirled around and shoved the blade into Flowers' back, high up on the shoulder.

The sudden pain made Flowers yell. He let Ginger fall to the ground, and with his right hand he pulled the knife out of his back. "You stinking sonofabitch," he screamed. Dropping the knife, his hand reached for the automatic in his pocket and, rage controlling his action, he cut Ginger almost in half with six slugs from the .45.

Breathing heavily, he stood there for a moment running his hand over the cut. It was only a flesh wound, the blade had not gone deep enough for anything more. Reassured, he set about getting rid of Ginger. There was no time to weight the body. He quickly stripped it of all identification, then used the knife to chop off both hands above the wrist. These he wrapped in the dead man's jacket, to be burned later. He then ran one wheel of the car back and forth over the face, smashing bone and teeth, making it totally unrecognizable. Finished, he pushed the corpse into the turgid water.

Back in the car he sat still for a moment, grimly satisfied. The bastard had deserved it. That evened things up for his brother. To Pete Montana he would explain how Ginger, mortally wounded, had died on the way back. The right thing was to get rid of the body, which he had done. He had even mutilated the corpse to make it look like just another revenge mob kill.

Heading back toward the city he wondered if anyone had heard the shots. It didn't really matter since the car was stolen. All he had to do was give the guns back to the drop, burn the hands and jacket, and get rid of the car. Then he'd take care of his cut.

Flowers raised his arm, wet with blood, in victory. There was no one to see him. He quickly brought the arm down.

This time I'm really going, he thought, weaving through traffic with his good hand. Nothing's gonna stop me now. I'm gonna be a big shot and go right to the top. The top, the top, the top.

By the time he had reached his destination, a wild euphoria had swept over him, a lightheadedness that proclaimed his greatness.

18

A FEW WEEKS AFTER the heroin purchase from Frank Taylor's men, Harry Strega moved in with Colie Rogers. He couldn't stand to be with Lucy Berg any longer, nor did he desire to remain in Mrs. Fugazy's house. He was tired of rooming houses, he had lived in them for most of his young life. He was also tired of living alone. What he needed, he had decided after meeting Colie Rogers, was to live with a real woman for a while.

Colie's two-room apartment was on the second floor of a four-story brownstone with carpets on the stairs and table lamps in the halls. The living room looked out onto a pocket park of planted trees and silvered children's swings, where winos regularly held court amid the half-dozen orange picnic tables.

In the tiny bedroom Harry and Colie made love, hungrily and with great zest, seemingly unable to gain enough of each other. They got up late most days, lazily discovering new sexual energy after exhaustive evenings. On her work nights, Harry would meet Colie afterward, waiting for her outside The Greek's, then walking to Journal Square for breakfast. Sitting at a table, watching her mouth open and forkfuls of food disappear, he was filled with a delicious anticipation. By the time they had eaten and taken a cab home, he was usually on the edge of orgasm. Colie never disappointed him.

Sometimes they stayed in bed all day, talking, sleeping, watching the television on a dresser at the foot of the bed. Hunger eventually drove them out to the pint-sized refrigerator in the kitchen alcove at one end of the living room. At other times they ate at nearby restaurants.

Both of them movie buffs, they haunted the local theaters, frequently seeing new pictures on the first day of appearance, often going on the bus to neighboring towns or even New York City to catch something they had missed, or just to see what was playing. Their taste was eclectic, their range virtually incomprehensible. They saw *Vanishing Point* as the great American epic of their generation, yet they could sit through monster pictures with almost equal delight. They loved all the old Fred Astaire musicals but wouldn't miss an Elvis Presley version either. Coming home from such films, excited and tense, they would often compare notes. On rare occasions they disagreed violently, and then the air was filled with verbal gunsmoke.

"Goddamn, can't you see it's all a stupid game," Harry would shout. "*Last Tango in Paris*, it don't *say* nothing."

"Maybe not to you," Colie would shout back.

"Not to *nobody,*" screamed Harry.

"It says plenty to me," screamed Colie.

"Like what?"

"If you have to ask, you wouldn't understand."

Colie banged a pan on the stove and retreated to the bedroom. Brooding, Harry wondered what he had seen in her. She obviously had no mind. A good face and a great body, but nothing upstairs. How could she be so dumb? He shuddered. That night they made no love.

The next morning they woke up touching each other and everything was forgiven. Men and women were different, after all, and it was silly to expect them to think alike or see things the same way. Harry realized how smart Colie was to understand that. She was not only beautiful but she had a great mind, at least for a girl. Lying there on her back, her long, slender legs tapering at the thighs to a V of brownish blond hair, her waist impossibly slim, her curved breasts pointing upward in defiance of gravity, she looked to Harry like the all-American wet dream. That she was his at that moment was a delicious thought. He fondled her, played with her, made her wet, and she, moaning, her head thrashing, her arms grasping for his shoulders, pulled him up onto her.

Afterward he lay on his side facing her, his arm draped over her flat belly, his nose buried in her wheat-honey hair. He felt better than he ever had felt with Lucy Berg. At least, he thought he did.

"That was super," Colie said as Harry nuzzled her ear. "Ummm. I like it all the time but sometimes it's even better."

"Me too," he said with strands of soft hair in his mouth. "I like it all the time too."

"Isn't it better with some people? I mean, than with others?"

"Sure, some people fit better together."

"That's what I mean. I think we fit pretty good."

He was sure of it. He would run his hands over her lithe body, the fingers trailing deliciously on supple skin. He caressed her nipples, stroked her clitoris, entered secret places incredibly alive to his touch. It was all so magical in a way. She seemed to open like a flower at his command, to bloom in his presence.

"I never felt like this," she confessed one day.

"Me neither," he lied.

She laughed. "Men always say that."

Taken by surprise, he thought furiously. "Maybe," he said finally, "'cause every woman wants to hear it."

"I don't. Not if it's fake."

One thing for sure, he told himself, she ain't like Lucy Berg. Colie was a real woman. She was honest and undemanding and passionate and very smart. And she knew her own mind, too. He liked that about her. She knew what she wanted and she didn't go around changing things every day. At twenty-one she was a waitress in a whorehouse, and if that's what she wanted to do at age twenty-one that's what she was doing. Harry wondered how Lucy Berg would do in a whorehouse.

Sometimes, alone in bed, he thought about Colie before he knew her. She had been with other men, gone with them, lived with them. What had happened to make her leave? Or had they left? She'd been through a dozen big towns across the country. Why was she always moving on? Would she leave him soon? He noticed that she had seemed impressed when he told her what he did for a living, but he wasn't sure what it all meant.

Around Colie he was careful to appear decisive at all times and to be authoritative in all matters relating to them. He sensed her appetite for strong men and he silently vowed not to be outdone. He exercised every day and practiced his karate. He dropped little hints about what was going on in the rackets, never anything too specific of course, but just enough for her to see that he was in the know. Above all, he didn't remind her that she was almost nine months older than he. Lucy Berg was, of course, almost nine months younger. At times Harry wondered if going around with an older woman was worth the effort.

When Colie worked, he went out to shoot a game of pool or get a few drinks in a neighborhood bar. Sometimes he took in a movie alone, liking the feeling of total involvement in the story without having to think of anyone around him. He was still living on his savings, and whatever he made from the jobs he did for Johnny Apples. Which wasn't much, yet. But Harry had plans. He intended to work himself into the rackets until he was a big shot like Zucco, and all the men feared him and all the women respected him. It was, he suspected, an ambitious plan. But he had plenty of time. He liked facts, and the fact was that he had been sent by Johnny Apples to make the drug buy with Frank Farrano. That meant something; that meant he was being noticed. Elated, he mulled over the thought each day. That he was on his way seemed evident by the whole Cloud

Nine episode, and by what was still to come, according to Farrano. Harry believed himself ready for anything. Every day he practiced his best scowl and grimace before the mirror.

One afternoon in a local bar that catered to a gambling crowd he saw Charley Flowers. In a corner booth, his hands cupping a beer mug, Flowers sat alone, staring morosely into the beer. Harry walked over.

"Hey, how's it going?"

Flowers looked up. "No complaints. You?"

" 'Bout the same."

"Come here much?"

"Few times. I moved up from Hoboken."

Flowers groaned. "From bad to worse, eh?"

"I like it better. More room to move around."

"Yeah, I know what you mean." He drank the rest of his beer. "Want some of this piss?"

"Might as well. Here, I'll get them."

"Long's you up."

Harry brought the beers back and sat across from Flowers in the hard wood booth.

"I heard you working for Apples," Flowers said.

"You heard right."

"He's OK but you got to watch yourself around him."

"How's that?"

"He'll dump you if he has to. Won't think nothing of it either."

"Don't everybody do that?"

"Yeah," said Flowers slowly, "you right about that. Only he'll do it a little quicker than most."

"I'll watch it."

"You do that."

"What about you?"

"I been a little busy."

"Too bad about Hymie Cole."

"That and other things." Flowers took a pull on his beer, thinking of the Yacavelli job and getting rid of Ginger. That was the best part, and he got away with it too. Pete Montana didn't say a word about how he handled it, not that the guy wouldn't have died anyway. Now if he could only get Zucco to use him regular so he could get away from that crummy bastard Al Parry.

"Looks like maybe we gonna make out OK."

"Huh?"

"I said we gonna do OK, me and you."

"Yeah, sure. Why not?" Flowers looked around and saw Art Hammis coming into the bar. "Hey, Art! Over here. Here in the corner. C'mon over."

Harry drained his glass. "Got to go."

"Stay and have a drink, for chrissake. What's the hurry?"

"No hurry. Just I got things to do."

"C'mon, one drink. That's Art Hammis."

"So it's Hammis. So what?"

"He's one of Zucco's own boys. You know him?"

"I met him."

"A good man." Flowers leaned across the table. "Sometimes he works for Zucco himself."

"Big deal. That don't mean I got to like him." He got up.

"One more drink. C'mon."

"No more. I'll see you around."

Harry passed Art Hammis on the way out. The two men nodded but did not speak.

Going home, annoyed at the whole idea of meeting Flowers and then Art Hammis, Harry stopped in another bar for a few quiet drinks. He liked Charley Flowers. It was Flowers who'd given him the idea of getting into the rackets that first time they met on the Spina job, who'd told him to go see Joe Zucco. Poor Hymie Cole had been in on that too. Thinking of Hymie, Harry wondered when Zucco would strike back at Alexis Machine. It was common knowledge on the street that Machine had ordered the killing to shake up Zucco.

That night Harry dreamed he was being chased by a man with a gun. The gun was as big as a tank, he didn't understand how the man could hold it. The more he ran, the closer drew his pursuer. He was in an old school building, running through the halls and up and down the stairs. All the doors were locked, he couldn't get out. The doors to the classrooms were locked too. He could see people inside but they paid no attention to his frantic banging. Somebody else was running in the halls. He didn't know who it was, he couldn't see his pursuer's face. Whenever he looked back, all he could see was the monstrous gun. As he turned a corner something struck him. Knives were being stuck into him. They were coming out of the walls of the narrowing corridor. Somebody screamed.

"Harry, wake up."

"Huh?"

"Wake up."

"What is it?"

"You screamed. In your sleep."

"So what?"

"You woke me up."

"So I had a nightmare. Go on back to sleep."

"What you scream for?"

"How do I know? I was asleep."

"Don't you remember?"

"No, and I don't want to. Now go on back to sleep."

"Who's Charley Flowers?"

"Did I say that?"

"And somebody called Hams or something."

"Forget it."

"Who are they?"

"Just some guys I know."

"Why are you afraid of them?"

"I ain't afraid of them. I ain't afraid of nobody."

"Then why'd you scream?"

"I don't know, Colie. I really don't know." He sat up, looked at his watch on the table. "Christ, it ain't even four yet."

"Must be something bad to make you scream like that."

"I suppose so."

"But you got no idea what it was?"

"I get a lot of nightmares. It don't mean nothing."

"Somebody was trying to kill you, wasn't that it?"

"How you know that?"

Colie shrugged, stuck a wisp of hair in her mouth.

"No, c'mon now. How you know that?" he demanded.

"Somebody once tried to kill me. I screamed just like you."

"When was this?"

"Three years ago in L.A. A man come after me with a gun. I ran and ran, it felt like a hundred miles."

"Why was he after you?"

"He said I took something that belonged to him."

"Did you?"

"No, just that I didn't go to bed with him. He didn't like that. When he caught me, he put the gun to my head. I screamed bloody murder."

"What happened?"

"Nothing. He pulled the trigger and nothing happened. There were no bullets in the gun. He laughed, said he just wanted to teach me a lesson I wouldn't forget."

"I hate wise guys like that."

"He didn't get away with it. In the morning, after he done everything he wanted with me and he was asleep, I went out and got some molasses and lye and mixed them up and covered him with it. Head to foot. Then I left for good. They didn't need no coffin to bury him in."

Harry looked at Colie with hooded eyes. She was wearing just panties. Her incredibly smooth slim body, fully ripened into womanhood, still had a childlike quality about it. In the moonlight she appeared inescapably innocent.

"You done *that?*"

"Served him right, didn't it? I mean, he could've killed me from a heart attack even without the bullets. I was just a little smarter than him and did a better job, that's all. Besides, for what he done to me that night I could've killed him twice. I still got the burn from where he spilled hot oil in me. You can bet I'm always going to be a little smarter than them."

"Who?"

"Anybody who's out to get me. Get them first, get them before they get you. That's the only way."

"Hey, I ain't out to get you."

Laughing, she put her arm around his neck. "I know that, silly. But somebody's always out to get you, me, everybody. The thing is you don't know when they're coming for you. So you always have to be ready, always a step ahead, or else you end up screaming like in that dream you had before."

Back in bed Harry lay awake a long time, thinking of his dream and what Colie had said. He was still a little shaky. Could it mean anything? He didn't believe in dreams, of course. But still, you never knew. But who would be after him with a gun? Not Charley Flowers or Art Hammis, they all were on the same side. It just didn't make sense. Just a crazy dream was all it was.

Slowly his thoughts drifted away, his legs jiggled, his hands loosened. Softly came the darkness stealing behind the eyes, sealing off the consciousness until all that remained of him was the slender breath of life.

19

HER NAME WAS CANDY PAGAN. She was second-generation Spanish-American, obviously virginal, and very beautiful. With a touch of makeup in the right places, she was eighteen. Except she was really only fourteen. Fourteen years and five months, to be exact. Unbeknownst to her parents, she was no longer virginal either, having been seduced some seven months earlier by one of her uncles. She had found the experience not wholly unrewarding, and became his mistress for several months until he was sent to jail for cashing stolen checks. She spoke excellent English, had a pleasant personality, and intuitively knew more about men than she had a right to know at such a tender age. Her self-assurance was monumental, her ambition unlimited, her hunger obvious. All in all, a normal, average, healthy, unspoiled, sweet, innocent youngster.

Standing now before Joe Zucco's large unadorned desk in her makeup, fantail shirt, and red flare jeans, Candy Pagan looked like a winner. Zucco had asked Moe Davis for a beautiful fourteen-year-old virgin who looked eighteen, who was capable of acting out a bedroom scene a few times, and whose parents were poor but respectable, and willing to let their virgin daughter sleep with a man for money. Zucco felt that Davis had delivered the goods. There was only one thing wrong, maybe.

"Will he go for a spic?" Zucco asked, the heavy lines across his brow deepening into a frown. "Suppose he don't like them?"

"You got to be dead to not like this," said Moe Davis. He sat in the big leather chair next to the desk, his face alert as always when business was being negotiated.

"That's you and me. Who knows about these Jew merchants? They're all nuts."

Davis, being Jewish and a merchant of sorts, merely smiled. Business was business. "He likes little girls, right? That's what you told me. So how can he pass this one up?"

"Hmmm." Zucco had to admit Davis was right. It'd be hard to let a trick like that go by. If he didn't respect womanhood so much, he himself would be tempted to take her over to the apartment. "You checked her birth certificate?"

"She's fourteen," Davis said. "Believe me, Joe, everything's legitimate."

"Yeah? What about her cherry? You check that too?"

Both men laughed lasciviously.

"She give me her word on that," Davis roared, slapping the desk. "Said it'd cost too much to find out for sure."

"She already knows what she got down there," Zucco said.

Candy found both of them disgusting, especially the balding Jew. But she found money delightful and she intended to have much of it in her life. For just being with someone a few times she was going to get a thousand dollars. She couldn't comprehend such a figure, it was more than she had ever seen. Her parents would be getting something too. She didn't know how much, and she didn't care. They'd never give any of it to her anyway. With her thousand dollars she was going to buy nice clothes and a record player of her own, and she might even run away.

Wetting her lips slightly with the tip of her ruby red tongue, she smiled sweetly at the two men. She did indeed know what she had, and she was going to use it all her life to get whatever she wanted.

Zucco dismissed Candy with a final lecherous look and turned to Moe Davis to talk money. He had been forced to tell Davis part of his plan, without mentioning names, of course, because he wanted to make sure he got exactly what he needed. The first two girls Davis had sent him were sixteen and already amateur hookers. Impatient, he had no time for any further mistakes.

"How much the kid's parents want?"

Davis fidgeted in his seat. "It's gonna cost a little more than we said, Joe. These people are highly respectable, they never done nothing like this before. Only reason they go along is 'cause they got a sick kid that needs an operation. You know how it is. They're very proud."

"Sure, sure. They're proud and they got a kid needs an operation. Stop the shit. How much?"

"They want four."

Zucco knew that meant two thousand for Davis and two thousand for the parents.

"That include the kid?"

Davis shook his head sadly. "She gets a grand."

"So the hit is five G's."

"That's about it."

"Where do you come in?"

Davis smiled disarmingly. "I'm just happy to do you a favor, Joe. You know me. Always like to pay my debts."

"Long's you can make a buck on it, eh?"

"Aww, Joe. C'mon. I done what you asked."

"Yeah, sure you did, Moe. You done a good job. Much obliged. Next time you in Vegas, say hello to the boys for me."

"Always a pleasure. You need anyone else, just let me know."

On the way out Davis rubbed his hands together in nervous habit. An easy two grand, for doing nothing.

"Goddamn Jew merchant," Zucco muttered in his office.

Three days later eighteen-year-old Candy Pagan was in Leon Harris's office seeking an interview with a successful businessman for her college freshman newspaper. Harris, flattered, his lecher's eyes drinking her in, was most cooperative. The more she ooh'd and ahh'd at his increasingly exaggerated exploits, the more cooperative he became. When he invited her out for dinner that evening, after tactfully ascertaining her age, she timorously accepted. They dined at one of the city's best restaurants, wined at the Blue Guitar, and ended the evening at a fashionable Boulevard apartment house. Not surprisingly, Leon Harris lived there. He had been a perfect gentleman all evening, taking no chances on frightening his quarry. She had been a perfect lady, taking no chances either. Once in the apartment, Harris stepped up the campaign. In the first half-hour, between drinks and talk, he had kissed and fondled her several times. When he coyly suggested that they might become better acquainted, she demurely informed him that she was a virgin.

Harris couldn't believe it. An eighteen-year-old virgin. Yet she *looked* so sweet and innocent and virginal that he just had to believe it. He began to talk: soft, soothing, relaxed talk, though he was anything but relaxed. Sweat formed behind his eyes, his tongue was dry, his ears were exploding. He was the hunter stalking his prey, the mighty tiger moving in for the kill. When he had calmed her fears, assuaged her doubts, assured and reassured her of his great feeling for her as a splendid human being as well as a woman, he slowly, gently, delicately led, escorted, and followed her into the bedroom, surrounding her with surety and smoothness. His footwork was excellent. Still talking, billing, cooing, he removed her final objections and then, at bedside, removed her clothing piece by piece. His patience and determination were rewarded. Shorn of their magic bra, her ample breasts tumbled out into his waiting eyes. Torn to shreds by his animal desire yet somehow stubbornly remaining intact, her blue panties were deftly removed to reveal a virgin forest of untapped wealth. Excitedly he touched her nipples, ran down her tight, flat belly into her lush womanhood. He couldn't believe his hands. He felt like Noah after the flood, or at least Columbus at San Salvador. Or was it San Cristobal? His breath came quicker, his whole penis throbbed. Caressing her, he lured her onto the bed until, straining every vital muscle of his fifty-four years, she had him. Gently, gently to honor her virginity he slipped himself inside, sliding easily along the wetness of her approach; she, meanwhile, moaned and tossed in the manner of virgins, while guiding him expertly, her hands firmly on his back. Entering, he felt with his organ the delicious tightness and then—magic moment!—the release of stretched tissue as his penis plunged forward into an unexplored world, not noticing that she had her legs jackknifed and her whole midsection taut to produce the spasms of tightness. With desperate animality, neck to neck, his head down, hers up, his eyes closed, he jiggled his body to an orgasm of sorts, exploding in a final burst of energy, while she, eyes open, stared at the ceiling, moaning and tightening appropriately as she thought of one thousand dollars.

Afterward, while he lay on his stomach, catching his breath and returning to his age, oblivious to all, she gingerly pricked herself with a pin she had stuck in the folds of her abundant hair. She allowed a half-dozen drops of blood to collect on the green sheet, then stuck the wounded thumb in her mouth and the wounding pin back in her hair. She lay down beside him, one arm flung across his flaccid back.

Leon Harris had deflowered a virgin; the first one, though he would never admit it, of his life. It would always, he intuitively knew in those first ecstatic moments, be for him the ultimate trip.

Two nights later Harris and Candy Pagan again used the bed for their own separate purposes. The bloodstained green sheet had been tactfully removed from the bed, though not yet washed. Harris was fighting a desire to have the one section framed, purely for personal reasons, of course.

Before the third love bout, which was planned as the main

event, Zucco called in a long-due favor from a maintenance man at the apartment house. He secured entrance to the Harris apartment, and installed a professional photographer to take pictures of the lovers. While Harris and Candy were grinding away on the bed, the photographer was grinding away from the rear fire escape through the open bedroom window. His zoom lens missed nothing. When the motion pictures were developed, the faces of Harris and Candy were as clear as the nature of what they were doing. If anyone wanted to press the matter, Leon Harris was up for statutory rape.

The next day Candy Pagan disappeared. She did not meet Harris at their usual place, nor did she live at the address given him. He called her college, only to discover that she was not registered as a student. He was mystified. Two days later he was shown the pictures and the mystery ended. The girl's real address and age were revealed to him, as was the fact of her parents' respectability. They would have him arrested as soon as they saw what he had done to their fourteen-year-old virgin daughter. Only money could save him. Twenty-five thousand dollars. He had just two days to get it.

Harris checked on the girl. She was fourteen, and her parents were poor but respectable. That she was a virgin, or had been, as he well knew, only made matters worse. The pictures doomed him. He went to Joe Zucco, who promised to get the same people to lend another twenty-five thousand on top of what Harris already owed. With the money he bought the pictures from the blackmailer and destroyed them; all, that is, but three which showed the girl in rather exciting positions. These he kept with the green sheet in a private safe.

The blackmailer, hand-picked by Zucco from out of town, kept half the money as his share. The other half he returned to Zucco before leaving town.

The net was tightening around Leon Harris. By the third week he was having trouble with his greatly increased payments. After five weeks he was way behind. During that fifth week he had an unexpected visit from Joe Zucco.

"You owe too much, Harris. My people are getting nervous."

Harris paled. "Money's tight now, you know how it is. But I'm good for it. They'll get their money."

"That's not the point. You made a deal. With the vig you're into them for over eighty-five thousand. They want it."

"But I haven't got it. They'll just have to wait for it."

Zucco sighed. "If it was me, I'd wait. I'm a businessman, I know about these things. But these friends of mine, they ain't businessmen. They don't like to wait. They want their money now."

"But I tell you I can't get it. I just don't have that kind of money."

"You own this place, don't you? Sell it."

"I can't sell it. This is all I have. It's worth over a half-million dollars." He chewed his lip. "No," he said firmly. "No, I won't sell it. I can't."

"Then give a piece of it to them."

"That's just as bad. I don't want any partners. No, no partners."

"Have it your way. Just remember, if you end up in the hospital or dead, it won't be worth nothing to you."

Harris, frightened, laughed nervously. "What will you do, kill me? Have me shot?"

Zucco looked startled. "Me? I'm just a businessman like you. I know nothing about that stuff. You asked me for a favor, right? You seemed a good guy so I done you a favor. That's all. I like to help somebody out when I can. People help me, I help them. That's all I know. You needed help and I come to you with a straight business proposition. Now you start waving guns at me. That ain't nice. What have I got to do with it? I'm just a businessman. I won't kill you." Zucco took a long, luxurious pull on his cigar. Smoke eddied about his head as he blew perfect rings upward. "But I know some people who will," he said softly.

The following week Zucco called in Charley Flowers.

"Charley, how's the boy? Al Parry tells me you doing great with the sharking."

"It's a living is all."

"Yeah, but living is you got to live, eh?" Zucco said, annoyed. "You got a beef with Al, or what?"

"No beef, just I ain't his big favorite."

"I give you a secret. Nobody is."

"Yeah, well, I kind of figured after the Newark thing maybe I'd get something special. You know."

Zucco smiled, a warm, engaging smile that hid the anger underneath. "You done real good on that," he said evenly. "The boys appreciate what you done. You know that, eh, Charley? You on the payroll, right?"

"Sure, Joe, sure," Flowers said hastily. "I ain't complaining. Just it's been a long time now, and I was hoping to get back to a couple years ago. Doing, you know, special things regular-like."

"Maybe you will, Charley. Sure, you're a good boy, right?" Zucco didn't like to be held up like this, and he didn't like any talk about jobs already done and forgotten. It was bad business, especially from someone who was on the drunk just because his brother got burned. He decided to keep an eye on Flowers. "Tell you what. I got a job right now I want you to handle. I need somebody I can trust on this one."

For the next twenty minutes Flowers listened to Joe Zucco tell him about a middle-aged businessman and a fourteen-year-old virgin. He asked no questions. Whatever needed doing he would do, or so he felt. Disappointed at not being elevated in the organization in the weeks after the Yacavelli job, or at least gaining some status as a shooter again, Flowers hoped that this job might do something for him. It was still strong-arm stuff, but it was for big money and it was for Zucco himself.

"You'll work with Art Hammis, he knows the score. All you gonna do is lean on Harris, get it? You lean, he folds. Simple."

"What about the girl? Where's she come in?"

"She's out. She took her money and ran."

Flowers nodded. "All I wonder is where Davis found her."

"Where else? Her sister's a high hooker on the circuit, but nobody knows about her. She turned Moe onto the kid."

"For a good price, I bet."

"Don't matter. Soon he'll have a sister act that'll lay 'em in the aisles."

Joe Zucco had personally negotiated with Leon Harris. He had demanded payment and Harris had refused. He tried reason, he tried flattery and cajolery. Nothing worked. Now he would send his subordinates to Harris. They would convince him to pay up. Since he obviously didn't have the cash, he would be forced to sign an agreement giving Joe Zucco forty percent of the business. Which was exactly what Zucco wanted. As a partner he could bring in his own people and methods. In six months he would own the store.

The next morning Leon Harris was visited by two men. They walked into his office unannounced. To Harris both men looked hard, hard and very tough. One of them had a small paper bag in his huge paw. They didn't bother to introduce themselves.

"You owe us ninety grand and we want it. Now."

"We know you ain't got it, Harris. We gonna give you a break. Just sign a paper and you're clear."

"We want you to sign the paper," the first man said. "You know how these things go. You sign or you get in bad trouble." He turned to his partner. "Tell him. Tell him what happens if he don't sign."

"We'll cripple you just for a start," said the second man. "We'll hack your ears off and smear your eyes with acid. We'll cut your hands off and chop them in pieces and send them around to your relatives."

"We can get real nasty, you know what I mean, Harris?"

"We don't like being nasty. Then we get mad 'cause we don't like it so much."

"Hey, maybe he don't believe us. Maybe he thinks we kidding."

"No, he wouldn't think that. Would you, Harris? Would you think that?"

Leon Harris sat stiffly at his desk, his knees bent rigid, his hands stark still and flat on the desk, his eyes transfixed. He was terror-stricken.

"Would you, Harris?" asked the second man again.

He tried to answer but nothing came out. His mouth shook, his lips quivered. He gulped and cleared his throat. Still nothing.

"Maybe we better show him," said the first man softly. "He don't seem too interested."

"Yeah, maybe you right." From the paper bag in his hand, the second man took out a pint bottle filled with fresh blood. He held the bottle above the cluttered desk, and with a deft motion unscrewed the cap and slowly spilled the cow's blood all over the desk. Harris watched in absolute horror.

When the bottle was empty, the man ceremoniously stood it next to Harris' blood-splattered arm. On the other side of the desk his partner produced a sheaf of papers, which he carefully placed on a small utility table. "Sign the papers, Harris." He turned the chair sideways. "There are three sets. Sign them all." He put a pen in Harris' hand. "And don't get no blood on them."

"I'm gonna count to ten," said the other man, now behind Harris, "and if them papers ain't signed, I'm gonna start cutting."

"He means it, mister. Don't make no mistake."

Harris, pen in hand, lunged forward to reach the papers. He signed them mechanically, the long blade, held from behind, pressing into his throat. He had visions of his throat being split open like a ripe melon, blood gushing out in torrents, rich warm blood oozing down, carrying bits and pieces of flesh torn from his savaged body. His breath sobbed, his eyes burned.

"That's a good boy," Art Hammis said, putting the knife back in his pocket.

"Now you got a partner," said Charley Flowers, stuffing

the papers back in his jacket. "You can relax and take it easy. Maybe get yourself a little girl and have some fun."

Both men laughed on their way out.

That evening Joe Zucco was met at the door of his townhouse by a beautiful blonde who kissed him extravagantly. Inside, he was treated to warm hors d'ouevres and chilled wine. Later, at an excellent champagne dinner prepared by the mistress of the house, Zucco told Cindy of his great good luck.

"Remember that business deal I told you about? The clothing store I wanted to get?"

"Ummm."

"It come through finally. So now we're in clothing."

"But not furs."

"Not this time. Maybe the next one be furs."

"Anything I can use?"

"Not unless you change everything you got."

"And why should I? Look at all it's got me."

Sitting in the cavernous living room, Zucco and Cindy spent the evening at home, drinking and talking. At some point he told her of the store owner and the young virgin. They had a good laugh over it.

"Does he know it's you?"

"By now he does. It's a dummy corporation on paper but he should be able to guess what the score is."

"What'll he do about it?"

"Nothing he can do."

"You sure?"

"I'm sure."

"He must be an awfully scared little man."

"I guess so," said Zucco.

"It's a funny story."

They didn't talk for a while. Cindy fixed another pitcher of martinis.

"I wonder why she did it."

"Who?"

"The virgin."

"She done it for a thousand bucks. That's what they all do it for."

"I wouldn't do it for just a thousand dollars," Cindy said drunkenly. "I mean, just do it like that for the money."

"Yeah?" said Zucco, equally drunk. "You cost me a hell of a lot more."

"If a man can't afford to keep a good woman," Cindy said heatedly, "he doesn't deserve her. After all, we have only a few years to make it."

"Well," said Zucco, "you sure ain't making none of it tonight."

Upstairs, too drunk to care, they fell out of bed twice.

20

THE FOUR MEN huddled around the table in the small meeting room above the Court Tavern. Joe Zucco, his face florid, his manner brusque, sat at the head of the rectangular table. Johnny Apples and Al Parry, like two bookends, flanked him. Pete Montana sat opposite. Across the long hallway, Gino Agucci, his arms relaxed at his sides, stood easy guard at the head of the stairs. Zucco anticipated no further trouble from Alexis Machine for the moment, but he was taking no chances.

He turned his attention to Johnny Apples. "You had—what is it now?—six weeks to get the nigger in line. Right? And so far we got nothing to show for it."

"I seen him twice, Joe, but he won't budge. He's willing to pay a little protection but he won't sell any part of the club."

"Why's that, Johnny?" asked Pete Montana.

"He says he don't want no part of the rackets. Once he pieces off the club to partners he figures he'll lose it. Says he'd rather burn it down first."

Zucco banged the table. "I don't want no protection. What I want is that club."

"Yeah, Joe, but how? I threw guys in there a couple times

a week to break heads. I had them threaten everybody in sight. But he keeps holding on. He's a tough boy."

"Whatever you doing ain't been enough. You said he was on drugs. So what happened there?"

Apples shrugged. "He just shut down the gallery and sent the junkies out on their own. Who would figure him for that? I guess he don't use the stuff himself."

"You guess," Zucco sneered.

"How should I know? When I seen the place I naturally figured he was one of them. What else could it've been, the way the whole thing was set up like that?"

"A shooting gallery just for friends is what else it could've been," Zucco raged, "and that's just what it was. When he seen trouble, he blew it up and took the loss."

"What happened to the rest of the heroin?" Parry asked.

"We got rid of it," Zucco said after a pause.

"Around here?"

"We done it quiet," said Apples. "A couple schools and some hangouts. Taylor don't know nothing about it."

"I hope so," Montana whispered. "We don't want trouble with him."

Zucco smiled. "No trouble, Pete. Frank's own man set the deal up for a piece of the take. Frank'll never know."

"Animals, all of them."

"Maybe," said Johnny Apples, "but what a profit in them drugs. I never seen nothing like it."

"Don't get too greedy," warned Zucco. "Like I told you before, you get too greedy and people around you start sweating. That ain't healthy for nobody."

"I only meant I was surprised at the take. I'm not thinking nothing, Joe."

"That's a good boy. You better off when you don't think."

Apples, defeated, sat scowling.

"Taylor's got a strong organization, real tight," said Zucco. "Maybe someday I knock him over but right now I need him on my side. I got plans." He was silent for a moment, lost in thought.

"Anything we should know, Joe?" Montana gently prodded.

Zucco shook himself. "Very soon," he said softly. "Any time now."

"Whatever you say."

"Now what about the nigger? I want that took care of first thing."

"Sure, Joe," said Apples, "but how? We leaned on him all the way and nothing worked."

"Then he goes over."

Everybody looked blank. Nobody said a word.

"OK. The drugs didn't work, even though we made money on the deal. Then he gets leaned on, and that don't work. Now I hear he's talking to the county prosecuting attorney."

"What?"

"Yeah. This punk nigger's talking to some asshole friend of his in the county office. I got it straight from inside."

"Talking about what?" Apples was suddenly sweating.

"What you think, dummy? About how we trying to muscle in on a legitimate business. That's called extortion. You ever hear of it?" Zucco sneered.

"Just talk so far?" asked Montana.

"So far. But I don't like it. When a guy won't bend, you can break him sooner or later. But if he's gonna open his big mouth, that's something else."

"Any chance of getting the club still?"

"There's still ways. If the nigger goes over, I can maybe buy it out of receivership. Or maybe work with the new owners. There's always ways if you got the time and the people. I'll get it. The point now is the nigger's talking. Plus I can't let him get away with waving his ass at me. Word gets around, it don't do us no good."

"So he goes over."

"He goes over."

For a few moments each man sat quietly, locked in his own thoughts. Pete Montana wondered what plan Zucco had in mind that necessitated having Frank Taylor friendly. Al Parry sulked because Zucco didn't give him the clothing store, especially since one of his boys was used on the job. Johnny Apples, still worried that Zucco might somehow know about his idea of dealing in drugs with Frank Taylor, resolved to be more careful. Zucco was still much too strong for any challenge from him. His day would come.

Zucco broke the silence. "Who you got to do the job?" he asked, looking directly at Johnny Apples.

Apples didn't hesitate. "Farrano. He's been on it from the start." He was still angry with Farrano for showing him up on the drug buy.

"Frank's OK, he knows what he's doing. Who else you got?"

"That new kid, remember he done the job on Spina that time? What's his name? Strega. Harry Strega."

"I remember him. How's he doing?"

"Aah."

"Think he can handle it?"

"What's to know?"

"You tell me. I don't want no slip-ups. What about a third man?"

"We don't need it."

"I want it. Insurance, you know? Set it up and get it done. Soon. I want this out of the way."

"Sure, Joe, sure."

"I just got a thought, Johnny. You be the third man, see?"

"Me?"

"That's right. You. This way it's clean right down the line." And more insurance, thought Zucco, in case Apples ever tries a double cross.

"Jesus, Joe. It's been a long time."

"What's a matter, you forget how it goes?"

"It ain't that."

"So what is it?"

"Just that in my position, maybe I shouldn't take them chances no more. That stuff's for the shooters and young punks. You know what I mean, don't you, Joe?"

"I know what you mean," Zucco said darkly, "and you know what I mean. This time I want you on the line, Johnny. You do this one for me, eh? For me?"

Apples sighed, unable to see any way out of it. "If that's what you want, Joe," he said regretfully.

"That's what I want." Zucco suddenly beamed. "Now let's talk about something going right for a change. Al, the take's been up these last couple months from the vig. Your boys are doing a good job."

Parry, always expecting the worst, merely nodded.

"But they could be doing even better. Anybody don't come up with their share, get rid of them. This is a tough business. People on the vig, they got to be pushed. Pushed and pushed some more. You and your boys are pushers, only you ain't pushing drugs. You pushing health. If they want to stay healthy, they keep up the payments."

For ten minutes Zucco and Al Parry discussed specific problems of the loanshark business. Then Parry was dismissed.

"You too, Johnny. Go 'head. You know what to do, eh?"

"I know what to do."

"Do it."

Left alone with Pete Montana, Zucco's manner changed abruptly. He relaxed, his eyes widened, his voice mellowed. Even his features and his very angularity seemed to soften. He stood up, stretched, walked across the room, came back, and sat down.

"We got problems," he said at length.

Montana remained silent.

"First off, Apples is getting restless. He seen the money in drugs, now he can't see nothing else. But he's a good man. I'm gonna move him around maybe."

"What about Al?"

"He's OK, he don't have that much imagination."

"Anything else?"

"We got to go more legit. It's one thing to have the rackets as your base but the dough's got to go into legitimate businesses. The lone wolf days are over, there's no more wild dogs burying their loot. That's why I'm trying to get into as many things as I can. I see it in two types. One is entertainment, like the nightclubs and bars. The other's services: gas stations and clothing and whatever else we can get. When Hymie ran them, he didn't do a goddamn thing. The problem is, all this legal work is too much. I don't know from legit business." He puffed on his cigar. "So I'm bringing my son-in-law into the organization."

"Which one?"

"My youngest daughter, Susan. Her husband's a lawyer. And he knows all about business, too. Got a business degree. He's gonna make all the service companies into one of them combines. He'll set the thing up with the legal stuff and the tax and like that. It's kind of an umbrella thing is how he explained it. Then at least some of the racket money got an easy outlet. And he can even make money deals in other countries."

"He gonna know everything we do, or what?"

Zucco frowned. "No way. He's strictly legit. He only knows about a company after we get it. And he handles only the service stuff, he got nothing to do with the clubs or anything like that. All he got to do is see them companies make money."

"When's he coming in?"

"A couple months at least." Zucco looked hard at Montana. "By then I want a lot of things changed around here."

For the next hour Joe Zucco told his long-time associate about the plans he had in mind. By the end of the meeting, Pete Montana had no doubts that his friend and mentor was still a man of brilliance and iron-willed determination.

That evening Frank Farrano, who lived with his mother, received an urgent call from Johnny Apples. They were to meet immediately in a downtown restaurant. It was raining and

Farrano's aged mother, who couldn't really understand why her executive son had to attend to business at night and in the rain, made him wear rubbers and carry an umbrella. His protests were of no avail. An hour later the two men were seated in a back booth at the Capri, plotting the execution of nightclub owner Philip Green.

The next morning Harry Strega was awakened by Colie Rogers.

"Harry, wake up. There's a call for you."

"Lemme alone."

"Wake up. He says it's important."

"Go way. Lemme sleep."

"His name's Farrano. He says he has to talk to you now."

Harry muttered under his breath, rolled over, and yawned a few times. Slowly he got out of bed. Legs first, then the back up, then standing. Looking like a scarecrow, with his tousled head and bleary eyes, Harry stood indecisively for a moment while Colie laughed.

"Throw me a bathrobe, goddamn."

Finding his slippers, dressed in the robe, Harry yawned his way over to the phone. "Yeah, Frank?"

"Got a job for you, kid. A big one."

"What the hell time is it?"

"Ten-thirty. Why?"

"Christ."

Farrano laughed. "Go to bed earlier, why don't you?"

"I did go to bed early."

"You gonna wear it out the way you going."

"Fat chance of that. Hey, can't this wait?"

"No."

Something in Farrano's voice shook Harry awake. "OK. Where?"

"I'll come over to your place. About a half-hour. Get rid of the broad for a while."

"She'll be out."

The phone clicked and Harry, putting down the receiver,

had a feeling that something important was about to happen to him.

When Farrano appeared, he didn't waste any words. "I seen Apples last night. Zucco wants the nigger to go over."

"Over?"

"That's what he says. The nigger's dead. His luck run out."

"Who's gonna do the job?"

"Me and you."

Harry, in sport shirt and jeans, still barefoot, sat in the chair and stared at Farrano. "Christ," he said softly, "I never done nothing like that. Just breaking heads and shit."

"You killed in that war, didn't you tell me that?"

"Sure, but that was different."

Farrano snorted. "Nothing's different. This is war too. What the hell you think it is?"

"I don't know. I never thought about it."

"Too late now. You wanted in, you got in. You ain't scared, are you?"

"I ain't scared of nothing. You just took me by surprise, that's all."

"Sure, sure," Farrano said quickly. "I know how it is. I felt the same way my first time out. But you got nothing to worry about, just think of him like he was one of them gooks you was killing over there. He's just a nigger anyway. Nobody's gonna care that a nigger got it."

"You and me?" Harry asked in a daze.

"And Apples."

"Apples? Why him?"

"I don't know why. Just he says he gonna be there. Maybe he don't trust us." Farrano sat in thought for a moment. "Or maybe Zucco don't trust him no more."

"What do you mean?"

"I don't know what I mean. He's gonna be there, that's all I know."

"When?"

Farrano hesitated. The kid was scared. Was Apples wrong in putting him on the job? Maybe he'd blow the whole thing. If he did, Zucco would blame Apples, and Apples would blame him. Maybe it was just nerves, the kid's first time out. Farrano thought back to his own first time. He was so nervous he didn't eat for two days before. On the job he pulled the trigger until the gun was empty and they had to drag him back to the waiting car. He never knew if any of his bullets even hit the victim, he was so nervous.

"When, Frank?"

Harry saw the hesitation in Farrano's eyes and he hated him for it. He was scared, sure. But now he was so mad he could kill the fat slob without thinking about it. Who did he think he was talking to? Some punk kid that never done nothing? He had killed more men than Farrano, the fat slob. He'd show him.

"It's set for tomorrow night," Farrano finally said. "Around the back of the place, where the nigger parks his car. He'll get a phone call just after closing that'll get him out of the joint. When he comes out, that's when we give it to him."

"Just like that?"

"Just like that."

Harry didn't eat for the rest of the day. Through the long afternoon he wandered aimlessly about the apartment, turning the TV on and off, picking up magazines and discarding them after reading a few words. By nightfall he was getting on his own nerves. When Colie asked him what was wrong, he screamed at her and walked out. The night air was cool on his skin. Not caring where he went, Harry walked the city's streets for hours: south, past Journal Square to Lincoln Park, east to City Hall and the river, northwest along the highways past gas stations and dismal diners. The city's outline was soft, steeped in shadowy moonglow. Houses shimmered before his eyes, streets weaved and undulated in rhythmic patterns, the passing cars glided noiselessly on rubberized roads. The lights of the metropolis were stars in a vast terrestrial firmament. Faceless people and disembodied spirits of unimaginable intensity accosted him, sought his attention, fought for it with noise or—intelligent beings!—with silence. All around him dogs barked, cats meowed, birds sang. Untired yet exhausted, Harry felt himself finally refreshed.

At midnight he went home. Between hurtful stares and halting words, he ate something and went to bed. In his dream he was standing by a tree, waiting to be executed by a firing squad. He awoke, sweating, just before the shots. In the absolute darkness of his uncertainty, he lay awake a long time before sleep rescued him.

He got up early, went across the street to the small park, was pleased to find it deserted in the graying light, and passed the morning hitting a red rubber ball against a stone wall. At noon he bought a sandwich and chocolate milk in a grocery store around the corner. Back in the park he decided he needed exercise, and so, for the second time in twenty-four hours, he walked to Lincoln Park, where he ran around the track, did pushups on the grass, and played softball the rest of the afternoon.

"I might be gone till morning," he told Colie that night.

"I'll be here." Her hair tied into two pigtails, her naked ears small and delicate, she was washing a dark stain out of blue panties. With an impatient groan she rubbed the spot energetically and rinsed it under the faucet. Bending over the kitchen sink, she seemed to Harry alarmingly like the typical housewife. Yet there was a smell of danger about her, a sense of animal excitement that attracted him. Her wide almond eyes and sensuous mouth spoke of cunning and lust and the primitive emotions.

"There's something I got to do. A job I'm gonna go on. Can't tell you more than that. Sometimes, you know, you do things maybe you don't like. Or maybe you just scared. Only it don't matter 'cause you got to do it anyway. Don't matter what you feel, the job's gonna get done."

While Colie smoothed out her panties over the back of a

kitchen chair, Harry went into the bedroom. He pulled down the shade and flooded the room with reflected light. The nondescript furniture was old and battered, contemporary Salvation Army. On the slab of mirror screwed to the closet door was the word "love," hand-lettered in red. The walls were filled with posters of animals and faraway places. From the ceiling hung odd little shapes of wood, some of them hollow, that made tinny noises when rustled. Other wood carvings rested atop the chest of drawers.

Taking his shoes off, Harry lay on the bed. "I ain't scared, don't get me wrong," he said when Colie came in and lay down next to him. "Nothing scares me, you know that. Just I have to get use to things. Like when I was in Nam, we'd be on patrol and I'd hear something in the brush and I'd go to fire away. But first time I seen somebody looking down my gun it took me a while before I fired. Just seconds, you know? But it seemed like forever. That's what I mean by you have to get use to things. It's the same here. People try to get what you got so they fight you. Or maybe you trying to get what they got. It's all the same. Everybody's fighting for something, to get it or hold it don't make no difference." Harry stopped. "Colie? You awake?" He felt her hand brush his arm. He didn't know if she understood what he was saying, he wasn't even sure he wanted her to understand. In the confusion of his mind, wanting only to sort things out, he babbled on. Sleep was out of the question, he had to meet Farrano at midnight. All that remained was time, and that was now the enemy. His hand touched hers. "Colie?" He squeezed it. "What you think?"

"About what?"

"What I was saying. Things that got to be done. You know?"

"How can I tell you what to do?"

"I don't mean that." He squeezed her hand again, gently. "I guess I'm just nervous."

"Whatever it is, you'll do it if you have to," she whispered. "You'll do what's right for you."

"Sure, sure I will."

"Want me to massage your back? Make you relax?"

"If you feel like it. Might help."

Harry rolled over. Her strong fingers on his shoulders made him think of the hostess in Saigon who had given him several rubdowns. Her hands were much the same: long thin fingers, bony knuckles, tight skin. She was a mother, working —so she said—to support her children and aged parents. But that was the story they all told. The only thing he really knew about her was that she had strong hands and a great body. And she enjoyed having her body used. Each time he had been with her she allowed him slight extra privileges which didn't appear on his bill as vitamins, the cover word for sex in the Saigon parlors. He had thought that very nice of her, and had always tipped her extravagantly. He liked Oriental women, their bodies seemed so much more supple and better conditioned for sex. Their sensuality was amazing, as he had discovered. Yet underneath ran a streak of cruelty, a taste for pain, that had shocked him. It was inexplicable, a force of nature perhaps, and something he could not comprehend. Now as he thought about the women of Saigon, he wondered if they really had been all that desirable. Or was it just a matter of time and place, and the excitement of the unknown? Harry turned over and put his hands on Colie, inching his fingers downward between her soft thighs.

"You got time?" she murmured. "You got that much time?"

"I'll make time." His hands were already wetting her.

"Umm. It may not be relaxing for you."

Her breathing, irregular now, excited him. He lost all thought of Oriental women, or anything else. "We'll see," he kept saying. "We'll see."

At 2:15 A.M. an inexpensive four-door Ford driven by one Petey Buttons pulled off Tonnelle Avenue onto the blacktop parking area of the Starlight Motel. It continued for about forty feet, then veered to the left around a long, low building before coming to a stop in back of the Cloud Nine club. Buttons switched off the lights. Next to him sat Johnny Apples, his beefy frame encased in an expensive Dacron tailor-made. In the back seat were Frank Farrano and Harry Strega. Nobody moved, nobody spoke. They had just fifteen minutes to wait.

Harry stealthily patted the revolver in his jacket pocket. It felt solid against his hip. He liked the feel. Farrano and Apples were also carrying revolvers. The guns, all .38-caliber police specials, had been stolen off a local pier months before, and were now untraceable. After the job, they would be returned to a gun drop, one of several Zucco used, until needed again. Members of the organization normally did not carry guns.

At two-twenty-five someone coughed.

"Keep the motor going when we out there," Johnny Apples blurted out. "I don't want nothing to go wrong."

Farrano thought Apples was acting very nervous. Petey Buttons was a good wheel man, one of the best around. He didn't need anyone telling him how to do his job.

Harry also thought Apples a little edgy. Either that or angry about something. Maybe it was just that a big shot like him had no business doing shooter work. Must be Zucco made him, for some reason. That was Farrano's idea, that Zucco made him do it to keep him in line.

Petey Buttons didn't answer Apples. He just kept on chewing his gum.

Two miles away a man picked up the phone and dialed the Cloud Nine club, humming as he waited.

"Hello? Lemme speak to Phil. This is Artie."

A moment later he heard a voice.

"Phil? Artie. Listen, I got Gloria over here. She's going nuts. Wants to knock herself off, says she can't stand it on the junk no more. You better get over here fast. What? Yeah, I'll hold her but get going. Yeah. OK."

Artie Baron, one of Phil Green's closest business associates and friends, hung up the phone. He had been well paid for that one call. And Green's death would benefit him, as well. A sound investment, he told himself as he opened the bedroom door and returned to the den. Gloria, in obvious good health of mind for a junkie, was fixing herself a drink. Her breasts, truly incredible in both shape and size for such a thin-waisted woman, reminded Baron of nothing he had ever seen before. He rubbed his hands in gleeful expectation.

Harry and Farrano and Johnny Apples were already out of the car. They waited near Green's new Cadillac hardtop, parked a short distance from the club's rear door. They stood abreast of one another, about four feet apart. Farrano was in the middle. Harry kept jiggling his left leg. His calves were shaking, his back was twitching. Sweat covered his hand. He swallowed and his ears popped. He blinked and his eye pulled. He was getting sick in his stomach and he knew it was just nerves but the hell of it was it didn't help to know it was just nerves, and if he ever got out of this he'd get himself a new stomach and to hell with the one he had now.

The rear door opened. In the darkness three men pulled guns. As Phil Green stepped out of the doorway into the night air, headed for his car, the guns opened on him. A dozen bullets splattered his body, tearing into the back, the head, the arms, the chest, ripping, gouging, crushing.

Harry stood calmly in the driveway firing at the figure in front of him. His nerves were steel, his hand was ice. He fired again and again, just a squeeze of the trigger each time. He felt nothing, thought nothing. His will was dissolved, his intellect erased. He was action itself, an extension of being, caught between time. A second was eternity, and all of eternity was the blink of an eye.

Harry Richard Strega stood calmly in the driveway firing at the torn body in front of him.

The shots suddenly ceased. In the darkness three men ran to a waiting car, its motor racing. In seconds it was whirling onto Tonnelle Avenue.

Harry held the gun in his hand. It was hot. He broke it open to check the cylinders. The gun was empty.

"Good work," said Farrano.

"We done real good tonight," said Johnny Apples.

With Petey Buttons driving in silence, the three men quietly relaxed their way home. Inside, Harry pulled Colie out of bed and they took a bath together in her porcelained tub, laughing and splashing each other.

21

CHARLEY FLOWERS stayed sober for three days after his mother was buried. Then he went out and got drunk for a week. It wasn't her death that bothered him so much as the fact that he was now alone. Father, mother, brother, all were gone. By the third day after her burial, his feelings of guilt and self-pity had become so acute that alcohol seemed the only answer. In his drunken stupor Flowers saw, or thought he saw, why he had been chosen to be the only survivor. He was the youngest. It was as simple as that. The race had to continue and the old had to die to make room for the young. That was the rule of life. That was the way it always had been and always would be. He felt so good about the rule of life that he had another drink. He was still young and so he would rise to the top of the organization, he just knew it. The old had to die out, Zucco had to die out. But the young survived. Suddenly he saw the way it had to be. He, Charles Francis Flowers, would become the number one man in the company. It was in the bag, just a matter of time. He quickly looked around to make sure no one was watching his thoughts.

"I'm gonna be a big shot," he mumbled into his empty glass. And banged it on the bar.

No one paid any attention to him.

"The biggest shot of all," he shouted at the figure in the mirror behind the bar.

No one looked his way.

"I'm taking over this town," he screamed at the screaming face in the mirror. "Zucco goes."

Four men moved down the end of the bar. Two others left. The bartender told him to go somewhere.

He told the bartender where to go.

In the men's room he missed the urinal and sprayed a stranger standing next to him.

"Watch your piss, mac," said the stranger. "Don't piss on me."

"I'll piss on anybody I want," growled Flowers. He was mad at everybody. Here he was alone in the world and about to become a big shot and nobody cared. It was enough to make a man drink.

"Not on me you don't," shouted the stranger. He turned half-left and squirted onto Flowers' pants and shoes. "Piss on you."

The two drunks stood there in purple rage, immobilized by their emptying bladders. Both tightened their muscles, strained their organs, forced, sweated, and grunted.

Flowers lost. In frantic haste, his movements blurred by liquor, he got his penis caught in the zipper. He yelped in pain just as the stranger hit him right in the mouth. He fell back, still holding his wound. While the stranger waited in common decency for him to finish dressing, Flowers disengaged the zipper and cautiously repaired himself. He then lunged at the stranger, sending him sprawling backward. Bobbing and weaving, the two drunks staggered around the small bathroom. Arms flailed, fists flew, curses rent the air. Then the door opened. "Excuse me," someone said politely and stepped past the startled men into the nearest stall. A moment later the door flew open again and the room was suddenly crowded.

"You wanna step outside?" muttered Flowers. "I don't fight in no shit-house."

"Neither do I," replied the stranger. "You first."

They walked outside into the bar.

"I been here before," murmured Flowers.

"I ain't," said his companion.

The sudden smell of whiskey dulled their anger and they decided to get one drink first.

"Long's we here anyway."

"Might as well."

"Can't do no harm, right?"

"Right."

An hour and a half-dozen drinks later they decided not to fight in their present condition.

"I'm too mean when I'm sober like this," Flowers said, his arm in friendly fashion around the stranger's neck.

"Me too," said his friend.

"I don't want to hurt you."

"Same here."

"If I ever hit you now, you'd be crippled."

"You'd be dead."

"I'm just gonna forget what you done."

The stranger looked at him. "What I do?"

"I forgot."

"No, tell me," insisted the stranger. "I wanna know."

"I already told you I forgot."

"Don't gimme that shit. If I done something, tell me what it was or else shut up about it."

"Who you telling to shut up?"

"You. Just shut up."

"Why, you dumb greaser," roared Flowers, "I'll break your scrawny head open."

"I'll split your empty skull," screamed the stranger. "That's what I'll do for you."

Squaring off, they left the support of the bar and quickly stumbled to the floor. Squatting there in a heap, they shook their heads in imagined hurt.

"You sure got fast hands," said Flowers. "I didn't even see that one."

"You pretty fast yourself," said the stranger. " 'Specially that right."

"I think you guys had enough," said the bartender, hauling them up. "Time to take a walk."

"Plenty of other bars," somebody mumbled.

"Bet your ass."

On the way out the door they staggered into a half-dozen people.

" 'Scuse me," said Flowers to an empty table.

Someone pointed to his pants. "Your fly's open."

" 'S all right," he said carelessly, "I wouldn't drink in a place that'd serve me anyway."

On the seventh day of his monumental drunk he rested.

In the afternoon he was visited by Al Parry. Awakened by a pounding on the door, not wanting to answer but unable to stand the frightful noise, he bellowed in desperation from the bed.

The pounding continued.

Maddened now, his head a reverberatory chamber, Flowers threatened to shoot through the door.

The pounding stopped.

Encouraged, Flowers withdrew his head from beneath the pillow. "Go'way," he shouted. "Nobody here." He held his breath.

A second later he heard the cold steely voice that told him he had lost.

"Open up."

There was nothing else he could do. He slipped into his pants and shoes and shuffled over to the door. Parry followed him back into the room.

"You ain't been on the job for a week, that's no good. People begin to wonder. They ask questions."

"I been sick."

"Everybody's sick. That don't mean nothing."

"My mother died."

"So your mother died. Everybody got a mother."

"We were very close."

"That's your problem. My problem is last week's collections ain't been made on your book yet."

"I'll do it first thing tomorrow."

"You'll do it first thing today."

"Al, I can't. I'm too shaky right now, you know what I mean? By tomorrow I be fine."

Parry looked at Flowers scornfully. He stuffed himself into an easy chair. "By tomorrow you could be dead. You know what *I* mean?"

"I do my job," Flowers said defensively.

"Listen to me, soldier. I don't like you, I never did. I don't think you can do a job to save your ass. But Joe wants you, so I'm stuck, but I ain't gonna be stuck long if you don't get it together."

"So I had a bad week."

"You had a bad life. All I care about is the collections."

"I got them in always up to last week, didn't I?"

"Now get them in for this week."

"I'll get them, OK?"

"When?"

"Today, ain't that what you said? Today and tomorrow. You'll have them by next day."

"I hope so for your sake. Now what about new money?"

"What about it?"

"Joe says we can do better."

"Christ, I got everybody on the book now."

"He says we should get more."

"I don't know from where."

"He don't care from where. Just so's we do it."

"I'll see what I can do."

"I'm telling all the boys the same thing. We gonna open it up, spread it around more."

"That'll increase the risks."

"So what? That's why we got muscle like you around."

Flowers wasn't sure how much Parry knew about the

Yacavelli job since Zucco never told anyone more than was necessary. He wanted to let Parry know that he was a shooter again, and not just some more cheap muscle. He wanted to tell Parry that he was doing the loansharking only until Zucco came across with the big spot for him, which would be soon. He wanted Parry to know that he had been chosen by Zucco himself to work on the clothing store deal, a really big money job. All this he longed to shove down Parry's throat, but he decided he couldn't take the chance. He said nothing.

"Ain't that right, soldier?"

"Ain't what right?"

"We got muscle like you to handle the heavy stuff." Parry laughed sarcastically. "All that dime-a-dozen shit, you really good at that. Like with Scottini. Eh?"

"I ran into some bad luck on that one," Flowers said softly. "Besides, I lost my own brother."

"You keep losing people around you. Maybe you just careless. Could that be it?"

"Maybe."

"Or maybe," Parry said darkly, "you just don't know what you're doing." He got out of the easy chair.

Flowers, watching him, sat on the bed picking his nose.

"It's like this, soldier." Parry stood by the door. "I don't trust you, you're some kind of jinx. You screwed up some jobs of mine a couple years back. Then you screwed up the Scottini thing so bad you almost blew it for me. Now you lose Ginger on that Newark job. Think I didn't know about that? Ginger was one of my men, remember?"

"He got hit. I couldn't do nothing else."

"Maybe," said Parry mysteriously. "But the point is this. Things seem to go wrong around you, so stay out of my way. Just do your job and don't make no more trouble for me. Or else you might have an accident. Them things happen, you know."

"I'll watch myself."

"You couldn't watch yourself in a mirror." Parry opened

the door. "You remember, just do your job and get them collections in." He turned around. "So long, killer," he said bitterly.

Flowers, unnerved, went back to bed. His head throbbed, his back ached, his muscles pulled, all his bones hurt. Coming down from a week's drunk was a very painful experience. He vowed never to do it again, at least not for a while. After all, he had nobody else to lose.

The next day he made his rounds. Encountering little trouble, he was able to increase loans for future collection by ten percent. After his initial surprise, consisting of a few mumbles and narrowed eyes, he concluded that money was extra tight in the straight world. That further whetted his desire to become the big boss he knew he would soon be. Not wanting to drink away his ambition, he buried it in tons of food. In one month he gained twelve pounds and had to buy a new belt. But at least, he reminded himself, he had cut out the heavy boozing.

In the weeks that followed, Flowers worked diligently and stayed out of Al Parry's way. The thought of what lay ahead for him drove his heart, warmed his blood, and filled his head. He marveled at his earlier complacency. Life without a goal now seemed almost suicidal to him. He felt so secure in his certitude of rising to the top that he began to daydream and fantasize about his future. His past life-style he regarded as hopelessly inadequate to his future needs.

He imagined himself once riding down the Boulevard in an impossibly long black limousine, his men following in other fancy cars. Motorcycle police preceded them, and men on sidewalks removed their hats as the silent procession slowly passed. He basked in the homage accorded him, and accepted it as fitting and proper. The musing pleased him and he thought of it often, until suddenly one day he noticed with horror that it too closely resembled a funeral procession. He resolved never to think of it again.

Each morning he read the newspaper, intent on learning about his near and distant surroundings, which heretofore he had regarded as of no serious consequence. He read about City

Hall and discovered that everybody was a crook. He read about the rest of the world and discovered that everybody was crazy. Soon he was sorry he had ever started reading the paper. His own way of life, he determined, seemed no different from anyone else's. Living was a hustle for everyone.

At night he would meet with people in bars or on the street, in small neighborhood stores and tiny fenceless parks. He spread himself thin, joined a few clubs, attended church-sponsored activities, participated in local political events. His desire to be known took him to some pretty strange places, but he handled all with the ease of a man destined for greatness. He wanted to be recognized in the community as a force, a power, a presence. Zucco was known by all, that's the way the big shots worked it. He, too, would be known. His ambition would drive him, his intelligence would direct. He noted with satisfaction that more people were smiling at him, talking with him, stopping him on the street. He beamed when they knew his name, little dreaming that many already knew him by a new nickname: Hungry Charley.

"Let's go to Hungry Charley's," someone would say jokingly. That meant to give all your money to the loanshark.

"That boy's going to be somebody, he is. God bless him."

"He's headed for big things."

"He got ambitions."

"He don't curse and he don't chase after women."

"He don't even smoke."

"He's hungry, that man."

"Hungry Charley."

To match his ambition and coming status, Flowers bought himself a half-dozen tight suits and an assortment of flowered shirts and turtleneck sweaters which he stuffed into the drawers of the painted dresser in his hotel room. The suits he hung in the narrow closet. To replace the missing doorknob he hammered a large nail into the closet door with an empty can. When he closed the door it broke off at the top hinge. Furious, he kicked the bottom hinge out and laid the door on the floor, then shoved it under the iron-sided bed. He was not ready to change hotels yet.

Eating well, sleeping well, Flowers went through the motions of routine, his eye on the future, a melody in his heart. He gave out money, at the usual rates; collected money, at the usual places. He had a word for nearly everybody. Many times it was no. But it was yes often enough for him to prosper in a small way. Best of all, All Parry didn't bother him. Though he longed for the big spot Zucco was assuredly grooming him for, he worked his side of the street and waited impatiently.

One evening toward the beginning of summer he attended a wake for a local stripper who had jumped or fallen out of a hotel window. Friday Knight, age twenty-six at her death, had been a stripper for four years and was known in most of the clubs from Baltimore to Chicago. Married twice, she was childless and penniless when she died. The wake, disguised as a benefit to raise the one thousand dollars in funeral costs, was held at the Flim Flam Club in the downtown section of the city. Friday Knight had been a local girl, born and raised on the South Side, and she was still remembered by some people in the area as a fresh young loner determined to make it big on her own.

When Flowers walked into the stark, dimly lit club, its shadowy interior glistening with ornate mirrors, a tall blond stripper was working the stage. Her costume folded into a napkin. Big-breasted, heavy-boned, her arms and legs fleshy, her abundant belly lined with stretch marks, she stood with a tassel on each breast, cupped tightly over the nipples, and slowly manipulated her torso so that the tassels were spinning in opposite directions, in defiance of all known physical laws.

At the table Flowers ate a steak sandwich drenched in fat. He drank watered whiskey out of plastic cups. After a dozen drinks he felt nothing, so he had another dozen. A chorus of near-nudes was simulating orgasm on the tiny stage. Spotlights bathed their bodies in harsh tones of whiteness, as if all color had been drained through the prism of the spot. At the edges of light, a luminescent haze, eerie and almost corporeal, flattened everything out.

Seated at one of the tables, Flowers drank cup after cup of fire water until he reached a comfortable level of incoherence. Acknowledging his presence at a wake forced him to think of his mother, whose memory he had successfully forgotten for many weeks. Now as he tried to remember her, his staggering mind ran into gaps and blind spots and covered corners. Undaunted, he turned all around to see if anyone looked like his poor mother. None of the strippers did, though one had his mother's eyes. Several of the older ladies at the table had a hair style or a palsied hand or a pair of glasses similar to his mother's. That made him angry. He didn't think it right that people should try to be like the dead. "Shouldn't be," he said to no one in particular. "It ain't right, ain't right," he repeated to himself until he forgot what it was that wasn't right. All around him was talk of city politics. As his head sank lower, he heard someone mention Barney Coyle who was once appointed the Director of County Weights and Measures even though Coyle admitted at the time that he had no idea how many ounces were in a pound.

Suddenly his seat shook. "Excuse me," a voice said somberly as his head snapped up.

"What's a matter?" he bellowed. "Can't a man hold a wake for his poor old mother no more?"

A few drinks later he left the Flim Flam Club, propelled by a sudden urge to visit his poor old mother. Sucking in the warm night air did nothing to dispel his internal fog. He started one way, stumbled back in a U-turn, continued a few steps and, with a wavering motion, unable to control his direction, staggered over to the curb. Hanging on to a parking meter he hailed a passing cab and told the driver to take him to the cemetery.

"What cemetery?"

"The cemetery my mother's in. What cemetery you think?"

"Which one?" asked the perplexed driver.

"She's only buried in one," Flowers shouted. "Just take me there. I need to see my mother."

The driver, needing another fare, decided to give it one more try. "How about Holy Name Cemetery?" he asked quietly.

"That's the one, that's the one she's in. Didn't I just tell you that?"

Twenty minutes later Flowers was awakened. They were parked at the cemetery's front gate. "Wait here for me," he ordered as he got out of the cab. "Right here. Don't move."

Weaving uncertainly, he trudged up the gravel path to the locked gate. After a few moments his shouts were stopped by the appearance of the elderly gatekeeper.

"What the hell you want here?"

"I wanna see my mother."

"We're closed now. Come back tomorrow."

"What you mean closed? My mother's in there."

"So what? She's dead, ain't she? She can wait till morning."

"Wanna see her now."

The gatekeeper shoo'd him away. "Go on home. You're drunk."

"I ain't drunk nothing all day."

"I told you we're closed now. It's 3 A.M. Come back tomorrow."

"I got to see her now."

"If you don't get away from here, I'll fetch the dogs on you. Now get."

"Open them gates, you old bastard."

"I'll open the gates," said the keeper excitedly. "I'll open the gates and let the dogs bury you next to your mother. How you like that, eh? Would you like that? Go on, you drunken bum. Get out of here before I lose my temper."

"I'll climb over these gates and ram your ass into the ground, you don't open up."

"You couldn't climb into bed, you bum. Now get away and let decent folk alone."

"You old bastard."

"Drunken bum."

Flowers watched the keeper disappear through the bushes. He hugged the gate a while, then walked unsteadily along the iron fence, his hand slapping each post. A short distance from the waiting cab he stopped and opened his fly. Kicking out a small hole next to the fence with the toe of his shoe, he urinated into the hole, chuckling to himself all the while. He had intended to urinate on his mother's grave, and this seemed to him to be the next best thing. Finished, he staggered back to the cab.

"Take me home," he mumbled to the worldly-wise cab-driver, who refused to be surprised by anything. Then Flowers promptly fell asleep again. Back in front of the Flim Flam Club he was awakened once more by the driver, who needed to know where he lived.

"Exchange Place Hotel," he murmured. "Where else?"

The question was left unanswered.

When he got up that afternoon, Flowers was shaken with remorse. He just couldn't understand his actions of the previous evening. His mother had been a wonderful mother, the greatest mother in the whole world. She had done her best for him and his brother, and had given them everything she could. It was his father who had been no good.

Now that it was too late, he saw that he could have been better to his mother. He didn't visit her enough, didn't take care of her enough. Maybe if he had been better to her, she wouldn't have died of starvation and dehydration all alone in her apartment, after suffering a stroke that made her unable to move or call for help.

He silently vowed to go to church sometime to make up for it.

That night he went out to celebrate his new prosperity and

returned near dawn full of good food and drink. He had a woman with him, and in the room, listening to her calculated animal noises, Charley Flowers wondered if he were indeed the only honest person left in the world.

THE WINDS DIED, black pitch streets turned soggy and stuck to shoes, garbage festered in sun-speckled slums spilling onto sidewalks bleached with fatigue. Summer lay at the throat of the city. When the heat-drenched rooftops and gutters flooded basements and seeped into walls of stone, Joe Zucco told Gino Agucci that the time had come. Zucco had waited impatiently through the spring of activity, a waiting he found difficult. Now the pace was slower, people with money were leaving the city and those who remained found their energies diverted to mere survival.

On a certain day of summer Zucco met with Pete Montana and gave him the OK for the first part of the plan. He was to use Art Hammis to knock over Alexis Machine's key numbers bank. It had been done before by Scottini on a small scale. This would be big, maybe a hundred thousand. Hammis was not known to Machine's men, so no one would be able to prove Zucco's complicity. But Machine, enraged, would know it was Zucco, and he would strike back. That would give Zucco the excuse he needed for the second part of his plan: to kill Alexis Machine and take over the city's gambling operation. How

Machine would retaliate after the robbery was unknown to Zucco, but he felt confident that he could weather it and carry out the plan. All he needed was some visible proof of Machine's move and he would be all set. Once the job was done, quickly and quietly, without any prolonged warfare, the syndicate would say nothing. And his would be the strongest organization in the city.

Hammis needed a partner. Gino Agucci suggested Harry Strega, the new kid. He had done all right so far. Zucco agreed. Montana was to inform Art Hammis and together they could fill in Strega. That was it.

Alone, Zucco relaxed. His simple plan would work. He had plotted and planned for too many years for anything to go wrong. All he needed now was to pick Machine's killers. Whoever they were, they would have to be expendable.

Two days later Harry Strega had visitors. The banging on the door woke him. Montana and Art Hammis, come to check him out.

"I like to sleep late," he said with a laugh. "My girl keeps me awake all night."

"Ain't she one of them whores?" said Hammis.

"Knock it off," Montana ordered. He smiled at Harry. "I want to talk to you about a special job I got in mind."

Montana pulled out a paper with some drawings on it. "This is a floor plan of an apartment that's a policy bank." He handed it to Harry. "Can you follow it?"

"Looks easy enough," Harry said after a moment. "Just a railroad flat, like a rooming house. I lived in plenty of them."

"Yeah, we know that," said Hammis. "That's why we come here, 'cause you such an expert."

"What about it, think you can take it?" Montana asked. "Alone?"

"Not alone. With Art here."

"No," said Harry, "I don't think we can do it. Don't look like it."

"Go on, I could take it myself."

"Shut up, Art," Montana said, "you talk too much." He motioned to Harry to sit down. "Here's how it is. The apartment's on the first floor. Four rooms. But all the big money's in only one room, the last one. There's a door leading into the room that's always closed, and another door to the hall. They keep that one locked."

"Any windows?"

"One. But it's barred."

"Where's it lead to?"

"An alleyway going around the corner."

"What about a rear door?"

"Bolted and locked."

"Then how can we do it?" Harry asked. "If we can't get in the room, what's the use?"

"Two of you can't get in," Montana said softly, "but one can."

"One?"

"That's right. All it takes is one man to pick up maybe a hundred grand."

"A hundred grand?" asked Harry.

"A hundred grand," said Art Hammis.

"And you're the one that's gonna do it," said Pete Montana. "A hundred thousand changes hands and everybody's happy. Everybody but Machine."

The plan was already worked out. Art Hammis would go through another building to the alleyway and get down to the window. It was summer, the window would be open. Meanwhile, Harry would walk into the building as if to go to an upper floor. He looked almost like a kid, and in jeans and a T-shirt he wouldn't be noticed. At a precise moment Hammis would shove a sawed-off shotgun through the bars of the open window and force the head bookkeeper to open the locked door to the hall. Harry, waiting there, would enter and scoop up the money. With the money in a shopping bag he'd leave through the same door, down the hall, and out to the street. A car would be waiting nearby. Hammis would keep everybody covered until Harry was out, then he'd cut through the alley and around the corner to another car. The whole thing would take only about three minutes. And that was the beauty of it. No one would know about the robbery until it was over and they were clear.

"Do everything right and you'll get a piece," said Montana.

"How much?" Harry asked.

"Ain't up to me," Montana said quickly. "But Joe's always looking for good men. He's got his eye on you."

"He has?"

"That's a fact."

"I was hoping to move up," said Harry.

"This is your big chance," the older man said warmly.

"I'll need a gun, won't I?"

"You'll need a gun," agreed Montana, "but just for emergency. Otherwise you won't even need to show it. Art, you take care of that."

"Sure. He's so dumb he'll shoot himself with it, that's how dumb he is." Art laughed as he spat the words out.

Harry wanted to rip into him. He licked his lips, thinking about it. Hammis hated him, he didn't know why. But the feeling was mutual. "Sounds OK," he said to Montana, "but do I have to work with him?"

"You think I wanna work with a punk kid like you?" Hammis snarled.

Pete Montana looked evenly at him. "You're too goddamn smart for your own good sometimes, Art. Now you just keep that big mouth shut. The two of you are gonna work this job."

There was nothing more to say.

Montana walked over to the door. "It'll be in the next couple days. Art'll let you know when." He gave Harry a warm, friendly smile. "We like to see young talent move up."

Hammis followed Montana out. At the door he turned around. "You should be glad working with a pro for a change, a punk like you."

When Colie returned home, Harry informed her that he was going to be working on an important job. There was, he hinted, a lot of money involved.

"Will you get some?" she wanted to know.

"Sure. What you think?"

"Is it dangerous?"

"I'm a dangerous man," he declared pompously, "so everything I do is dangerous."

"But can you get hurt?"

He shook his head in dismay at the naïveté of women. " 'Course I can get hurt. You think that bothers me? That's part of the job. Anybody goes to hurt me they just better watch out."

He wasn't sure that Colie fully appreciated him, or even understood him. Here he was moving up in the rackets, making a name for himself, and she wanted to know if he could be hurt. Why, he was already a shooter and not just some punk muscle man. He had been in on the Cloud Nine hit. He had paid his dues. If she couldn't see how exceptional he was, how unique, then maybe she didn't deserve him. On the other hand, she was just a girl. They couldn't be expected to know much.

For the next several days Harry walked around with an air of megalomania. He believed himself destined for big things. He had long had the feeling, so he reminded himself, that he was going to be a power in the rackets. Events were now beginning to prove him correct, he felt. The fact that he had been scared and nervous at Phil Green's execution meant nothing. It had been his first job as a shooter. But from it he had learned something important about himself. He was not afraid to kill. Nor did he particularly like it. In truth, he didn't seem to feel anything at all. It was just a job, exactly what it had been in Vietnam. He would not, of course, kill children or animals. But men who deserved to die or who stood in his way were just bodies to be pushed aside. It was a war and he was a soldier, looking out this time not for country but for himself. Out of it would come power and prestige and all the things big money could buy. He thought of Zucco, with all that money and all those women. He wanted to be like Zucco. Better, he wanted to *be* Zucco. No, by God, he would be even *bigger* than Zucco. It had to come. He was on his way.

The day finally arrived. The big money was waiting and the weather was warm. Art Hammis picked him up, they collected the guns and drove to the numbers bank. Petey Buttons was the wheel man. A second car with a driver was parked around the corner. Hammis went into an adjoining building, the shotgun in a bag. Harry waited five minutes, then walked into the building with the policy bank, a revolver in his pocket and a shopping bag under his arm. At exactly the right moment the locked door opened to the hall. He entered the room and filled the shopping bag with bills. In two minutes he was back on the street. No trouble, nobody hurt. A perfect job.

A half-hour later, Joe Zucco received a cryptic phone call. "Tomorrow's gonna be a good day," said Pete Montana. "How's that?"

"My big toe hurts," Montana said. "You can count on rain."

That evening Art Hammis left for Canada. The next day Harry Strega was told to go to Florida for a couple of weeks, all expenses paid. It was a vacation and he was expected to enjoy himself, nothing more. He would be told when to return.

Harry arrived in Key West at dusk, after a jet flight out of Newark to Miami and a prop shuttle the rest of the way. Colie was with him. They took a cab from the small airfield into town, Harry directing the driver to the address given him back in the city. It was a large two-story white frame house off Duval Street. Four filigreed columns across the front of the house supported the second-floor open porch. Curtains hung from all the windows, and in the front garden bloomed a dozen different flowers of intricate design. Tall willowy grass sprang suddenly beyond the white picket fence and in cracks of concrete reaching almost to the curb. In an airy upstairs corner room, with a windowed alcove and private bath, Harry would be lodged during his stay. All arrangements had been made.

Sluggish from the confinement of the planes, already feeling the pull of the southern sun, Harry and Colie briefly inspected the rooms before rushing out for drinks, leaving their luggage unpacked on the bed. Inside were bathing suits, a few pairs of jeans, some dresses and skirts, shoes, sweaters, and Harry's one suit. He would not, he had insisted, go anywhere unprepared. For what, he refused to say.

Duval Street, running north-south for about a mile, was noisily shaking off its daytime torpor as they strolled the narrow sidewalks. Bars were plentiful, as were checkered-tablecloth restaurants and diners of indeterminate origin. Young people of every sex in colorful rags promenaded the area. Sailors from the naval base lounged dreamily in Irish bars or listened politely to wild tales of incredible sex repeated endlessly. Blaring uninterrupted out of lower Duval, Cuban music mingled at some indefinite point with the slower native rhythms. In a small waterside hotel cocktail lounge at the end of the street, their eyes looking out over the blue-green sea, Harry and Colie sat drinking rum Cokes. The air, the sea, the very rustle of the waves, all was so very peaceful they found it hard to accept their whereabouts. Neither had ever been to Florida.

"That's the Gulf of Mexico out there," said Harry, pointing seaward.

"Out there?" Colie asked, distracted. "Is it big?"

"Big enough. The nearest land is maybe a hundred miles away."

"Where's that?"

"Cuba."

"Oh," she said, disappointed. She had thought he was going to say South America or maybe even China. "Harry?" She looked at him gazing out over the water.

"Umm."

"Why are we here? I mean, it's great and I love it. But why'd we come here so suddenly?"

"I already told you. The people I work for, they thought I needed a vacation. You know, lay in the sun and all that."

"Is it the job you told me about?"

"I done it already. Now I take a rest. That's the way it goes."

"You're not in any trouble, are you?"

"Trouble?" He put his empty glass down on the table and turned to her, exasperated. "Listen, little girl, I'm the one gives the trouble. You follow? I mean, I'm gonna move up and make all that money. Anybody gets in my way, bang, I squash 'em."

"You be careful, though. I'd hate to lose you now."

"Nobody loses me," he bragged. "I lose them."

Colie was quiet while he ordered another round.

"What about my job?" she asked when he finished. "I didn't even call them."

Harry smiled benignly. "You don't work there no more. I don't want you to."

"But the money?"

"Don't mean nothing. From now on I got enough for everything."

"You sure?"

Harry didn't answer. He wondered if she would be another Lucy Berg, always nagging him, never understanding anything he did. He hoped all women were not like that. But in his heart of hearts he believed he already knew.

After a long while they walked back up Duval, hand in hand, homeward bound, a box of fried chicken in her bag. They went to bed tired and got up tired, walked back to the tiny beach by the lounge, splashed each other with warm blue water, and spent the day lying on a pier in the Gulf of Mexico. For lunch they bought burgers and sodas from a pleasant old man in a shack on the beach. At night they walked Duval Street, stopping in different bars, meeting people, leaving people. It was for both of them a lazy, liquid existence, a respite from the world, and a time of youth.

"I hope this lasts forever," Harry said one day, wondering what was happening back in the city.

"Nothing lasts forever," said Colie as she put on her shawl. "You'll see."

THE MAN in the pork-pie hat was one of fourteen passengers who boarded the 9 A.M. eastbound flight out of Denver. He wore a black suit, tightfitting, short at the sleeves and waist. His shoes also were black, as were the socks. A brown suede shirt, cut Western-style with cinch tie and snap buttons, fit snugly across the chest. In his hand he carried a small blue canvas bag.

Midway down the coach section of the almost empty jet, he chose a window seat on the right. The pork-pie hat and blue canvas bag were placed carefully on the middle seat. Loosening his shoe laces, he stretched his long legs as best he could, settled his large frame into the soft upholstery, and closed his eyes. Flying was not his favorite pastime, nor was it something he actively disliked. As a quick way to get somewhere, or to get quickly away from somewhere, flying was dependable and he used it as such. The time spent on the plane itself was for dozing or for rehearsing future moves or examining past ones. In this instance he decided to let his mind wander to the point of sleep. He was already tired and he had a long day ahead of him.

He checked his watch. Nine-ten. With an involuntary sigh, Julian Gogordo closed his eyes and squirmed farther into the plush seat. Ten minutes late and not ready yet. How sloppy! He could never stand such sloppiness in his business.

At 9:25 A.M. Flight 419 left for New York. Silvered wings aglow in the Denver sun, the big jet taxied to the far runway and roared alive. In the tiny cockpit switches were set, levers pulled, dials turned as the graceful bird skimmed the surface and rose swiftly toward a cloudless sky, its plumage swirling behind in graying curls of pollution. Within a minute it was soaring eastward on waves of wind. Inside, at a window seat midway in coach, Julian Gogordo released his safety belt and swallowed to relieve the blockage in his ears. With fingers looped under his belt, his hands relaxed, he sought sleep amid the passing of the world beneath his shoeless feet.

Julian Gogordo was a gunman out of Cheyenne. At thirty-five, he had been in the rackets most of his life, first in Pittsburgh and then gradually drifting west in search of a dry climate for his diseased lungs. He had moved through St. Louis and Kansas City before settling on Cheyenne. There he opened several clubs and wormed his way into some choice business deals. He was affiliated with, but not officially a part of, John Spinoza's organization in Denver. He did occasional contract work for Spinoza, and his Cheyenne operation had the protection of the Denver combine's long reach. Known in the right circles as a close-mouthed loner, Gogordo's gun-for-hire was regarded as about as dependable as Spinoza's protective arm. It was a healthy relationship.

Over the phone he had simply been told to report quickly for a rush job. In Denver he was informed of the location and target. It was a loan-out: somebody who needed an out-of-town shooter had asked Denver for a favor, and Denver had picked him. The job was to be done in the next few days, with details supplied on location. He was to leave the following morning. He returned home that afternoon to attend to affairs and to prepare for his short business trip. Into the blue canvas bag he put an extra shirt, underwear and socks, a light raincoat, his shaving kit, and an electric alarm clock. That was all he needed.

The gun would be supplied at the site. Because of skyjacking and the subsequent electronic surveillance of passengers, guns were no longer delivered by couriers to major airports. Gogordo found this reasonable. He had never been arrested for possession of a gun.

At 4 A.M. on the day before his death, Julian Gogordo silently rode his black Mustang through the deserted Cheyenne streets. Of all the towns through which he had passed on his westward journey, Cheyenne impressed him the most. From the beginning he had felt strangely secure in its surroundings, as though he had been born to its open spaces rather than in a crowded Pittsburgh tenement. In six months his coughing stopped. By the end of the first year he was considered a successful businessman. After three years he was a leading citizen, a force in the community. He intended to keep it that way. Pulling into the small bus depot next to the old Union Pacific station, Gogordo doused the lights and got out of the car for a few moments. He stared into the darkness around him. This was his favorite spot in the old section of town; he often came late at night to stand by the famous rail line and revel in fantasies of frontier life in the wild West, when the Indians roamed the land, and later. He imagined himself in the West of a hundred years ago, with the cattlemen and sodbusters. He yearned for the days of Jack Wilson and the other Cheyenne gunfighters. That had been his time, and he felt somehow cheated that he had been born too late. He looked up at the star-infested sky. In Pittsburgh he had hardly ever seen stars, yet here the whole Wyoming sky was blazing out of control. He laughed nervously, after three years still not entirely convinced that it did not present a threat to him. He wondered how people could continue to live in Pittsburgh.

At 4:30 A.M. Julian Gogordo again mounted his Mustang and rode slowly out of Cheyenne for the last time. No one witnessed his departure, which was exactly what he had wanted.

From Cheyenne to Denver could be a two-hour drive

down U.S. 87, full of dips and rises but with few winding passes. Gogordo took his time, enjoying the empty roads and hilly landscape. With the tape deck playing favorite arias, he watched the dawn steal across the highway from his left. By seven-thirty he passed the outskirts of the city and stopped for a breakfast of bacon and eggs. At eight-fifteen he parked the Ford at the airport and settled himself in the departure lounge with a newspaper. His round-trip reservation, purchased under an assumed name, was in his pocket. The return date was open. He fought the nervousness within him, as he had done each time he was forced to leave his adopted home on a job. What caused those nervous spasms was not clear to him. He fingered the ticket, knowing he would soon be home again.

Over Ohio, Gogordo suddenly awakened. His mouth was dry, his lips parched. Recovering his shoes, he went to the toilet and relieved himself, then splashed water on his face. In the aisle he was met by a stewardess who asked if he wanted coffee and rolls. He accepted the offer of coffee and returned to his seat. For the next hour he stared out the window and tried to concentrate on the job ahead.

About his victims he had known little and cared less. Not even the faces mattered unless there were no spotters. Then he'd memorize a face quickly, without thinking about it. Over the years he had found that the best policy was not to get involved. He was sent somewhere by someone and ordered to do a specific act, but the reasons behind the order didn't concern him. He thought only about the mechanics of the job. The approach had to be investigated and verified. There were invariably only so many moments available to him to execute the order. The escape route had to be planned, with an alternate prepared for emergency use. Even with everything calculated to the finest degree, there was still the unexpected. That was his biggest worry. There was simply no way to prepare for the unexpected.

For his present job he had been told only that the man was in the rackets, the head of a local organization in some Jersey town. Gogordo had not been surprised. New Jersey's reputation as a mob paradise was known even beyond the East, and he had heard much about it in the old days in Pittsburgh. Nor did the fact that his intended victim was mob-connected bother him, he had handled that kind of assignment before. They died just as quickly and as surely as any civilian. Since it was always just a matter of business, there was never any question of personal revenge against him. He was merely carrying out orders, much as would any soldier. If he violated policy and someone needed him dead, he could expect the same treatment. But as a soldier on a job he was not responsible, except for the completion of his orders. That was a matter of survival, and he had survived now for many years.

Flight 419 from Denver arrived at Kennedy International Airport at 3 P.M. New York time. Among the last passengers to depart was the man in the pork-pie hat and black suit. In his hand he carried the small blue canvas bag.

To preserve anonymity, he boarded the Carey bus into the city and then took a cab across town to the Port Authority terminal. There he paused briefly to eat a quick steak at the downstairs grill and gaze into some of the indoor display windows. At a newsstand he bought a local paper, folded it under his arm to blend in more readily with the commuters, and rode the escalator upward. On the crowded second level he suddenly heard someone scream for help. Nearby, he saw two black youths running away from an old man down on his knees in front of a stone stairway. People rushed over amid cries of anger and shaking fingers. The youths were down the escalator and racing for a side exit, bowling over those in their way, before anyone on the lower level could react.

Julian Gogordo shook his head in disbelief. He had just witnessed a near-mugging, and he had been in town only a half-hour. The stories he had heard about New York were all true. Crime was out of hand and vicious young punks were taking over. He wondered how anyone could live with that kind of thing going on. Nobody was safe. What he had just seen had occurred in a crowded place. What was it like where there were no crowds? On darkened streets or in parks? Where were the police? What the hell were they doing about it? He just couldn't believe it. Why would people put up with such crimes? He and his business associates would know what to do, all right. New Yorkers, he decided, must be crazy.

The interstate Public Service express bus to Journal Square left the Port Authority terminal as soon as it was filled. Gogordo, relieved, was glad to rid himself of New York City. Too dangerous. He stared out the bus window all the way down the ramp and into the Lincoln Tunnel.

Twenty-five minutes later he stepped out, the last one, at Journal Square. Following directions, he walked to the Stanley Theater, then one block past it going east. When he got to the corner, a quiet residential area, he spotted the dark green Ford that had been parked for him on the street. Rented earlier in the day for his use, the keys had been left under the driver's seat. He got in and moments later was headed west, again following verbal instructions. At Tonnelle Avenue he turned north and quickly sped by a half-dozen communites. He soon entered Bergen County.

In twenty minutes he arrived at the Palisades Motel in Palisades Park. A room had been reserved for him, under an assumed name. Inside, he laid the extra shirt and alarm clock on the dresser, hung the raincoat on the closet door, and put his shaving kit in the bathroom. He then dialed the number given him in Denver. His voice on the phone was low and coldly impersonal. "This is Tuesday. I'm here for the view."

Leaving the door open, he went out to the car and drove a short distance to a main street, where he quickly found a liquor store. Returning with the bottle, he had two fast drinks while he shaved. Afterward he turned on the radio and eased himself into a chair facing the door, now locked. The whiskey sat within reach. His mind a million miles from home, he closed his eyes and waited.

First the knob was turned, slowly. The knock, when it came, was soft. When he unlocked the door, two young men, hard-faced, stared at him. They wore tailored suits and flow-ered shirts. Both were hatless.

"Tuesday?"

"Yeah."

They followed him inside without a word, their eyes pick-ing over the room carefully. Behind them entered a third man. He was tall, solidly built. His well-groomed shock of white hair gave his florid Mediterranean features an aristocratic cast. Without a trace of smile, he turned his colorless eyes on Julian Gogordo.

"I sent for you. I'm Alexis Machine."

24

JOE ZUCCO had just finished lunch with Julie K on this cloudy and dismal Wednesday afternoon. They had discussed business, told some jokes, relived the past, and generally enjoyed themselves as usual. Lin Fong, new owner of the Pagoda Gardens —having won it back from crazy Fred Riley in a sudden-death game of Chinese checkers—stood at the doorway and bade them good luck. Outside, they chatted a few moments as close friends do, while Gino Agucci went to fetch the car.

"Real lousy day," said Julie K, looking at the sky.

Zucco agreed.

"Good day to be home. Just where I'm going right now." Julie K buttoned his baggy jacket. "You gonna be home tonight? The country, I mean?"

Zucco smiled at his friend. Julie K was always so very discreet when it came to relationships with women other than wives, almost puritanical. He never mentioned any affairs of his own. For all anyone knew, he never saw a woman other than his wife, whom he obviously adored. He always referred to the Metuchen house, where Zucco officially lived with his invalid wife, as the country.

"You know I never go there on Wednesdays."

"That's right. I forgot, tonight's when you play cards with the boys," Julie K said sarcastically. "Ain't that it?"

Zucco laughed. "Play with something, anyway."

"Does she still live in your townhouse?"

"Cindy? Sure, why not? She takes care of the house and I take care of her, you better believe it."

"A beautiful woman." Julie K sighed. "And tonight you're gonna take care of her in the townhouse."

"Wrong again," Zucco said, frowning. "Tonight I got to break the schedule and go on home."

"So you will be going to the country," Julie K said quickly.

Zucco shook his head. "Nobody knows it but tomorrow's our twenty-fifth anniversary and I got a little surprise for the wife tonight."

"What is it?"

"One of them electric wheelchairs," said Zucco proudly. "Got everything on it but the kitchen sink. All custom-built, too. Cost me an arm and a leg for the goddamn thing."

"Why not give it to her tomorrow?"

"She's gonna see some people in the morning. If she uses it, she got to practice first."

Julie K looked up at the sky again. "Roads are gonna be bad. Get home early."

"Got some business first, but I should make it by ten."

Gino came around with the car. The two close friends parted as always, arms around each other's shoulders and a final fond handshake.

"I'll call you for lunch," Zucco said, getting into his car. "We'll make it real soon."

"You do that," said Julie K warmly. He peered into the window. "So long, Joe."

While people hurried along the streets to their secret destinations, and traffic waited impatiently at stoplights or moved slowly along crowded arteries, the sky suddenly brightened for a minute before the sun lost itself for good behind a solid bank of black clouds. Somewhere in the far distance thunder pealed ominously.

Heading north along the Boulevard toward home, Julie K dreaded entering his desolate house. He drove slowly, his heart heavy.

In a sumptuous three-story home on the Heights, Alexis Machine waited to hear from his men whether Joseph Zucco would die or live for another day. Either way he was a dead man. He had been pushing Machine for a long while. This time he had pushed too far. Sending punks like that Scottini to steal nickels and dimes was bad enough, but at least that kind of thing was easily handled. But knocking over the biggest policy bank in the city for a hundred grand was a personal insult, a slap in the face that went far beyond his killing of Hymie Cole. It was a message that could not be ignored.

The day after the robbery Machine contacted syndicate friends, but he received no encouragement. There was no definite proof that Zucco had ordered the job. Even if proof were available, the area was too dense for any jurisdictional dispute that could erupt into a local war. Such wars would not be tolerated, would be put down mercilessly. The syndicate, in effect, had disapproved of any action.

Machine understood that message as well. Either do nothing, or do something quickly and efficiently. Any prolonged conflict would mean failure. And failure meant destruction.

The logical course of action was to regain the money, perhaps in some similar robbery of Zucco's men. Kidnapping Zucco for the amount was a tempting idea but was quickly ruled out. For obvious reasons kidnapping of organization personnel had long been outlawed by the National Commission. Disobedience meant immediate death. Yet Machine's instincts told him that he must go all the way. If kidnapping was forbidden, assassination was not, provided it was successful and no further trouble ensued. Machine knew that Zucco would expect some robbery attempt. Without syndicate approval he would not anticipate an attempt on his life. Surprise would ensure success. Once done, Machine would be the strongest power in the city.

His decision final, Alexis Machine began his search for the assassin. He could not trust any Jersey shooters, or even any from the East Coast. It had to be someone unknown locally, someone who could slip in and out unnoticed. Two weeks after the robbery of his policy bank, Machine reached more than halfway across the country to Denver. John Spinoza, head of the Denver organization, was a distant relative by marriage. A trusted lieutenant was sent to see Spinoza. The man returned to report that Spinoza had agreed to help. Someone would arrive within a few days, Machine had only to prepare his way.

In a motel room in Palisades Park, Julian Gogordo waited to hear from Machine's men whether Zucco would be returning home that night. He had spent the previous evening, the evening of his arrival, being driven past the Zucco estate in Metuchen. That was the best spot for the job, much better than any place in the city. By the fourth pass he had seen enough. There were two possibilities: either at the street as Zucco's Cadillac slowed for the turn into the driveway or all the way inside the grounds, perhaps at the start of the circular drive where the cars were parked in front of the house. A walk along the edges of the property confirmed the wisdom of the second possibility. After the shooting, a short path through some bushes would bring Gogordo to the side street, where his wheel man would be waiting. The chances of being seen by passing cars would thus be eliminated. It was perfect.

He lay face downward on the bed, his long bony hands propped under his forehead. How many would this make? Twelve? Thirteen? He had lost track. After the first few times they all were the same. All of them needed to be dead; needed, at least, by someone. Different faces, different names, different towns, but all of them had one thing in common. They all were in the way. Whatever their sin—whether treachery or greed— they had to be destroyed. Treachery was unnatural and must be punished. Greed was natural and must be curbed. Unless, of course, the greed was on the part of the one ordering the kill. Then the victim was guilty of the third, and last, type of sin. He was still breathing.

Gogordo was glad he wasn't like any of them. He didn't covet unlimited power. He didn't double-cross anyone or stand in anyone's way. All he wanted was to be left alone. He was a professional: one who did a job for money, with no questions asked and no reasons given. He was a mechanic who fixed things without knowledge, a computer that was programmed without thought. None of which bothered him. As a professional, rather than a politician, he was no threat to anyone, and therefore safe. He performed a service that could be bought, and that all could use. His kind would always be around.

He poured himself some whiskey. If everything went right, this time tomorrow he would be home. Home and gone from this hellhole. He began coughing again. Cursing silently, he quickly reached for more whiskey. One day in this climate and his lung was already acting up. He couldn't believe it, but here he was coughing. He downed the burning liquor, shuddered as it passed his throat. Rising from the bed's edge he turned on the television and patiently watched a group of people facing a crisis. Apparently, someone couldn't bake a pie and six lives were being destroyed as a result. He sat there wondering how some people could live that kind of life.

No more than a mile away, a retired electrical engineer was putting the finishing touches on a custom-built electric wheelchair. It had two forward speeds and a reverse; it could turn halfway or completely around, all at the flick of a switch. The control console was built into the right arm. Equipped with a heating system, oversized tires, front and back lights, and a plexiglass bubble that protected the occupant from wind and rain, the motorized chair was usable just about anywhere. The backrest could be leveled, the foot section raised to form a bed. There was a fold-up writing table, and a reading stand and reading lamp. A radio and cassette tape deck were built into the left arm. The rechargeable nickel-cadmium batteries were at the lower rear of the chair, right behind the portable toilet facilities. The master craftsman had no doubts that the wheelchair was the only one of its kind in existence; he had built it from the ground up at the express order of a man for whom he had done other custom-built work. But that had been chiefly in cars, nothing so intricate and precise as this. Money, he had been told, was no object. He believed it. For such a man, money was merely a means to an end. What mattered was perfection. Patting the chair as if it had life, the elderly electrical engineer beamed within himself. It was a work of art, this creation of his, and it was finished on time. In a few hours Mr. Zucco would be here to look it over. He patted the chair again, like a proud and gleaming parent.

In his office atop the funeral parlor, Joe Zucco was not thinking of the chair he was shortly due to pick up for his invalid wife. Nor was he bothering with plans for his twenty-fifth wedding anniversary. What troubled him at the moment was Alexis Machine. Here it was two weeks since the robbery and Machine hadn't made a move. Nothing. No stickups, no beatings, no harassment. He didn't like it. Machine should have made some move against him by now. Something was wrong but he couldn't figure out what it was. He had sent men out all over town in an attempt to pick up some feelers about Machine's intentions. They had returned empty-handed. Nobody knew a thing. Two of Machine's runners had been picked up by the cops, a bookkeeper was fired for stealing, an errant topcoat was found shot to death, a Machine lieutenant disappeared for a few days but turned up in Las Vegas, another went into a hospital. A bunch of little things, but nothing that seemed to have any hidden meaning. All of Machine's key people were where they should be, and nobody new in town was seen talking to any of them.

The one thing Zucco knew for sure was that Machine had gone informally to the syndicate for backing, but had received none. Exactly as he had anticipated. Nobody wanted unnecessary trouble, at least not without some visible benefit. But no benefit for the syndicate was attached to Machine running the city's rackets, or for that matter, Zucco running them. And a gang war was eminently nonbeneficial.

A horrible thought crossed Zucco's mind. Suppose Machine had somehow learned of his intention, and so purposely took no action. What then? He had been told he could move against Machine only if Machine struck first. He had fixed it so Machine would appear to move first. Now the bastard refused to move at all. It was frustrating. He could, of course, go ahead without syndicate approval, but it would be taking a big risk. If anything went wrong he might be through. No, the risk was too great. He'd be patient and wait it out.

Gino came in to remind him of several business meetings, then the trip out to Fort Lee to get the wheelchair.

"Yeah, that I got to see."

"It's four-thirty now. We should be there by seven."

"The old guy's a genius, you know? What he done to the car that time ain't nothing to this chair he built. It's got everything in it."

"You think it'll work?"

"It better work," Zucco said ominously, reaching for his jacket. "The goddamn thing already cost me more than the car."

In his home Alexis Machine smiled broadly into the phone. "Good. Good. Then we go ahead. Yes, now."

He cradled the phone gently, a surprising feat for a man of his size and temperament. Still smiling, he fixed himself a drink. He had just been told by one of his men that Joe Zucco would be returning home that night at about ten o'clock.

In a motel room a few moments later, Julian Gogordo lifted the phone and heard from one of Machine's men that Joseph Zucco would be returning home that night at about ten o'clock. Gogordo would be picked up at eight-thirty.

He replaced the phone and went in to take a shower, glad that it had worked out for that evening. That meant he would soon be home.

On the way to the business appointments Gino Agucci told

Zucco that he had a funny feeling something was going to happen.

"Like what?" asked Zucco.

"I don't know. But I don't like the feeling I got."

Zucco settled back in the seat. "Don't worry about it," he said calmly. "Just keep your eyes open."

Gino intended to do just that.

At seven they were in Fort Lee. Zucco was delighted with the chair. He sat in it and tried all the gadgets, like a kid with a new toy.

By eight they were back in the city. Gino parked the car in the garage, the chair tied in the Cadillac's enormous trunk. With the trunk lid up, it just fit. They walked around the corner to the townhouse. Gino ate in the kitchen while Zucco spent an hour with his mistress, eating a delicious dinner and relaxing a bit in the bedroom upstairs.

At eight-thirty a black car pulled up in front of Room 19 of the luxurious Palisades Motel. Julian Gogordo got in. He was handed a .38-caliber revolver by the driver. He went back into the room, removed the five bullets, took the gun apart, oiled it with a small can he got from his shaving kit, felt the hammer, reassembled the parts, clicked the trigger several times, then loaded each cylinder carefully and returned to the waiting car, the gun now in his pocket. As they sped off, his coughing began again.

By nine o'clock Zucco was ready to leave. He kissed Cindy goodbye. She, peeved that he was not staying the night, merely brushed his face with her full lips. He and Gino walked back to the garage and headed for Metuchen and home.

At nine-thirty Alexis Machine, dressed in a new suit and soft white shirt with flamboyant tie, entered his chauffeured car and was driven to an expensive and well-lighted restaurant. He was going to dine with friends, and would make certain that he was seen by many people.

The night was damp and miserable, the roads fog-bound. Joe Zucco and Gino Agucci spoke little on the tedious drive.

Zucco sat in the back, comfortably smoking a cigar. Gino kept his eyes on the slippery road.

At five minutes to ten they turned into the driveway, past the always opened iron gate. The sky was clearer in Metuchen. As Gino inched the car forward, his headlights picked out dew-laden trees glistening in the moonlight. Following the curve of the driveway, he bore right and soon began the swing into the oval in front of the big white-columned house.

Julian Gogordo stood behind a clump of bushes at the head of the oval. An expert marksman, he intended to shoot Zucco through the huge rear window of the Cadillac. At that brief distance, with the car barely moving, there was no chance of missing. He would be able to get three shots into Zucco's head before the driver could get out of the car. By then he would be well on the path to his own waiting car. It was a perfect setup. He had never missed a shot at ten feet in his life.

As Zucco's car approached, Gogordo raised his gun and waited. They passed by, only feet away from his covering. He leveled the gun, his finger already beginning the press of the trigger. Steady, steady.

Something was wrong. He could not see Zucco's head. The trunk lid was up, covering the rear window. A machine of some kind lay in the trunk.

Cursing his luck, Gogordo ran out of the clump of bushes and along the rim of the shrubbery toward the side of the house, intending to shoot Zucco as he stepped out of the right side of the car. He got to the best spot just as the door opened. Angry now, excited, nervous, and out of breath, he began suddenly to cough.

Gino Agucci turned the ignition key off just as Zucco opened the door. Alerted, on edge because of his feeling, he suddenly heard someone cough in the noiseless country air. He reacted instinctively. In a split second he turned the ignition key back on and pressed a special button on the panel. His hand was already reaching for his gun as overhead floodlights, specially connected to an electronic device in the Cadillac by the retired electrical engineering genius, bathed the entire oval area in hot light. Shouting to Zucco to get down, Gino kicked open his door and was out of the car and crouched on the balls of his feet before Gogordo knew what was happening. Hugging the left rear of the car for cover, Gino peered around and found his man at the tree line about fifteen feet away. Gogordo was standing in the naked light, gun in one hand, the other shielding his eyes trying to see. Finding the car he fired once, hitting the open door, as Gino sent three quick bullets into his body. Blown backward by the impact, the body seemed to wrench in mid-air, as if hurled there by a giant hand, before sagging listlessly to the wet ground.

As Zucco crept out of the car and cautiously approached, Gino Agucci walked over to the inert mass and calmly sent a fourth bullet spiraling through the brain and lifeless body of Julian Gogordo, a gunman late out of Cheyenne.

SEATED AT the head of the table, his face a sequence of scowls, Joe Zucco shouted, raged, pounded his iron fist, stamped his feet, cursed, swore, banged his chair, stormed, ranted, and raved in what had to be one of the angriest performances of his life. Only the aftermaths to the much earlier attempt to kill him and the successful double cross perpetrated upon him when he was young could equal the present moment in the importance of his anger.

"Machine!" he screamed.

Around the table Johnny Apples, Pete Montana, Al Parry —all three hastily summoned for this extraordinary 3 A.M. meeting in the big house in Metuchen—and Gino Agucci sat stone-still. Each knew that to speak now would be to court disaster. Best to let a hurricane work itself out.

"Machine," he screamed again, pounding the table as he rose. "Machine done it. You bet your ass he done it. That horse-faced northern rat, that miserable woman-sucking sheep-screwing *scungill* tried to have me killed. *Me.*" He stopped for a moment, unable to comprehend how anyone could have such insanity. "He wants to take over. He's greedy, wants everything for himself. He don't understand how we share things in this country. He don't understand how the organization works for everybody. *Everybody.*" He banged the table again. "Not just one man named Machine. When our people come to this country they had to organize to get anything. They done a good job. Now we got organization everywhere. It works 'cause we *make* it work. Now this animal, this *schifoso,* wants to destroy us, take everything for himself." Still shouting, Zucco was nevertheless arguing his case as though before a syndicate commission. "Greed. It killed off half our friends in the old times. They couldn't see things were different here. Here you make it only if the other guy makes it. Then everybody got a deal. That's the American way. But there's always somebody like Machine that don't wanna be American. That don't wanna be organized. That don't wanna be our friends. What they want—" He paused, looked at the faces in front of him. "What they want," he said in a booming voice, "is to see us *dead.*" He suddenly cleared his throat and spit right on the table in front of the men. "But what they gonna *get,*" he made the sign of the gun, "is this." He shook it in the air. "That's what Machine's gonna get. And that's all he gonna get."

With his left hand Zucco hunched up his pants. "Charity," he said loudly. "That was my mistake." He nodded his head. "Charity. I let that degenerate bastard steal from me all these years. I felt sorry for him. I let him grow fat on my blood. And how does he repay me? He sends some scumbag to knock me over. If it wasn't for Gino here, I'd be dead now." Everybody at the table looked at Gino Agucci, who sat there immobile as always. "You see what you get for charity?" It was a rhetorical question. "But no more. No more charity. What he done, he made me know who I was. *Joe Zucco.* Now Machine's gonna wish he never heard of me."

"What you gonna do, Joe?" blurted out Johnny Apples.

"Un'azione brutale," said Zucco, eyes bloodshot. "Kill him."

In the privacy of his locked study Zucco spent another hour with the four men, discussing the task of Alexis Machine's permanent removal. He had called them together, once the police had dispatched the body and taken statements, to have a captive audience for his show of rage, and to satisfy himself that Johnny Apples and Al Parry were not involved. Then too, he wanted it on the record, at least with Apples and Parry, that he was a reasonable man who had had no thought of killing Machine until the attempt on his life earlier in the evening. Gino Agucci and Pete Montana already knew the truth, of course.

Angered as he still was, Zucco was somewhat relieved that the move had finally been made. He was now free to carry out his plan. In fact, the attempt made his plan perfect. Machine had moved for execution without syndicate approval. It was a desperate gamble that had lost. Now he could repay in kind and the syndicate would say nothing, even though some wouldn't like it. All he had to do was make sure that the job was done right.

"Johnny, who you got for this? We need the right men."

Apples thought for a moment. "What about Durk? He's my top gun. Or Rocco Slick? They worked together on that—"

"No good," Zucco cut in. "Machine's got their faces. They'd never get near him."

"Tony Pro. He's sore at Machine anyway, for doing the job on his sister that time."

"Same thing. These guys got to be new. No faces. Nobody knows them."

Apples snapped his fingers. "Machine don't know Farrano. He never worked that side of the street."

Zucco looked at Pete Montana. "What you think?"

"I don't like it, Joe. Frank's a good man, the best, but for a big job like this he's too easily spotted. They don't have to know his face to watch somebody like that soon's they see him."

"Yeah, that's just what I'm thinking."

"Why don't we go out of town?" asked Al Parry. "Bring in somebody from Buffalo or Detroit."

"Looks like Machine done something like that."

"No, I don't want nobody coming in on this," said Zucco. "Nobody's gonna know for sure what happened but the five of us right here in this room. That's the way I want it. Nobody else."

"Except the two shooters," Parry suggested.

"Yeah, them too."

"But who they gonna be?" Apples asked, perplexed.

"What I want," said Zucco, "is a couple boys people don't know about. Maybe they just coming up. Or maybe they just ain't going nowhere. But they already done some jobs and they know what goes. Now who we got like that?"

"Charley Flowers," Gino said after a moment's silence. "He done the job on Yacavelli."

"That's right. Pretty good, too."

Al Parry snorted. "He lost a man."

"So what?" replied Zucco impatiently. "Nobody's perfect."

"Do we use him?"

"We use him. What's he doing?"

"Some loansharking you give him through Al."

"That's right." Zucco turned to Al Parry. "Get someone else on it. He's off as of now."

"For good?" Parry asked hopefully.

"For good. Pete, you'll handle the job. Gino'll get word to Flowers to see you. I want it all set up this week."

"What's the rush, Joe? Let Machine sweat a while."

"I don't want him to sweat. I want him dead."

"Whatever you say. But you know he's gonna be tough to get to, now that you knocked over his gun."

"I'll get the sonofabitch. I don't care what it costs me, but I'll get him." Zucco spit out the words slowly, almost one by one. "I swear to Christ I'll get him."

"You mean I'll get him," Pete Montana whispered.

Johnny Apples had an idea for the second shooter. "Farrano's partner on the Cloud Nine hit. Tall guy, young, knows that karate shit. I can't never think of his name."

"Harry Strega."

"That's him. He done OK on that job, and nobody knows him."

"Except he knocked over the policy bank," said Gino, "so Machine's people seen him."

"In a couple minutes, with guns on them? What could they see?"

"Enough."

"No, wait," interrupted Zucco. "I think Johnny's got something there. How many were in that room, Pete?"

"Four, counting the bookkeeper. But Art had them facing the wall."

"How long was Strega in there?"

"About two minutes."

"Two minutes, with a shotgun pointing up their ass, and their backs to him. Ain't much chance to see."

"Don't forget the bookkeeper, he let the kid in before he went to the wall. And them guys all got good memories. They don't need long to make you."

"So he told Machine the kid's make. Tall, young, hair color, maybe clothes. What else? It fits a million guys. And besides, he ain't gonna be riding shotgun for Machine. He's just a lousy bookkeeper, right?"

"It's still risky," said Gino, who liked Harry Strega and didn't want to see him get hurt.

"I don't think so. What about it, Pete?"

Montana looked at Zucco, then at Gino. "I'll go along with you," he said as his eyes returned to Zucco. "A couple minutes ain't much and like you say, the guy won't be around Machine anyway. They know we pulled the job all right, but Strega's new. He ain't known to nobody really. They probably figure he was outside talent." He rubbed his chin in thoughtful decision. "I guess it's safe enough."

Zucco turned to Gino, who nodded his head in affirmation. He had said his piece and would say no more, now that Zucco had made up his mind. That was the way it had to be.

"Where's Strega now?"

"I sent him down to Florida right after the job. Key West. He's there now."

"Get him."

The matter was settled. Alexis Machine, head of the numbers and most of the gambling in the city, would be hit sometime, if possible, in the following two weeks by Charley Flowers and Harry Strega. The hit would be Pete Montana's responsibility, with Apples and Parry giving any needed assistance. There would be no trouble from the syndicate, providing everything were done smoothly and without prolonged conflict. Machine's operation would be taken over by Zucco, whose organization would thereby become the strongest in the city. Frank Taylor might not like it, but would not be able to do anything about the takeover. Immediately after the execution, Machine's three top lieutenants would be given the option of joining the Zucco organization or retiring. If they chose neither, they would be killed. They had no standing or power of their own to cause any trouble.

Some reorganization would be necessary. Pete Montana was to take over Machine's position as the operative head of the numbers. In effect, he'd control the city's major gambling activities as a new branch of the expanding company. "Get whatever you need," Zucco had told him. "Set it up separate, just like we done with the others. Everything works through you."

Johnny Apples would take over Montana's slot as head of the nightclubs and bars, including the one in South Jersey. He'd also continue Montana's efforts to open up the South Jersey town for gambling. This was an important deal that could lead to casinos and become a focal point for heavy mob money. Perhaps eventually even another Miami Beach or Las Vegas. Zucco had begun to suspect that Montana might not be the right man for the job. He had always regarded the show business aspect of Apples' personality with a certain degree of contempt, but now he saw a spot where it could be put to good use. It would also, he hoped, help to keep the restless Johnny Apples in his place.

To replace Apples, Frank Farrano would be elevated to full partnership and made head of all extortion activities. This was a key position because of the monies and dangers involved, and required somebody of imposing force and ruthlessness. Zucco liked Farrano's style and bulk. And remembering how the ex-longshoreman had come to him from time to time with misgivings about Johnny Apples, he regarded Farrano as eminently loyal.

Al Parry would remain where he was as head of loansharking. It was a job for someone with little imagination and a lot of quietly sinister authority. Parry seemed perfect for it.

Gino Agucci was to take over the cigarette smuggling, which was prospering mightily. He would also manage all future smuggling activities, including several that were in the works. It was a full partnership, and one that Zucco believed was well deserved. Gino would remain a traveling companion as much as possible, though Art Hammis would take over more of the role of bodyguard and chauffeur. The move would free Zucco to devote more of his time to special projects like the clothing store deal, and to oversee the whole operation even more closely. He intended to pay increasing attention to the legitimate end of the business, to be run by his son-in-law.

Under the reorganization there would be five separate but equally responsible branches: gambling; nightclubs, food, and liquor; extortion and labor racketeering; loansharking; and smuggling. Each had an operative head analogous to an executive vice-president. In theory each man had equal command, but in reality Pete Montana remained the most trusted and Gino Agucci was closest to the seat of power. That power was vested solely in the president and chairman of the board, Joseph Zucco. As with the chief executive officer of any growth company, Zucco's primary function was to actively seek new business.

After Johnny Apples and Al Parry had left the meeting, Zucco spoke further with Montana and Agucci. The local police would cause some minor embarrassment but no real trouble concerning the shooting earlier that evening. The dead man was obviously a hired gunman from somewhere else. He had been carrying an unlicensed revolver, probably stolen, with which he had tried to kill one of the town's leading citizens. The bullet hole in the car door proved that. Gino Agucci had a permit for his gun in the township of Metuchen and he had used the gun, reluctantly but legally, only in the protection of his own life and that of his employer. Naturally, neither man had the slightest idea why anyone would want to kill the owner of a funeral parlor. Perhaps a deranged member of some client's family, or an overly bereaved soul whose mind suddenly snapped. Perhaps it was merely a case of mistaken identity. Neither man could say. But under the circumstances the official disposition of the matter would of course have to be justifiable homicide. Meanwhile, when Zucco learned the identity and home base of the shooter, he'd know more about who released the trigger to Machine, and who he would have to watch out for in the future.

Into the early hours of the morning the three men discussed the specifics of killing Alexis Machine. It would be an execution, grand and simple. Guns, of course. There'd be no torture or mutilation; he was, after all, a chief. Timing was crucial. A kill of that type needed to be made within a few weeks to get the maximum impact. But Machine would be closely guarded during that time. His own plan of execution gone awry, Machine would be on the defensive. He'd get no help from the syndicate. He'd get no more easy chances at Zucco, who would himself take special precautions. Without help or hope, Machine would have to hide. He'd surround himself with his bodyguards, remain indoors, not appear in public. He couldn't run away, couldn't just disappear for a while; that would cause too much loss of face. He couldn't start an all-out war between the two groups; that would doom him with the syndicate. He'd just have to wait it out, sweating, planning for a truce arranged through third parties, or another crack at Zucco. Both would take time.

Zucco had no time. He needed to get at Machine fast. The home would be too well guarded, with men posted at all entrances. Same for the offices. Restaurants were out, they'd be searched beforehand and carefully watched during any stay. Machine's cars would be garaged and guarded, and checked for explosives each time before use. One early possibility had been a machine-gun nest across the street from the home or office, but this was ruled out as too public. Besides, it was not foolproof, and entirely too reminiscent of the early days of mob warfare in Chicago. Zucco wanted a clean job, executed with some imagination and flair, that would have high prestige value with the syndicate and public alike.

What was needed was a moment when Machine would be virtually alone in a place accessible to Zucco's shooters. Over the years much had been learned by Zucco's men about Machine's habits and movements through the city. As with any organization head, the times when he was alone in public were few. Now they would be fewer still, if at all.

By the time the sun rose in the Raritan River east of Metuchen, the three tired men in Zucco's study had ruled out all possibilities but one. In only one rare instance was Alexis Machine virtually alone for a moment in public. It was this moment that would be seized upon.

"That's where he goes," Zucco said confidently.

Pete Montana looked skeptical. "You sure, Joe? I mean, in *there?*"

"Why not there? Who'd suspect?"

"Yeah, but can we get away with it?"

Gino coughed delicately. "It's the only chance we got at him alone." His voice was very soft.

"I know," said Montana anxiously. "I just hope we don't get too much trouble from the big shots."

"Any trouble from the city, I'll take care of it with money in the right places," said Zucco. "But that's where he goes."

"In there," Montana agreed reluctantly.

"In there."

26

ALEXIS MACHINE was worried. His plan for the death of Joe Zucco and the takeover of Zucco's organization lay in ruins, at least temporarily, and he himself was now in danger. He would of course take all necessary steps to ensure his own safety, but his ambition to become the city's strongman would have to be stilled for a while. He could not count on getting another crack at Zucco until things quieted down. Meanwhile, he'd try to arrange for a truce through syndicate friends. The worst part of the whole mess was that his ambition was now out in the open. The fact that he had not succeeded meant only that he would have to try again. It was that kind of business. And next time he'd make sure to hire a top gun to do the job and not somebody like that nobody Spinoza had sent him from Denver.

When Zucco learned the day after the shooting that the dead man—whose name apparently was Julian Gogordo and whose age was listed by police as thirty-five—had been from Cheyenne, he had only one public comment to make. "Where the hell is Cheyenne?" he asked a local reporter. Afterward, he was told by Gino that Gogordo's Cheyenne was evidently just a stone's throw from Denver. "Spinoza," Zucco exclaimed bitterly, and then he knew whom he would have to watch out for in the future.

Harry Strega returned that same evening from Florida. He had left Colie Rogers in Key West to swim and sun during the daytime and drink in the bars at night. "I'll be back in a couple days," he told her. "We'll go to Miami Beach, see what that's like." They had spent a relaxed, almost deadened, two weeks in Florida, and Harry returned eagerly. "Don't forget about me," Colie had said to him at the last minute. "I wouldn't want to be stuck down here forever."

Charley Flowers heard about the attempted wipeout of Zucco that afternoon when he got up. He didn't know what it all would mean but he had this funny feeling in his gut. When he heard Gino Agucci tell him that Pete Montana wanted him at a meeting, Flowers knew something important was on and he was in it.

Gino himself was busy that day, informing interested parties that Zucco was alive and well, reassuring friends, gathering support. He said nothing about who might have done such a thing, it was known by those who should have known and unimportant to any others. On much of his rounds he took Art Hammis, returned from Canada, who would shortly be taking over some of his duties.

For Pete Montana the day, after a sleepless night, was one of frenetic activity. In somber mood he set about organizing the details of the coming execution of Alexis Machine. He inspected the site, noting places and positions, routes of escape, and the like. Everything had to be done first by him, since nobody was to know of the plan except the seven men, at least for now.

Both Johnny Apples and Al Parry spent the day working, after sleeping away the morning. Zucco had let them know in the strongest terms at the close of the late-hour meeting that he wanted business to go on as usual. Nothing was to change, no suggestion was to be made that anything was different. Both men knew what was to happen, though neither one knew the details nor the final part of the plan.

In Denver, John Spinoza received word at about noon of the death of Julian Gogordo. He was angry, vowing never to send another man east if that's the kind of thing that went on there. Gogordo had been a good man, one who never failed him. The mistake must have been made by Machine and his people. After his anger subsided, Spinoza set about planning for one of his men to move to Cheyenne to take over Gogordo's rackets.

In Cheyenne, Julian Gogordo's death became known at about the same time. His mistress of two years fainted upon hearing the news. His business associate swore publicly but gloated privately, and moved quickly to stabilize the business in his hands. He had the working knowledge but lacked certain paper information. Before nightfall, Gogordo's mistress had recovered sufficiently to negotiate a tenuous relationship with his successor.

In Kansas City, knots of men met informally to discuss how the slaying of an insignificant shooter in New Jersey, sent there by the Denver organization, could be used to their advantage.

The next morning at eleven o'clock, Pete Montana met with Charley Flowers and Harry Strega in the upstairs room of the Court Tavern. He told them of the plan, going into the details of their part. He also told them some of the background of the attempted assassination of Zucco on Machine's orders. As he spoke, the two young men stole glances at each other. Neither had ever been involved in anything this big. It meant that they were being recognized, that they were moving up. Both men smiled inwardly. Their day had come.

"Tuesday's the big day," said Pete Montana. "Tuesday morning at eight. A car'll pick both of you up around six-thirty, take you to get the tools. That's where I'll meet you. You leave for the hit at seven-thirty. Art Hammis will be your wheel man, Gino will drive the backup car. You'll be in and out in a few minutes and on your way."

Montana gave them pictures of Machine to study. There would be no lookouts or fingermen at the scene. They'd be on their own, and so would have to spot Machine immediately. It would not be hard: in physique and bearing he was easily recognizable. Both men had seen his picture before, they would have no trouble spotting him.

"Over the weekend you can case the location," Montana told them. "But do it separately. Just drive by, go around the block, get the feel of it. Then take off. And whatever you do, stay away from there on Monday. He might have spotters of his own around." Montana smiled at them. "We know you gonna do a good job."

The two men left the Saturday morning meeting exhilarated. There were no doubts now: they were on their way.

By Sunday Alexis Machine was more than worried. Too many people in the business were treating him as though he were a leper. Some had looked right through him. The meaning was clear. To them he was a dead man. He went to Frank Taylor for help.

"Can't do it. I can't help you," Taylor said bluntly. "The word's out on you."

"What is it?"

"You didn't get permission for what you done. That put everybody uptight. Then you blew what you was gonna do anyway. That made it a hundred times worse. Now everybody's on edge, watching and worrying."

"What for? I ain't gonna start no all-out war, I ain't crazy. I'll just forget the whole thing."

"That's you. What about Zucco? Suppose he don't forget? He ain't exactly the kind to forget something like that."

"What can he do? He won't start a war either, he knows everybody'd be down on him same as me."

"Even so, it's still shaky," said Taylor. "You screw up the balance in one city, and that shakes up a lot of people in other places. They don't like that."

"C'mon, Frank. How long we been friends, eh?"

Taylor looked at Machine as if he were dead. "It's a syndicate thing now," he said slowly. "There's nothing I can do."

Sunday night Machine called some of his other friends around the state. Not one of them was home. In desperation he tried to reach Jimmy Rye but was told that Rye was out of town. "Anytime he calls," Jimmy Rye had told his man, "I'm out of town." For the moment, the mob was going to wait on the sidelines and watch.

By Monday Zucco was feeling good. One more day and it would be over. Twenty-four hours more and he'd be boss of the city. No, not boss but certainly the number one man. He'd give Taylor a few things to keep him happy. He'd give the syndicate a little more so nobody would be uneasy. And there'd be a lot more for himself, including more prestige downstate and with commission members.

It was a good life.

Charley Flowers and Harry Strega took Monday off, relaxing in the afternoon with a couple of young ladies. Colie Rogers was still in Florida and Flowers had no one waiting for him at his hotel. Their spirits were high, as was their nervous energy. They had already checked out the location, and were anxiously awaiting their hour.

Gino Agucci, always relaxed, spent a little bit of Monday explaining another part of the plan to Art Hammis. Then he made final preparations, checking everything thoroughly. Cars, guns, oil drums, rocks, baling wire, all in order. The boat, a twenty-eight-foot inboard cruiser, was gassed and ready to go.

Pete Montana used Monday to catch up on some business he had been neglecting all week. He trusted Gino to look after the details of the coming execution, now that he had assembled all the pieces. In his mind the deed was already done. He found himself thinking of the next step.

For Johnny Apples and Al Parry, Monday was a normal day since they didn't know when Machine would be hit, or where, or how. They made their rounds, pushed their men. Neither one had any business scheduled for that night so they relaxed, each in his own home, as befits a man after a hard day's work.

Joe Zucco spent Monday evening in the city, at his town-house in the company of his blond mistress. Gino and Art Hammis were posted as bodyguards in the house. At ten o'clock he was visited by Pete Montana, and the four men settled down to a final meeting. Zucco intended to remain in the city over-night, and to be at a local construction site at seven-thirty in the morning. A new parochial school and parish hall, to which he had contributed heavily, were being built for St. Mary's. The visit had been hurriedly set up, and he would be seen by many workmen. At eight he was due to have breakfast with his close friend Julie K at one of the city's more posh early-morning restaurants. Again he would make a point of being seen. The breakfast had also been hurriedly arranged, Zucco telling Julie K that he was leaving that morning on a trip and needed first to confer with his friend about an important business proposition, a joint venture that would mean much money for both of them. The matter was too crucial to wait until his return, and he would be gone before lunch. It had to be breakfast. Julie K had reluctantly agreed.

By midnight the four men had disbanded, Gino and Hammis remaining in the house to sleep, Montana returning to his own home. Zucco had a last drink with Cindy Woods and shortly thereafter accompanied her to bed, where he fell asleep in her arms. By one o'clock the townhouse was silent.

THE DEVOTION of Alexis Machine to his wife, while she lived, was total and complete. A brutal man in most ways, with a killer's instinct for survival, he yet remained tender to his beloved wife all the years of their marriage. Never questioning him or interfering in his activities, she consoled him in his failures and rejoiced in his successes. He adored her, and his devotion did not go unnoticed by friends and enemies alike.

When she died eight years before, he was grief-stricken. At one point there was fear for his sanity, but he soon regained his balance and returned to the wars seemingly unimpaired. If anything, he became even more ferocious in his dealings, the one soft influence on him now being gone. The only outward sign of his continued bereavement was the monthly mass he offered in her memory.

For those eight years, on the tenth of each month—the day of her death—Alexis Machine attended a memorial mass for the repose of her soul. The mass was always held in the same church, Our Lady of Grace, in the city's north end, and always at eight o'clock in the morning. As was the practice in that church, holy communion was given to those parishioners, mostly workmen, who desired it before the start of the regular mass; the host having of course been consecrated earlier, at the seven o'clock mass. Alexis Machine always received holy communion on that day, before the start of the mass commemorating his dead wife. He would arrive at a few minutes before eight, walk up to the center altar rail for holy communion, then retire to an empty pew. One or more of his men would be settled unobtrusively in a pew farther back. After mass he would hurry out to a waiting car, always parked directly in front of the church.

On this tenth day of the month—a Tuesday—Alexis Machine arrived at five minutes to eight. Two burly bodyguards got out of the car first and looked around carefully before Machine walked hurriedly up the front steps between them and into the church. Inside it was cool and uncrowded. The church itself, built in the early years of the century, was huge, and more nearly resembled a cathedral, stretching a city block in length. At the front were three separate altars, served by any of five assigned priests and others from outside the parish. Half as wide as it was long, the church had three doors at the rear, with the choir loft over the center door. Two more doors were located in the front part of the church, near the altar rail and confessional boxes, the left door leading to the street, and the right to an anteroom set next to the sacristy, from whence the priest entered the church proper to celebrate mass. The anteroom itself had two exits leading to a small courtyard in back of the priesthouse. To the right of the courtyard was a fenced area that served as a playground and ball field for the grammar school immediately in front of it. At the rear of the fenced area was an open archway that bordered the street.

It was through this archway that Charley Flowers and Harry Strega had already entered the parish grounds, and from which they intended to make their escape. Seated in the lead car was Art Hammis, parked at the curb, with Gino Agucci in a second car behind him. The street on which they waited was around the corner from the church at the other end of the block, and was one-way going away. If the job were done swiftly, pursuit would be almost impossible.

As Alexis Machine walked toward the altar, his bodyguards slipping quietly into a pew three-quarters of the way up the center aisle, Flowers and Strega were donning cassocks and surplices. They had minutes earlier entered the sacristy through the anteroom, and had bound and gagged the surprised priest and two altar boys. They were now ready. Flowers put the priest's stole around his neck and slipped the gun into his belt through the side opening in the cassock. Strega put his gun in the same position. Under the loose garments nothing showed.

"Let's go."

With Strega as the altar boy in front of him, Flowers walked into the church from the sacristy, his hands clasped devoutly, his head bowed. Out of the corner of his left eye he saw about twenty people at the altar rail, waiting to receive communion. He couldn't find Machine.

Strega stopped at the carpeted bottom stair of the altar. Flowers walked past him and up the four steps. He stood in front of the tabernacle for a moment, hesitantly, then opened the gold door and withdrew the chalice with his left hand. He turned around to face the people and with his right hand he drew out one of the hosts and held it up and made the sign of the cross, meanwhile moving his lips as if in prayer. He then descended the stairs and walked toward the altar rail, Strega following him with the silver plate.

Alexis Machine was the sixth along the rail.

Still moving his lips, Flowers placed a host on the extended tongue of the first communicant. He moved on to the second. Sweat was running down his back and legs. The third. His eyes were misting, his head buzzing. The fourth. He almost dropped the chalice. The fifth. His vision was going, he knew he'd never make it. He somehow took a step to the right and came face to face with Alexis Machine. Suddenly his vision returned, his body cooled. All the waiting was over, and it was too late to turn back.

Machine's head was raised, his face thrust forward, his eyes closed, his tongue extended. It was a pose, a moment in time that Flowers thought would last forever. Everything became for him slow motion. He moved as though in a dream. His right hand drew out the gun. *"This is for you, Machine,"* he heard himself say as he pulled the trigger. Strega's gun spoke at the same instant. Those kneeling nearby looked up, stunned. Others, having quicker reflexes, already were opening their mouths as six bullets ripped into Machine's face and neck and chest. He had received his last holy communion.

Then the screaming began.

Dropping the chalice onto the thick green carpet, Flowers ran, gun in hand, Strega next to him. Back through the sacristy entranceway, into the anteroom, out the door to the small courtyard, into the fenced area, across it, and out the archway. Hammis was already pulling away as they piled into the car, guns still out, cassocks and surplices still on.

"We done it," Strega gasped, out of breath.

Flowers couldn't talk.

Behind them, Gino's car kept its distance.

"You sure you got him?" Hammis asked.

Flowers nodded emphatically.

"We got him good," said Strega. "He ain't going nowhere."

"Except a cemetery."

"That's about it."

Hammis looked in the rearview mirror. "Get out of them costumes," he told the two shooters. "It don't look right."

"We didn't have time," Flowers snapped breathlessly, his voice coming back. "We didn't have time to change, remember?"

"So do it now is all I'm saying."

Hammis drove steadily, neither too fast nor too slow. He skirted the city along its eastern rim, moving southward through a dozen different streets before hitting Garfield Avenue. Somewhere along the way, waiting for a red light, he had stuffed the church garments into a weathered old mail sack on the seat next to him. He had also collected the two guns used in the killing and put those in the sack as well.

"Relax," he said as they approached the Jersey City–Bayonne line. "We'll be there soon." They had been riding for some twenty-five minutes, with Gino's car tailing them expertly.

In Bayonne, Garfield Avenue turned into Broadway and Hammis followed it south. For Charley Flowers, seated quietly in the back now that his initial exhilaration was over, it was like going home again. He knew the area well, had lived in its tenements and fought in its streets. Gazing out the window at the incomparably dreary landscape, he hoped he would never have to see it again.

Harry Strega, silently looking out the opposite window, also found Bayonne familiar. It was for him just another Hoboken, where he had come from originally. He had always thought of Hoboken as Jersey City North and Bayonne as Jersey City South. Both were border towns: rough, hard-drinking towns whose men were quick to take insult and even quicker to give it. To Harry it seemed at that moment that he would always live in such places. The thought didn't upset him, but he wondered what it must be like to have lived elsewhere.

"We're almost there," Hammis announced, breaking into their separate thoughts. "Another five minutes or so."

"Is the boat ready?" Harry asked.

"All set to go," Hammis said. "It'll take you around the other side of the bay and down the Jersey coast."

"I don't know why we couldn't just drive down there," Flowers whined. "Who needs a boat?"

"What are you complaining about? You're getting a free cruise like you was one of them millionaires."

"And a whole week in world-famous Atlantic City," Harry laughed. "Don't forget that."

"We could've rode down there," Flowers persisted.

"Zucco didn't want to take any chances," Hammis explained patiently. "Suppose they watching the Parkway and them other roads. Eh, what then?"

"So we just taking a ride."

Hammis looked at Flowers in the rearview mirror. "Just taking a ride," he repeated softly. "In a stolen car with phony plates, a couple of guns, and some church shit in a mail bag." He glanced at Flowers again. "You got some smarts."

"I don't like boats, they make me seasick."

"Are you kidding me or what? This boat's gonna hug the shore all the way down. You won't be in no sea."

"If it ain't a sea, what is it?"

"Just a bunch of water," Hammis shouted. "How should I know what it is? Just some water."

"We come back in a week, right?" asked Harry. "My girl's still down in Florida waiting for me."

"You'll be back in about a week," Hammis said carefully. "Montana'll let you know when."

Following Broadway to the end, they came finally to their destination. Turning right, Hammis drove along the waterfront for several blocks before stopping on a bulkhead at the water's edge. The white cabin cruiser lay in front of them, shimmering in the morning light. There were no other boats in sight. No one was around.

The three men got out of the car and stood by the boat, waiting for Gino Agucci. Hammis tossed the mail sack on board.

"You sure Gino knows how to operate this thing?" Flowers asked Hammis suspiciously. "Suppose we get stuck out there and he don't know what to do? It ain't like land, you know. You can't just crawl in something and hide."

"He knows what to do, he's worked the boats a hundred times. No problem."

"I hope he knows what he's doing," Flowers insisted.

"You ever see him when he didn't?"

"I like the water," Harry Strega declared suddenly. "My old man was a seaman."

"That's nice," Art Hammis said absently.

Charley Flowers just looked at him.

A few minutes later Gino Agucci drove up. He checked his watch. Eight minutes to go.

He grimaced. One more job and it was over, at least for this time. But that was the name of the game in his business. There was always one more job, and it was never really over.

He formed his face into a smile and opened the door. "Great job," he said as he got out of the car. "Great job."

AT 8 A.M. Joe Zucco was sitting down to breakfast with his good friend Julie K. Recognized, they were given a desirable round table toward the rear of the tastefully furnished restaurant. Business was brisk, yet there was no commotion or unruly noise. The Captain's Table catered to high-level businessmen, politicians, and professional people of every stripe. Its menu was varied and expensive, its service leisurely, its decor elegant. In its twin dining rooms there were no booths or counter service, and heavy drapes lined the walls. All tables were covered with Irish linen. The water goblets, refilled instantly from bottled spring water kept in a separate refrigerator, were of the finest crystal. The serving plates were bone china. People came to dine rather than merely to eat.

Zucco, biting into a croissant, looked up. Two of his men occupied a smaller table nearby. Their eyes patroled the room constantly, seeking out faces, alert to the slightest deceptive movement or unusual behavior. Nodding imperceptibly to a business acquaintance at another table, one who had been a source of profit in the past and might be sometime again, Zucco turned his attention to his close friend seated across from him. Julie K seemed apprehensive, uneasy.

"You look worried. What's a matter, business problems?"

"No, no," Julie K said quickly. "Just I don't like these early hours. You know I never get up before ten or eleven." He laughed, a little too loudly, a little too shrill.

"You're nervous about something. I can always tell when you get nervous. You know why?"

"It's nothing, I tell you. I just was up most the night, couldn't sleep." Julie K spoke rapidly, his eyes occupied with his English and eggs. He kept sipping from the water glass.

"I can always tell when you nervous," Zucco persisted, " 'cause you slow-sip your water to death. Just like you doing now."

Julie K's hand jiggled and knocked over his water glass. A waiter appeared instantly. Zucco's men noted the incident and passed on. Julie K apologized to the waiter, who smiled idiotically. Zucco said nothing.

"Guess it just ain't my day," murmured Julie K. He ordered the waiter, returning with a fresh glass of spring water, to remove the breakfast dishes. Sweat glistened on his forehead, which he repeatedly wiped with a small breast pocket handkerchief. The carefully folded handkerchief was initialed J.K. in large blue script letters.

"You said you had some business deal in mind," he prompted Zucco nervously. "Something that couldn't wait. Now that's the kind of business deal I like, eh Joe? You always make money when you got somebody who can't wait." He smiled.

Zucco smiled.

"One time I had this joker needed a certain chair for his collection," Julie K babbled. "Had to have it. I told him to wait till prices went down 'cause right now there's none around. Meanwhile, I'm sitting on a dozen I made up special. But he says no, he got to have it right away. So I give him one, and not for nothing either. It cost him plenty."

Julie K swiped at his forehead, sipped from his water.

"Another time somebody wanted some new stock in a big

hurry, I said wait till it finds its own level. He don't listen, he wants to make a quick killing. Six months later the stock's worthless and he's broke. I buy out his whole warehouse for next to nothing. All 'cause he couldn't wait."

Julie K swallowed hard, wet his lips with his tongue.

"There was even this one guy who—"

"Why'd you do it, Julie?"

Time stopped for Julie K. He sat there, ageless, immobile, suspended in eternity. His heart stopped beating, his blood stopped flowing, his temperature plummeted to zero, all bodily mechanisms ceased to function. He was a dead man.

"Why'd you do it?"

His senses returned. With the next breath his heart resumed its beat, his blood flowed, his temperature rose. Sweat poured down the lined brow into his bushy eyebrows. Nervous spasms gripped his thighs. Unable to control his fear, Julie K sat there, stunned.

"*Why?*"

It was more an accusation than a question.

"What's that, Joe?" he squeaked out, his voice a naked cry of anguish.

"You set me up, Julie. Why?"

"Set you up?"

"For Machine," Zucco said impatiently. "Outside of Gino, you and Cindy were the only ones knew I was going home that night. I never go home on Wednesdays, remember? Not only that, but they knew what time I'd be there. A guy checks the grounds for me every hour. Nobody was waiting around earlier. It had to be you."

"What about your mistress? She could've told them."

Zucco shook his head. "No good. She didn't even know I'd be going home till the last minute. Much too late to set everything up." He looked hard at his close friend, his eyes dreadful. "No, Julie. It was you."

His hands cupped tightly around the water goblet, the knuckles white against the fleshy pink skin, Julie K shuddered and tried to clear his throat. His face was twisted into a half-smile. "Guess there's no sense trying to fool you, Joe, is there?"

"Why'd you do it?"

Julie K brushed his hand absently over the empty table. "My wife. They took my wife. Said they'd kill her if I didn't help them."

"You should've come to me."

"For what? They were gonna kill her, Joe. They had her hid somewhere and they would've killed her if I didn't find out when you'd be home."

"But what you done, Julie, you marked me for murder. Your closest friend."

"I know." He shut his eyes. "I know. But I couldn't think. It was you or her, and she never done nobody wrong. I love her."

"Your closest friend," Zucco repeated.

"I'm sorry, Joe."

Zucco sucked in his breath. "You're sorry. That's a good one. You know something, Julie, you wanna know something? I should cut your heart out and feed it to the rats for what you done. I should let the boys chop you into little pieces and stuff your balls down your throat. I should have you peeled like an orange." Zucco's face was distorted in controlled fury. "But you're a friend of mine, right? You're my closest friend, my lifetime buddy, my pal," he said in a mocking tone, "So I can't do any of that."

"Joe, leave my wife out of it. She had nothing to do with this. Please, Joe, don't hurt her."

Zucco fumbled in his jacket pocket, ignoring his friend's pleading. His hand came out with a small plastic vial. "There's four pills in here," he growled, slamming the vial on the table in front of Julie K. "You supposed to take one every six hours. If you take them all at once, they kill you."

He abruptly stood up, shoving his chair backward.

"Take them all at once, Julie." He leaned over the table. "If you're still around tomorrow, your wife gets it with you.

That's a promise." He straightened up. "There's no place you can run we won't find you."

Reaching again into his pocket Zucco pulled out a roll of bills and threw the top one, a twenty, on the table. "Your last meal's on me," he said viciously as he passed by Julie K toward the front of the restaurant.

At a small table nearby, two men got up noiselessly and followed him out the door.

Outside, Zucco found himself shaking. He was furious. He clamped his teeth together, trying to control the rage. It won't last, he reminded himself; in a few minutes it will be gone. He was, all in all, pleased with himself. Twenty years ago he would have killed Julie K with his bare hands, in a crowded restaurant if necessary. Now, as a man of position and power and wealth, as a man, finally, of *respect,* he could no longer afford to do such things.

The black limousine, double-parked, waited for him. He stepped in, sinking into the deep cushioned backrest. Closing his eyes, he sat eerily still for ten minutes, letting his mind wander, allowing his body to cool.

Afterward, through the warm and wakening city streets, beginning to swell with workers, he was driven to his office atop the funeral parlor.

There was only one more thing to be done.

Zucco, frowning, checked his watch. He didn't like having his own men killed, it wasn't good business practice. But this was different, a special case. Too much was at stake for him to take any chances now. There was just too much danger involved in letting Charley Flowers and Harry Strega live. At nine o'clock they would be shot by Gino Agucci and Art Hammis, and their bodies stuffed into oil drums weighted with rocks and taken by boat past Staten Island, where the drums would be dumped into the ocean. They would be killed for the good of the organization. It was as simple as that.

Joseph Zucco, age fifty-one, a self-made man who now headed the most powerful organization in the city, sat in his

black overstuffed chair in his office atop his world, waiting for
the phone to ring. . . .

The time is now eight-fifty-nine of a beautiful midsummer
morning.

Stepping on board the cabin cruiser, their happy eyes not
yet sighting the weighted oil drums, Charley Flowers and
Harry Strega feel great. They have just finished the most important job of their lives. They are moving up in the organization.
They will someday soon be really big.

They have everything to live for.